ATTENTION! WARNING!

You are holding a haunted book.
You may set it down right now and no possible causal effect can beset you;
however,
if you read farther, I cannot be held accountable for whatever may affect you— for good or ill.

This volume was fashioned from several manuscripts set down long ago at various times by people in the throes of huge events and huge emotions, who could not help but to infuse, that is, print upon, these assorted writings strong impressions, exactly in the manner that some houses and other locales have been imprinted with intense personalities or incidents long passed. Such impressions, or recordings, as it were, are sometimes observed to repeat themselves over and again—phenomena often interpreted as "ghosts." In other words, this volume contains the haunted descriptions of several incidents, but especially of one in particular. The different documents that make up this book have been, in turn, lost and forgotten for ages, only to be found for a time, mulled over, then passed on, only to be lost again from both view and memory. *They have passed through diverse hands, always affecting the lives of whoever touches them or has been touched by them.* Furthermore, each individual to whom Fate has dealt these awesome and sublime manuscripts has felt obliged to add a marginal word or attach a note, sometimes of explanation, sometimes of warning, before Providence set to work burying again each in turn, only to later have them surface and move on to the next person by whatever happenstance or means. And it is I—and I alone— who has been fated to act as the focus or locus wherein all these several texts have been brought together. While the actual disparate manuscripts from which this book has been derived are without a doubt haunted in their own right in the manner described—except perhaps my own jottings—I have reason to believe that the essence of the haunted thoughts and accounts contained therein have been transferred to this entirely new work by virtue that the ideas and histories are in themselves haunted, regardless of the medium in which they are presented.

All things considered, then, it is only natural that the book you are holding consists of many layers. If you feel compelled to read this book, I suggest you read all of it from beginning to end— carefully and attentively—or else there is no point reading it at all.

T.K.M

Praise for *Sherlock Holmes on the Roof of the World*

"A delightful story!"—Rozonda (Goodreads)

"Very well written, it explores new territory in the fascinating life of this larger than life character."—R. Bennett (Amazon)

"I urge anyone who's reading this review to go and get this book."—Daniel Baldridge (Amazon)

"[E]njoyable and interesting.... I found Millers' knowledge of Tibet and Buddhism fascinating.... [H]e writes a fine story, in what is quite obviously a labor of love. A must book to obtain."—Gary Lovisi in *SHERLOCK HOLMES: The Great Detective in Paperback* (1990)

"[T]he solving of the crime by Holmes-Sigerson was true Canon indeed. A pleasure!"—John Bennett Shaw, Holmes authority.

Praise for *Allan Quatermain at the Crucible of Life*

"Immensely enjoyable!"—John Betancourt, Publisher Wildside Press

"Really quite a good deal of fun...strikingly unique."—Jim Sanderson (Goodreads)

"I've just finished reading....and I must say it's one of the best books I've ever read. It's absolutely amazing."—N.G.

"RECOMMENDED: A sheer joy!"—Gary Lovisi in *SHERLOCK HOLMES: The Great Detective in Paperback and Pastiche* (2008)

"I couldn't wait to finish the book and at the same time not wanting it to end."—JWC (Amazon)

"I won't say I couldn't put this book down. Of course I did, several times, to eat, to sleep. But I didn't WANT to!"—Anonymouse (Amazon)

"There is humour, horror, action, suspense, mystery and history. But above all, there is an open challenge to all the readers to go through this complex web of stories and get to the end to work out one's own solution for the mystery of life. Are you up to it? Go on, give it a try. If nothing else, you will enjoy a jolly good story."—Riju Ganguly (Goodreads)

"[A] masterful tale...Quatermain's narrative is actually 'revealed' several times over in the course of the document's existence.... I found the book to be very entertaining and difficult to put down. I have this nagging itch for stories that reveal the mysteries of time, and THIS LITTLE EXFOLIATE especially provided me gratification as I sifted through its many layers."—Golden Fleece (Amazon)

Praise for *Allan Quatermain at the Dawn of Time*

"Tom's meanings run deep and like deep water sometimes take time to play out. It'll be worth your time to read this book."—Raven (Amazon)

"The author has given us another singular adventure."—Riju Ganguly (Amazon)

"Any lover of Rider Haggard's works will be intrigued to see the innovative use of his main hero in what is a most unusual and original book.... [I]f you want a real challenge and an intriguing thought-provoking read then this is worth a try."—Roger Allen (Rider Haggard Society)

"One outer document leads to another, and these to further, inner documents, so that the reader experiences the book as if going through a series of doors in a labyrinth of secret passages. This approach is supported by the pleasing design of the book, which gives each document a charming verisimilitude.... [W]e must regard the book as like a curious crystal, which reveals some new dimension as each facet is caught in the light of our understanding."—Mark Valentine (Wormwoodiana)

SHERLOCK HOLMES IN THE FULLNESS OF TIME

Or, Adventures on Three Roads Less Traveled

THOMAS KENT MILLER

Rosemill House

SHERLOCK HOLMES IN THE FULLNESS OF TIME
Or, Adventures on Three Roads Less Traveled

To Jayne Marie—My Ariel
and
To Douglas Preston Michael—My Son
and
Ellen Rose—My Granddaughter

Also to Adrian Nebbett, Ray Riethmeier, Gary Lovisi, Robert Reginald,
and John Betancourt

Illustrations by Linda Villareal, Sheila Marie Comerford, Elizabeth Davies,
Thomas Kent Miller

Published by Rosemill House
P.O. Box 7692
Redlands, California 92375
thomaskentmiller@gmail.com
Trade Paperback ISBN 978-0-944872-77-2

SHERLOCK HOLMES IN THE FULLNESS OF TIME

Or, Adventures on Three Roads Less Traveled

Contents

The Potala—that most spectacular of Asian palaces—in Lhasa, Tibet.

SHERLOCK HOLMES ON THE ROOF OF THE WORLD;
Or, The Adventure of the Wayfaring God

From the Journal of
Leo Vincey, Esq.

Being a Further Chronicle of the Exploits of Horace Holly
and Leo Vincey, as Previously Published in the Volumes
"She" and "Ayesha: The Return of She"
By Horace Holly

Edited and with a Foreword and Notes by
Thos. Kent Miller

Foreword

As I prepare Leo Vincey's manuscript for publication, there is one thing, I find, that especially saddens me: namely that, in this entire heretofore unknown Sherlock Holmes adventure, there is only one oblique reference to Watson—Dr. John H. Watson, friend, confidant, and biographer of the great detective. What, I ask myself, is a Holmes story without his trusty Watson?

As is known, nearly all the lost adventures that have come to light since the passing of the principal characters have been through an agency connected somehow either to Watson or his estate, or to Holmes's estate. But even that cannot be said for the tale you are about to read. It is apparent, I think, that Watson never had any knowledge of either the manuscript or the incident which it describes, and that Holmes kept the matter entirely to himself, as he was in the habit of doing with so many particulars of his life.

Be that as it may, I will now explain how the manuscript came to the attention of this editor. My wife and I lived in a secluded part of a rustic town midway between San Francisco and Silicon Valley. In April of 1984, our neighbor up the court from us, Jan Needleman, was preparing to travel to Nepal. As an employee of an airline, Jan could travel virtually anywhere without cost. The day before she was to take off via British Airways to Calcutta, she called us and asked if we would keep an eye on her house for three weeks and bring in her mail. At the time, we were still fairly new to the neighborhood; I barely knew Jan and had no idea that she was about to embark on such a grand adventure.

As it happened, as I spoke to her over the phone in my basement office, I was surrounded by stacks of books about the Himalayan region—*Seven Years in Tibet* and *Return to Tibet* by Heinrich Harrer, *The Secret Exploration of Tibet* by Peter Hopkick, *The Third Eye* by T. Lobsang Rampa, *The Trekker's Guide to the Himalaya* by Hugh Swift, *The Way to Shambhala* by Edwin Bernbaum, and *The Arun: A Natural History of the World's Deepest Valley* by Edward W. Cronin, Jr., to name a few. As coincidence would have it, during the several months previous, I had developed an interest in that part of Central Asia called the

Roof of the World and had done extensive research on the subject with the intention of parlaying the information into some sort of book. The fact is that Himalayan trekking had become a popular pastime among young urban professionals, and interest in the region had simply picked up appreciably. It seemed to me inevitable that a new travel book of some sort or a reference book about northern India, Nepal, Tibet, and the Himalayas was virtually guaranteed to succeed.

Such was my background in the subject when, out of the blue, Jan called to say she was leaving the next day. Naturally I was very excited for her and was about to summarize all of the above for her and to ask her to be alert on my behalf for anything of interest of an anecdotal nature that I could use in my book. But before I could broach the subject, my wife drove in from the market beeping the car horn, indicating that she needed help unloading the car. Knowing where my duty lay, I simply wished Jan fun on her trip and agreed to look after things for her while she was gone.

Life went on as usual, and at the end of the third week Jan returned—at once enchanted by her experience and disappointed. Don't ask me how she did it, but despite all her research into the trip, two critical facts had evaded her: April may be the best time of the year to witness the miracle of Nepal's rhododendrons, but it is also the month that the entire Himalayan range is socked in by mist and fog so that not even the slightest pinnacle is visible.

She enjoyed herself nonetheless, especially her excursions in the towns and cities on her trip, and she returned with a small gift for us for our trouble: a packet of handcrafted stationery.

The stationery was in a lovely ten-inch-by-seven-and-one-half-inch envelope covered with a blue and red stencil of what appeared to be a conch shell repeated innumerable times so that very little of the beige paper showed through. The flap on the envelope was secured by a strand of red string tied in a bow knot. As I handled this token of appreciation from the other side of the planet, I was immediately impressed with the craft involved and the brilliant colors. I undid the string tie and pulled out the contents—several sheets of red-stenciled "Dambar Kumari" paper with black-stenciled matching envelopes. An enclosed rough explanatory note indicated that the paper was named after "a famous beauty in the Nepalese court" who had been the first to wear printed cloth, and explained that "two hundred years ago in the Himalayan Kingdom of Nepal a group of men started the tradition of textile printing," having learned the technique from the Muslims of northern India.

As I riffled through the stationery, I saw that there were several consecutive sheets in the back that had already been written on. These sheets proved to be much older than the others, of a different paper altogether, and brittle besides. The writing was in English and in an elaborate hand. Questioning Jan, she had no idea how these sheets got into the stationery packet. She had purchased this gift, as well as a number of other souvenirs, trinkets for friends and family, and the like, from various street vendors and market bazaars on her travels. One can only guess how the sheets got into the hands of a Nepalese peasant, or of what went on in his or her mind: probably some notion of economizing or something of the sort. It was impossible to say.

What follows is the contents of those sheets *in toto*, edited only to improve the title from the original "Journal of Events in Lhasa" to one of a more Watsonian cast, to add a few applicable epigraphs, to correct or update spelling (*e.g.*, "Tibet" for "Thibet"), and to add appropriate chapter titles and notes.

Whether the manuscript is authentic and whether the events it chronicles really happened is anyone's guess. Whether what it records has any basis at all in reality or is just the rambling writings of a delirious man also is anyone's guess. For my part, I believe that the manuscript is authentic, was penned by one Leo Vincey in 1891, that the events chronicled did in fact happen as described, and that it was left in the safekeeping of Sherlock Holmes himself. How it passed from Holmes's hands into a packet of stationery ninety-three years later is a tale that may never be told. We may simply be pleased that it did reach our world intact so that its contents can be shared with our generation.

But one fantasy persists. What if Holmes had in fact delivered the manuscript into the hands of his friend, Dr. Watson, as he had no doubt intended? How would the good doctor have edited it? What would have been his approach? What sort of droll commentary or imaginative framing device would he have included to temper the impact of the story, as he was wont to do with the more sensitive of his friend's exploits? Perhaps such questions are pointless, but they are seductive.

Two points, it seems to me, are clear. This is one of the few stories to come to light regarding events involving "Sigerson," the fictitious name Holmes went by during the nearly three years of his Great Hiatus (a point that he discusses in "The Adventure of the Empty House," and which is elaborated on at great length in Baring-Gould's biography of the sleuth and also in his *Annotated Sherlock Holmes*). Besides this extraordinary claim to fame, the following tale also has the distinction of being the true first sequel to Horace Holly's famous journal, *She*, which was published in 1887 under the byline of Holly's agent, Henry Rider Haggard. The only heretofore known sequel, *Ayesha: The Return of She*, was published in 1904 and records events that occurred some twenty years after *She*. This new tale is a record of events that occurred *between* the previously published adventures.

For those unfamiliar with the events that precede this new story, I have included the following synopsis of *She* and the pertinent early sections of *Ayesha*.

The adventures of L. Horace Holly and Leo Vincey as recorded in She, *in brief, plus some early incidents from* Ayesha:

Late at night, Ludwig Horace Holly, a student at Cambridge University, is studying in his rooms when his friend, Vincey, unexpectedly arrives with a heavy strong-box. Vincey explains that he is dying, and asks Holly to act as guardian to his son, Leo. Vincey does in fact die, and the years roll quickly by. When Leo turns twenty-five, he opens the box his father had left him. In it he finds a broken potsherd inscribed with ancient writings.

The inscriptions tell a weird story: Leo's ancestor Kallikrates, a priest of Isis, had broken faith and fled Egypt with a young princess, Amenartas. The inscriptions also tell of the queen of a savage people—a white goddess—and a strange Pillar of Fire, which she had shown Kallikrates and Amenartas. The queen fell in love with Kallikrates and, in a fit of jealousy, slew him, but Amenartas escaped to give birth to Kallikrates's son. The writing ends in Amenartas' plea that the son she was leaving behind, or another courageous descendant, avenge her against the Queen of the Pillar of Fire.

Leo and Horace take up the quest and after many trials come to the hidden African city of Kôr, carved out of solid rock, where reigns the mysterious Ayesha, She-Who-Must-Be-Obeyed. Ayesha explains to Horace that she has been living in her hidden city for two thousand years without news of the outside world. Time means nothing to her; nor can death touch her.

The next day, Ayesha visits Leo, who is dying of fever from a wound. When she enters his room and sees him for the first time, she draws back in astonishment. Leo has the features of the dead Kallikrates: *He is the man she has loved and whose rebirth she has awaited for two thousand years.* Ayesha then restores Leo's health.

Eventually she persuades Leo and Horace to see the Pillar of Fire for themselves. Leo, though, hesitates to enter the flame as it shoots up from the bowels of the earth. To assuage his fears, Ayesha enters the fire where she bathed only once before two thousand years earlier. Her features begin to shrivel, her arms grow scrawny and wilt, and before the stunned audience, she shrinks into a small bundle of skin and bones. Why? How? No one knows. Perhaps the flame's magic can only be used once in a lifetime. Three weeks after they penetrated the African interior, the two men emerge and make their way to England.

During a period of morbid isolation in England, Leo and Holly strive to wring some meaning from the joke called Life. Leo's despair is so great, he contemplates suicide. However, a Universal Power greater than his intervenes, providing two separate but related signs—one a dream, the other the sun bursting through a particular cloud formation—that give our adventurers hope once again. At once they arrange to leave for Central Asia. They travel through the snows and mountains of that region for a number of years seeking the solidly *real* manifestation of the symbols they saw in the signs . . . and seeking the meaning of Ayesha's last words: *"I shall come again."* For a while they tarry in Lhasa.

T. K. M.

I traveled for two years in Tibet . . . and amused myself by visiting Lhasa, and spending some days with the head Lama.
—SHERLOCK HOLMES in
"The Adventure of the Empty House"

We are . . . going away again, this time to Central Asia, where, if anywhere upon this Earth, wisdom is to be found . . . .
—L. HORACE HOLLY in *She*

Introduction

It is Horace who is the incurable chronicler, not I. I'm afraid the arts of writing have never been to my taste, except in regard to the mundane affairs of life. Pen and paper have more often been foreign to me than not despite my university days, but those days are long past and seem remote beyond ken, at least in the light of the events of subsequent years. Indeed, I am writing this account now for two reasons only: The first is that Horace is incapacitated with an ailing heart, or so he believes it is, for we must make do here without Western medicine of any sort. Also, the resident medical authority, who is more a priest than a doctor, concurs with Horace, but, in any event, my friend and foster father is hardly well. Frankly, I believe that his Christian soul has suffered a severe shock of the most profound sort. I can say this with some certainty because I suffer as well, even as I write.

Which brings me to the second purpose for this account. That which Holly and I and a Norwegian chap named Sigerson learned or deduced in recent weeks is of such incalculable import that a record of the whole affair must be made, for better or for worse. Of course, there is the temptation to simply disregard the evidence and to "let sleeping dogs lie" as they say; yet I cannot in conscience simply abandon a point of knowledge of civilization-shaking import. I suppose that this is the university training coming out in me, or perhaps it is simply a respect for knowledge and truth that I never dreamed I possessed before now. On the other hand, the very prodigious and threatening nature of our discovery could well shake civilization in fact and not at all figuratively. Do I want, I must ask myself, to be accountable for the maelstrom of confusion that must inevitably follow the release of a manuscript such as I am about to set down?

So, there are the two poles of the problem with which I am confronted. If only Horace was strong enough now to guide me in this matter as he has guided me in so many matters over the years.

Yet I dare not impose on him any part of this quandary, at least at this time, for fear of aggravating his condition. In any case, I have made my decision: While they are still fresh in my mind, the circumstances must be set down as well as I understand them. At the least, this is my duty as an intelligent man.

Yet, neither do I rate lightly my current circumstances: Where am I? In the vicinity of Lhasa, Tibet, where to my knowledge no other Europeans—and no other Westerners—other than Horace and Sigerson have been allowed to sojourn during this century. What am I doing here? Even more importantly, when do I intend to return to England or, for that matter, to any part of the world that is considered "civilized," "a safe harbor," "a port in a storm," et cetera? The answer to that is of course when I find Ayesha, which may be next week or in a thousand years. Knowing these facts, then, an ordinary man would be naturally prone to ask further: If even the manuscript were to be written, what is the probability that it would even reach a discerning world? What chance will such a fragile thing as a manuscript—written on old notebooks—ever have of reaching the world beyond these encircling mountains? So it is that I've determined to do what I must, and then let the dice fall where they may. I cannot say for certain whether or not God intercedes in human affairs, yet I believe He must, at least in matters of consequence, as this affair must be considered.

I will write, the dice will roll, and the rest is in Hands far greater than mine.

Five or six years ago, following our return to England from Kôr, Horace busied himself recounting in some detail the adventures we experienced both approaching and in that fabulous land, which we were the first white men to enter in two thousand years, or so Ayesha led us to believe. And though this woman, who is so much more than a mere woman, may be the veritable sun lighting my path, I have known her on occasion to alter the truth to suit her own needs. Thus, whether this bit of information is totally accurate or not, I know not.*

In any case, after Horace had completed setting down all the strange things that happened to us, we deliberated for some time to decide what to do with his "book," as we were wont to call it at that time. We mutually decided that nothing would happen to it so long as either one of us lived. But since it contained an account of things we believed to be of "unparalleled interest," which was, I believe, the phrase we bandied about all during this time, we would make arrangements with a certain agent for it to be made public following our demises, however and whenever those may occur. Then, in the end, we decided to leave with the agent the final determination. As it turned out, however, circumstances arose quite unexpectedly the result of which was that Horace and I prepared to leave England in some haste. I understand from Sigerson that this agent found the script worthy enough to publish and that it enjoyed some popularity.

I mention these particulars only so that whoever may come into possession of this journal will understand that there is a long preface, already published, which may be of some interest or use insofar as it may put into some kind of perspective the nature of events that brought us to Tibet in the first place.

But I am wandering; I have a tale to tell and all of the preceding is tangential at best, only casting light on how it was we were in the chief library of the capital city of Tibet in the year 1891.

L. V.

---

* Editor's note: Allan Quatermain of *King Solomon's Mines* fame, records in *She and Allan* an adventure he had in Kôr in 1872.—T.K.M.

CHAPTER ONE

Sigerson the Norwegian

Horace and I were again deep in the archives of the library of Lhasa. We had made up our minds that this would be our last visit to those stone catacombs; but we had little hope of finding what we were looking for. For nearly half a year we had virtually bivouacked in the venerable institution, opening countless books, unrolling some few scrolls, scanning line after line and page after page, seeking some clue as to the whereabouts of, or any reference at all to, the volcanic peak above which towered the symbol of Life of the Egyptians—the crux-ansata,* which Ayesha led me to in a dream. Indeed, it was this dream—and a waking vision that Horace and I shared fast on the heels of the dream—that prompted our sudden leave-taking from England. It had been made quite clear to us—by what powers I cannot say—that Ayesha was keeping her oath to come again, and that we would find her in Central Asia. All we need do is go there and seek her.

As it turned out, five or six years of seeking have succeeded only in determining where she is not and haven't given us a clue as to the location of the Loop of Life, the visionary symbol of which we are certain was given to us as a sign, rather as an X that marks the spot, the spot being, of course, the true and ennobling love which I must seek to find fulfillment, at least in this life, which, despite Ayesha's tales, is the only life of which I know; and I cannot live without this woman. After all, didn't our Lord say, "Seek and ye shall find; knock and the door will open" or words to that effect? Well, if ever there is an award given for seeking, certainly Horace and I should win the prize.

*

---

* Editor's note: More commonly called an Ankh.—T.K.M.

As I was saying, Horace and I were searching for the last time for any possible clue in the books, for none of the lamas or any of the other estimable locals to whom we had spoken had any knowledge or the slightest concept of that which we sought. Fortunately, our backgrounds in language and the long years we have spent trekking about this land and its high terrain have given us sufficient familiarity with the Tibetan language—both spoken and written—so that we were quite able to pick our way through the books and scrolls and such things with confidence. We were, in fact, looking over again some volumes which had seemed promising some months previously, but which had proved barren, at least at that time. Our intent was to take a last look at these works and then depart, that is to say, plunge ahead, or over, the most prodigious mountain country on the planet with the intention of continuing our quest.

We were intent on this business in a corner of an antechamber, which had evidently been hewn from solid rock and which branched off a main corridor, when there came to us the sound of scuffling not unlike rats in a wall (not likely in this rocky place), then a muffled curse in English, more scuffling, then the unmistakably pungent smell of a waxed Vesta being lit, and finally the totally incongruous yet delightfully familiar aroma of smoking shag. Horace and I became aware of the first scuffling at the same moment and we both looked up from our respective volumes and glanced quizzically at one another.

At the sound of the English voice, our eyes opened wide together and I mouthed silently, "What the devil!" Then as the succession of extraordinary little events seemed to reach its conclusion, in a hushed voice I said to Horace, "It's been years since we smelled tobacco like that. Heavens! It's like being in an English drawing room again. Who on earth could be smoking the stuff in this place?"

🔹

Horace's reaction was to place his finger along his nose, indicating quiet. Frankly I was irritated by this gesture. This seemed to me to be a time for exclamations and such, not the nervous concealment of a scared rabbit. I was about to say as much, when there came a clear voice across the stacks calling out in English.

"Hallo! I say, is anyone here? That is, are there Europeans here? There are, after all, quite a few Tibetans about." Following this, there came a chuckle.

Horace put his hand on my arm as I was about to impulsively reply. For a while there was silence, then the voice came again.

"Well, of course, I can understand your timidity. We are a long way from home, aren't we . . . ? Yet, I can't help but feel somewhat put off. Frankly, I long for a Western face."

Well, even Horace's customary caution melted under such sentiments, and we both called out.

"Hallo. Stay still. We'll come to you."

It must be understood that it was hardly a matter of simply stepping over to the source of the voice. The library was, or is, a virtual maze, and one moved from one place to another only by trial and error. Over the months, Horace and I had learned our way about the place, but still it was not wise to go rushing off in some direction without taking one's bearings, noting landmarks, so to speak, and so forth.

"Most certainly, my dear fellows," came the voice. "I wouldn't dream of moving. I'll just chatter on till we meet. My, my, it certainly is unexpected to discover in a remote place like this, if not one's countrymen, at least Westerners with whom a man can share a smoke and perhaps some gossip of matters of mutual interest." He kept talking like this for a couple of minutes as Horace and I picked our way through the dusty stacks of long board-covered books. Then, "Hallo, there, you're getting warm . . . around the next bend then . . . and there you are!"

There standing languidly before us, his back against a shelf, was a tall man, somewhat over six feet, with piercing eyes that had a bit of humor about them. Beneath these eyes was a straight, sharp nose and then a full growth of dark beard, much as both Horace and I possess. (Shaving is a civilized custom that one soon learns to do without in a remote and bitter land such as Tibet.)

"My name is Sigerson," the fellow said, and he put down the book he was holding and held out his hand. "I'm a Norwegian up to no good, I'm afraid."

Horace and I shook the man's hand, Horace saying, "But your English is so good." But before either Horace or I had a chance to introduce ourselves, Sigerson went on.

"Oh, that is easy, you know. Much of my adult life has been spent in England. I'm rather a free spirit, flitting between the two countries and points between and beyond as—" he indicated the space around him "—you can see readily enough. But I must know, how did you find the workmanship of the gold work at the market this afternoon? It is most satisfying to know there is, after all, some craftsmanship and pride and such things left in the world, even in this day and age, though one must look for it in Tibet!"

Horace and I gave one another a questioning glance, then Horace looked up at the man, fixing him hard in the eye.

"Now, see here, sir! If you saw us there, why didn't you come forward? It seems to me the only proper thing to do, after all."

Sigerson smiled impishly. "But, my good man, I did not see you there today. In fact, it's been days since I've been to the market. No, no. I saw clearly that the two of you had been at the goldsmith's today from the minute specks of gold dust I see glinting on your fingertips, from that and from the orange mud staining the edges of your boots. That particular mud is comprised of a soil rich in ocher clay, and in my wanderings to date I've noticed it only in the vicinity of the open-air market. That the stains show signs of still being wet indicates that you were there only this afternoon. Quite simple, actually."

"Impertinence is more like it!" Horace harrumphed. My foster father, as I do, likes matters straightforward and simple. We both understand "simple," and Sigerson's idea of "simple" was clearly not ours.

"Now, now, old chap, there is no need to take offense. It's a bit of a hobby of mine to make deductions from the obvious things that few others heed. For instance, it is apparent that having achieved your ends at the goldsmith's shop, you strolled up to Palkhor Street for a nourishing repast of yak cheese and buttered tea."

At this point, I was aghast. Horace, I could see, was quite as dumbfounded. He inhaled and exhaled a deep breath. "'Impertinence' I said, and 'impertinence' I meant, dash it all! What right do you have snooping on us, following us about as though we were a couple of criminals! A fine how-do-you-do this is!" Horace's voice was quite naturally raising. It was my turn to put a restraining hand on his arm. After all, we had only just met the man, and it was certainly too soon to get into a brawl.

"Perhaps, Horace, Mr. Sigerson would be kind enough to explain."

"Certainly. I must learn either to keep my little revelations to myself or to broach them in a more subtle fashion. Actually, I can't blame you for your agitation. There are those who say I am somewhat smug, but I honestly can't help myself. It seems to be a part of my natural condition. In any case, responding to your query, in your beards are numerous morsels of yak cheese which indicates what your last meal must have been, and the mule dung covering in spots the previously cited mud on your boots is evidence that from the market you traveled, by what route I'm not entirely clear, to east Lhasa where the mule traffic is centralized by ordinance, and I happen to know of a fine little cheese shop in the vicinity, which happens to be on Palkhor Street."

"And the buttered tea?" I asked.

"My good man, who in this country doesn't drink vast amounts of the stuff at every available opportunity?"

"A point well taken. Horace, I believe we both owe Mr. Sigerson an apology. He certainly seems on the up and up."

Horace colored and held out his hand. "I suppose so. But this sort of legerdemain or mental prestidigitation or whatever you may call it will get you in trouble some day, Sigerson, mark my words, unless you learn to curb yourself. But I'm afraid Leo and myself have been in error ourselves by not introducing ourselves. I am—"

"No, no. Let me guess. You are the indomitable Ludwig Horace Holly and this is Leo Vincey."

"Why man," I said, grasping the man's hand again, "did you read that from the mud and dung?"

"Not at all. Leo Vincey and Horace Holly hot on the trail of She-Who-Must-Be-Obeyed, no doubt."

There was no end to the shocks that this Sigerson presented. As a man, Horace and I stepped back in surprise, our jaws dropping. Though we may have at times asked directions to certain geological or architectural landmarks which we had reason to believe marked our goal, never during our travels in Asia had we mentioned what that ultimate goal was.

"Gentlemen, don't be so surprised," Sigerson interjected. "In this year 1891, I would venture to guess that half of Europe and much of America besides know exactly who you are and have reveled and despaired vicariously with you on your adventure into Central Africa."

Then I understood. "So the man to whom Horace sent his account of those days has seen that it was published."

"Yes, and to worldwide acclaim."

"My word," Horace said.

"And, I'm sure, insomuch as your agent is by all indications a man of honor, I would think that he has set aside some percentage of the royalties for the event of your return. Quite a few quid, I would venture."

Horace was about to interject, when Sigerson continued, "No, no, my good man, I know what you are about to say: that you had specified to the man that he could do with the manuscript as he pleased and that he could keep whatever monies might be derived from that decision. True enough, for that is also common knowledge, yet as I said, I feel certain your agent, who has surely become a rich man acting on your behalf, has made arrangements so that the author of the book can enjoy some of those fruits as well."

I chose this moment to speak my thoughts. "Mr. Sigerson, this is news indeed, though I must say it is a bit disconcerting to know that half the world is privy to one's most intimate desires." Here I looked at Horace. "Horace, when I agreed to let you send your manuscript to that agent, I never thought that our quest would be held up to public inspection to be talked of and bantered about as though we were the subjects of some tasteless governmental scandal."

"Nor I, Leo. I am decimated to hear this."

"My man!" exclaimed Sigerson. "I am telling you that you are a wealthy man now. You need only to return to Europe to claim your own."

"Ah, but there are catches here," Horace said. "I am, and I'm sure I can speak for Leo as well–("Here, here!" I said)–quite content being where I am doing what I'm doing. Neither the money nor the suggestion to return home interest me one jot."

"Please," Sigerson said, "I did not intend to upset either of you. These matters of which I spoke are, as I said, common knowledge to all except the principals involved, and I ought to have been more sensitive than to have callously brandished this knowledge at your expense. I ask your forgiveness. But, also, I must ask, how fruitful has the sequel been?"

"Fruitless," I answered, hardly able to stifle a groan, whereupon I described the nature of the dream that sent us to Asia and how to this date we had succeeded not one whit.

"We had hoped to find here in Lhasa some clue to the location of the looped pillar. We have been here for six months to no avail. It was our intention to set out tomorrow to the northeast. These last six years have been utterly futile except to chalk off a bit of territory."

"Excuse me, gentlemen, but I can't help but wonder that, despite the nature of your previous adventures, you would spend your lives tramping about the Tibetan wilderness on the strength of a dream."

"But, sir, there was more!" I ejaculated. "Following my dream, there occurred a most spectacular display in the heavens that affirmed the dream without question. It was the moment of dawn and the English sky was clouded over. But as we looked, the clouds broke apart and formed the definite shape of a Loop of Life at the rim of a fiery crater, the fire being the sun breaking between the clouds, and as it broke a sharp ray of crimson light shot through the hole in the loop. I assure you the phenomenon was quite spectacular, though in a moment it was gone. It is on the combined strength of the dream and the vision—which obviously was more than a vision since it entailed somehow rearranging the fabric of the very heavens—that we have based our quest, and it is this memory which girds us daily."

"Indeed," Sigerson said, "it seems odd that a mere coincidence would provide the impetus for a quest that has already lasted five or six years and Lord knows how much longer, not to mention the privations and tribulations."

"My good man," I said, "you cannot know the power that that 'mere coincidence' had, nor the influence it had on our very souls. Believe me, sir, that was no mere coincidence . . . no, not by any means. If anything, I for one consider it the very Grace of God."

"But sir," Horace said after a pause in our conversation, "you have the advantage knowing all there is to know about us, but we know nothing of you."

"Oh, that is easily rectified. I'm a world traveler, a bit of a naturalist, and have received a special commission from the combined crowns of Scandinavia to explore the nature of the Yeti, or the so-called Abominable Snowman, as the press back home is wont to call the beast. Perchance . . . have you had experiences or heard tales in your travels that I might catalogue?"

"No, sir, we have not," answered Horace.

"Pity."

At this moment, we were interrupted by the sudden appearance of the lama whose responsibility it was to oversee the library. He was grimacing and seemed quite shaken.

"Gentlemen," he said in his native Tibetan, "I smell smoke. No, no. That is not allowed. No smoking in the library. This is strictly forbidden. Please leave; it is time to go now. Go, go."

Sigerson held up the pipe, which he had been sucking all through our conversation, and used it to gesture to the nearest of the many yak-butter lamps sputtering and smoking along the walls, and which Tibetans universally use to brighten the dark.

"I don't understand," he said in fluent Tibetan, "How could a little smoke from my pipe be of concern when the entire library is lit by flaming lamps under far less control than—"   At this point, the lama interrupted Sigerson with a great sweep of his yellow robes.

"Blasphemy! Oh, we will rue the day we ever allowed white men into our midst. But that is not the point. I am head lama of this library and I say that you must go. Now go! Do not ask questions. Go! Do not interrupt. Go!"

Sigerson looked plaintively at his pipe, which had now gone out. "I'm terribly sorry," he said. "This is my error entirely. I was so involved in my research that the pipe came out by reflex. Be assured it will not happen again." He stirred the shag ash in his pipe with the untreated end of a Vesta, knocked the pipe empty against his boot heel, and pocketed the offensive instrument.

"Without delay," the lama, whose name was Brother Paljori, said emphatically. He waved us on as though we were so many goats. "Out, out, out! Now, be gone! The Library of Lhasa is closed to you. Begone!"

It was at this point that I lost control. "Now see here, Brother Paljori, what is the meaning of this? My foster father and I have been studying peacefully amongst your stacks for almost six months. We have done nothing wrong. Why are you being so rude over an oversight made by our friend here? Besides that, we intend to leave Lhasa tomorrow, as you well know for we have spoken of it often these last days. I don't understand why you have chosen this moment to be immensely rude and to upbraid us about a matter so small as smoking a pipe."

Horace put a cautionary hand on my arm. I shook it off and glowered at the lama who held his ground, neither elaborating nor explaining our offense or his desires any more than he had already done. Well, the upshot of the matter was that we consented to leave and Paljori shepherded us out. As we exited, and just before the vast bronze doors closed behind us, we saw Paljori bow to us, from force of habit I suppose, since he wasn't particularly enamoured of us at that moment.

CHAPTER TWO

The Fate of Poor Paljori

"Most peculiar," I said as we made our way down the long staircase, "I wonder what got into him."

"I believe the man was more agitated than he let on," Sigerson said. "His distress over my smoking was largely a ruse, and was symptomatic of a more troubled underlying condition. Of that I am certain."

"Whatever the case," Horace said, "if that's his attitude, I'll be glad when we leave tomorrow."

We continued to discuss Paljori's peculiar behavior, not making any headway, but, caught up in conversation, strode off to that very same cheese shop that Sigerson had named when observing our boots. We found a rough table, ordered the simple fare available there, and began to exchange news and experiences. It was heartening to hear from Sigerson that Gladstone had come to power soon after we left England, for I am frankly all for Irish home rule, but I was disheartened that he lost out to Salisbury shortly thereafter. Certainly Salisbury is a fine man, but I always felt he was a bit of a pawn, working for the great commercial interests. Sigerson says the man has been much involved in the partitioning of Africa, at least to the time Sigerson left Europe. It seems, also, that Queen Victoria's jubilee was a gala event, not to be missed by any except by the likes of us. And so Sigerson brought Horace and me up to date concerning our native England and other matters of interest to the Western world of which we were abysmally ignorant due to our long absence, and, for our part, we gave Sigerson our views of our ports of call in Central Asia.

Sigerson seemed just as pleased to meet us as we did to meet him, and eventually we went off to his tiny apartment in the Doring district where he smoked prodigiously and we talked and drank buttered tea into the wee hours.

Sigerson's room was, as ours was, palatial compared to the transient accommodations provided for pilgrims and such, which were generally loathsome at best, small, rancid-smelling, cramped mud affairs with only a ragged scrap of cloth for a door, sleeping half a dozen or more at a time on whatever rough mats they themselves provided. We three, at least, were provided by the head lamas on our respective arrivals with clean rooms. Horace and I shared one at some distance from Sigerson's, equipped with sufficient cots and bedding. I noticed the other accouterments, or what passed as such, in Sigerson's room were similar to those in Horace's and my room: a rude wooden bench, a simple wooden shelf attached at chest level to the wall with nails, a butter lamp, and a real door comprised of two vertical planks held together by two traverse planks.

As for Sigerson's personal effects, there was little enough: a bag under his cot, a second pipe and a row of books on the shelf, and various bits of apparel scattered about. We spoke of many things that night, but mainly of the power of love, of Ayesha, and of a woman in Sigerson's past named Irene.

It was just before dawn, when they say that the hour is the darkest and when we three began to show signs of exhaustion, that we first heard the faint sounds of men yelling and general far-off pandemonium. Of course we were concerned and curious, but not for a moment did we suspect that we would soon be the central characters in a drama of genuinely earth-shattering dimensions.

The sounds of running and men crying out came closer. Suddenly Sigerson's door burst open and an army of yellow-and-maroon-clad police monks fell upon us, man-handling us in an uncouth manner, and dragging us out into the street without so much as a word of explanation. My first inclination, of course, was to fight off the wretches, but Horace was able to communicate to me by his expression and a few chosen words that he thought we should stay calm, that there had obviously been a misunderstanding, and that struggling at this time would only lead to further difficulties. Sigerson, at the start of this dismal affair, had struck a stoic expression and merely let himself be dragged. Reflecting that perhaps Horace and Sigerson had reasons for their quiescent attitude, I, too, ceased my struggles and let myself by dragged. (I don't believe we were even given an option to walk.) And dragged we were, through the mud and dung of the street and then east across the Bridge of the Pleiades and on to the Jo-Kang, the Tibetan cathedral.

We were rushed through this temple, the holy of holies of all Buddhist Asia (with an interior to match) then along several corridors and down numerous staircases (I lost track of the turns and switchbacks) and eventually found ourselves in the presence of the High Regent himself. The Dalai Lama was at this time only fourteen-years-old; and since it would be some years before he would be able to govern for himself, the secular aspect of the Tibetan state was run by the Regent, effectively the Dalai Lama's guardian.

He looked little different, to my eye, at least, than the rest of the monks in the room, with shaven head and clad in the traditional brocade robes. It was his bearing that betrayed his high role. He sat behind a plain table, looked at us sharply, and asked us what we meant by killing his librarian.

It can be imagined how we reacted to this query!

"My God, sir, what are you talking about?" were the next words I heard, and they from Horace. "We have hurt no one, let alone killed anyone. Paljori! Are you talking about Paljori? My God, he was fine when we last saw him. Is it he? "

"Of course we are talking of Brother Paljori. His heart was pierced obscenely no more than six hours ago, and a most precious holy relic has been stolen. It is certain that you Europeans are responsible and you must die, but first we must have the book returned to us. Please, if you would be so kind to tell us where you have hidden it, we will then expedite your departure from this incarnation."

"Thank you, your grace." Sigerson now chose to speak up. "It is kind of you to be so considerate of our eternal souls; however, I must disappoint you by enlightening you to the fact that neither my friends here, nor myself, have entertained any violent notions toward any of your kindred, let alone actually hurt anyone, least of all your librarian. Whatever his faults, Paljori certainly didn't deserve to die so horribly. May I ask why it is you believe we are the culprits, since I know that we have been only eating and talking since we last saw Paljori?"

At this point, another lama disengaged himself from the knot of monks standing near the Regent and stated coolly, "Why, it is self-evident! You three are the worst criminals imaginable to accept our hospitality only to murder us at your leisure and steal our most precious belongings."

"At this point," Sigerson said, "I have two questions more: Who, my good man, are you? And what is this precious book of which you speak? Some account of a previous incarnation of the Dalai Lama, no doubt?"

The Regent spread his arm in a grand gesture and said just as grandly, "Why, Mr. Sigerson, this is Wan-Po, Tibet's greatest police monk and solver of crimes. It was he who, ten years ago, solved the mystery of the Dalai Lama's stolen slippers. On his behest, a certain nurse of that time was skinned alive and blinded with burning yak butter. You can believe that no slippers have since disappeared."

I, for one, winced at this terrifying image, but I was determined not to show the least fear. I concentrated on studying our accuser, who bowed and grinned malignly. "Harrumph," snorted Horace, and then in English, "A fine how-do-you-do this is. Falsely accused by a sadistic swine and no recourse at all but trying to talk some sense into the Regent's head. Yet I can't help but think that the cards are stacked against us. Quite a pickle! It appears, Leo, that we will have to fight our way out of this scrape much as we had to fight off the perverts who wanted to burn our heads off with white hot pots.

"Gentlemen," injected Sigerson, "don't give up hope yet. I suspect that the Regent will see the light before long and realize the extent of his mistake."

The Regent made a gesture and the beefy monks who had brought us here tightened their circle around us and were about to lead us Lord knows where, when Sigerson spoke up again:

"My God, man, who do you think you are to accuse us of mischief when you yourself, only minutes ago, were consorting with the Snake Queen, which you know fully well is against all Tibetan law?"

I wish you, dear reader, could have seen the Regent's face at that moment. His mouth fell open and his eyes popped as though he had seen a spectre. In any case, Sigerson seemed successful in catching the man off his guard. Wan-Po first looked at Sigerson and then looked at the Regent and said, "Don't be insane. You are talking to the High Regent himself, sitting in the stead of the Dalai Lama. How dare you talk like that? Absurd! Insane!"

The upshot was that we were dragged off into what was, for all intents and purposes, a dungeon.

"I seemed to have touched a sore point," Sigerson said.

"Bravo, Sigerson!" Horace said. "Here's to having put one over on that bloke. Here! Here!"

"I'm afraid you may have missed the point, Holly," Sigerson replied. "I didn't 'put one over' on that fellow. I simply stated what I knew from evidence readily perceivable to the trained observer."

I saw that Sigerson, despite our situation, was on his high-horse again. Frankly, I was finding his attitude a bit tiresome.

"Well, for goodness sakes, don't leave us dangling," I remarked trying to sound sarcastic. "What did you see that Horace and I were so blind to?"

"Why, it is perfectly straightforward! When we were standing close to the Regent, I smelled an incense that I have reason to believe can only be burnt in the Snake Queen's chambers. Coupled with his disheveled appearance and the rouge on his lips . . . well, there was only one conclusion. But that is neither here nor there. What is important is that Wan-Po will soon be sending for us when he realizes his error."

"But how can you be so certain he will come to that conclusion?" asked Horace.

Sigerson looked at Horace incredulously. "Why, because we didn't murder Paljori, of course!"

CHAPTER THREE

The Dalai Lama Beckons

We bided our time for three days, and, truth to tell, the guards did come for us. But they did not take us directly to Wan-Po. Instead, we were led across the entire city of Lhasa and brought before the fourteen-year-old Dalai Lama himself in his royal quarters in the Potala—that most spectacular of Asian palaces.

I say "brought," but it was hardly this simple. One does not simply step into the Dalai Lama's quarters for a chat. There is a certain protocol or etiquette that must be maintained. The guards were hardly the type to impart this sort of learning to us; monks they may have been, but it seemed to us that some of them were short on the spiritual side of the scale and considerably heavy on the brawn side. So they led us through the unexpectedly drab corridors of that Buddhist Vatican, around and around until we eventually came to a portal, which we passed through, and were brought before a good-natured looking fellow, another monk, of course, for that is the only species of man there, save lamas, who are but high monks, who introduced himself as Brother Sigme.

"Gentlemen," he announced with a flourish, "I am to be your tutor. You are to attend the Presence of the Most High, and I am to instruct you."

Needless to say, we had mixed feelings about this announcement. On one hand, we were flabbergasted that we were to have an unexpected audience with the high lama, but sufficiently angry about our general treatment that none of us reacted in any but a cynical "who on earth do you think you are to be telling us anything?" manner. But, the man was sufficiently pleasant that soon we softened and allowed him to instruct us.

"Enter the room with your eyes down. Walk to a point just five feet from the Dalai Lama. Stick out your tongue, drop to your knees, and bow three times. This is a form of salute. Then kneel with your head bowed and place this silk scarf across His feet. He will then put a scarf across your neck. Finally, slowly rise to your feet and step backwards to the nearest cushion. Now you, Vincey, try it."

I went out of the room, and the lama clapped his hands as a signal for me to enter.

And so it went, with each of us practicing in turn (all the time feeling terribly silly) until several hours went by, though at one point we stopped for a quick lunch of tea and barley. Sigerson and I seemed to get the hang of it fairly quickly, but poor Horace seemed to think the whole business was contemptible and muttered under his breath constantly. Though I couldn't help but think that part, or most, of his resentment stemmed from his awkwardness in trying to manipulate his comparatively squat frame into the necessary positions.

But finally, the time came for our audience, and we were herded in front of two gigantic bronze doors. A gong sounded, and the doors began to open slowly of their own accord—probably due to some hidden mechanism. Frankly, the three of us were startled into breathlessness when the royal chamber doors were opened and there, beyond any doubt, was the supreme head of Asian Buddhism.

For a moment, we were stunned into a sort of paralysis, but soon enough we looked at one another as though deciding what we should do next. Then Sigme coughed loudly from the corridor outside and we began our entrance one by one, first Horace, then myself, and finally Sigerson.

When after a long while we were finally seated with our eyes averted, we heard the Most High's adolescent voice speak: "Mr. Holly, Mr. Vincey, Mr. Sigerson, I am very happy to see you." We were surprised by these, the first words we heard from the young man, who is, in effect, the Buddhist pope. "Please, don't let Brother Sigme's lessons intimidate you. I invite you to look at me."

We three looked up at once, and Horace, perhaps because he felt the wisest among us, rushed to speak next. "Your Highness, the pleasure is all ours, we assure you. Speaking for Leo and myself, we never expected to be honored by your presence during our sojourn here."

"You do yourselves an injustice," the High Lama said sternly, "and myself a disservice. I am neither completely rude nor are you representatives of distant empires completely below my notice. As for Mr. Sigerson, he is a special case; and it was inevitable that he...

as a...er...an official representative of that esteemed nation Norway... would be welcome in my rooms."

Horace and I both looked at Sigerson with querying lifts of our eyebrows, for the reference to him left something to be desired, but he responded only with a shrug, then spoke to our host.

"Your Highness, you are supremely thoughtful as is expected and inevitable, for though you appear young in body, you measure your age not in years but in centuries . . . indeed, millennia . . ." (At this point Horace and I couldn't help but look at one another knowingly, for such a person—one who counted her years in this same fashion—we had known before) ". . . and your wisdom and compassion are correspondingly perfected."

Of course, here Sigerson was referring to the traditional Tibetan belief that each Dalai Lama is the latest incarnation of the previous Dalai Lama all the way back to Buddha himself. When a Dalai Lama dies, it is thought his spirit enters the body of a newborn boy, and monks search the country for a boy born the exact moment the High Lama stopped breathing. That baby is then taken to Lhasa and is raised to fulfill his destiny as the new Dalai Lama.

"It is so, but I did not have you brought here to exchange pleasantries. My uncle, the Regent, was perilously close to resorting to torture, and I thought it prudent to intervene lest such methods prove inadequate and your bodies be maimed to no avail. In fact, it was my hope that I could induce you to speak freely with an offer of gold, jewels, or other such trifles equal in sum to the value of the volume's cover, the acquisition of which was no doubt the reason you committed the crime to begin with."

"I'm sorry to disappoint you, Treasured King," Sigerson said quite calmly, "however, neither my friends nor myself have had any aspirations toward the item in question, and I'll repeat as I have many times before that we had nothing whatsoever to do with the murder or the theft."

"How am I supposed to believe that when all the evidence points clearly against you Europeans?"

Horace at this point spoke up. "Excuse me, Your Grace, but we have been accused and confined without being told a word about this so-called evidence. Exactly what is its nature so that we, too, can understand how it points so inexorably to us?"

"Certainly that is a fair question," the boy responded. He pulled a scrap of parchment from the fold in his robe that served as a pocket and referred to the document as he listed the evidence against us.

"First, near Paljori's body were found ashes of the noxious tobacco Mr. Sigerson enjoys so well. Second, in front of the cache where the sacred book was kept were footprints in the dust that only your European boots could have made. Thirdly, it is well known that your respective sojourns here in Lhasa have been spent very nearly entirely in the said royal library. For what possible reason but to search for the sacred book and its jewel-encrusted cover? Fourth, it is well known that Europeans as a rule are mercenary, ruthless, and always liable to take the road that leads to riches when given the opportunity.

"My priests and I were lulled into an uncharacteristic letting down of our guard by Holly's and Vincey's talk of peculiar pillars and stone symbols, but rest assured, it won't happen again. Henceforth, our country will be absolutely closed to all non-Tibetans. There will be no exceptions. This will be so because I have said it!

"You sit before me and are accused, and you have heard the unassailable evidence against you. What have you to say?"   As the Dalai Lama spoke, I couldn't help but notice that Sigerson struggled to restrain himself from smiling. Apparently this was noticed by the High Lama as well, who said, "Mr. Sigerson, you find the facts amusing, I see."

"I only find amusing, sire, that so many good, intelligent men make so much of so little. A man trained in the powers of observation and reasoning could reach a far different conclusion from the same facts."

"Explain" The boy looked especially grim at that moment.

"Since no one actually saw the crimes in question, someone who wanted to put my friends and I under suspicion could easily have planted the evidence you listed. Do you truly think I am so stupid that I would empty my pipe at the site of a murder I've committed? Or leave incriminating footprints? No, Your Grace, we did not leave behind those clues . . . but I assure you that someone did."

"Who would you suggest?" the boy asked.

"That would be difficult to say without a thorough investigation, though I do have some ideas along those lines. Your Holiness, it so happens that in my professional duties in my home country I have dabbled in police work . . . investigations and such . . . and I have had some luck. You might say I have something of a knack in clearing up crimes. I beseech you now, if you are truly interested in finding both the guilty party and the missing tome, to take the shackles off me!"

The Dalai Lama was quiet for a time. We three merely stood before him. I for one felt rather foolish and was glad when the youth spoke again.

"Sigerson, I'm not sure why, but I am inclined to trust you—or rather, I'm not so stupid that I don't understand that if you three are executed, we may never find the sacred book. At least if you have a degree of mobility, you may lead us to the prize either out of carelessness or luck or skill. We will see what we will see."

"Your Grace, you will not regret this decision," said Sigerson.

"Naturally, however, your two friends must remain incarcerated to guarantee your reliability."

Horace and I both reacted sharply to the news. I don't think it is necessary to go into detail except to say I don't think I ever saw Horace so hot under the collar—the presence of His Holiness or not—except with the possible exception of his reaction to hearing the accusations against us some days earlier.

And, also, any idea that we might have had that we were alone with the Dalai Lama was quickly dispelled by the sudden appearance from around the entire perimeter of the room of a score of guards—who then vanished as rapidly as they appeared at a sign from the boy.

Sigerson, as to be expected, took both this news and the appearance of the guards with aplomb.

"Your Holiness," he said, "that would be inadvisable. I gather you wish to recover your property. I can guarantee that you will never see it again unless I aid you, and I will not aid you unless I can have the assistance of my two friends."

Well, you should have see the look on the young High Lama's face. It was rather as though he had just been informed that he had just ingested poison or had been bitten by a snake. The internal conflict wafted across his face: He was unsure whether to recall the guards and have us thrown into irons or to hold his royal temper and submit to Sigerson's demand. Fortunately, his last signal apparently had been a command to the effect that the guards leave the room entirely, for I'm sure that had any Tibetans been in attendance, the act of saving face would have been paramount and perhaps none of us would have seen another day. As it was, the young fellow seemed to count to ten, take a breath, look at Sigerson with renewed respect and finally say, "Your terms are difficult, Sigerson, but not impossible. You may have your assistants, but there will be three royal guards accompanying each of you at all times."

Sigerson smiled. "Agreed, Your Holiness. Capital!"

CHAPTER FOUR

The Dalai Lama's Story

As chaotic—almost dreamlike—as this whole episode seemed as we lived through it, the interview of the Dalai Lama by Sigerson that followed remains in my mind as the strangest, the most dreamlike. As I sat there in this Oriental hall on the far side of the world, surrounded by Golden Buddhas and all manner of alien accouterments, I watched Sigerson stretch out his long legs and steeple his hands below his thick beard, close his eyes and thereafter fasten on every word the boy uttered.

But here is the worst of the dream: As I watched the scene, I suddenly had the strongest impression of an English drawing room. I blinked and for a moment I thought I saw upright chairs with red velvet seats and backs, fine china set on a polished table, and newspapers scattered about. All during the interview, so long as Sigerson's eyes were closed and his attention was rapt on the Dalai Lama, I felt drawn to that room.

But that is neither here nor there; the things said by the boy should be the focus of this narrative at this point. The starting point of the Dalai Lama's story was Sigerson's query: "Pray tell me about the missing item and the circumstances of the death and theft."

That which follows is the boy's story. As you will see, it left much to be desired.

"Paljori was our honored and most revered librarian since the passing of Brother Tzu, Paljori's mentor, forty-five years ago. Part of Paljori's glory was—and this has never been mentioned to a non-Buddhist, non-Tibetan in millennia—was in the guarding of a holy book that has been handed down through many generations of librarians. The book itself is virtually worthless except for a few high lamas, for whom, of course, it is priceless. Its main value is its cover and box, or case, which are inlaid with gold and encrusted with jewels and are worth a fortune (from a Western perspective). But, what good are gold and jewels to a good Tibetan? None! That is why suspicion fell on you Europeans.

"What is your saying? It is worth a king's ransom. It's no wonder you would take it. But I forgot, in order for you to 'find' the missing item, I should not judge you in advance."

(You notice I felt it necessary to place find in quotation marks above. The reason is that the youngster's tone was such that he made it clear he never doubted our guilt.)

"However," he went on, "Brother Sun-Li, Paljori's apprentice, entered the library, as is his habit, two hours before dawn of the morning in question and found poor Paljori dead with a ceremonial sword through his heart. He was slumped over his prayer rug.

"Brother Sun-Li immediately told the first monk he encountered and in short time, Brother Wan-Po, our revered chief police monk, whom I believe you've met, was at the site of the murder. In short order, he had deduced the guilty parties . . . and the rest you know."

The Dalai Lama fell silent and observed the three of us with a kind of twinkle in his eye; I suppose because he considered the whole thing a game.

Well, my feeling about this is, if you make a child a god, then you have a childish god. But as has been mentioned before, the young Dalai Lama is not the real power; his powers are limited until he comes of age. My God! What if a fourteen-year-old boy became Prime Minister of England! Can you imagine it? It beggars the imagination!

But this aside is not pertinent to our situation, so I'll go on. Needless to say, our lives were in the young fellow's hands and any inclination toward mercy that he showed was appreciated. In fact, his show toward us was the only indication of mercy at all that had been granted us thus far. Despite his immaturity and his behavior with us, it was not he who had put us in this predicament. It was Brother Wan-Po.

Sigerson opened his eyes at the conclusion of the High Lama's tale and stood up abruptly.

"Well then, let us be on our way. I must see the scene of the crime. Call your guards or whoever you wish to accompany us. The game is afoot. Time is being wasted."

CHAPTER FIVE

The Monk of Long Ago

So it was that half an hour later, we were once again in the great Lhasa library with its thousands of ancient texts-one-time domain of the late Brother Paljori, Head Librarian.

Our nemesis, Wan-Po, was already there with his retinue. As we entered, I couldn't see that he was doing anything other than swaggering pompously hither and thither, his yellow robe swishing and his nose stuck in the air. It seemed probable that his presence was due to some messenger being sent out to inform him of our mission, and he saw fit to be there at our arrival, more to hinder us, I suppose, than to help us.

"The murderous Europeans, I see, come to obliterate the clues pointing to their guilt."

Sigerson would not be baited, however. He merely looked coldly at the rogue and asked, "Where precisely was the body found? In order to pursue my investigation I will need your cooperation. Tell me what you can, every detail you remember. This is by order of your most revered Dalai Lama."

Wan-Po didn't appear concerned by this information. Doubtlessly, he already had received word to the effect that Sigerson was to have his way. Wan-Po would obey his sovereign's command, but he wouldn't like it.

"So be it!" he said a bit too sweetly for my taste and shot to attention but not, as I said, with a bit of sincerity in his attitude. "Over there is the table at which Paljori sorted and catalogued new volumes as they arrived from the various monasteries of the realm. Beyond that is the alcove where he customarily prayed. There, slumped forward, a sword in his heart, his body was found."

Sigerson proceeded to the spot and surprised one and all by pulling a small magnifying glass out of a pocket, then, falling to his hands and knees, examining the floor and walls between the table and the alcove.

He occupied himself thus for about ten minutes, totally ignoring the varied sounds of consternation that emitted from Wan-Po, who grumbled and moaned and stamped his feet for the duration about his time being wasted and similar pointless concerns. I say pointless because the chap was such an inferior sort by any standard that, so far as I was concerned, Tibet would be better off if he found elsewhere to spend his time.

In any case, Sigerson was now examining the table and the books that were neatly piled at both ends.

"These books!" Sigerson shot. "Have they been moved since the incident?"

"All is as it was," Wan-Po replied. "Only Brother Paljori's remains have been removed."

Sigerson's reply was, "Harrumph!" Then he continued inspecting as before with his magnifying glass. Horace and I were dumbfounded by Sigerson's behavior. We spoke between ourselves and agreed that his mere physical presence and level of energy seemed to fill the place.

Finally he stood, turned abruptly to Wan-Po, and asked, "Where was your precious volume kept? A secret cache perhaps?"

The monk didn't seem to want to respond. He delayed his response sufficiently long that Sigerson made another noise of frustration.

"Are there exits, or doors, or rooms or other secret portals in the immediate vicinity?"

Wan-Po still didn't reply, though it appeared as though he was trying to say something. Finally, Sigerson stepped over to a shelf behind the table, where there were piled many long books with board covers from goodness knows when, reached behind and did something, and suddenly, a section of the wall adjacent swung open on a kind of hinge, revealing a passageway behind.

Wan-Po and all the other monks in attendance gasped in astonishment, then spoke rapidly amongst themselves. Wan-Po exclaimed, "More proof of your guilt! How would you know of the cache unless you had been here before when it was open . . . and stolen its contents?"

Sigerson didn't even honor this remark with a rebuff. He grabbed the nearest sweet-smelling butter lamp and crossed the threshold, glass in hand. We all made our way slowly down the passage, which was about forty feet long, following Sigerson. At the end was a wonderful room, a true secret chamber, hung with gold fabric and elaborate rugs and infinitely detailed paintings of historical scenes. As the lamp flickered, the metallic contents of the room sparkled, highlighting different quarters at different times. As interesting as the general ambiance of the room was, the nature of the scenes depicted in the paintings and rugs drew our special attention.

The main character was a Buddha-like figure, but not Buddha—that is to say, not the typical Buddha image. And the scenes were of this figure speaking to crowds. And there was another figure in attendance, a sort of compatriot to the thin Buddha.

Sigerson glanced around, didn't seem at all surprised by anything he saw, and stepped over to an elaborately carved wooden chest which was centered on a shelf along the back wall. He moved the chest aside and revealed a niche in the wall just big enough to hold a typical Tibetan book. Of course, it was empty.

Now Wan-Po positively gloated. "What more proof do I need?" he asked of those clustered in the small room. "With each passing minute, the man establishes his presence at the scene of the atrocious crime."

With admirable restraint, Sigerson continued to ignore the man's pompous remarks. Horace and I looked at one another as though to say, "My, my, he does seem more than passingly familiar with the layout of the place . . . ." Finally, after a few minutes of crawling around on the floor and peering into literally every corner of the room, Sigerson stood, positioned himself against a wall, folded his arms, and said, "Please, explain to me what this room held . . . in precise detail, if you will." Wan-Po opened his mouth, with the intention of objecting, I'm certain, when Sigerson made a quick reference to the Dalai Lama, and the inspector monk groaned, and relayed the following history:

"For many centuries, a particular text, detailing the life of a beloved monk who lived long ago has been hidden in the very niche you see there. During the life and reign of each Dalai Lama, only three people at any given time know of its existence: the Dalai Lama, the head librarian whose duty it is to guard the text, and the chief of police monks.

"The text is of little importance except for ritual purposes; however, the boards that have covered the volume have over the centuries been inlaid with gold and decorated with jewels. It can't be imagined that the text was stolen for its own sake, but more likely for the value of the cover."

"Who was the monk whom you think so highly of?" Sigerson asked.

"His name was Issa. He lived long ago. It is said he knew Buddha himself, but that is only a story."

Sigerson mulled over what he had heard for a while, dropped his glass into his pocket, took one last look around and said, "I must see the body."

Wan-Po was taken aback by this. "Why, that is impossible. The vultures have taken him to heaven."

I suppose that for those uninitiated into the ways of Tibet that an explanation is due at this point. Because Tibet has little ground worthy of agriculture, most of it being rock, or rocky moraine, centuries ago the natives developed the pragmatic ritual known as "sky burial." It is simple enough: In lieu of ground to bury them in, each dawn undertakers chop to pieces the bodies of the recently deceased and feed them to carnivorous vultures, which Tibetans believe to be sacred beings that take the souls of the dead to paradise.

CHAPTER SIX

An Undertaker and a Doctor

Shortly thereafter, we found ourselves in the southeastern corner of Lhasa, where Sigerson sought to interview the "Disposers of the Dead," or morticians, at the sky burial site. Despite our familiarity with the subject, having tarried in Tibet at length, Horace and I exchanged glances of disgust. There had apparently been a "service" only recently, as there was a pool of blood in the middle of the clearing, and the air still smelled of the pine and cypress that was burnt to attract the vultures.

Wan-Po, who had belligerently accompanied us, spoke to one man explaining our mission. Sigerson, as might be gathered by now, was not one to waste time. He immediately introduced himself and began to fire a barrage of questions. He then took the undertaker aside by the arm and the two of them spoke in muffled voices for a time, the undertaker occasionally looking towards Wan-Po, as though seeking guidance, though not receiving any from the disgruntled monk.

While they spoke, I looked around. On three sides we were surrounded by gray outcroppings. A swarm of perhaps twenty-five vultures circled high overhead. Probably they had only just finished their meal as we had arrived.

Certainly, the vultures of Tibet are uncannily spoiled. Beyond what I've explained in passing, there are also these details to share, gentle reader: Following the dissection of the corpse, the first thing the undertaker does is remove and pound the bones, mixing them with tsampa-roasted barley flour. This mixture is fed to the vultures first. In this way, no mortal remains are left. Once every morsel of the corpse is devoured, the birds take flight. The soul is set free.

Finally Sigerson grunted approval and ventured back to our group.

"Capital!" He seemed to actually gloat. "Now I must see Paljori's rooms!"

Paljori, it proved, lived in a small one room apartment adjoining his precious library.

Wan-Po showed us through with a contemptuous bow. Sigerson proceeded as before, instantly taking command, bustling about, glass in hand, peering in every corner, crevice, and crack. The room itself was similar to other monks' rooms, so far as I could see, which is to say, it was identical in sparseness.

We were there about five minutes when Sigerson rushed through the opening that served as a door and demanded of Wan-Po to see the chief medical monk. Once again we traveled the breadth of the city, and we were introduced to Brother Linga, the very fellow who helped diagnosis Horace's heart condition. The meeting proved to be the twin of the one with the mortician—hushed whispers out of earshot.

Finally Sigerson came back to our group and told all present that he would like to spend a quiet evening with Horace and myself in his rooms, and that in the morning he would announce who, without doubt, the murderer was and also locate the missing priceless tome.

CHAPTER SEVEN

Sigerson's Solutions

So it was that we three Europeans found ourselves in comparative comfort for the first time in several days, albeit with guards stationed in the hall outside Sigerson's door. Truth to tell, we were all exhausted. For the life of me, I couldn't imagine how Sigerson could be so confident that he'd solved the riddle, when I certainly saw nothing that pointed in any direction other than toward ourselves.

During the hours that preceded our retiring for the night, Horace and I engaged Sigerson in an intellectual debate, the point of which was Horace trying to knock Sigerson off his high horse. However, Sigerson maintained his irritatingly haughty attitude, and there was nothing for Horace and I to do but hope that tomorrow would be a better day.

Yet, part of me believes (in retrospect, mind you) that Sigerson was terribly lonely that night. We were invited to his room to share time with him, but his attitude rubbed us the wrong way and distanced us. I wonder, in light of later events, how that night would have gone if Horace and I had been more agreeable and open to the man. Perhaps it was we—faced with the unbelievable—who were rude and insensitive, and not he, who was merely justifiably proud of his abilities. A man looking back on his life often regrets decisions, and wishes he could reverse some—this is one of those times for me.

Regardless, the following describes our discussion that night:

When we were settled down, Sigerson on his rough bed, Horace on what passed for a chair, and myself on the dirt floor, Sigerson asked, "Well, what do you think? Did I run these rascals ragged? Do you have any ideas?"

Horace said, "Frankly, Sigerson, I have to admit I'm impressed with the energy expended in your efforts; however, I'm at a loss to understand what you could have possibly learned. A lot of chasing after wild gooses if you ask me."

Sigerson laughed, which, of course, may as well have been calculated to set off poor Horace. Whatever else Sigerson does or doesn't have, or can or cannot do, I can say with assurance that his social graces leave much to be desired. I never knew a man who could so easily upset all those around him with a mere flick of the wrist or toss of the head or a slightly-off tone of voice.

But before Horace could even open his mouth to object, I jumped in, stating, "Well, it's all still a mystery to me. What could those horrid vulture feeders have been able to tell you, or for that matter, how could the dust in the corners of the rooms have made any difference? I only pray that we can get out of this with our skins."

"My feeling," continued Horace, "is that there is more here than meets the eye. I don't believe that you are what you say you are, Sigerson. So out with it. Who are you? What are you doing here? What is all this hocus-pocus you've been trying to pass off as deduction and detection—?"

"My good man! Holly, I dare say, please. You are getting yourself overwrought! You yourself speak of 'more than meeting the eye.' My avocation is simply spying those details—sometimes remarkable, sometimes not—that nine hundred ninety-nine people out of a thousand don't see. The details are there, sometimes blown into corners by draughts, sometimes as isolated bits of information taken for granted by one person but not even known to another. I look for all these disparate pieces and assemble them. Sometimes the process is simple, like pieces of a puzzle neatly coming together, and *voilà*, there is the answer! Other times, the solution is more difficult to ascertain." "Skullduggery is more like it!"

"Horace, honestly, I, too, am beginning to lose my patience with your fears. The man has just successfully bought us some time. We need now to plan our escape."

"Perhaps, as a fallback, that is a good idea," Sigerson offered. "However, if we can accept the word of the high lamas here, we will be able to walk away tomorrow, if such is our desire."

"How can you possibly say that?"

"Obviously, I'll simply tell them who killed Paljori and lead them to their sacred book. When they have everything they want, they will release us."

"Do you mean to say you actually know these things?"

"Of course."

The absurdity of it struck me as funny. Therefore, I knew what Horace's feelings must be. I had to hurry to think of an idea to circumvent his wrath.

"Well, then, let us try to guess the answer," I ventured. "We were with you today, saw nearly everything you saw, met the people you met. I know I have a theory, as must Horace. Let's compare our ideas."

"Capital!"

"I believe there are Chinese spies among us." "Now, why on earth would you think that?"

"Well, obviously since the Dalai Lama is involved, it must be some big political brouhaha, which indicates international intrigue. At present, there are only three nations interested in Tibet from a political point of view—Britain, Russia, and China. Holly and I are the only representatives of Her Majesty here, and we are certainly not spies, let alone killers. That leaves the Russians and the Chinese. But since there has been no evidence of non-Orientals lurking about, then the culprit or culprits must be Chinese disguised as Tibetans."

"Most impressive, Vincey. Yes, yes, a most impressive feat of mental derring-do. Unfortunately, you could not be further from the truth."

"And why do you say that?"

"Well, for one thing, the Russians could easily have utilized Mongolians, or border Tibetans for that matter, but it is a more fundamental problem than that. What about you, Holly?"

"Frankly, it is as much a mystery to me today as it was when we first heard about it. I don't see where it all leads. I only hope we get out of this fix somehow. In fact, I hope that you are right in whatever it is you reveal tomorrow, Sigerson."

"So be it!"

We retired late that night and slept restlessly. Indeed, I think that sleep was denied Horace entirely, for I would awaken intermittently through the night and hear my foster father muttering to himself.

But at last, the guards roused us the next morning and off we went to confront Wan-Po in the temple. There was some arguing between him and Sigerson, then the Norwegian suggested we all return to Paljori's apartment, which we did in short order.

"Wan-Po, please give me a description of the book."

"It is two feet long, perhaps four inches thick, and eight wide. The cover boards are the rarest mahogany inlaid with gold, emeralds, rubies, diamonds. This ornamentation was created centuries ago in the form of a dragon eating its own tail by a master artisan of such high caliber the world has never seen another like him. The pages are a kind of parchment, brittle now and so brown the text is barely discernible."

"Admirable. Admirable, indeed."

Just at this point, without so much as a whisper to warn us of his approach, and with a grand flourish consisting of piercing tones from six-foot-long ceremonial horns, conch shells, various reed instruments, and drums, the young Dalai Lama entered the room. It was a most unexpected and awesome entrance.

"Excuse me, gentlemen, but I was curious," said the boy.

Sigerson's eyes glowed with fire. "Ah, you are just in time, Your Grace!" he said triumphantly.

And then with a dramatic turn, Sigerson thrust aside Paljori's rough cot and pointed at a section of the wall.

"There is where you will find your precious document."

Astonished, I peered at what he was pointing to, but could only see the blank wall. The others in the room appeared equally confused.

"What manner of nonsense is this?" Wan-Po erupted. "Do you take me for a fool?"

"Humour me, my good man, and touch that section of wall and then the surrounding sections."

Reluctantly, the Dalai Lama's head police officer did so.

"This section is rougher than the surrounding areas. So what?"

"I do believe that if you were to set men to gouge out a hole at that spot, you'll find your document."

Not to drag out this narrative longer than necessary, they did just that, and, as God is my witness, in a cache in the wall, wrapped in the finest silks, was the book in question, housed in a box and between covers every bit as fine as we'd been led to believe.

Horace groaned and whispered to me, "Don't you see it? Sigerson was the guilty party all the time. How else would he have known where to look? He is the murderer. And how clever he is to have hidden it where no one else in the world would have dreamt to look for it."

I looked at Horace with horror. I couldn't believe he actually believed what he said. To my mind, however idiosyncratic Sigerson might sometimes seem, he wouldn't have allowed us to be falsely accused. No. It was unthinkable!

Sigerson, for his part, though he must have heard Horace's frustrated remark, chose to ignore it, and instead confronted Wan-Po. The police monk was tenderly looking over the volume when Sigerson interjected. "You have your volume now, and I can safely presume that it is in fact the tome for which you were so desperate, not the elaborate cover and box. Gold and jewels are replenishable; whatever this manuscript may be, is not."

Wan-Po ignored Sigerson's statement and looked up with suspicion in his eyes. Then he made, in his own language, a remark nearly identical to Horace's, denouncing Sigerson as the ultimate culprit.

"On the contrary. 'Twas not I," Sigerson calmly responded. "But I know who is, or was, rather."

We waited. All eyes inevitably drifted to the Dalai Lama's expectant expression.

Sigerson drew out the moment, slowly meeting the gaze of each and every person present. For a moment, I felt I was immersed in a stage production. Finally, he spoke again.

"Paljori was deathly afraid of Vincey there, and Holly and myself—for no other reason than we represented the different. But worse than his fear of us as individuals, he feared what we represented—our home-lands, the Western world, our governments. He could not allow us to leave your country to report, so that others would follow us. There was no greater threat in the world to the man, and he plotted how to be rid of us. He needed for us to enrage those Tibetans who had the power to triple and quadruple the civil effort to prevent foreigners from penetrating your borders. He had to guarantee that no non-Tibetan would ever again enter Tibet, let alone travel all the way to Lhasa."

I realized my jaw was hanging open. Horace, I saw, was pale.

"Paljori, gentlemen, hid the book himself where he felt no one would ever look, planted evidence that pointed clearly and irrevocably to my friends and myself, then simply killed himself. His faith in his convictions was so great."

Wan-Po was too taken aback to speak.

"Proof? You will want proof for such an apparently outlandish conclusion, of course," Sigerson continued. "I can quickly provide it. Will the undertaker and the medical monk, who are waiting outside, please step in?"

Whereupon the two indicated persons stepped in from outside, clearly uncomfortable to be in the presence of their revered spiritual leader on one hand, and to be the centers of attention on the other.

"You'll have to excuse this little surprise," Sigerson went on. "Your Grace, you'll remember, you gave me the power to question these men. I took the liberty, as well, to ask them to be available here at this time. Now, I'll have them clear up this last sticky point."

Whereupon, in response to queries from Sigerson, the medical monk described the nature of the wound, as did the mortician, both indicating that the slash was just deep enough to have been inflicted by the wielder of the sword in question, but not so deep as one would expect if a second person had wielded the weapon.

Finally, Wan-Po was convinced, as was Horace. The Dalai Lama was clearly impressed.

As a reward, Sigerson asked only that we three foreigners be given the opportunity to learn the contents of the document that was so important to our hosts and so nearly disastrous for us.

The boy granted Sigerson's request. Unexpectedly, the volume proved to be written in Aramaic. Horace, being familiar with the written form of the language, volunteered to read it aloud. Though there was Tibetan annotation, he read directly from the original. I wish to God he hadn't read it at all. But it is not mine to pick or choose as God might. Here is a copy of the old Tibetan book. Make of it as you will.

The Gospel of Issa

1. Is it God or is it I who guides this brush? God fills me as milk warm from the goat fills a cup to overflowing.

2. Long ago I ceased to be merely the man who is the son of my parents. I was young when God showed Himself to me:

3. That was the time I ceased to be the son of my parents. I became then an instrument of the Lord. I, Issa, son of Joseph, the carpenter of Nazareth, ceased to be.

4. My whole will from that time forward focused on the fact of God's gracing me with the indisputable awareness of His presence.

5. Why me? What did I ever do to deserve the acquaintance of God? My time and my life have been for these last eighteen years fully a matter of trying to understand what was and is happening to me.

6. I am filled with God. But tell me, if you empty a fig of its meat and fill its skin with mandarin orange pulp, are you left with an orange?

7. Then I am no more God than the fig is an orange. But as that fig, transformed, knows more of oranges than a natural fig, so I know more of God than a natural man.

8. They will say, I think, that I am the son of God. Others will say I am a fraud!

9. I know that the Lord has chosen me for some other than ordinary purpose. I can see glimpses of it, but the details elude me.

10. These things are fact, not to be ignored by me or anyone.

11. I know clearly how the prophets must have felt; what they must have known. As God spoke to Abraham and Moses and Isaiah, so He speaks to me.

12. I truly know that I am to do my Lord's bidding; I am to be the instrument of His will.

13. My Lord wants me to wander through the East and absorb everything I see and hear.

14. So be it. Such is what we have done for nearly eighteen years. Here I am with my brother Didymus Judas Thomas in the land of the Bon,* the mightiest mountain country that my Father has created.

15. We have traveled far, about as far from home as is imaginable.

16. I have learned much: the tenets of Hinduism, Buddhism, Confucianism, yoga. These are all fonts from which I have drunk mightily.

17. What is it now that I am supposed to do? Is it time to return? Home has beckoned for months now.

18. Is there anything else to learn in this high land of false magic and superstition? Will I know what to do when the time comes?

19. Now, however, I write this account as You have asked, or, rather, ordered, for my Father does not ask.

20. I am here, Lord; but I don't know why. I have learned much, but I don't know why. We have traveled far, and I don't know why.

---

* Editor's note: An ancient name for Tibet.—T.K.M.

21. Everything is so different than that which I was taught as a child in Nazareth.

22. Is it that I am loath to admit to myself what your purpose is for me?

23. In our wanderings, I have noted a common theme. A tenet that explains so much—that answers so many of your children's unanswered questions.

24. Whether in China or India or here in the loftiest mountains, so long as I am in the East, I hear of death and rebirth, and of the soul using the body much as I would ride in a vehicle:

25. How after death, the soul must be born again. Though in a new vehicle, or vessel, according to the merit that the soul exhibited in its previous existences.

26. It is a meritorious approach to existence certainly. Much as a school boy moves from one level of learning to another higher level, so, too, a death marks the potential for a move, for the coming to a crossroads;

27. But as some children need to repeat an entire season of lessons due to slothfulness or poor behavior or inattentiveness, so, too, a soul must sometimes repeat a wasted life in order to attain the merit to move on.

28. Attainment of merit is simple, surely. To do onto others as you would have them do onto you.

29. If a man or a woman follows this tenet for a lifetime, he or she will achieve merit and be closer to God for having done so: In this life and in the next.

30. To be One with the Father, that is the purpose of existence: base man must rise above his baseness to sit at the right hand of the Father.

31. Yet it is slow. God's time is not man's time, nor woman's. A human lifetime is but the single beat of a fly's wing in God's measure.

32. The miracle is that God notices, and more than this, that God cares.

33. But God does care. If God was not Love Incarnate, perhaps all of human existence could have begun and ended without the Father even knowing.

34. But God does know and God does love.

35. Patience is the foundation.

36. An hour, a day, a month, a year, seven years, a single lifetime is not enough.

37. I have had arguments, or, rather, discussions with my brother Thomas.

38. It is self-apparent, I will say to him, that the punishment for the curser is that the soul will forget its previous life and will be cast down into a body that will spend its time continually troubled in its heart;

39. That the punishment for the arrogant and over-bearing man is that the soul will forget from whence it came and will be cast down into a lame and deformed body so that all despise it persistently.

40. Then Thomas will ask, "And the man who hath committed no sin, but done good persistently, but hath not found the mysteries, what will happen to him?"

41. And I reply, "He will seek the light and will find it."

42. *Surely, then, my destiny is to teach of these matters and others, such as the righteousness of humility and of seeking and others of which I have learned during our long sojourn.*

43. *But to whom? Surely, the people of our fathers, the people of Abraham will make naught of such matters.*

44. *Oh, my brother and I have seen so much in these last years.*

45. *By caravan, we followed the silk road to Bactra and from thence to Kabul and Palitara. I have seen the holy cities of Juggernaut, Rajagrina, Benares, and Kopilavastu.*

46. *We have journeyed through many nations and supped with many peoples.*

47. *I am filled to overflowing with the wisdom of the ages.*

48. *You told me that I am Your tool. Well, use me! I have much knowledge and have acquired marvelous techniques. What is it all for? I am tired.*

49. *(Could it be that it was I who wrote here of patience?)*

50. *I know now that I am to teach. Well, then, let me teach! How much more must I learn? I have seen your many faces!*

51. *Eloi, Eloi! I am lonely. Despite the companionship of my brother, Thomas, I am tired of being a stranger in a strange land.*

52. *I have learned without doubt that You are Love, but I do not love. I have teachers but no friends.*

53. *I am feeling sorry for myself, for I am lonely and too wise.*

54. *I know God as well as I know Joseph, the husband of my mother, Mariam.*

55. In the beginning, when I was very young, He would speak to me, and I would respond.

56. He spoke to me and it was clear enough. Not in words would He speak, but in signs and symbols and, sometimes, in dreams, too, He made His wants known. Learning the language of the signs was the challenge.

57. What is school if not a challenge for the student?

58. As a child who does good is rewarded, and is punished for having done bad, so, too, God shows pleasure when a sign is read correctly and displeasure when a sign is misread.

59. Usually some coincidence that inspired wonder would be my reward for right interpretation; a sense of foreboding being the clue that there was misreading.

60. I needed always to plumb my feelings and try to understand what God was trying to say. In time, I built a whole vocabulary.

✦ ✦ ✦

61. My brother, Issa, is dead. I, Didymus Judas Thomas, who has been my brother's companion for nearly eighteen years as we traveled through the strange lands of the East, am now alone. I am afraid. God has deserted us.

62. Issa was attacked in a dark alley by robbers and was clubbed to death. The morticians here, who feed their dead to the birds, have him in their care now.

63. I cannot bear to stay in this foreign land one day longer. I am leaving for home, Judea.

64. I have much to carry; I leave behind much; my burdens are heavy.

[Thus ends the manuscript.]

Conclusion

Horace was silent for a time, as we all were. Eventually, he seemed to awaken as from a trance and carefully picked up the loose leaves he had been turning over as he read, straightened them neatly, and replaced them onto the back cover, then replaced the top board, effectively returning the volume to the state in which we found it.

Then Horace folded his hands over the book and bent his head. I think he was praying. Sigerson was sitting with his back against the wall, his hands steepled as he so often held them, and appeared in deep concentration.

The young Dalai Lama, to whom, presumably, the story was familiar, sat calmly on Paljori's cot watching us passively.

For myself, I felt dazed, confused—only dimly aware of the impressions I've recorded above.

Finally, Horace looked up. I saw a hopeful glow on his countenance.

"Issa died here in Tibet," he said. "Obviously what we are all thinking . . . must be a case of mistaken identity. The man we've known as Jesus and this Issa must not have been the same man, since Jesus continued to live for some years."

Before anyone could respond directly, a thought suddenly loomed in my mind. I suppose my face must have registered some sort of shock for suddenly all eyes in that room were upon me.

The thought was so startling that I didn't want to speak it aloud. But I saw I had no choice.

"There is a conclusion that naturally follows from the narrative we have just heard: If the real Jesus of Nazareth died here in Tibet, then someone claiming to be him appeared in Palestine sometime afterward. This brings up the possibility of an impersonator."

"My God," said Horace. "That can't be! For that would mean that all of Christianity is based on the work of an impostor. Could the entire faith of the Western world be predicated on a sham? No, by God!"

No one in the room responded.

Horace continued, "No, Leo. You forget, when Jesus returned, he was accepted by his family, by his mother, and by Thomas his brother, who apparently was the last to see him, at least according to this narrative."

To which I said, "Jesus left the fold when he was twelve. Eighteen years later, a man returned claiming to be Jesus. An imposter, I believe, could have successfully perpetrated this fraud under those circumstances."

"But what about Thomas?" Horace countered. "He would have been in the best position to recognize the fraud and didn't . . . ."

Horace's voice faded. Surely he remembered that it was, in fact, Thomas who was the most vocal with his doubts.

All this time Sigerson maintained his silence, and Horace finally demanded of him, "Well, man, what do you think?"

Sigerson put down his pipe. "Yes, yes, what do I think indeed? I think we've heard all that is necessary to deduce the truth. It is straightforward. Issa spent much time in India where he no doubt was a disciple of Hindu yogis. He became adept at controlling his respiration, temperature and pulse, and when he was attacked by the hoodlums, with no chance to escape, he feigned death to avoid a further beating. Thomas, who was not privy to the extent of his brother's spiritual prowess, in low spirits quit the East and immediately returned home.

"Following his brother's departure, Issa, that is, Jesus, roused himself from his self-induced trance, and, finding himself alone, continued his adventures and education for a little time, and then he, too, returned."

Horace closed his eyes tightly, then opened them and spoke: "You're saying that Jesus made himself appear to die, then sometime later awakened and continued his business."

"Yes."

"Then, assuming what you say has some basis in truth, that which he accomplished once, he could accomplish again, couldn't he?"

Sigerson didn't reply, merely sucking on the pipe that he'd pulled out and lit at some point. The young Dalai Lama chose this moment to interject his thoughts.

"Gentlemen, it is quite clear, I think, that the results of this investigation, if taken in a certain light, could be the death knell of your Christianity. It is my understanding that belief in Jesus' resurrection is the foundation of your faith. Take away resurrection and suddenly there is no foundation. If your Jesus did not in fact come back from the dead, but pretended to—"

"No, no! Don't say it, Your Grace! I cannot bear to hear it."

Horace was beside himself with grief. For myself, I reeled with confusion. What did it all mean? Could Jesus Christ have been a fraud? Was he a mere charlatan who successfully duped half the world, and all of Western civilization? Could all sanctity and piety be nothing more than a joke? Sigerson must have read the thoughts on my face. Certainly Horace was as pale as a ghost. I doubted I looked better.

"Now see here, men, straighten up," Sigerson said.

Whereas to this point he had maintained his smug, self-satisfied posture, for once he became thoroughly serious. He knocked his pipe out onto the dirt floor and drew Horace and I close.

"Now the way I see it," he said, "Issa, or Jesus, was not a fraud—was hardly a villain—and was every bit as good a man as we all take him to be—but he was a victim of circumstances. I believe he eventually returned to his home where he reestablished himself in his family and began to share his acquired wisdom with his neighbors. As word got around about this man and his radical views, people flocked to him and he found himself thrown into the position of teacher.

"Doubtless, he had no intention of dying before his time, and when he found himself arrested and condemned, he realized that he had within himself the means to survive. Whether or not he planned to be discovered walking about later, it is hard to say. But he was spotted and, no matter his explanation, to the great unwashed of Palestine his continued existence seemed a miracle.

"Poor Jesus, I'm sure he would be appalled to learn that what was likely an act of self-preservation has been misinterpreted through the ages."

Horace and I didn't feel much relieved after hearing this. Perhaps Jesus wasn't a fraud per se, but the alternative proposed by

Sigerson nevertheless toppled the pillars and shattered the foundations of Christianity.

The Dalai Lama spoke again: "It seems so strange that a misunderstanding could root itself and become so integral a part of a faith for millennia."

"Your Grace, you should well know why the concept of resurrection has held for so long. It was because there was, after all, some basis of truth in it."

For myself, after having had my soul, my very identity as a Christian, dashed to the ground, this little bit of news seemed to hold succor. I waited hopefully.

"After all, resurrection is merely a form of rebirth. And it was a different doctrine of rebirth that Jesus no doubt shared with his people. It is clear, I think, what Jesus' message was when he returned from the East. Jesus saw his people suffering under the Roman yoke and shared with them the laws of karma. He taught them to do onto others as they would have them et cetera. Seek and you will find.

"Quite clearly, within the remnants of his thoughts that have been preserved to the present, these notions are paramount. He taught that to do good was all important and that, whether or not they were rewarded in this life, they would be in the next. These are clearly karmic concepts.

"But it appears that following the delivery of his message, much was lost, forgotten, misinterpreted, deleted, changed, appended, and amended; still, doubtless a fair number of references to karma and metempsychosis still existed. But even those—all but a few fragmentary references such as those I just indicated—were purged from all Christian writings after 553 A.D."

"Why 553 A.D.?" I asked petulantly.

"It is rather a convoluted story. I will see if I can summarize it: Our orthodox versions of the New Testament date no further back than that year, when the Byzantine Emperor Justinian called the Fifth Ecumenical Congress of Constantinople in 553 A.D., supposedly to condemn the writings of a certain early church father.

"During that congress, events were initiated that caused the relatively few Bibles then extant to be edited or destroyed and all competitive gospels and histories of Christ to be likewise destroyed.

This appears to be largely the doing of Justinian's Empress, Theodora, who, it is said, started out as an actress and prostitute. How a commoner became an empress is another story. Suffice it to say she was world-wise and greed-driven, and she beguiled Justinian. Before long she was running the Empire as Justinian sniveled at her side.

"It was Theodora's great hope that upon her death, she would be instantly elevated to divine status. Since the doctrine of metempsychosis, with its slow cycles of birth and rebirth, opposed such an immediate destiny for her, she set about obliterating every reference to that doctrine that existed in the Empire and beyond. The fact that Christ's very teachings contradicted her desire did not matter. There was a conflagration that lasted decades as books were burnt across the civilized world. Thus nearly all references to Christ's Eastern teachings were deleted from the bible or altered to reflect a view that did not offend the Emperor and Empress. The latter, by the way, died in 547, six years before the congress in question. Apparently Justinian was determined that his consort would get her way posthumously.

"Beyond this, you must remember that the various books of the New Testament were pieced together totally independently of one another from a potpourri of pieces and sources. God only knows what was lost before Justinian and Theodora did their damage!"

Horace and I listened to all this sullenly. What were we to say? What further comment could we make? Sigerson spoke again. He said, "I live by a philosophy that has done good service for me. Namely, when all possibilities have been eliminated and all that is left is the impossible, then the impossible is the solution.

"Frankly, it appears obvious to me that metempsychosis is the only logical solution to the great mystery of the Injustice of Life—how it is that the good are allowed to suffer while the wicked roll in blessings, that innocent children should die, that plagues devastate populations and war destroys all. Otherwise Life on earth is a travesty . . . otherwise Life on earth is a mockery . . . otherwise Life on earth has no meaning at all."

"But how could God," I was prompted to ask, "have allowed the Bible to be so tampered with?"

"Because," Sigerson shot back, "though altered and watered down, it still served His purpose: The vision of Christ's resurrection and the festival of Easter still gave people hope—and certainly Christianity taught that we're all responsible for our actions. The root moral concepts underlying metempsychosis were still there, just obscured. The altered message still served God's plan."

And so it continued until I was numb with exhaustion. And finally there came a time when we all retired to our respective quarters.

Once we were back in the solitude and quiet of our apartment, thoughts came without my prompting:

Were we to accept reincarnation in place of Christ's resurrection? Certainly, I, Leo Vincey, of all people, had something to say in the matter! Am I not—even now—searching for a woman—my true love—who I know beyond a doubt is dead, for I saw her die with my own eyes? Isn't it true that Horace and I are searching for Ayesha's new incarnation, though we've never gone so far to admit it quite in that fashion before? Didn't she claim that I myself was the reincarnation of one Kallikrates, an Egyptian priest? Certainly, during our encounter with Ayesha, I believed none of her stories; but now I ask myself time and again, if I don't believe, why then am I searching for her now? Why have I spent six good years of my life looking for her who has already died? I suppose I must believe in my heart, or these last many years have been a waste!*

Then again, even if I were to admit belief in reincarnation, does that necessarily mean that Jesus had anything at all to do with the doctrine? Does that invalidate resurrection? What does my belief or disbelief have to do with Jesus and the birth of Christianity?

So many questions. So much muddle in my mind. I have no answers.

It was shortly after his reading of the sacred text that Horace fell ill. I believe the foundations of all that he believed in were battered

---

* Editor's note: Ten more years will pass before Leo and Horace find Ayesha.—T.K.M.

irreparably. Can I blame Sigerson? Part of me wishes we never met the man with his cold insufferable logic. Yet part of me is also aware that Horace and I shared a fabulous adventure with the man. I hold nothing against him. We all must do what we must do.

So I have done what I set out to do; I have recorded an incident that might have been better left unrecorded. Still I could not sit back and pretend it didn't happen. Horace and I will linger here in Lhasa until he recovers sufficiently to continue our trek, or return home, whichever seems appropriate at the time. Sigerson is preparing to leave—in search of Yeti he says. I wish him luck.

There is nothing more to tell.

Addendum

Upon returning to Lhasa three months after the incident last recorded in this narrative—from an interesting and hardly fruitless quest into the Nepalese Himalayas—I was given the Vincey journal by His Holiness the High Lama, who said Vincey left it with the request that I deal with it as I saw fit, or for the fates to deal with it as they will if I had no interest in it.

I note that Vincey did an adequate job of relating the circumstances and facts much as I recall them, though it is odd to read of another's sentiments toward oneself. Be that as it may, I will take this journal back to England, where I'm sure Watson will be interested in it, and possibly arrange through his or Holly's agent to have it published as a worthy footnote to Holly's and Vincey's original adventures.

It should be noted here, therefore, for the benefit of those who will not be content until they understand the reasoning, how it was I knew where to find the hidden latch that worked the secret door opening onto the chamber of Issa's journal. It is really very simple. We know that the library—which is contemporaneous with the Potala Palace—is many centuries old and that many generations of librarians have guarded the volume, checking it probably daily. In point of fact, the stone floor had been worn down over this period by the countless tread of librarians' feet so that a wide, shallow groove led right to the latch, and, similarly, the stone hollow where the latch was hidden was worn smooth and shone brightly as a result of myriad handlings.

Notwithstanding the above, I—*

---

* Editor's note: Here the manuscript ends. One can't help but wonder why "Sigerson" did not in fact carry the journal back to England with him, since its coming into my possession via Nepal would indicate the notebooks remained behind. Perhaps Holmes had a change of heart. Or perhaps they were stolen from him by Nepalese highwaymen. Regardless, we of our time and our heirs must be grateful that "the fates" saw fit that these pages eventually fell into sympathetic hands.—T. K. M.

ALLAN QUATERMAIN AT THE CRUCIBLE OF LIFE;
Or, The Adventure of the Rose of Fire

From a Memoir As Told By
Allan Quatermain
Author of "King Solomon's Mines," "She and Allan," "Marie," ETC.

1881 Manuscript Recorded, Edited, and Supplemented By
John H. Watson, M.D.
Author of "A Study in Scarlet," "The Hound of the Baskervilles" ETC.

Edited, Supplemented, and Annotated By
Thos. Kent Miller
Editor of "Sherlock Holmes on he Roof of the World" ETC.

A red light, a burning spark seen far away in the darkness, taken at the first moment of seeing for a signal . . . and then, as if in an incredible point of time, it swelled into a vast rose of fire that filled all the sea and all the sky and possessed the land.

—Arthur Machen in "The Great Return"

Travelers afoot in hot deserts should set their course toward shade!

—*Junior Woodchucks' Guidebook*

Remember, most loving and compassionate Virgin Mary, it has never been said or heard that anyone who turned to you for help was left unaided. Inspired with this conviction, I run to your protection and stand before you penitent of my wrong doings, for you are my mother and the mother of all. O Mother of the Word of God, neglect not my prayers, despise not my words of pleading, but in your mercy, please hear and answer me. Amen.

—*The Memorare:* A Prayer to Mary

Hurt and you will be hurt, love and you will be loved, cause someone to cry in suffering and you will be made to cry with your own suffering. This circle of doing followed by God's response may be experienced immediately or may be held off for a future. or even a past, lifetime, according to the will of God for his own reasons.

—*The Gospel of Gaspar*

Dedication

To Sir Henry Rider Haggard (1856-1925)

My Dear Sir:

As you so often with sincerity dedicated your books to those you admired, I would like to offer this volume to you, though, as I place these words down, you have been gone from us for nearly a century.

Let me accomplish this by meandering a bit. During the early 1950s when I was a child, my father and older brother read Uncle Scrooge *comic books (published for ten cents at the time by Dell Publishing Co., Inc.). I received them as hand-me-downs and was enchanted and enthralled by the adventures of Uncle Scrooge McDuck and his nephews, Donald Duck and Huey, Dewey, and Louie. Though it was obvious that my father and brother enjoyed these stories, at some point I realized that somehow these illustrated tales of lost cities and civilizations touched a special chord in me that transcended mere enjoyment. I knew this because my reaction to them was fundamentally different; my father and brother forgot about them and lost track of them, whereas I treasured every panel, turned the pages reverently as I read and reread the stories, and considered them my most precious possessions.*

On the cover, prominently displayed above the title was the name of Walt Disney. What I did not know as a child was that during that era of comic book history the actual writers and artists who created the comic stories were anonymous. As an adult, I learned that Mr. Disney had little or nothing to do with Uncle Scrooge. *Scrooge was the creation of a man named Carl Barks and the best Scrooge stories—the ones that haunted me, such as the Ducks's stumbling upon the Seven Cities of Cibola, the lost continent of Atlantis, and Tralla La—were written and drawn by Barks.*

Furthermore, I didn't know—and didn't learn until still more time had passed—that it was you, Sir Henry, who was the man behind Barks. He drew from you as surely as desert nomads draw from an oasis well. The magic he touched me with—as glorious as it was—was, in a way, recycled magic. You invented the magic—the subgenre of fantasy that has come to be known as the "lost race adventure."

Let me quote from the passionate historian and editor of fantasy literature, the late Lin Carter. In the introduction to a reprint of one of your novels, he wrote that you were the right man with the right idea in the right place at the right time, that time being the end of the nineteenth century at the height of a succession of momentous historical and archaeological discoveries.

"For even more exciting," Carter said, "than the discovery of lost cities of the past, dead and buried and forgotten for thousands of years, is the discovery of an ancient city tucked away in some far corner of the world—still inhabited!"

I cannot say why this subgenre you invented affects me so, but I suspect that somehow these matters are prearranged by a power far greater than ours, as perhaps you would agree. Be that as it may, because of the great joy I have experienced both from you directly in the form of your many "lost race" novels and indirectly through Mr. Barks (and not only Mr. Barks because it turns out that there are a multitude of others you have touched, among them writers named Arthur Conan Doyle, Edgar Rice Burroughs, A. Merritt, Talbot Mundy, John Taine, James Hilton, and, more recently, Ian Cameron, Lin Carter, and, of course, Michael Crichton)[1], I ask you to allow me to set your name upon these pages and subscribe myself,

Gratefully and ever sincerely yours,
Thos. Kent Miller

Introduction
H. Rider Haggard's Character Hans the Hottentot*

By *Thomas Kent Miller*

H. Rider Haggard

There are sides to H. Rider Haggard that aren't generally recognized but are manifestly interesting for those who look beyond his reputation as an adventure writer. Here I will explore three such sides, namely that he had a "secret love" who, for good or ill, fueled nearly all his fiction; that he had a very real mystical side, an intense current, that drew from fatalism and the occult in equal measure; and among his most vital characters there is one, a little Hottentot, who is universally and unfairly overlooked, yet who, I believe, symbolized for Haggard all that was good and noble in humankind.

In 1973, I chanced to read H. Rider Haggard's *The People of the Mist.* This was my first encounter with Haggard, and it affected me deeply; there was a mysterious *something* permeating the novel that I found refreshing and illuminating. My immediate reaction was to begin collecting Haggard's books, hoping that lightning would strike twice, and I was not disappointed. It took me a while, but I

---

*This introduction originally appeared in somewhat different form as "Fate as a Character: H. Rider Haggard's Secret Currents" in *Wormwood: Literature of the Fantastic, Supernatural and Decadent* Issue 20, Spring 2013, edited by Mark Valentine and published by Tartarus Press.

finally put my finger on the quality that had so excited me. It was that Haggard successfully made Fate a character in many of his books. It seemed to me that his stories did not come alive due to characterizations or plot developments so much as they did to turnings of Fate.

After a while I realized that Haggard had a cosmic view that was the tent pole from which he draped most of his stories. Usually his characters didn't exist in a logical universe that they could depend on, where B clearly followed A or where predictable effects followed causes. Haggard biographer Peter Berresford Ellis noted something of the kind when he recognized "Haggard's concern with man's ambiguous status in the universe, a universe of chance and change, and his probing towards an elucidation of purpose and establishment of a 'great end', if indeed there was one to be found."

✦ ✦ ✦

H. Rider Haggard's *King Solomon's Mines* and *She* have been continuously in print since 1885 and 1887 respectively, with *She* alone selling about 85 million copies. Nonetheless, this eminence of *She* notwithstanding, it is the title *King Solomon's Mines* that has become so much a part of western *Zeitgeist* that people who have never heard of H. Rider Haggard, or Allan Quatermain, or Ayesha, or even *She* will perk right up at the mere utterance of the syllables "King Solomon's Mines." I've seen this happen time and again during the last 40 years as I've tried to turn conversations toward Haggard.

Still, usually a reader who happens upon and reads *King Solomon's Mines* would be hard pressed to fully realize that the novel is only the first of 14 novel-length "romances" featuring Allan Quatermain. Neither would that reader know that Allan Quatermain's loyal companion through six of those novels is an old native southern African fellow named Hans, or Hans the Hottentot. Most especially this reader would be ignorant of Hans because all six of those books quickly went out of print in the United States and were not reprinted (except for the brief reappearance of *She and Allan* in the mid-1970s) until the advent of print-on-demand and ebook public domain publishing toward the end of the 1990s. In the United Kingdom, the situation was only a little better.

Allan Quatermain's career began in 1885 with *King Solomon's Mines*—and then Haggard improvidently killed him off in the speedily written sequel that was published two years later in 1887 as *Allan Quatermain*. However, the popularity of Quatermain's first two published "memoirs" necessitated that Haggard quickly resuscitate his hunter/trader and the next two consecutive years saw the publication of two novellas, *Maiwa's Revenge* and *Allan's Wife,* tucked amongst the dozen novels that poured from his insanely successful pen from 1885 to 1889. However, because an important conceit of the first two Quatermain best sellers was that they were accounts of real adventures, the only way to maintain this fiction with regard to the novellas was for Haggard to posit them as "found" manuscripts (mainly prequels), which then became a requirement for all the follow-up books.

Thus it is important to note that the first Allan Quatermain books were:

King Solomon's Mines (1885)
Allan Quatermain (1887)
Maiwa's Revenge (1888)
Allan's Wife (1889)

And then Haggard put Allan Quatermain on a shelf for 23 years! (That is, 23 years if reckoned in terms of publication dates, but it was *only* 20 years in terms of composition.) During those years, Haggard published more than 30 books of many different stripes, but Allan Quatermain was not among any of them. This in itself may not be unusual; after all, it may be as simple as Haggard wanting to move on to other things, much as Conan Doyle famously needing to distance himself from Holmes.

But then, beginning in 1912, came an outpouring of Quatermain books (titles featuring Hans are marked with an asterisk):

Marie (1912)*
Child of Storm (1913)
Allan and the Holy Flower (1915)*
The Ivory Child (1916)*
Finished (1917)
The Ancient Allan (1920)
She and Allan (1921)*
Heu-Heu or the Monster (1924)*
The Treasure of the Lake (1926 posthumously)*
Allan and the Ice Gods (1927 posthumously)

There may be nothing surprising about this that can't be explained by falling royalties and publishers' demands. Nevertheless, there were special factors in Haggard's life just then that almost dictated the rebirth of Quatermain. One such factor was that Haggard was keenly sensitive to the fact that his first-hand impressions and experiences of the period 1875 to 1879 in Natal, South Africa, as well as the voluminous native history of the region that he'd learned directly from older, more experienced colleagues, demanded recording. His friends of the period some thirty years earlier were passing from this earth one by one. He understood that his privileged position as one-time general factotum to Sir Henry Bulwer, Lieutenant-Governor of Natal in South Africa and then later as a Lieutenant of the Pretoria Horse, made him privy to knowledge and experiences of that turbulent period of the British/Boer/Zulu wars that were not only unique and invaluable, but would soon be extinct.

Thus, having just completed a 14th century historical novel set in England involving the Black Death titled *Red Eve*, and beginning about April 1909, he dictated a one-off Zulu novel titled *Child of Storm* about the rivalry between the Zulu princes Cetywayo and Umbelazi from the point of view of Allan Quatermain, and around the same time, he declared in his autobiography, which he was writing simultaneously:

> I always find it easy to write of Allan Quatermain, who, after all, is only myself set in a variety of imagined situations, thinking my thoughts and looking at life through my eyes.

Child of Storm was finished in August, but at some point during or after its writing, Haggard decided to make *Child of Storm* the middle volume of a Zulu/Quatermain trilogy examining the fall of the Zulu House of Senzangakona (i.e., Shaka's father). Upon completing *Child of Storm*, he began *Marie*, which would become the first volume of the trilogy (the third being *Finished*, 1917), dealing with the coming of the Boers to southern Africa and their bloody conflict with the Zulus.

> It is in *Marie* that Hans the Hottentot first comes on the scene . . . . The humor, unscrupulous cunning, savage wisdom, and devotion of the bibulous and ragged old "tottie" accompanies Allan through the pages of [five additional adventures].
> —Lilias Rider Haggard in *The Cloak That I Left*

Once resurrected in *Marie*, Allan Quatermain dominated Haggard's fictional output until the author's death. From 1912 until his passing in 1925 and beyond, of his 18 published books ten were Allan Quatermain chapters and six of those featured Hans the Hottentot.

It is my belief that Hans was not entirely, or merely, a character that Haggard invented to help move his plots along or to provide "local" color to his African stories. Just as Quatermain himself was Haggard's self-declared alter ego, reflecting his pragmatism as well as his innate skepticism, Hans, consciously or not, became the manifestation of Haggard's loyal, true, honorable, dependable, and faithful character, which, we will see, was likely the essence of Haggard's self-image and value system.

Marie was published in Britain more than a century ago in 1912. Therefore, some background as to H. Rider Haggard's expectations for his readership would be in order. At that time, though dwindling in popularity, "freak shows," which had been the rage for much of the previous century, were still in evidence. During the heyday of these entertainments, one of the most popular attractions was a woman from southern Africa known as "The Hottentot Venus." For the purposes of this introduction, it suffices to say that the exhibit did not reflect well on "Hottentots," serving to fuel the negative racial attitudes of the time. If Haggard wanted just then to use the medium of a popular novel to parody and castigate these attitudes, he would have justifiably assumed that the collective "mind's eye" of his audience would call up a certain image at the mere mention of the word "Hottentot"—an image, an assumption, that he could then turn on its head. Thus, he made Quatermain's sidekick a Hottentot. To put this into clearer perspective, here is what noted biologist Stephen Jay Gould tells us of the racial divide of that period.

> In an age before television and movies made virtually nothing on earth exotic . . . the exhibition of unusual humans became a profitable business . . . . Supposed savages from faraway lands were a mainstay of these exhibitions . . . . On the racist ladder of human progress, Bushmen and Hottentots vied with Australian aborigines for the lowest rung, just above chimps and orangs . . . creatures[s] who straddled that dreaded boundary between human and animal . . . .

Nowadays, we would say that Hans was of the closely related southern African ethnic groups that—during the internal timeframe of the Quatermain series—comprised the pastoralist Khoi (known then as Hottentots) and the hunter-gatherer San (known as Bushmen), both of which spoke Khoi, a clicking language. However, there was no love lost between the groups and for centuries they were periodically at war.

Now let's take measure of how Quatermain (that is to say, Haggard) viewed Hans. This passage is from *She and Allan*:

> "Hans, I should say, was that same Hottentot who had been the companion of most of my journeyings since my father's day. . . .

"One good quality he had, however; no man was ever more faithful, and perhaps it would be true to say that neither man nor woman ever loved me, unworthy, quite so well.

"In appearance he rather resembled an antique and dilapidated baboon; his face was wrinkled like a dried nut and his quick little eyes were bloodshot. I never knew what his age was, any more than he did himself, but the years had left him tough as whipcord and absolutely untiring."

This next passage is from *The Ivory Child* in which Hans sacrifices his life for Quatermain's sake:

"The truth is that after the death of Hans . . . there was no more spirit in me. For quite a long while I did not seem to care at all what happened to me or to anybody else. We buried him with honor and when the earth was thrown over his little yellow face I felt as though half my past had departed with him into that hole. Poor drunken old Hans, where in the world shall I find such another man as you were? Where in the world shall I find so much love as filled the cup of that strange heart of yours? . . . Now Hans never cared for any living creature, or for any human hope or object, as he cared for me. There was no man or woman whom he would not have cheated, or even murdered for my sake. There was no earthly advantage, down to that of life itself, that he would not . . . forgo for my sake . . . . That is love in excelsis, and the man who has succeeded in inspiring it in any creature, even in a low, bibulous, old Hottentot, may feel proud indeed. At least I am proud and as the years go by the pride increases, as the hope grows that somewhere . . . I may find the light of Hans' love burning like a beacon in the darkness, as he promised I should do, and that it may guide and warm my shivering, new-born soul before I dare the adventure of the Infinite."

Haggard authority Gerald Monsman has concluded that "Hans [is] doubtless modeled on Haggard's own South African servant

Mazooku" during Haggard's attachment to the colonial government in the 1870s, which Zulu servant was devoted to Haggard and who saved Haggard's life by doggedly seeking the injured man in the wilderness when all others had given up the search as a lost cause. This suggestion is easily supported by Haggard reminiscing in his autobiography:

> Where, I wonder, is Mazooku, who saved my life when I was lost upon the veld? . . . or if my Mazooku should be dead, as well as he may be, and if there is any future for us mortals . . . then I'm quite certain that when I reach that shore I shall see a square faced, dusky figure seated on it, and hear his words, 'Inkoos Indanda, here am I, Mazooka, who once was your man, waiting to serve you'.

Mazooku, Haggard's Zulu servant from his days in South Africa.
—Photo from *Diary of an African Journey: The Return of Rider Haggard* (New York University Press), edited by Stephen Coan

Thus, it appears we know whom Haggard modeled Hans on; but, could there have been a deeper reason why Haggard created Hans *just then*? To my way of thinking, Haggard's need to create Quatermain's Hottentot companion *at that moment in time* is far more complicated than the cataloging of all the facile explanations just enumerated.

✦ ✦ ✦

It is always tempting to describe H. Rider Haggard in a nutshell. Mike Ashley is straightforward in his assessment of Haggard, saying that he was "one of the greatest adventure writers who ever lived." Lin Carter says Haggard was the "unchallenged master of the adventure romance." And Otto Penzler sums up the matter with "The name of no writer is more closely or affectionately connected to adventure fiction than that of Sir Henry Rider Haggard." Doubtless, it is these kinds of pronouncements that casual readers take away from their first encounters with Haggard.

Indeed, Haggard novices may not be in the least aware that there is much more driving his fiction than adventure for adventure's sake. At the root of Haggard and his fiction is a more or less consistent cosmic view that permeates all his writing. Haggard's recurring theme has been importantly pointed out by Glen St. John Barclay in *Anatomy of Horror: The Masters of Occult Fiction*:

> The greater part of [Haggard's] enormous output . . . is composed of stories which either deal directly with the occult, or in which occult interventions play a fundamental part of the evolution of the plot. Moreover the assorted occult aspects can be related to one another as integral parts of a generally consistent if not always coherent philosophy which provided the inspiration for Haggard's own life . . . . Haggard's incoherence is indeed virtually a source of strength, in the sense that it reflects an attitude to human experience apparently free from any kind of dogmatic constraint or preconception . . . . [T]he whole basis of Haggard's approach to the occult was that precise statements were necessarily inappropriate in an area not subject to the limitation of the physical universe.

Alan Sandison, in his *The Wheel of Empire*, viewing Haggard's work from the more prosaic perspective of culture and humanism, comes to a remarkably similar conclusion:

> Given the fact that things were in continuous process, in a state of Becoming, there were for Haggard three possibilities. These were firstly that there *was* a principal of order in the universe and that it was dictated by God; secondly, that there *was* a principle or order in the universe, but its determination was purely mechanical with accident as its first cause; thirdly, that there was *no* order inherent in the universe and that chance dominated all . . . . Though he feared the worst, Haggard's restless urge to penetrate the flux and discover its secret for himself remains to be either the subject or a large part of the subject of practically every book he wrote.

This philosophy that "precise statements were necessarily inappropriate" is constantly being manifested in Haggard's fiction. One can see in his works the view that there is no such thing as certainty and that irony and fuzziness are the coin of the realm. This is the source of the overall befuddlement that is at the heart of Horace Holly's and Leo Vincey's depictions in the first two Ayesha novels and, too, of Allan Quatermain's, as he is constantly confronted with truths that he dismisses and prevarications that he wastes energy grappling with. Thus we have Ayesha's endless and contradictory claims that she may or may not exist on multiple plains of divinity all at once. Thus we have Quatermain's two dear wives being senselessly killed. Thus we have Leonard Outram in *The People of the Mist* enduring a fearful adventure and rescuing and marrying a woman all by virtue of wrongly interpreting the "Delphic oracle"-like last words of his brother, which led him to material success but also to an everlasting sorrow and a never-to-be-bridged emptiness between him and his wife.

If St. John Barclay and Sandison have accurately summarized Haggard's world view, and that these are merely somewhat different ways of describing an *effect*, what might have been the *cause*?

I believe that the root cause has been unearthed. While researching his biography of Haggard, D.S. Higgins noticed this vague reference in Haggard's autobiography:

I fell truly and earnestly in love. If all goes well, this, I suppose, is one of the best things that can happen to a young fellow. It steadies him and gives him an object in life: someone for whom to work. If all goes ill, it is one of the worst, for then the reverse is apt to come about. It unsteadies him, makes him reckless, and perhaps throws him in the way of undesirable adventures. In my case, in the end all went wrong, or seemed to do so at the time . . . Some thirty-five years later I was present at her death-bed—for happily I was able to be of service to her in her later life—and subsequently, with my wife, who had become her friend many years before, was one of the few mourners at her funeral.

This, plus various other omissions and vagaries, sent Higgins on a classic quest, effectively a prolonged forensic investigation into who this mystery woman must be, searching musty birth records in out of the way districts, "hours going through the annual indexes of The Times," and examining some twenty graveyards and countless gravestones. He eventually solved the mystery and explains his findings in his essay "Rider Haggard's Secret Love":

When Rider Haggard was nineteen he fell in love, as young men often do, with a beautiful young woman [Mary Elizabeth Archer Jackson, known as "Lilly"]. Unlike most other men, however, Haggard was to remain in love with her throughout his life, even though they were soon separated and subsequently married other partners. His idealistic love for this untouched, untouchable woman influenced much of his writing and was in part responsible for the brooding melancholia that so often overtook him.

Haggard seems to have responded to this loss of love (via the post, no less!) in a manner many would consider out of proportion. He seems to have allowed the resultant grief to absolutely color his views on the nature of reality. How could a love so profound and real (or so he believed) be yanked from him so callously? Where was the sense in that? If such a thing could happen, what other universal laws could be swept aside in a heartbeat by whatever power or powers? How could he trust anything at all? The enormity of his feelings seems to have transmuted into that classic of endless love, *She*. As historian Victoria Manthorpe muses, ". . . full of autobiographical signposts . . . [d]rawing deeply from the well of his passion for Lilly Jackson, he produced [in *She*] the theme of a love which transcends death itself." Further, there is something of Lilly and the loss of her love in nearly his entire oeuvre, often overtly, as in *She* and its follow-up books, sometimes subtly. As publisher Douglas Menville has recognized—without benefit of Higgins' insights:

> If we examine Haggard's work carefully, we can see the White Goddess appear in all his adventure novels in one guise or another; sometimes more prosaic . . . other times more remote and mysterious . . . . Throughout all the Allan Quatermain novels, this feminine archetype appears again and again as a kind of spiritual foil to the cynical, joyless, pragmatic side of Haggard represented by Quatermain.

Mary Elizabeth Archer Jackson (Lilly)
—Photo from "Rider Haggard's Secret Love"
By D.S. Higgins

Tragically, Haggard's view of callous fate was only given more credence when in 1891, six years after he had indisputably attained the position of one of the world's most successful writers, his only son died of measles at the age of 11, when Rider and his wife were in Mexico. One can only imagine Haggard's grief and reactions on every level. Where was the sense there? *What was the point of attaining the absolute pinnacle of success only to have all joy extinguished forever?* All this only convinced him of the cruel workings of destiny and the underlying futility of life, views that couldn't help but infuse *The People of the Mist*, the second book he wrote after the loss of his son and which was, as you recall, my introduction to Haggard.

✦ ✦ ✦

Much later, having written dozens of books, the period 1908–1909 proved to be a watershed for H. Rider Haggard, as he lost his brother Jack and took upon himself the care of Jack's family, his finances became untenably strained, and his first grandchild died at age six months.

Yet there was another event in 1909 that likely eclipsed these losses and downturns, at least on some primal level, that I suggest triggered the creation of Hans the Hottentot. This event was the drawn-out death by syphilis of his Lilly.

Supposing that his being jilted by Lilly when he was 19, exacerbated by the death of his boy, did in fact cause him to forevermore doubt the value of existence, it only seems reasonable that Lilly's slow dying and death would have compounded that feeling. Remember now that in the year 1909, Haggard wrote three books: *Red Eve* as Lilly was wasting away, *Child of Storm* immediately after her death, then *Marie*.

With regard to *Red Eve*, Haggard authority Roger Allen muses thus: "At the time of writing, Lilly, his early love, was dying of syphilis, and Haggard often passed through the marshes near Blytheburgh to visit her at Aldeburgh. Not surprisingly he was rather depressed at this time and it is not fanciful to compare Red Eve's illness and the effects of the Black Death to Lilly's situation."

Of *Child of Storm*, Higgins says, "Significantly, the heroine is a beautiful and extremely clever black girl, Mameena, and the real story is about her life and tragic end. It seems that after Lilly's death, Haggard's thoughts returned to the African girl of his memories and once more re-created her in his fiction." But when one considers that Haggard's 1892 all-Zulu rendition of the reign of Shaka is titled *Nada the Lily*, it may be that for Haggard black/white distinctions were not especially relevant.

Thus, we see the pattern of strong feelings having to do with Lilly's demise reflected in his fiction during that year of 1909. So it is not unreasonable to seek something of Lilly in *Marie*, the third book written that year. And in fact, in this novel Allan Quatermain, at about 19 years of age, falls in love with a beautiful young woman, whom he marries, and who tragically dies at the end. This much is obvious. However, in this story, Quatermain's life is falling apart all around him: He is betrayed endlessly; he saves Marie literally hours from starvation; he witnesses Dingaan, the Zulu king, invite a large contingent of peaceful Boers to his kraal, then betray, torture, and massacre them all; he is falsely accused of plotting the massacre and is put on trial, and so forth.

> "Yes, Baas," said Hans, twirling his hat in his vacant fashion, "I understand that the Baas, as is usual when he is in a deep pit, seeks the wisdom of Hans to get him out—of Hans who has brought him up from a child and taught him most of what he knows; of Hans upon whom his Reverend Father, the Predikant, used to lean as upon a staff."
>
> —Hans in *Heu-Heu or The Monster*

> ". . . O little yellow man who are so great and white of heart. Behold! I give you a new name, by which you shall be known with honour from generation to generation. It is 'Light in Darkness.' It is 'Lord of the Fire.'"
>
> —Mavovo (Zulu captain of hunters)
> in *Allan and the Holy Flower*

In the very dark *Marie*, wherein Quatermain can't trust anybody or anything and whose cup is full of disappointment, I suspect that Haggard simply couldn't leave Quatermain to face all this all alone, so he created a companion, a character on which he could *"lean as upon a staff"*—a character who was 100 percent true and faithful and noble and upon whom Quatermain could depend entirely—in effect, it seems to me, a character with the qualities that Lilly, the woman who had broken his heart and for whom he pined his whole life, *ought* to have had, qualities that Lilly *ought* to have embodied. Qualities, in fact, that he saw in himself, for hadn't *he* been forever true and noble and patient? Therefore, it is not to be wondered at that he created Hans, a character who had not existed during the previous quarter-century history of Quatermain's literary existence—to be Quatermain's *"light in the darkness."*

✦ ✦ ✦

Bearing in mind that Hans' role is at once vital and pivotal in six Quatermain novels, especially the final books, a poignant fact is that Hans is not so much as mentioned in the major Haggard biographies by Cohen, Ellis, Higgins, and Pocock; and neither is he brought up in the major commentaries by Coan, Etherington, St. John Barclay, Sandison, and Stiebel. Then, to make matters worse, Peter Haining in the introduction to his *Hunter Quatermain's Stories*, states "there are, of course, several other memorable characters to be found among the total of 18 novels and short stories . . ." whereupon he lists Sir Henry Curtis, Captain John Good, the Zulu warrior Umslopogass, and the wizard Zikali, but not a syllable about Quatermain's number one sidekick.

Furthermore, when I sought an illustration of Hans to use with this introduction, I could find only one drawing, by Hookway Cowles, in my 1973 impression (copyright 1958) of Macdonald & Co.'s *The Ivory Child*. Unable to locate anything else, I contacted Roger Allen, editor of the Rider Haggard Society's *The Haggard Journal*, and asked if he knew of other images, and he responded:

> I have checked through all the relevant titles including the serialisations (I do not have every one) which have many pictures not in the books. None has a picture of Hans . . . I suspect that Hans was such an ugly character that artists shied away . . . . That Hookway Cowles decided to depict him is a bit surprising in so far as he would not be an "attraction" to the reader . . . . Perhaps we should see [Hans] as an ugly amalgam of the worst traits of the natives Haggard met, but with superlative redeeming features: RH was way ahead of his times in realizing that colour was irrelevant in many cases . . . obviously nothing to be found pre-1940!

Which means that it may well be that the following drawing is the only published illustration of Hans in existence, despite his being featured in six novels over 13 years.

From all this unfair neglect, I conclude that Haggard did such a good job of portraying Hans as a disreputable, no-account, profoundly superstitious, drunken old scoundrel (while really trying to show that appearances can be deceiving), that Hans has gone unnoticed and has been effectively skipped over by both the literary and art communities, while some of Haggard's other native

"We shall beat him, Hans," I said looking at the broad river which was now close at hand.

Detail

characters, such as Mameena and Umslopogaas, were much discussed and well-represented while their respective stories were in the spotlight. Regardless, the fact remains that the final words Haggard had Hans the Hottentot say to Quatermain were (and, frankly, it would not be a stretch to imagine that Hans was here standing in for Lilly): "Baas, I understand now what your Reverend father . . . meant when he spoke to me about love last night [in a dream]. It had nothing to do with women, Baas, at least not much. It was something a great deal bigger, Baas, something as big as what I feel for you!"

In my experience, many readers, even fans, of Haggard don't often look beyond the exotic settings, bloody battles, and thrilling treks that punctuate his stories, but if they tried putting on hold their own skepticism and shelved for a while their own "cynical, joyless, pragmatic" natures, it may well be that Haggard's spiritual side would suddenly "pop" for them, and they'd ask themselves why they never noticed that before.

Bibliography

Allen, Roger. Red Eve. *The Haggard Journal* (No. 103). Deneholm: Rider Haggard Society, December 2011.

Ashley, Mike. H. Rider Haggard, *Who's Who in Horror and Fantasy Fiction*. New York: Taplinger Publishing Co. 1977.

Carter, Lin. Introduction: Lost Races, Forgotten Cities, *The People of the Mist* by H. Rider Haggard. New York: Ballantine Books 1973.

Cohen, Morton. *Rider Haggard: His Life and Works*. New York: Walker and Co. 1960.

Ellis, Peter Berresford. *H. Rider Haggard: A Voice from the Infinite*. London: Routledge & Kegan Paul Books 1978.

Etherington, Norman. *Rider Haggard*. Boston: Twayne Publishers 1984.

Gould, Stephen Jay. The Hottentot Venus, *The Flamingo's Smile: Reflections in Natural History*. New York: W. W. Norton & Co. 1987.

Haggard, H. Rider. *The Days of My Life: An Autobiography*. London: Longmans, Green and Co. 1926.

Haggard, H. Rider. *She and Allan*. Hollywood: Newcastle Publishing Co. 1975.

Haggard, H. Rider. *The Ivory Child*. London: Macdonald & Co. 1973.

Haggard, Lilias Rider. *The Cloak That I Left*. London: Hodder & Stoughton 1951.

Haining, Peter (ed). Introduction, *Hunter Quatermain's Story: The Uncollected Adventures of Allan Quatermain*. London: Peter Owen 2003.

Higgins, D. S. Rider *Haggard: A Biography*. New York: Stein & Day 1983.

Higgins, D. S. Rider. Haggard's Secret Love, *Haggard's Secret Love & 2 Other Haggard Articles*: Kindle Edition, 2009.

Manthorpe, Victoria. *Children of Empire: The Victorian Haggards*. London: Victor Gollancz 1996.

Menville, Douglas. Introduction, *Allan's Wife* by H. Rider Haggard. Hollywood: New Castle Publishing Co. 1980.

Monsman, Gerald. *H. Rider Haggard on the Imperial Frontier: The Political and Literary Contexts of His African Romances*. Greensboro, North Carolina: ELT Press 2006.

Penzler, Otto. Introduction to "Hunter Quatermain's Story." *The Big Book of Adventure Stories*. New York: Vintage Books 2011.

Pocock. Tom. *Rider Haggard and the Lost Empire: A Biography*. London: Weidenfeld & Nicolson 1994.

Sandison, Alan. *The Wheel of Empire*. New York: St. Martin's Press 1967.

St. John Barclay, Glen. Henry Rider Haggard, *Anatomy of Horror: The Masters of Occult Fiction*. London: Weidenfeld and Nicolson 1978.

Stiebel, Lindy. *Imaging Africa: Landscape in H. Rider Haggard's African Romances*. Westport, Connecticut: Greenwood Press 2001.

Contents

ALLAN QUATERMAIN AT THE CRUCIBLE OF LIFE

List of Illustrations

Editor's Note to the
Fourth Edition

The publication of this fourth edition of *Allan Quatermain at the Crucible of Life* coincides with the official joint announcement by the African states of Eritrea, Ethiopia, Djibouti, Somalia, Kenya, Uganda, Rwanda, The Democratic Republic of Congo, Burundi, Tanzania, Malawi, Mozambique, Zambia, Zimbabwe, and South Africa that great swatches of their countries are being set aside for the establishment of a vast African continental preserve—The Great Rift Valley Paleoanthropologic Preserve. The preserve, in principle, follows the East African Rift System that cuts north and south through most of these countries. The park extends a bit further beyond the southernmost aspect of the rift valley into South Africa and is roughly 3,500 miles long, averaging about 75 miles wide, for a total of about 265,000 square miles.

Given that much of this area has been in extreme political turmoil for years, and that death, civil war, and even genocide have been the windows by which the world has assessed much of the area, this unprecedented alignment seems little less than a miracle. This near-impossible task was, in fact, accomplished through the supreme efforts of the Wildlife Conservation Society, the board of directors of the Peace Parks Foundation, and United Nations Secretary-General Nicholi Lorenzo and a significant percentage of the staffs of the U.N. Environment Programme, the Institute of Human Origins, the National Science Foundation, the National Geographic Society, and the thousands of dedicated volunteers who believed in the unique value of this preserve.

The motivating principle behind the creation of the park is to preserve that unique spot on this planet where the human species arose. It has been shown over and again through a succession of historic paleoarchaeological finds (beginning in South Africa with Raymond Dart and Robert Broom early in the twentieth century through the redoubtable Leakey family in Tanzania and Kenya; Donald Johanson, Tim White, and Yohannes Haile-Selassie mainly in Ethiopia; and numerous other investigators) that beyond a reasonable doubt, primates stood tall on their legs and walked fully erect all over this area beginning between six and three million years ago. Despite the fact that researchers are constantly quibbling about the details, timeline, and branches of our family tree, there is complete consensus that these first walking primates came into existence in East Africa. Then, through the ages, they lived their lives, slowly changing in response to changes in their environment. The general outline of this evolution is *Ardipithecus* to *Australopithecus* to *Homo hablis* to *Homo erectus/ergaster,* some of this latter group leaving Africa about 2 million years ago and spreading across the Eurasian continent—yet failing to survive as a species due to the subsequent much-later development in that same East African Rift Valley roughly 150,000 years ago of *Homo sapien,* which in its turn left Africa about 70,000 years ago, also spreading across Asia (thoroughly replacing *Homo erectus/ergaster*), then Europe, and finally the Americas to populate the world.

In a sense, we are all Africans, which has been proven time and time again beyond a shadow of a doubt through advances in mitochondrial DNA and Y chromosome research. And now this fact has finally been acknowledged by the modern countries that include and surround the rift system.

But, of course, it is far beyond the realm of possibility or even of the wildest dreams to expect such a preserve to have a literal, physical fence around it with admission gates, souvenir shops, and the like. Something so vast as this preserve, which crosses so many political boundaries, even to the extent of absorbing entire countries—Rwanda, Burundi, and Malawi to be specific—must be something altogether different than what we are used to thinking of as a preserve.

There is no doubt that The Great Rift Valley Paleoanthropologic Preserve exists. But if there are no fences marking its outermost boundaries, what is the nature of its existence? This preserve exists:

- In the minds of the leaders and politicians of the fifteen governments who set it up at the urging of the agencies already mentioned, it exists as an entity within certain geographical points of longitude and latitude as measured by the Global Positioning System (GPS).

- In the eyes of the United Nations, it exists.
- As a designated area on all new maps of Africa and of the world, it exists.

And to underscore its existence, each of the preserve nations is even now setting up preserve offices staffed with scientists of all sorts, preservationists, administrators, and an "army," as it were, of preserve rangers, who, like similar personnel the world over, will educate and entertain visitors while also protecting their charge.

By now, I'm sure, some of the new readers of this book are wondering what this astonishing accomplishment has to do with *Allan Quatermain at the Crucible of Life*.

I'll satisfy that curiosity by briefly discussing the evolution, as it were, of this book and show how it has changed over its previous three editions.

In the beginning, by a circuitous route, the manuscript came into my possession *(see my original preface below beginning on page xiii)*. Given the state of publishing these days, it was in itself a miracle that I was able to get first my agent, Gail Morgan Hickman, and then a publisher to even look at the book. Even so, once the publisher was persuaded to print Quatermain's story, for purely commercial reasons she balked at printing the rather extensive front matter and ancillary material, much of which was my contribution. Thus, the book was released as a paperback original with a print run of 10,000, and all concerned assumed that it would sell enough copies to make a modest profit or break even and then fade from memory, the unsold copies of course being stripped and recycled. But by one of those flukes that can never be predicted, nationally syndicated radio talk show host ("shock jock") Randy King by chance read the book and mentioned on his program that he had enjoyed it and found it thought-provoking. The net result was that the paperback publisher went back to press seventeen more times over the next two years.

The inevitable movie was released, of course . . . and then tanked. The film version (*The Rose of Fire*, starring Michael Caine, Gene Hackman, Sigourney Weaver, and introducing young Nigel Knox as "Will Scott," and costing in the neighborhood of $75 million) had a disastrous opening weekend, acid reviews, and then quickly disappeared. It came and went so fast that most people weren't even aware of its existence. Indeed, as of this writing, it still has not appeared on video, DVD, Blu-Ray, VOD, or streaming channels.

But, naturally, the eventual fortunes of the film were not known while its advertising and promotion campaigns were being prepared. As the movie-tie-in edition of the book was being planned, I used my by then not-so-insubstantial clout to suggest very strongly that the book be published as I had originally planned. As the publisher was quite distressed about this, I quietly reminded her of a particular clause in my contract, whereupon she sighed ever so deeply and made no further protest.

And then, in another twist of fate, the movie tie-in version of the book took on a life of its own.

Whereas the original paperback was accepted and thought of as a rather light true-life adventure story, the second (annotated and enlarged) edition (at first only a paperback, then reprinted in hardcover but with no further changes, as I had nothing more to add at the time) became a magnet for study. (In due course, a third edition appeared that contained some astonishing and important newly discovered data.) It seems the notion of a continental park was not new, that the groundwork had been prepared by many of those visionaries mentioned above, among others, and all that was wanting was a straw to cave in the camel's back, so to speak . . . and this little memoir of Quatermain's adventure proved to be just that. Educators, scholars, politicians, and heads of state, many of whom were affiliated with conservation groups around the world, found that Quatermain's record of the events in 1872 included an aspect that underscored the reasoning and the arguments that they themselves had pursued to no avail for so many years. Slowly, others of influence gravitated to the book, discussed its implications, and eventually more and more world leaders were persuaded that certain points brought up in the book warranted serious study.

In time, the East African Coalition came into being and the world community was able to provide certain inducements and guarantees to the fifteen preserve nations. The joint announcement is the unprecedented result of all that focused interest.

This fourth edition is, therefore, intended for those readers who are coming to the book for the first time. *Allan Quatermain at the Crucible of Life; or, The Adventure of the Rose of Fire* has taken on a life of its own, to be sure, but I hope that it never be forgotten that it began as a true story of "rip-roaring adventure" shared among cultured friends before a crackling fire in upstate New York.

T.K.M.

Editor's Note to the Third Edition

Since the publication of the second edition of Allan Quatermain's memoirs concerning his first adventure in East Africa, some vital new material of a revelatory nature has come to light that mandated this third edition, which entailed appending a long footnote to Chapter Ten and adding a new Chapter Eleven).

T.K.M.

Editor's Note to the Movie Tie-In (Second) Edition

Now that Allan Quatermain's history of his adventure with Sherlock Holmes will soon arrive to silver screens and multiplexes worldwide—but in drastically altered form, as is frequently the case when books are translated into film—I feel obliged to take advantage of this movie tie-in reprint edition to prepare the definitive collector's edition that I originally planned and include the original introductory material, which explains how the manuscript came into being and just how it came into my hands.

Many readers may remember that the book was originally published as a true-life adventure memoir beginning with what is Chapter One in this book. This seems natural enough, but unbeknownst to those readers, that edition omitted Quatermain's introduction, Watson's foreword, and this editor's preface, as well as much other ancillary material, the publishing wisdom of the time (and still is for that matter) assuming modern readers wanted only to jump into the story—front matter be damned!

I am grateful to my publisher for this new edition, allowing me to rectify that disservice to the shades of the principal parties.

What follows, therefore, is the complete manuscript that I had the good fortune to receive. As editor, I have made certain cosmetic changes according to practical and commercial decisions, such as incorporating a more appropriate title and eschewing the original:

Record of A.Q.'s narration concerning certain adventures that unfolded in east Africa during the early part 1872
As set down by John H. Watson, M.D.

In addition, for the sake of the modern reader, I felt obliged to add a few applicable epigraphs; to correct or update spelling (e.g., "Ethiope" to "Ethiopia" and "Chaka" to "Shaka"); to add clear editorial attribution to the many internal notes made by the several contributors; and to add appropriate chapter titles, footnotes, endnotes and other corroborative supplementary material, including my original preface.

In this vein, I am particularly grateful that this edition of the book will carry the title I originally gave it rather than the abortive, abbreviated version that both the original edition and the movie carry. Let's face it, *The Rose of Fire* makes it sound like yet another sequel to *Romancing the Stone* such as that silly confection *Jewel of the Nile*.

Let us embark, then, on a miraculous journey and enter the minds of some of the nineteenth century's most exciting individuals—but in a manner that I hope is more in alignment with their expectations of how their adventures should be presented to a discerning readership, and also in a manner that does no disservice to this editor's far-from-slight investigatory efforts aimed at putting the whole affair into the historical perspective that seemed wanting and which begged to be resolved.

T.K.M.

Preface
The Prodigious Phone Call

By Thomas Kent Miller, Editor

There is no doubt in my mind that there is a force in this world that some call "serendipity" and others "synchronicity."

It was my birthday, a Tuesday in October 1994. I was sitting at my desk rereading for the hundredth time a yellowing correspondence from the late Judy-Lynn Del Rey, who was up until her death in 1986—and still is, to be sure—considered one of science fiction's most admired and important editors. It so happened that this missive—which, in point of fact, was a rejection letter—was one of my prized possessions. It reads thus:

Del Rey Books
An Imprint of Ballantine Books

September 18, 1985
Dear Mr. Miller:

Your idea of writing a double biography that blends the lives of Allan Quatermain and his literary representative H. Rider Haggard is indeed interesting. Unfortunately Lester's and my attempt to resurrect Haggard recently was an unmitigated disaster. Therefore, I must say that taking on your project would be economically unwise for us at this time. I sincerely hope your project finds a home elsewhere.

Best to you,
Judy-Lynn Del Rey[2]

I prized this letter for many reasons, but the most important was because Judy-Lynn had clearly *reluctantly* rejected my idea. It was gratifying that a person of her stature saw the merit in my idea.

For those of you who might not know, Allan Quatermain was the prototype "great white hunter," who in the early 1880s wrote the enduring memoir *King Solomon's Mines* (published in 1885). It is his self-portrayal in that classic that propagated the likes of Jungle Jim, Ramar of the Jungle, and all those rifle-toting, safari-leading heroes such as Clark Gable in *Mogambo*, Gregory Peck in *The Macomber Affair*, John Wayne in *Hatari*, and even Pete Postlethwaite in *The Lost World: Jurassic Park* and Ernie Hudson in *Congo*, not to mention Indiana Jones!

My idea was to take the eighteen published histories that Allan Quatermain wrote (or related) mostly during his three-year hiatus at his estate, the Grange, in Yorkshire, England, and subsequently left behind (all except the last), and condense them into a formal biography. Listed in internal chronological order, these works are *Allan's Wife, Marie, Child of Storm*, "A Tale of Three Lions," *Maiwa's Revenge*, "Hunter Quatermain's Story," "Long Odds," *The Holy Flower, Heu-Heu or the Monster, She and Allan, The Treasure of the Lake, The Ivory Child, Finished*, "Megepa the Buck," *King Solomon's Mines, The Ancient Allan, Allan and the Ice Gods*, and *Allan Quatermain*.

Yet, the story of Quatermain must always be intertwined with that of his friend, Henry Rider Haggard, through whose tenacity and great strength of personality Quatermain's histories saw the light of day. I think it can be said without fear of argument that Quatermain and Haggard were in many ways doppelgangers of one another, mirroring as they did each other's life so neatly—thus, my vision of blending the lives of the great adventurer and his literary executor into a single volume.[3]

So there I was, rereading Mrs. Del Rey's note, mourning the project that never happened, when the phone rang. That call was the first domino in a series of events that changed the direction of my life and now, it seems, the entire world.

I had taken the day off from my job as the editor of a respected trade publication. It was ten in the morning, and the call proceeded in the following manner.

"Hello, are you Thomas Miller, the editor of *Sherlock Holmes on the Roof of the World?*"

"Yes, I am," I said, delighted, for heaven knows I've received little enough feedback on that particular labor of love.

"Well then, I'm Jim Turner . . . ."

Excitement welled up within me and before he could finish his thought, I blurted out, "The editor of Arkham House!"[4]

"Why yes. I'm flattered that you know me."

"Mr. Turner, I've been a fan of Arkham House for most of my life. Of course I know your name. What can I do for you?"

"Please call me Jim. May I call you Tom?"

"Of course."

"Tom, I'm not sure if this will interest you, but it turns out that a box of H.P. Lovecraft material was misplaced and went unnoticed for seventy some years after his death and has turned up in the Brown University archives—in the John Hay Library to be exact. Naturally, I was among the first to be notified.

"Among its contents was a book-length manuscript that Lovecraft had apparently received as a commission to revise or 'fix up' as he used to call it. It appears the manuscript was originally set down in script in 1881 and was received by Lovecraft in 1925. Lovecraft's revisions, such as they are, are rather sparse and unenthusiastic with the exception of a section dealing with meteorites. They are in his handwriting, so we know he started the job. We have no idea why it apparently was never completed."

"You are most definitely sparking my interest, Jim."

"It seems that in 1925, Lovecraft, with his wife Sonia, had traveled up to the Hudson River Valley area of New York state and had visited an unusual and rather lavish house called Olana—"

"I'm sorry to interrupt again, Jim, but you're speaking of the home of Frederick Church."[5]

"Yes. I'm gratified you know that as well. You seem to be knowledgeable in a number of fields."

Ignoring the compliment, I hurried on to say, "This is marvelous! Before you go any further, I must tell you that my wife Jayne, our son Douglas, and I made what I call 'a pilgrimage' to the National Gallery in 1990 to the Church exhibit."

There was a long silence at the other end of the line.

"Jim?"

"This is fortuitous indeed."

"Please go on."

"Yes. While at Olana, Lovecraft and Sonia met with Sally Good, Frederick Church's daughter-in-law, who with her husband inherited the home at the time of Church's death in 1900. During the visit, when Sally learned of Lovecraft's vocation as a revisionist, she asked if he would be interested in undertaking a commission—namely to revise for publication a peculiar manuscript that she and her husband possessed, that they had inherited along with the house. Apparently Sally, though by no means feeling it was an urgent matter, nonetheless sensed that the manuscript had some historical or literary value and chose this opportunity to act on that intuition.

"Lovecraft seized the opportunity and took the manuscript home—and then it disappeared for more than seventy years until the archivists at Brown unearthed it last month."

"This is truly wonderful, but I don't understand what all this has to do with me."

"Yes, I suppose I ought to get to the point. The manuscript in question purports to detail an expedition to Ethiopia a century and a quarter ago. Indeed, the names of Allan Quatermain and Dr. John Watson are prominent. Naturally, as a publisher, I was overjoyed. You can imagine all the permutations of publishing possibilities that flashed in my mind."

"Allan Quatermain! Dr. Watson!"

"Despite my excitement, I must be realistic. In a short time I will be leaving Arkham House to start my own publishing company. Arkham's plate is currently full, and my new company has more than enough to do at the moment. And this volume, as undeniably exciting as it is, and though it certainly has merit, is nonetheless a bit of an odd duck, and, as such, must wait in queue for some time, perhaps years, before we could get to it.

"When I began to think of who else might shepherd this volume into publication, I began to list editors with backgrounds in the subject. The list was very short. Then I remembered Leo Vincey's journal [*Sherlock Holmes on the Roof of the World*] and also recalled that Vincey's literary executor was H. Rider Haggard, as was Quatermain's. And, insofar as fate had once arranged that you take up Haggard's baton, I realized that you of all people would be the most perfectly equipped to properly prepare this remarkable story to share with the world. May I send a copy to you?"

Somehow, through my breathless excitement, I was able to assure Mr. Turner that I would be delighted to receive the manuscript and take on the project.

In due course, a photocopy arrived at my door via UPS. On opening the box, the first thing I found was a sheet of Arkham House stationery with a cordial note from Mr. Turner more or less repeating what he had told me over the phone.

Below that . . . .

How can I express the pristine joy that filled me at what I saw next.

There, below Mr. Turner's note was a photocopy of an original typescript of an actual letter written by H.P. Lovecraft and addressed to "My dear Smith:—" who could only be Clark Ashton Smith, the northern California painter, sculptor, poet, translator, and author of whom Lovecraft once wrote, "In sheer daemonic strangeness and fertility of conception, Clark Ashton Smith is perhaps unexcelled by any other writer dead or living." As the letter I was looking at was dated June 1925, Lovecraft and Smith by then had been regular correspondents for slightly over three years.

Turner had scrawled at the top of the photocopy, "Derleth and Wandrei left this note out of the *Selected Letters*. I assume that was because the manuscript referred to could never be located and the letter would have meant nothing out of context. Of course, the original letter (which is lost) would have been in Lovecraft's dense, spidery script. This is a copy of the typescript they had prepared, as they did for all of HPL's correspondence that they were able to locate. If it had been printed, it would have started on page 19 of volume II where letter #188 to Frank Belknap Long currently is."

Let us, dear reader, simply be glad that the typescript remained in the publisher's files. The letter reads thus:

169 Clinton Street

Brooklyn, N.Y.

June 21, 1925
My dear Smith:—

On this cosmic & splendid Solstice Day, I bid you greetings. I bear news of the grandest sort! By way of preface, I will begin at the beginning & come to the delicious details in due course.

. . . .[6] Upon my wife's return from Saratoga Springs[7], we chose to celebrate in a most uncharacteristic manner. (But I mustn't prevaricate. The following voyage extraordinaire was also initiated, in part, with the transparent and terribly self-conscious goal of heading off my funk—or that part of it that remained following the burglary of my clothes.) Ol' S.H.G. & I were able to prevail upon the good nature of one Mrs. Renshaw, a client up from Washington, who seemed more than happy to act on behalf of this Lady & Gentleman in the role of chauffeur.

You may recall that last year I mentioned to you something to the effect of my having a real affection for scenes—landscape & architecture—as opposed to the company of transitory mankind. In point of fact, recently the craft & home of Frederick E. Church has come to my attention. You may recall that he was quite the rage three-quarters of a century ago, a veritable pinnacle of the Hudson River Valley School of landscape art. He built his retirement home not too terribly distant from here.

Thus, it turns out that our destination this very day—O! prodigious day!—was the Church home, which is built on a hilltop overlooking the Hudson River. Furthermore, "Olana," as the place is named, is one of the few places on earth where the separate disciplines of landscape & architecture cross with a vengeance.

The purpose of our visit was part satisfaction of architectural curiosity, part holiday, part celebration at S.H.G.'s return to health & home. Our host & hostess were expecting us, once again due to the good graces of the ever resourceful Mrs. Renshaw.

Even before we viewed the house, as we drove up the circuitous drive, at every bend we encountered the most fabulous scenes of the Hudson River or the Catskill Mountains. The man had actually planted thousands of trees in such a manner as to purposefully frame choice vistas just as though they were landscape paintings. Quite ingenious! Thus, you can imagine that when we made that last bend, the house itself was like a veritable jewel in the crown. Trust me when I say that when the house ("mansion" perhaps is too large a term) first came into view, I caught my breath at the audacity of it.

Though the underlying purpose of Olana was that of a sanctuary for his family, Church designed the house himself fueled by inspiration derived from travels to Persia & other exotic Middle Eastern states. The name Olana I was told by Church's daughter-in-law, is a variation on "Olane," which she said was a fortress/treasure house in ancient Persia. The

Oriental windows, the graceful pink & blue tile work, the bell tower & embellished doorways . . . . Believe me when I say I felt transported into the likes of F. Marion Crawford's "Khaled," or William Beckford's "Vathek," or George Meredith's "The Shaving of Shagpat." One would not do badly by quoting from "Vathek" in attempting to give the flavor of the place:

> "The palace named 'The Delight of the Eyes, or the Support of Memory,' was one entire enchantment. Rarities collected from every corner of the earth were there in such profusion as to dazzle and confound, but for the order in which they were arranged . . . . Here a well-managed perspective attracted the sight, there the magic of optics agreeably deceived it; whilst the naturalist on his part exhibited, in their several classes, the various gifts that Heaven had bestowed on our globe."

We were treated lavishly to be sure, fêting us not in the parlor but in the family's own sitting room. Though this lovely room had many features of significant note, the eye was perpetually drawn to, & eventually anchored by, a lavish, tallish painting above the marble fireplace of Petra's El Khasne, whose astonishingly detailed façade was carved, as you know, from a rose-colored sandstone cliff, & which in the painting, only a glimpse can be seen beyond the converging walls of a mountain cleft.

In due course, though, there came a time when the ever-merciless spectre of vile "business" appeared like a fungus & would not be shaken off—to blazes with mixing metaphors! Once our hostess learned that I made my livelihood primarily by revising the prose & poetry of others, she verily leaped at the chance to offer me a commission, that of, as she said, "turning an old manuscript into something worthy of publication."

I demurred, of course, but she was insistent. Between that & the equally insistent prodding of S.H.G's elbow into my side, the end was that I agreed to see the MS. She was gone from the room for quite a while. When she returned, she had with her a rather dusty & discolored leather portfolio that had the appearance of being hurriedly wiped & which *still had the silken strands of spider webs clinging to its accordion folds!*

I took the portfolio, set it on my knees, & extracted a disorganized stack of heavy foolscap. Believe me I had no idea what to expect. I spent a moment straightening the sheets. They were written upon in ink in an inconsistent script—sometimes large & round, sometimes small & squeezed. It was difficult to determine if they were the same hand. As hackneyed as it sounds, it actually did take a few moments for me to realize what I held on my lap. That title page, which merely bore the fact that it was a "Record of A.Q.'s narration concerning certain adventures that unfolded in east Africa during the early part 1872" actually had the shattering audacity to additionally state "As set down by John H. Watson, M.D." Talk about an unexpected state of affairs.

These poor people, for all their acumen within their particular social strata & business interests, really did not seem to appreciate—nay! simply had no idea— what they had, & which, I soon learned, had been occupying a convenient cubby in their wine cellar for a quarter of a century!

As you know, I am immune to so-called matters of providence, yet I swear a tingle possessed my spine for those few moments when all this first made itself manifest. Providence or not, coincidence or not, the fates of the whole known Universe or not, I—me!—myself!—happened to be the right person at the right time in the right place when this particular MS. changed hands!

I took the commission, of course, & I have to tell you I was in quite a state, an uncharacteristic one, I assure you—S.H.G. tells me I even flirted with rudeness—until I could focus on the thing.

But to conclude Olana . . . . Our hosts toured us around their home, or at least the downstairs—the upstairs being strictly personal—& we left after dark.

O! most dire of circumstances! Understand that Renshaw, gracious lady that she is, has installed within her automobile a splendid lamp to satisfy the nocturnal reading requirements of her sundry passengers during longish rides. Yet the lamp this night was not functioning! I had no choice but to wait before I could peruse the document further. In due course, over the lonely roads, I found myself mentally framing this missive to you &, having come home only minutes ago, have set it down forthwith, knowing that first to last you'd appreciate the magnitude of this . . . this . . . *discovery!* Having said that, I will now get back to the MS.

    I can hardly contain myself. Wait a bit . . . .

* * *

    I calmed myself down enough to look over the MS. & I have now had an opportunity to study the document well enough to give you the broad outlines. As I said, it is authored by Watson (or claims to be). But, as I scan through the first half, I must admit to being puzzled. Throughout, as you would expect, there are references to "Holmes," but as far as I can tell, they don't refer to the correct Holmes, but another one entirely. Indeed, the person of Sherlock seems altogether absent.... Furthermore, the document is primarily a memoir of Allan Quatermain. (You remember him, of course—he penned 'King Solomon's Mines' back in the '80s.) It seems Watson's role here was that of transcriber.

    O! This will be fun! A new Quatermain adventure in Africa. I was promised a fair wage for my dabbling; but I feel almost as though I'm stealing from Church's relations. I do see, however, much need for my poor workmanlike efforts. Watson was always a bit quick, don't you think?

    I am posting this immediately & will offer the sequel (when there is one) "in the fullness of time."

                  Yr most oblig'd & obt. Servt.
                  H P L

My eyes reached the end of this epistle and lingered on HPL's abbreviated closing. I must say that I was deeply affected by being so privileged to have access to this otherwise unknown letter. Silently I thanked Jim Turner to the skies—and then found I didn't want to turn the page.

I was gripped by the plethora of the emotions one feels when delving into the unknown. Eventually I mastered myself and did in fact turn the page, finding another sheet of unadorned stationery on which Turner had scrawled the following:

Sad to say that no "sequel" to this letter has yet turned up, and it is unknown why HPL apparently made no further mention of this commission again in other correspondence. Neither is it clear why he didn't pursue, let alone complete, the project. You'll note that his crabbed scribbles—not even finished edits—are most evident on the pages dealing with meteorites and astronomy.[8] Perhaps it is no coincidence that his accepting this commission predates the writing of "The Colour Out of Space"[9] by almost exactly two years. It is certain, however, that his initial enthusiasm must have waned rapidly, otherwise his revision would have been far more extensive. The more interested he was in a project, as you know, the more likely he would have undertaken nothing less than a complete rewrite. Perhaps he was intimidated by the notion of rewriting a proven master, or, perhaps, just the opposite, he felt himself above dabbling with the work of a senile hack who couldn't even keep his dates, wounds, and wives straight[10] and who frequently diminished himself to the level of a mere romance writer.[11] Doubtless we will never know. Thanks for your interest and your agreement to help.

Agreement to help! I would have paid handsomely for this opportunity!

I flipped the page and came to another sheet of paper—yet another one that affected me profoundly. There lay before me this note written in, one must assume, Dr. Watson's own hand:

Dear Mr. Church,

The account given by Mr. Quatermain in your sitting room seemed to impress and affect us both to such a degree that I took the opportunity presented by our long sea voyage back to England to set it down on paper. This effort was made all the easier due to the presence of Mr. Quatermain himself who indulged me by responding to my every question.

In memory of your delightful hospitality and your boundless enthusiasm for Mr. Quatermain's tale, I have arranged to have a copy of my ms. be made for my files and I enclose the original herewith for your pleasure and also as a memento of that fine evening.

I have notified Mr. Quatermain of my intent and he sends his regards.

Yours ever faithfully,
John H. Watson
4th Feb. 1881

Whereupon, I settled in to read the manuscript from beginning to end and found that it was frequently interpolated with marginal notes by Watson and Allan Quatermain—and then realized the ultimate irony of ultimate ironies. What neither Lovecraft nor Turner had mentioned—and therefore probably didn't realize—was that Watson had indeed recorded a real Sherlock Holmes adventure—*a full month before he had even met Holmes!* Their famous encounter at St. Bartholomew's Hospital on March 4, 1881, had not yet happened! Yet this was undeniably a full-length account of a teenage Sherlock Holmes traversing the hellish deserts of Ethiopia.

Can you imagine my state? I was holding a manuscript-length document—penned mainly in the full round script of Dr. John H. Watson himself—that was, without doubt, *both* a new Allan Quatermain memoir and a new Sherlock Holmes tale. Furthermore, it was a story of the most prodigious journey the mind of man could fathom—dwarfing in its way even Magellan's circumnavigation of the earth and Apollo 11's journey to the moon—*for the adventure described was nothing less than a journey to the City of God!*

All and all, the sensations I experienced couldn't have been much different, I suppose, than those I would feel upon stumbling onto a priceless, lost Christian gospel!

T.K.M

Foreword

By John H. Watson, M.D

Feb. 1881

My dear Church,

As I prepared a copy of the following ms. for your special enjoyment, it occurred to me that it would be advantageous for you to understand exactly in some detail how it was Quatermain and I happened to appear on your doorstep last month, and then I will summarize for posterity (or perhaps for no more than merely our own faulty memories) the gist of that evening.

It was with great delight that I heard my new friend, Mr. Allan Quatermain—only shortly after he had settled into the Grange, his new home in Yorkshire—invite me to join him on a transatlantic voyage to America. We had been introduced only a few weeks earlier by his son, Harry, a medical student at St. Bartholomew's Hospital, and we had found that we had much in common.

"John," he began, "I have business to transact in Boston and New York City, and I fear that such a trip alone to lands unknown I would find daunting and I would be honored if you could contrive a way to join me."

I found amusing the thought that this man who had trekked over all of the wilds of Africa—to and from since he was but a mere lad—would find anything at all daunting. Nevertheless, I myself had only just returned from war duties in Afghanistan and found London sufficiently stultifying that this proposed adventure to the New World had much appeal. Unfortunately, such meager finances that were my wound pension allotment at the time, and my sole income, prevented my accepting Quatermain's invitation.[12] I muttered something banal in an attempt to obfuscate my way out of this embarrassing situation that my friend had inadvertently placed me in. But before I had completed the lie, Quatermain said, "Of course, I understand the financial imposition such a trip would entail, and Heaven knows that it was only a short time ago that I lived so close to the land that supper enough to fill my stomach only became a reality if an antelope happened to wander by or if I could strike up a trade with whichever tribe happened to be in my neighborhood. But I've made my pile now, and I can afford to be generous. Consider my invitation to be on me, and, pray, please accept this without a second thought and don't let it be a matter of discussion. Any further discussion on the subject I will take as a personal affront."

Well, when faced with this decree, I can honestly say that I threw polite humility to the wind and without further hesitation I agreed to put my affairs, such as they were, in order so that I could indeed join Quatermain for the requisite amount of time, which would be about four or five weeks. I did insist, though, that once my practice was established and running smoothly I would repay his generosity.

Before a month was out, and after an uneventful ocean voyage of ten days, we found ourselves disembarking the steamship *Virginian* in Boston Harbor. Quatermain's business, having to do with investments involving the diamonds he brought back from the mines of King Solomon, took us to New York as well, and it was concluded within a few days. Eventually we found ourselves with time on our hands. It was a Friday night, then, when we were strolling down a lane quite bursting with a variety of entertainment choices when we came upon an art gallery. We entered and walked slowly through, gazing upon paintings by Monet and Renoir and Cézanne and the like. Though he was silent, I could tell that Quatermain was disgruntled.

"Allan," I ventured, "you're restless."

"John, what am I to make of these pictures? What are these blurs and blobs? What has happened to art? Isn't the point of a picture to represent *something*—some reality?" He fell silent and I could see the muscles below his left eye twitch slightly as he mused. "I remember there was an exhibition when I was last in London about ten or eleven years ago.* Now that was art! Straightforward,

---

* Editor's note: This would have been before Quatermain's retirement to England, of course.—T.K.M.

clear, no doubt what you were looking at. I forget his name . . . it was a Mexican scene, I think, of a raging volcano with a jungle and a waterfall in the foreground. Blast, I wish I could remember the artist's name. It was one of those names that is also a word, something like Temple or Hall."

The proprietor of the gallery happened to hear Quatermain's remarks and said, "You must be referring to Church, Frederick Church. He did a number of South American scenes, some of which toured Europe. *Cotopaxi* is the name of the work you mentioned; the volcano is in Ecuador He lives just upstate, you know, in the Hudson River area."[13]

"He does? Now there's a man whose hand I would like to shake. In fact, his pictures would fit well within the Grange. Now there's an idea! Where, sir, could I purchase one or two?"

The proprietor's face shifted from a smile to a frown. "Well, now, his work has been out of favor for some years now. Also, it isn't so easy to find one available these days."

"Well, then," I offered, "Perhaps we can trek 'upstate' and see if we can get one from the source, and then you could indeed shake the man's hand!"

Of such small resolutions, big things happen and, within four days, after making inquiries, we found ourselves approaching Olana, which we first perceived as an exotic palace set on a snowy hilltop surrounded by trees.[14]

Let me set the stage once again, the better to savor memories of that most pleasant evening. You had been alerted by wire of our visit and awaited us in the foyer of your home. In short order we met your wife and four children, ate a sumptuous supper and retired to your perfectly appointed sitting room.

As we entered this room, and Quatermain's and my gaze took in our new surroundings, something peculiar happened. It was a small thing, and I doubt anyone else would have noticed. I did because I was already medically attuned to my friend's smallest behaviors. His gaze stopped abruptly at the painting above the hearth, and I saw him start. He quickly regained control and we continued in. I quickly forgot it, and remember it now only because, in retrospect, its significance is clear.

As the evening progressed, the fire bloomed, warming your guests as did the delightful spirits clinging to the sides of the crystal goblets in our hands.

"I dare say, Mr. Church," Quatermain said, "that your hospitality and fellowship have made our journey to America more than worth it."

"That is very kind of you to say, Mr. Quatermain," you replied. "Likewise, the company of one as worldly as yourself gives me inestimable pleasure."[15]

As I relaxed, I couldn't help but notice that the entire decor of the sitting room was clearly chosen to complement the painting that was over the mantle and that had riveted Quatermain's attention. Judging from the extreme care of rendering of minute detail, this work, I determined, must be one of your own.

I said as much and inquired as to the subject.

"Ah," you said, "this is the ancient treasury house—carved in red sandstone—of El Khasne in Petra. Some call it 'the rose red city half as old as time.' It is quite the amazing place, located as it is amongst some cragged mountains in the middle of a desert wilderness south of the Dead Sea. We traveled there thirteen years ago. The place has special meaning for me, but I suppose that's obvious."[16]

I noted aloud that the rendering of the painting seemed somehow unusual, showing as it does a mere fragment of the glowing treasury house on the far side of what looked to be a great crack in a cliff face, the rock sides of the crack dominating two-thirds of the painting and rendered in a dark, opaque, almost oppressive fashion.

"But, you see," you said, "that is just the way it is. The gateway to Petra is a crack in the mountain wall. The crack leads into a narrow canyon a thousand feet deep where the sun seldom shines, and the canyon leads into the city. That is part of the wonder of it. An entire fabulous city hidden from view, protected from enemies. Besides which, it is also the very spirit of civilization, or, at least, so it seems to me, which is why it is so central to this room. From the point of view of the artist, the dark cliff walls force your eye to the sunlit façade beyond, which was my intent."

For a few moments, we were all lost in our thoughts. Then Quatermain broke the silence, venturing, "Though hardly a connoisseur of art, Mr. Church, I have nonetheless formed a distant and great admiration for your paintings. I am a straightforward man, and take my enjoyment in a straightforward manner. This new impressionism is simply a confusion, if you ask me. But, sir, when you paint a leaf, a leaf it is and nothing more. When you draw a mountain or valley, there is no doubt of what you have represented. By chance do you have a work in progress you would care to share or, perhaps, even one that I may purchase for my own home?" Then he added almost shyly, "I'm in the position now of being able to afford the finer things in life."

You smiled wistfully. "Perhaps I should have mentioned it at the outset, but I have retired from the business of landscape painting, as my arthritis makes it increasingly difficult to ply my craft. For well over a decade it's been now. Which is not to say that I have stopped painting altogether. In fact, in the corner behind you, Quatermain, propped on an easel by the window is a new one. It is, I'm sorry to say for your sake, spoken for already."

You rose, crossed the room, and removed the covering from the painting. My first impression was that its oils still looked wet in the firelight. The image portrayed a fairy city, noble and pristine in the brilliant distance, while in the deep shadows of the foreground a man stood at a curious fountain.

You were saying that your plans for Olana would eventually include a formal art studio with proper lighting. In the meantime, you still dabbled, as it were, in your Manhattan studio, and that you had brought this nearly completed landscape to Olana to view it in the light of the country, since you never considered a painting complete until you had viewed it in the light of both city and country.

As for the subject matter, you said it presented an idealized view of Constantinople with a fountain called El Ayn. It was realized from sketches and notes you had placed in your sketchbook some thirty years earlier during your journey to that part of the Old World. "I call this one *The Fountain*," you said.[17]

I recall that Quatermain studied the picture at length and finally sat back down with his brandy. The three of us were quiet for a time. For my part I was content in the company of these world-class men. I noticed that Quatermain's eyes returned over and again to *The Fountain* and also to Petra's ancient treasury house over the fireplace.

"I must admit," he finally said, "that these particular works of yours, Mr. Church, call to mind an interesting interlude in my life, wherein I was required to traverse through a mountain cleft much as you've rendered there . . . only to encounter a most fabulous city and a fountain as well—but one of a very different character, I dare say." Then he shook his head as though shaking off the memories that had intruded themselves into his mind.

"But that has nothing to do with anything," he said with finality. He abruptly stood, saying, "Mr. Church, I fear we have overstayed our welcome. I merely wished to make acquaintance of a man whose artistic technique so closely parallels my own concept of an organized universe. That and to perhaps purchase a painting, but I can see that that is easier said than done."

Somewhat taken aback by the abruptness of Quatermain's leave-taking, I was about to rise, but you would have none of it. "*Mister* Quatermain, please sit back down. Humor me, please. Your comment interested me. I am flattered that my work would evoke memories in one—that is to say an adventurer—such as yourself. I hesitate to be so bold, but may I inquire about this 'interlude' you mention?"

To this Quatermain at first demurred, but our insistence prevailed and thus it happened that we sat before that wonderful fire, partaking of your delicious spirits long into the night. Quatermain turned back the hands of time while you and I sat enthralled, experiencing vicariously so many entirely new sights, sounds, and feelings.

Thus, because his experiences seem to me worthy of permanent record, I have set them down—and I only hope my attempt will be deemed acceptable in your eyes and in those who may chance to follow in time to come.

J.H.W.

Record of A.Q.'s narration
concerning certain adventures
that unfolded in east Africa
during the early part 1872,
as set down by
John H. Watson, M.D.
Feb. 1881

Introduction

As Told By Allan Quatermain

It was Christmas morning 1871 [Quatermain began] as I was preparing to leave the Black Kloof, the dreadful, dark and haunted gorge that was the home of Zikali, "The Opener of Roads," the formidable and clever black dwarf who was the wizard Zulu kings most held in awe, where he'd had me stay for several days and nights telling him every last detail of my recent adventures to Heu-Heu land—where he had sent me to procure a certain medicine for him. As I say, I was preparing the oxen and wagons to leave the area when two of his immense guards came to me and explained very politely in their Zulu language that Zikali wished to see me one additional time before we rode off.

Now, when Hans, my faithful Hottentot*[18] servant, heard this, he clamped his hands to his head and moaned, "Baas! Oh Baas, leave now while we have the chance. No Baas! The Opener of Roads must have another grocery errand for you down another long road and I am sick to death of his errands."

Hans was a little Hottentot fellow who had been my companion through most of my adventures, even when I was a lad. Indeed, my very first memories include him, as he was aide-de-camp for my father. Hans was strong, quick, and agile, also clever—extremely so—and quite astute when the need called for it. Otherwise, he remained quite content to drink when he could, and when he couldn't, he tended to get himself into mischief in the most ingenious ways. In any case, his eyes were always bloodshot from the drink, which was, if he had any choice in the matter, gin, which he called "square-face" after the shape of the bottle it came in. Nevertheless, he was devoted to me, as he was to my father before me. Sad to say, he is gone from this world now and I miss him, but that is another story, and neither here nor there, and has no pertinence to my tale.[19]

---

* Editor's note: Please see the "Intoduction: H. Rider Haggard's Character Hans the Hottentot" earlier in this volume.—T.K.M.

So it was that I looked at the two enormous men who stood waiting patiently and said to Hans, "If you think either or both of these fellows will take 'no' for an answer, then you may be my guest in the execution of your plan."

"No, Bass, for I think now that you have a point and because I think 'execution' is just the right word to describe our poor futures if we deny these huge fellows."

The end of it was that I was soon once again seated before the shriveled old dwarf, who said, "Macumazahn"—which means "Watcher by Night" and is what the natives call me—"thank you for returning to speak to this Old Cheat, as I know you call me at every opportunity. There is another matter of which I wish to speak.

"The reason I called you back is this: Last night as I slept, my spirit flew much farther than it does most times—halfway to the stars it seemed—and when I looked down upon the face of the world, I saw not the world of forests and mountains and deserts that are the coin of the world, but instead a giant bowl, its edges aflame. Then fiery stones fell from the sky with horrible roaring sounds and poisonous smoke and crashed into the bowl."

I sat listening to this nonsense, wanting only to be on my way, for the truth is I become impatient with Zikali and his ilk very quickly. "So what does this have to do with me?" I asked. "Do you have another errand for me?"

"Why, Macumazahn, I am talking about how your life, as pale and feeble as it is, as humble as it is, will soon have an encounter with the gods, or rather, a god. That much I know from the dream. But let's look further into the matter."

Here he grabbed some ashes from the circle of dying embers that surrounded the small fire that burned forever it seemed before his crouching figure, poured them on the dirt floor and patted them flat. I should say here that my acquaintance with Zikali began when I was quite young, hardly a boy, but even then he looked much the same as he did during this encounter, a shriveled dwarf with eyes of fire and an enormous head from which granite white hair fell in lavish braids. I have often thought that this particular posture of his, which I dare say is the only one that I can recall seeing, made him look much like an evil, aberrant toad.

He clapped his hands, and a servant appeared, one of those who had requested our return, with Zikali's catskin medicine bag and handed it to the wizard, who rummaged inside and pulled out his yellowed knuckle bones, those that he kept near him at all times and used for divining, or at least supposedly so, for I don't take much stock in such tricks that are the stock in trade of Africa's wizards. Then he shook the bones in his cupped hands for a bit and threw them down into the ashes.

Here he did something that I certainly didn't expect, and can say in truth I never witnessed before or since. He actually flinched as though startled. This was especially unusual because Zikali's whole existence was one of control. In many ways, he was like the puppeteer who controlled the marionette strings of his minions over all Zululand and beyond. I pretended I hadn't noticed and he continued to peer at the bones in the ashes.

"Ah!" he said, "more than a mere encounter. Much more. You will become an honored familiar to a great goddess. No, not a great goddess. *The* great goddess," he said, cocking his head and glancing at the bones from a somewhat different angle. Here he began to chant under his breath in a hypnotic wavering drone and rocked back and forth on his haunches. I sat impatiently for several minutes waiting for him to say what he had to say. I must have dozed, for the next thing I remember is seeing that he had a figurine cupped in his hands. The figurine, only about three inches in height, was one of those fertility goddesses that one sees so often these days in drawings of artifacts that have been dug up from archaeological sites all over the world. This, as those, possessed heavy drooping breasts, wide hips and a pregnant, prominent belly. Zikali dug a small indentation in the ashes and there placed the figure carefully before him. He then waved his hands in wide large movements, fanning the fire and bringing some of the smoke up from the fire to himself where it circled his head then drifted down to the figurine and began to encircle it, a horizontal ring of smoke that formed a kind of halo above that bit of carved black stone. All this while he had been chanting, and after some time, it was almost as though he had gone to sleep himself, with only the occasional audible mutter communicating that he may be alert still.

His murmuring eventually stopped, and he stirred himself and coughed. Then he reached into his medicine bag again and withdrew a handful of roots that he began to deliberately place into the fire, one by one, and each flared with a different colored flame and smoke. In a few moments, a rainbow of flames emanated from the little fire and the small hut was thick with the complicated, changing patterns created by the intermingling columns of many-hued smoke.

Before long I thought I was seeing an image in the congealing smoke. It was really quite a complicated illusion, and I must admit that for a short time I almost believed the image was real. What I thought I was seeing was this: I was standing alone on an enormous plain, when suddenly a burning stone fell from the sky with a shriek, hitting the ground and setting fire to a nearby thorn bush. Then, lightning flared all around the flickering flames of the bush and a voice like thunder spoke my name, "Allan, O Allan!"

And I responded in my dream with, "My Lord, why have you brought me hither?" At this, I began untying my boots and awkwardly slipping them off my feet, for it seemed the right thing to do, though I felt rather foolish.

"O Allan, she who is mother to all, she who is mother to all the world needs your aid. Go to her and I charge you with her care while you are with her. I also task you with discharging the great responsibility that she will require of you."

"What responsibility, Lord?"

And the response was an enigmatic one. The voice from the fiery bush said, "You are but a cog in the wheel of life and in the fullness of time you will exercise my will, though mayhap you will not know it."

At which point the fiery bush began to smoke terribly, and then the smoke was the smoke in the hut. It was choking me and I had no choice but to jump up and run out into the air.

When I returned some minutes later feeling somewhat better but still confused and shaken, the smoke had cleared, by what manner it was done so fast I don't know. I returned to my sitting position in the dirt before Zikali. I noticed that though the fire still flickered, for it never went out entirely, it was now mostly glowing embers, and the bones and small idol and medicine bag had been cleared away. Zikali himself was motionless but making a peculiar sound. In time I decided he was laughing, "Ho, ho, ho, ho!" When he quieted down, he said, "O, White Man, who is so brave as is his whole race, I can see into your mind. You are saying, 'He is nothing but an old repulsive Kaffir cheat and magician. I saw nothing of consequence except that which was suggested to me while I was somehow drugged and made to dream.' But you are also wondering now how can 'the thing that should never have been born' know of such things?*

"Verily, Macumazahn, I had little to do with any of this. I have heard that your people have something called a magic lantern that projects pretty pictures that you all gather round and make surprised sounds at. Consider then that I have only been a magic lantern through which one greater than I caused you to see that which you were intended to see."

By then, I was vastly confused and said as much. But it really came down to one simple question: "Zikali, why did you want to see me and ask your messengers to bring me back here before you? Always you want me to help you for some selfish end. What do you want of me?"

The old wizard finally stopped laughing and peered at me with his infinitely black eyes. "O, Macumazahn," he began, "you always think so poorly of me! I have nothing to gain, nothing at all. The information I convey will merely be of use to you, that is all. It appears the goddess has honored you and requires you to carry a grand message outside the bowl, for that is where you will meet her, that bowl that I saw in my dream last night."

"What is this bowl?" Then skeptically, "What is the nature of this message?"

"Ah, Macumazahn, as always you doubt your friend, the Old Cheat. But perhaps this time you are more justified than usual, for I

---

* Editor's note: "The thing that should never have been born" was a title mockingly given to the wizard some fifty years before by the great Zulu emperor, Shaka, as there was "bad blood" between the two.—T.K.M.

can tell you no more. The fiery stones, the bowl, the queen of the gods, the message . . . these are all that I am allowed to be privy to and no more, no more details at all, for a vast black shield blocks my arts. It is as though something or someone wished to whet both our appetites, and, once having done so, withdrew.

"Now begone with you. Though we are friends of decades, at the moment you tire me, and I want to consider what power it is that can turn the great 'Opener of Roads' into a mere tool."

Shortly thereafter, Hans and I were soon back at the wagons, where my men had made the final preparations. The oxen and the wagons were ready to go, for which I was thankful because I wanted to be away from the Black Kloof as fast as my feet and the feet of our oxen could take me.

I spent the better part of several days trying to understand what had happened. The most amazing thing of all is that, for the first time, I saw the great Zikali seem contrite and not in control. Never in my presence before or after that affair did he seem so unsure of the ground on which he stood. I alternated between shaking my head in wonderment at that and trying to make sense of the vision I saw, or thought I saw. It was almost as though the Hebrew God "I am that I am" took a moment off his busy schedule to ask a favor of me!

Dash it all! My head hurt when I pondered all this, so after a while I pushed all else out of my mind except the glorious image of a hot bath in the simple tub in my small home in Durban, the small home I had not seen in nearly a year, for that was the length of Zikali's little grocery trip!

"So, gentlemen, that is merely the beginning of the story. It is but the preamble to a journey that seems in retrospect as unlikely as, say, bumping into the honest-to-goodness Pearly Gates while strolling through London's West End. For myself . . . perhaps I am a doubting Thomas or perhaps I am merely pragmatic . . . ."

[Watson note: Quatermain did not finish the thought, but instead sighed deeply and said, "But the telling of the rest will take some time. Should I continue?" Well, you (Church) and I were both quite caught up and adamant that it was out of the question that he just stop there. The end of it was that Quatermain asked for more brandy, which request you happily obliged, and there was quiet all around except for the crackling fire in the hearth. Quatermain rolled the amber liquid in his glass, catching the glow of the fire through the glass. In time, he heaved another great sigh and continued his story. —J.H.W.]

Ethiopia shall soon stretch out her hands unto God.
                                        —Psalm 68:31

In some older strata, do the fossilized bones of an ape more anthropoid (manlike) or a man more pithecoid (apelike) than any yet known await the researches of some unborn paleontologist?

—T.H. Huxley

CHAPTER ONE

Allan's Unwanted Guests

As we approached Durban on the very day of Epiphany, 6th Jan. 1872[20] [Quatermain continued], the town had a merry appearance, still in the throes of Christmas celebration. I remember how all this Christmas atmosphere and a generally melancholy mood (somehow imposed on me by that damnable wizard!) put me in mind of the history of the area. Europeans had first troubled themselves to notice the southeastern coast of Africa on a Christmas morning in the fifteenth century and the area had been called Natal ever since as a consequence.[21]

I remember too how I mused that Lieutenant Francis George Farewell would hardly have recognized the trading community he founded in May 1824, which he called Port Natal, but which name was changed a few years later to Durban, after the then new governor of the Cape. Not only had it become a prosperous and bustling town (rather than the half dozen or so poor structures that Farewell's people had thrown up) but, at the moment in question it was so festooned with decorations of the season that it appeared more a carnival than a serious community.

"Baas," Hans said while rubbing his dirty, sparsely stubbled chin, "I hope the Big Baas in the sky can forgive you your sins for which his Son was pinned to a tree, since you don't look like a man who is in the mood to celebrate anything at all, least of all His Son's birthday."

`This was only nine years ago—it seems like a lifetime ago, but of course I've done a great deal since then—but I'm never likely to forget the reason for the frown that had so changed my face that it prompted Hans's remark: There in front of my house stood four men, three of whom were very serious, business-like men, which was precisely what I did not want to see at that time. I was tired after a very long trek and only wanted to settle into my little house, but somehow I knew that that particular small reward would be denied me.

"Look yonder, Hans, and tell me what there is to celebrate."

He did as I bade and seemed startled, I presume because he had missed this new circumstance even though it was as evident as the nose on his face, something he subsequently wrote off by saying he was distracted by all the holiday ribbons and festive colors, though I knew he secretly admonished himself about it for days to come.

"Oh, Baas, those four have faces like the Predikant, your reverend father, when he would find me drunk behind the shed—stern and unsmiling—but your father never had a face pale like plaster as these do. All my poor life I have known white men, both high and low, but these men are more white than any of the others, and therefore all the more ugly for it." Then he grinned, "But they also look rich, which can only be good news, as I have heard you mutter to yourself that our purse is poor and even more so since we have used up so much on this journey and gotten no reward for our grocery errand except a pat on the back from The Opener of Roads."

"Hans, I don't care if they offer me a golden platter heaped with diamonds, I intend to rest and intend to do exactly so and nothing more."

By this time, we had arrived at the proximity of my front porch, and the men in question approached. One separated himself from the others and held out his hand to me. "Mr. Quatermain I presume?"

"You are correct," I said as we shook hands.

"Mr. Quatermain, my name is Richard Holmes. I am with the British Museum on some rather urgent business. These are my associates Thomas Huxley, Will Scott, and Sergeant Cuff."

Mr. Holmes looked as though he represented a museum. He was average height—meaning that he was somewhat taller than myself—middle aged and scholarly. His cheeks held thick tufts of graying hair and his hairline receded, but he was otherwise clean shaven.

Huxley would have been tall, if he wasn't so stooped. His face was nearly covered with thick white whiskers, though his chin and cheeks were clean shaven. It seemed to me, too, that Huxley was beginning to grow somewhat stout about the middle, a fact that put a clear strain on his handsome red silk waistcoat. But I remember his eyes especially—so piercing and intense that when he shot a glance at you, some part of your mind had to remind yourself that you had not in fact been shot. This contributed to the great power—almost that of a youth in his prime rather than a man in his middle years—that I felt emanating from the man and I decided that he was not a man to be toyed with. Beyond that, I remember thinking that his high forehead and the smooth cut of his exposed cheeks above his beard bore an odd resemblance to those of the young man who had been introduced as Will Scott.*

I said, "Mr. Huxley, your name is familiar, but I fear that I can't immediately place it." But then I remembered, "Oh! I have it now. Aren't you the man who has stood at Mr. Darwin's side through thick and thin?"

Huxley seemed pleased with this perception and my phrasing of it. "Indeed I am," said he. "Though I must admit some surprise that in a spot so remote you would have heard of my humble efforts on behalf of my friend and his conclusions. I suppose, my being a fellow of the Royal Society and all, that my name creeps into public awareness now and again."

To which I responded, "Though I may be a backwoodsman, I've read of your championing Mr. Darwin, sir, and I admire your courage for standing up for what you believe. Though my reading of books is limited mostly to the Old Testament and *The Ingoldsby Legends*, I have read abstracts of Mr. Darwin's book and

---

* Editor's note: William Baring-Gould, who has done much to fill out Sherlock Holmes's life beyond Watson's biographical and anecdotal sketches, tells us in his biography of the sleuth, *Sherlock Holmes on Baker Street*, that Holmes's parents had three boys, Sherrinford in 1845, Mycroft in 1847, and Sherlock seven years later. Holmes's father wished to name their third-born son after the 17th century theologian William Sherlock, but his mother preferred naming the child after her favorite author, Sir Walter Scott. "At last," says Baring-Gould, "a compromise was arrived at. The boy was baptized William Sherlock Scott Holmes." —T.K.M.

have seen enough in Africa to admit that his notions have given me much food for thought, at the least. I have read about you more than once in the various publications that make their way here to Durban. Though I haven't been near a newspaper in almost a year, I recall that 'survival of the fittest' is the phrase that the gentlemen of the press seemed to enjoy trumpeting about."

"Yes, indeed, sir. 'Natural selection' is still quite the topic these days."

My response was to smile politely.

The boy, Will Scott, was hardly more than seventeen or eighteen years and extremely tall and thin. In fact, he was nearly the tallest European I have ever seen, though I have seen some Watuzi of comparable height, if not taller. So thin in fact was he that I feared for his health. His arms, too, seemed unusually long, but his grip was firm, which tells much about a man.[22] Also he stood upright and straight, and with his solid determined chin, he had a singular air of purpose about him.

As for the last member of the party, Sergeant Cuff (and now that I think about it, I don't believe I ever learned the man's Christian name—how odd!), he was of advanced age and average height. But my initial reaction was for this man's health as well, for he was hardly more than skin and bones. Beyond this, it was clear that he had not shaved for several days, his hair was gray and cut extremely short, and his complexion was severely wrinkled and dry.

Just as these thoughts crossed my mind, Hans, who had been able to stealthily come up behind me, whispered in my ear: "Oh, Baas, this one you must be careful with. He is like a dead man who still walks and talks. Do you think he might be one of the spooks who belong to The Opener of Roads?"

"Hush!" I said as unobtrusively as I could. Then to Cuff, "Mr. Holmes introduced you as Sergeant, sir. Are you retired from her majesty's service?"

"Oh, no, Quatermain. I'm a policeman."

"A policeman! What on earth?" I shook my head in confusion. "Gentlemen, gentlemen! I'm afraid I am most perplexed."

"Mr. Quatermain," Cuff rejoined, "it falls upon Mr. Holmes to explain the details at this early juncture."

Holmes opened his mouth and I'm sure would have told me all about it, about Cuff and all the rest of their business, but I would have none of it. Just then, suddenly, I was filled with a sense of defeat and perhaps a little foreboding, and it was all I could do to smile politely. I was not pleased at this uninvited, unwanted attention, but I could see that these were determined men with a mission, though at that moment I had no idea what that mission might be.

"Gentlemen! Not yet!" I said, surrendering to the feeling of fate about to overwhelm me. "I'm sure you have far more to tell me than my poor head can hold for the moment. Please allow me! As you see me this moment, I have not crossed the threshold of my house for nearly a year, and there it is, just a few feet away, beckoning me, and I'm afraid its allure is far more than I can handle."

This statement shocked them all into apoplexies of apologies, and they quickly stood back and let me through.

"You see," I began, actually enjoying the tiny bit of power I was able to assert just then, "I am anxious to take off my boots and sit in my chair. And the last thing I want to hear at the moment is your purpose. I beg you, therefore, to indulge me while I settle back into the domestic life."

With only a little comment, they were kind enough to oblige. I invited them in and they made themselves as comfortable as they could in my modest accommodations.

These, then, were my first impressions of these men with whom I would journey far and share experiences the nature of which it will be extremely difficult to communicate [but for the sake of you two gentlemen, I will try]. Among these impressions was the sense that though Holmes initiated the talking, Huxley was the man in charge. In addition, though Cuff might have looked like a cadaver, I quickly became most impressed with the man's energy, an energy that entirely belied all my first impressions.

After we all shared a simple dinner of buttered rice and mutton, washed down with native beer, I finally consented to hear out my unwanted guests. Hans, who had disappeared at the start, as he was wont to do when "customers" first made their appeals to me, reemerged and silently settled down onto his haunches unnoticed in a corner.

"Well," I said to Mr. Holmes, "what business does the British Museum have with me, not to mention the police?"

Here, young Will Scott chose to speak. "I'm afraid much of the blame falls on me, sir. I'm sure you don't recall, but we met almost two years ago at Castle Ragnall. It was at a rather large garden party."

He waited for some light of remembrance from me. "I'm sorry, young man, I don't recall having seen you there."

"But of course, since I was only fifteen or sixteen then. I had been invited by my dear friend Luna, Miss Holmes.[23] You may recall that you made quite an impression on her."

"Yes, of course, I do remember that. She pumped me for every detail of every trek I had ever undertaken in southern Africa. A lovely young woman. How is she?"

"Quite fine. She and Lord Ragnall married not so long ago. It was when Richard here mentioned to me his desire to hire the 'best damned guide in Africa' that I remembered you and went so far as to recommend you."

I looked at Richard Holmes and said, "Might you be a relative of Luna?"

"Oh, no. Just a coincidence of names. I have yet to meet this young woman, who one and all refer to in the most reverent tones. But, yes indeed," Holmes added, "after inquiries, I determined that you were just the right man for the job."

"And just what is the job you have in mind?"

"You know of course, just four years ago, Britain sent a large force to Abyssinia for the purpose of rescuing hostages from Emperor Theodore."

"Yes, I was upcountry during those events, but I learned of the Ethiopian campaign belatedly."

"Some 280 ships unloaded 32,000 men and 20,000 mules, and materiel enough to keep them all going. Quite an astonishing expedition. Field-Marshal Lord Napier marched his army into the highlands for some three months. In the end, Theodore took his own life (or seemed to, which is one of the reasons we're here). A certain amount of bounty was acquired for the purpose of paying the men. I can proudly say that I accompanied this expeditionary force and was there when the emperor's treasury was cataloged."

"Plundered is more like it," broke in Huxley. "I hear the soldiers went through the place like mad beasts."

"True enough, I'm afraid," responded Holmes, frowning with the memory. "In the end, however, I was able to retrieve some 900 manuscripts and other historical documents to return to the museum for preservation. It has been my great and fortunate honor during the interim to examine and determine just what we found."

He had paused, for effect, I think, but since he failed to continue, I felt obliged to speak. "And this has to do with me in what way?"

"After the demise of Theodore," Holmes continued, "the three chief contenders to the throne warred amongst themselves, and still are for that matter. Her Majesty's government, for various reasons, supports one by the name of Kasa Mercha, who has been extending his influence for well over a decade. In fact, in about two weeks, it is intended by our government that he ascend to the throne. I believe he has chosen the name Yohannes IV. Naturally, this has been a long time in development.

"But the fact is that in recent months rumors have reached Mercha, and thus to the top levels of the British government, to the effect that Theodore is not dead. That the dead man we came upon on the steps of his fortress Magdala was that of a fanatical look-alike. There is talk amongst Ethiopians that Theodore still lives and rules from some secret location. The talk is that the King of Kings has risen from the dead and rules.

"Mercha, as you can imagine, is a bit nervous about these rumors. His own attempts to send agents to determine the truth have failed. Her Majesty thus feels a responsibility to make the effort to put the lie to the rumors or find Theodore if he lives. We—" he took in the others with a sweep of his arm, "—are her tools in this regard." At that, Holmes ceased to talk and there was silence.

Finally, I said, "This is all well and good, gentleman, but, I repeat, what does it have to do with me? And what does this purely political matter have to do with a noted biological naturalist like Mr.

Huxley here? Or a policeman such as Mr. Cuff? Or, for that matter, a museum curator such as yourself?"

All eyes turned to Richard Holmes. He seemed to blush for a moment. He cleared his throat and continued.

"You see, Mr. Quatermain, Napier's expedition had some corollary effects. Several, as a matter of fact. First things first, though. Sergeant Cuff is here in the official capacity of determining whether Theodore is alive or dead. He was chosen because his methods of deduction have proven over and again to be of great service to the Crown. The official determination of Theodore's continued existence or not is in his hands."

Here I looked at Cuff, but he merely rubbed the growth of gray grizzly beard on his chin. As I had nothing to say to the man at that moment, I was about to give my attention back to Holmes, when Cuff addressed me.

"I see that you have climbing roses around your porch, Quatermain."

"Why, yes. I'm afraid I don't have much chance to enjoy them, though."

"Ah. Of course. Perhaps if you were around more, then they would be better cared for. I couldn't help but notice that they're only one step from the wild state."

I was stunned. I had no idea how to take this comment. Was it innocent? Was it meant critically? If so, how dare he, who hardly knew me? Such thoughts filled my brain as I stared astonished and wide-eyed at the man.

It was Will Scott who jumped to the man's rescue. "Quatermain, please understand that beyond police work, Sergeant Cuff's primary passion in life is the cultivation of roses. That is all we heard about on the voyage here."

"I'm sorry if I offended you, Quatermain," said Cuff. "It's just that roses poorly tended rub me the wrong way. A year is a long time to be away, though, to be sure. And, yes, it is my affidavit that may very well put an end to this Theodore affair."

Not quite knowing what to make of all this, I took a long quiet, and what I hoped was an unobtrusive, breath and then slipped on my bartering face, the blank expression I always wore when trading with the various peoples one encounters in Africa. Unfazed by the interruption, Holmes was continuing. "Huxley's role is one of an entirely different character."

Huxley took up the tale: "You can imagine what it must have been like, 32,000 men and tens of thousands of animals crossing the desert and thence into the highlands. Though I was not there, I can see in my mind the cloud of dust. Richard was there, however, and he has described the scene. No matter the details. You see, once the army had accomplished its goals and marched back through the village of Zula to Annesley Bay, the harbor from which the expedition had been mounted, one soldier, Corporal Saint James by name, knowing it would take several days to dismantle the camp, decided to do a bit of sightseeing. You understand, his activities at that time were strictly contrary to orders, but he rationalized that he would never be in Ethiopia again and that he had a small boy back home in India for whom he wanted to find a proper souvenir. His route took him into some barren, terrible areas, as he describes them. At one point he found something of particular interest. Not being an ignorant man, he knew he had found something of interest to more than just his young son."

Huxley slowly reached into his inside coat pocket and removed a leather pouch. He opened it, extracted some wadding, which he unfolded, and produced a piece of bone, which he then held out to me. Taking note of the wadding and extreme care with which it had been packaged, I took hold of it very gingerly and held it up into the light from a beam that poured through the window into the room from the setting sun. I turned the bone every which way, showed it to Hans, and so on. But in fact, it wasn't bone at all but rock in the shape of a bone, so I knew it to be some sort of fossil.

Huxley continued, "He spotted a dozen or so pieces just such as you have there just lying on the desert floor, exposed to the elements. He picked them up, protected them, and, of course, intended to get them aboard ship without anyone noticing."

I examined the piece closer, saying, "It looks to be the forearm bone from a monkey of some sort." I looked at Hans, who was nodding his head vigorously. "Fossilized," I added, "which implies great age. However, aside from that, I am not clear as to its significance."

"Ah, you are quite right, Quatermain," said Huxley. "It does in fact originate from a primate of some sort. You see this is but one of the several pieces that Saint James found. It is a convoluted story, but Saint James's escapade did not go unnoticed and his souvenirs were commandeered. Fortunately, they made their way into my hands. I shudder when I imagine what could have happened to them if they had been the responsibility of less learned men. Suspecting an unusual provenance, I brought them to the attention of Darwin. He and I have spent days, weeks, with the bones, measuring, weighing, comparing, conjecturing, mulling over the whole set. The upshot is that we are convinced that these bones belong to a primitive ancestor of Man—perhaps as old as a million years.[24] The very sort of creature Darwin hypothesizes about in *The Descent of Man*, which in fact was being printed in February just as these fragments came to our attention."

[Friends, Huxley's words startled me to the core, as I was dead certain I myself had stumbled onto the Missing Link *still living!* some months before in Heu-Heu land—the creatures called the Hairy Folk of the Woods. But I kept that to myself!]

"However, our conjectures are meaningless with so little to go on, so it quickly became imperative that a team be assembled to go to Ethiopia and more closely investigate the region Corporal Saint James stumbled upon. Through official channels, it was determined that both the needs of the British government, as relayed by Mr. Holmes, and that of Mr. Darwin and myself intersected and that it would be mutually beneficial if we teamed together. Feeling grateful that there was a chance to hastily join an expedition of an official nature that was in itself being hastily prepared, I, as Mr. Darwin's representative, became part of the group you see before you today. In fact, as I had pressing responsibilities, it was necessary that I feign illness from overwork." Here he grinned. "I was so successful that my doctor prescribed therapeutic travel. Only Darwin and a few others in the government know where I truly am. To the rest of the world, I'm on holiday in France and Germany. In addition, young Will Scott, here, has agreed to accompany me as my assistant since a fair amount of tedious digging and methodical record keeping will no doubt be necessary, regardless of the outcome. And let me say that he volunteered to do this at no small inconvenience to himself, as he was about to take up residence at Christ Church, where he will begin his first year at Oxford in a few months, when these circumstances became known to him." Huxley looked over at Scott and fairly burst with pride and affection.

Scott blushed at the mention of his name and said quickly, "Yes, I'm Mr. Huxley's assistant." He smiled broadly. Then he opened his mouth again as though to say something, but Huxley's demeanor instantly changed and he gave Scott a quick look, at which the young man snapped his mouth shut. This, of course, aroused my interest and I remember thinking that under different circumstances I would have determined what exactly the boy had wanted to say. As it happened, though, I was simply tired and really did not care.

During this entire conference, I was sitting in my rocker, one of the items I missed the most while traveling. I rocked. And I rocked. I must tell you, there was a profound silence in the room. I rocked because I was thinking.

Eventually, I looked again at the group's spokesman and said, "Mr. Holmes, I must admit that these various tales I'm hearing are interesting. Though, as I said, the notions of Mr. Huxley here and Mr. Darwin have given me pause, actually, I tend to lean toward the Old Testament in such matters, and besides, it seems to me that a monkey bone is merely a monkey bone. And that is the end of it. As I said, this is all very interesting, but it doesn't explain your presence, Mr. Holmes."

The face of the museum curator suddenly glowed; his eyes grew wide and he exclaimed, "Mr. Quatermain, I am present for no less reason than a miracle . . . ."

"My dear Mr. Holmes!" I exclaimed, for I was not used to being associated with such terminology.

"Mr. Quatermain, are you familiar with the Great Library of Alexandria?"

I'm afraid that my education, being rough and administered in the wilds of what is now the Cradock district of the Cape Colony, lacked some subtlety and the particular institution to which Holmes referred meant little to me. I said as much.

"Indeed, the Great Library of Alexandria was planned by the first Ptolemy and developed in the third century B.C. by Ptolemy II.

Its goal was no less than the accumulation of all knowledge, and it seemed to have succeeded in that regard. Within its walls were some 700,000 papyrus scrolls containing the wisdom of the Macedonians, Romans, Egyptians, Jews, Indians, Persians, and Phoenicians, all their religion, science, and history. Over six centuries, this library evolved into the intellectual core and splendor of civilization, the crowning achievement of human life on earth. But, at the end of the fourth century A.D., the Christian Emperor Theodosius ordered it all burned."

"My word! What on earth for?"

"Well, Christianity was so sufficiently new that Theodosius was fearful of anything pagan, which is how he thought of the library and its contents. It was not one of the prouder moments of the Christian era, to be sure." Here he paused. "Yet, as I studied in the British Museum the hundreds of volumes from Theodore's treasury, I found several references, delicious hints, if you will, that inferred that a portion of the library, or at least many of its important scrolls, were secretly packed up, removed to Abyssinia, and hidden from the book burners. Preserved, in other words. And there is every reason to believe that that remnant of the library has not been touched since, that it is waiting to be rediscovered . . . perhaps to help humankind enter a new renaissance."

Holmes then pulled a paper from an inside coat pocket. "Quatermain, let me give you one small example of the nature of the sorts of things this library may hold for us. What I have here is a translation from a fragment of a scroll I found in Theodore's treasury. It, in turn, is a copy of a scroll far older that was part of the Alexandrian Library. Now, please indulge me and read this."

Reluctantly, for I knew that by doing so I was enmeshing myself further than I desired into this venture, I reached for the paper.

Yet, before I was able to touch it, Holmes drew his hand back, saying, "Quatermain, have you not heard of the Synoptic Problem?"

"The what problem?"

"In the Bible, man! Mark, Matthew, and Luke are called the Synoptic Gospels because they have such similar elements. Of Mark's 661 verses, more than 600 of Matthew's and 350 of Luke's are the same. But Matthew and Luke have 200 other verses that are the same but that do not appear in Mark."

"I'm afraid I had no idea," I said.

"For years, scholars have hypothesized that Matthew and Luke were independently compiled, or drawn, from Mark and from *another* and *unknown* source document. This would be an entirely new gospel."[25]

"Yes . . . I can see that," I said noncommittally.

"What you are about to read could well be a fragment from that new gospel. The author purports to be one Gaspar, which is the name tradition has given to one of the three Wise Men. Many scholars believe that if the Magi existed at all, they were probably Zoroastrian priests from somewhere in Asia Minor. It is also claimed in tradition that Gaspar was the youngest of the Wise Men and that he was Ethiopian."

He handed me the paper, his eyes wide with expectation, and I began to read:

[Watson note: Here Quatermain closed his eyes and, struggling only a little, recalled from memory the gist of the document.— J.H.W.]

[Quatermain note: Later, Mr. Church, at the end of this strange trek, I was able to secure from Holmes a copy of the paper I had read at this juncture, which I still have amongst my mementos, and I am asking Dr. Watson to have it reproduced and to attach it to the narrative he is preparing for your enjoyment.—A.Q.]

[Watson note: Which I have happily done at this point.— J.H.W.]

"Thus Gaspar says:

"These are the words of Gaspar the Ethiopian.[26]

"I am dismayed. A significant portion of my life has been given to the study of one man, and more and more frequently I hear reports concerning him that are blatantly false or twisted far beyond the simple truths.

"Why is this? Can there be so many whose self-interest outweighs the simple truth?

"In all things, Jesus the Nazarene said, 'Treat others as you would have them treat you. Do good and give as you can without expecting a thing in return. Your reward will be great, and God will call you his children. Show mercy even as your Father shows mercy. Do not judge, for how can you judge? What right do you have to judge when you have no understanding why a person is the way that person is? Remember, the standard you use will be the standard used toward you.'

"The one God is real, a spirit that is at the core of everything and everyone. God is always observing how you treat and judge others and how your actions and words, or inaction for that matter, affect others. This spirit doles out according to your actions. Hurt and you will be hurt, love and you will be loved, cause someone to cry in suffering and you will be made to cry with your own suffering. This circle of doing followed by God's response may be experienced immediately or may be held off for a future, or even a past, lifetime, according to the will of God for his own reasons.

"Jesus explained the way of the world in a simple manner, with parables that even children can understand. He was proud of his ability in this respect. He told his followers and all those who would listen, 'Blessed are the eyes that see the things that you see, for I tell you that many prophets and kings have desired to see those things that you see and have not seen them, and to hear those things that you hear and have not heard them.'

"And yet I, Gaspar, mourn, as none of this do I hear from the caravans. Instead I hear about magical wine and multiplying loaves and fishes. Where is the word of Jesus the Naserene, who told us not to worry about our lives, what we will eat, about our bodies, or what we will wear, for isn't life more than food, and the body more than flesh? Did he not remind us of the way lilies grow, that they do not work or spin, but that even Solomon, in all his splendor, was not as glorious?"

And thus the document ended, and when I had finished reading, I looked at the men grouped in my house. I wasn't sure what they expected me to say or do. I wanted to say something like, "Mr. Holmes, surely you have better things to do with your time than to dabble in romance writing of this inferior sort" but I thought better of it. Instead, I looked at them all and said, "I don't understand."

Holmes looked exasperated. I must chuckle to myself when I think back on it. He took the sheet back, neatly folded it, and returned it to his pocket. Then he continued as though I had said nothing. "This is only a fragment. If the full Gaspar document had been in circulation about 50 A.D.—which is when we believe it was written—then it would certainly have become part of the Alexandrian Library. Alternatively, if Gaspar was Ethiopian, then it's not entirely unlikely that a copy of his writings would have found its way into the library of an Ethiopian 'king of kings.' In either case, the full document, if we considered it and nothing else at all, would be priceless beyond discussion. And if it turns out to be the lost source document of which I was speaking, decades of arguing would be put to rest." Holmes let that sink in for a moment, then said, "But that could all be moot because we are not looking for one document but a library, or at least a significant portion of one."

As preposterous as all this sounded, I was beginning to realize that these important people hadn't come all the way from England to test my patience. "I repeat for the *third* time," said I, "what does all this have to do with me?"

"We want you to help us find the surviving remnants of the great Library of Alexandria," said Holmes.

"To help locate King Theodore II, if he still exists," broke in Sergeant Cuff.

"And to help locate the region where I can find more primitive bones," said Huxley.

I took a deep breath, calmed down. When next I spoke it was some minutes later. "Gentlemen, I assume your passage from London to Durban was done at the expense of the British government. That is all to the good. Because what you are proposing is lunacy—pure lunacy on a grand scale on a myriad of levels. I would have thought that men of your backgrounds would have realized the total futility of these sundry ventures, not to mention the cumulative lot, and would have given it up no sooner had the thought entered your collective minds.

"It would be one thing if you had maps or directions—though heaven knows I have seen enough suspect maps in my day!"[27]

Holmes then muttered something, a characteristic that did not seem to become the man, though I had only just met him.

"I beg your pardon," I asked.

"Quatermain," he began again, but with less conviction, "we did bring some statements that might be of navigational assistance." He drew some more papers out of his coat pocket. He shuffled through them a moment, settled on one, and continued, "Corporal Saint James described his journey as well as he could. Let me read some extracts from his account:

[Watson note: Here Quatermain again closed his eyes, remembering the substance of the document that Holmes read at that point. —J.H.W]

[Quatermain note: As before, despite Holmes' predilection to hold these documents extremely close to his vest, I was eventually able to persuade him to let me copy this one, as well.—A.Q.]

"Our thousands had been steering down from the highlands into the base camp. I was near the end of that long column, a fact that allowed me to move around somewhat more than others without being observed. At an opportune time, when the front of the column arrived in the vicinity of the bay, I took off at dusk heading at first due south into the desert, then following the easiest path, which turned me a bit to the east. I didn't know what I was looking for, only that my boy would like a fine souvenir. But the further away from the column I got, a kind of giddiness took over. I felt a kind of freedom I hadn't known since I was a boy myself. I kept telling myself I'd best be going back, but my body would not obey my mind. The funny thing is that I didn't feel at all worried at being found out. Instead I felt more like a kid at play. Anyway, seeing that you want to know my route, after some time the moon came up and I could see my surroundings pretty clearly. I'd say it was about twenty miles from the start that a range of mountains kind of popped up on my left. Even though I could see, on account of the moon, I couldn't see much. I just knew they were there . . . how far away I couldn't be certain. So far my path presented little more than broken rock and sand from the start. Then I saw something that chilled my soul. In the distance, southwest of my position, the sky was glowing with redness, I couldn't help but aim toward the spot and after several miles I could see what looked like a boiling cauldron at the top of a large hill. "I'll be daft," I thought, "a volcano!" That I wasn't expecting! I looked around at the ground thinking a volcanic stone or two would suit my purposes, and indeed I did grab a couple, like chunks of black glass. I stared at the fiery sight for a time, then, instead of turning back, which would have been the sensible thing to do, I decided to see what other wonders this strange land might reveal. Before long the cauldron had turned back into a glow on my rear horizon. Everything I've been describing took up most of the night, and as the sun rose, I felt like an egg in a pan. It was well over 100 degrees it was, maybe 120, 130, something like that. I found some shelter in a sort of cave formed by two boulders and was properly grateful for it, to be sure, and here I rested till night again, using my water sparingly. When I started up again, I continued on in more or less the same direction, that is to say south, southeast. I think that I forgot to say that the range of mountains I'd seen to the east did nothing but grow during my entire journey. All the while, I could see those mountains, sometimes dipping toward the horizon, sometimes looming so close it seemed like they were the whole world, if you catch my drift. And the volcano that I had left behind had merged into another, lower range of mountains off to the west, so that I was making my way through a sort of valley, I guess."

Here Holmes looked up at me. "And he goes on like this describing what he saw. He was asked some pointedly specific questions having to do with the kinds of rocks he noticed, type and degree of vegetation, etc. Unfortunately, he wasn't able to provide more than a middling amount of specific information, not being a naturalist of any sort. But in broad outlines, his expedition has been documented up to the point he found the fossil bones, which is the point at which he finally determined he should return. Now it is fairly certain that the volcano he encountered was Mt. Erta Ale, the location of which, obviously, is well known and mapped. The point is that his journey can be extrapolated and his probable positions placed on a map. So you see, in effect, we do have a map of sort leading to the general vicinity of his wonderful find."

I opened my mouth to express my incredulity, since the "vicinity" he so blithely spoke of was no doubt equivalent to hundreds of square miles, but I was cut short. "But there's more, Quatermain." Here he shuffled more of his papers. "Those rumors about Theodore still being alive include some geographical detail, namely that his (if it is his) base camp is probably near a ridge that is approachable from the east on a path that leads between two volcanoes. The entrance point of this path is about three days northwest by horse from the tip of the peninsula that is the African side of the Strait of Bab el Mandeb. Once again, extrapolating from the available information, we have reason to believe that the volcanoes in question are the Dama 'Ali and the Kurub Koma, two of a complex chain of mountains and volcanoes that dot that country. The camp itself is on the western side of the volcanoes. And here it gets a little tricky. No one can say if the camp is approachable from the west."

Abruptly, young Will Scott broke in. "It is very exciting actually. If the camp is approachable from the west, then it would be in a spot just about due south of the fossil find, perhaps fifty or seventy-five miles. Our proposal then is to use Saint James's information to locate the fossil beds, and then we turn south and try to approach the camp from the west, and if we can, determine if Theodore is still with us or not. If that proves impossible, then we merely circle toward the south and east to find the path between the volcanoes."

To say I was dumbfounded would be an understatement. Tomfoolery, tommy rot, suicide, the whole venture was. And I said as much. "Young man, I have heard nothing but a lot of very vague terms in the last few minutes, words like *might provide, middling information, broad outlines, fairly certain*—you see, I have been listening!—*extrapolated, in effect, general vicinity, rumors, reason to believe,* and now you just uttered the most foolhardy of them all. One does not *merely* circle around a pair of volcanic mountains in singularly unknown territory."

Young Scott seemed abashed and his face flushed red, but this lasted but a moment, for he cleared his throat and launched right back into his justification for the expedition, "You see, it is perfectly obvious that there are some correspondences here that may be of use. The map extrapolated from Saint James's account seems to fit nicely into the particulars of the camp location, which are more than rumors, I believe, being actually the intelligence appropriated by spies, and, therefore, that much more credible. So you see, there is some sense to this enterprise. We only need to put all this disparate information into focus."

I looked helplessly at these unwanted guests of mine. I looked at each face in turn, at once trying, I suppose, to communicate with my eyes the hopelessness of this plan, and at the same time gain some sense of their degree of purpose. Indeed, all I saw was their passion and determination.

I looked at the papers still in Holmes's hands that told of two completely unrelated aspects of terrain in a part of the world of which I knew precisely nothing and uttered my exact sentiments.

"Gentlemen," I said testily, "I don't see how these fool scribblings will help one bit. Furthermore, what on earth do either of these sets of directions have to do with your great library or a new gospel? What is the connection?"

Holmes was the one who spoke. "Quatermain, this base camp we have been speaking of . . . Theodore's hideout . . . we think it is one and the same place where the remnants of Alexandria's library were sequestered. At least, that is the working theory of some who are positioned in the government just to make such informed conjectures. The reasoning goes thus: if thousands of books could exist there safely for almost fifteen hundred years, why not one man for four years?"

I was already so numb from this veritable landslide of nonsense that this new pebble hardly affected me at all.

Here Holmes looked pointedly at Lieutenant Cuff. "It is Cuff's job to officially put the lie to this whole untidy affair, or, if true, give Theodore certain communications and promises. The problem is," he continued, "that so little is known about Abyssinia in Europe. We have the limited knowledge derived from the Napier expedition, of course, but they pursued a course into the highlands and stuck to it, while ours will lie in the other direction into the desert. Ideally, we need the services of someone with perfect knowledge of the country's geology, climate, peoples, and natural history."

"I hope you don't think I'm such a person."

"No, of course not," Holmes said. "However, we do think you are the next best thing. You, Quatermain, as very few others, are intimately acquainted with Africa, its moods, its pulse, and its people and cultures. We need you to help us in our endeavor to navigate its exotic and strange nature."

I was quiet for a time, then I said, "I'm flattered your opinion of me is so high, yet the fact is I know nothing of Ethiopia. As I have said, gentlemen, it's out of the question. Admittedly, I would not ordinarily refuse a commission, but I'm tired and want nothing more than to spend some time quietly in my home."

During this discussion, Hans had maneuvered himself closer to me so that now he was just below my ear.

"Whoa, Baas!" he whispered in Zulu, "We were only a little while ago talking about the Big Baas in the sky, and I see that he certainly knows more than you about your own pocketbook for he is sending you even now that big gold plate full of pretty rocks of which you were also talking so recently."

And the truth of it was that Hans was correct. Our financial situation was sad indeed. The long trek into Heu-Heu land may have provided Zikali with his great medicine, which Hans was pleased to call "groceries"—by the way, did I explain that this medicine consisted of leaves from a grand old tree called the Tree of Illusions, which Zikali required for his black arts?—but all I profited was memories, most of which I would have just as soon done without, for there was much fighting involved and death and much sorrow . . . but that is a whole 'nother tale.[28]

Anyway, Hans's talk had a sobering effect on me, and I found myself saying, "Gentlemen, let me try to summarize. You, Mr. Holmes, have found evidence that at least a portion of the Alexandrian Library may still exist in Ethiopia and possibly a fifth gospel, as well. Also as a result of the same expedition of 1868, evidence has surfaced that the earliest ancestors of Man may have once lived in Ethiopia, and Mr. Huxley and Mr. Scott are determined to return to the scene of Corporal Saint James's explorations to seek more such fossils. And over and beyond that, there is the hope to determine that King Theodore did in fact "go to the spirits," as the Zulus say, or not, as the case may be, and this is Sergeant Cuff's role."

Holmes grinned. "Yes, yes, to kill three birds with one stone so to speak!"

"And you have come to me to be your guide, despite my never having been to that region and having no familiarity with it or its people at all."

"Mr. Quatermain, the British Museum, indeed, the British government—Her Majesty herself, I might add," said Holmes, "as well as others—have every reason to believe that if anyone in Africa can help us, it is you, sir! They have the greatest faith in you!"

"I am indeed flattered," I said, looking at young Will Scott. "What on earth did you tell these people?"

He grinned and said, "Though I might have brought you up, it was Lady Luna and Lord Ragnall who convinced the authorities that you were the most practical man for the job."

"But what if I hadn't just arrived back to Durban, not to return for a year or more, as I am wont to do in my business—as I have just done?

"But that isn't the case—is it?—we are happy to say," Holmes responded. "But now that you have a notion of what we want to do, shall we discuss terms? For your services, to begin in due course after you have had an opportunity to rest for a time, the British authorities will pay you—" whereupon he mentioned a sum so prodigiously ample with terms so fair that I would have been a fool to have turned it down.

Hans, who had been watching and listening the whole time, took this opportunity to whisper to me, "Whoa! Baas, such a pretty number I have never heard. Yes, our trek has been long and my feet need to rest, but perhaps our feet only need a very little rest after all."

Frankly, I was beginning to think along those very lines myself, and the end of it was that I agreed to attempt what seemed at the time to be the most ridiculous proposal I had ever heard in my entire life.

CHAPTER TWO

Allan's Headache Grows

Within twelve days I was able to settle my affairs and was readying my house once again for an extended absence and preparing to board the *H.M.S. Deborah*, the British Navy vessel that had brought my clients. With Hans, I was returning from town with an armload of supplies, my home being on the outskirts of Durban, when I became aware that someone was sitting on my porch. A giant of a Zulu had made himself comfortable on the little swing that I had there for decorative purposes. I don't know what possessed me to buy and install the thing except that it reminded me of similar device that hung from a certain other porch that I knew well in my youth, being part of a home and farm called Maraisfontein. This farm belonged to a Boer named Henri Marais[29] who was our closest neighbor in the Cradock district of the Cape Colony, being only fifteen miles distant from the station where my father had established himself as a Church of England clergyman. I never used the thing, that is to say the swing, first of all since I was seldom home but more so because the act of swinging seemed somehow frivolous, while I am at heart a practical man.

But I don't know why I am getting off the subject. I was speaking of the Zulu. The man jumped up when he saw me. He was naked, of course (imagine if you will a black *David*), except for an animal skin about his middle and various ceremonial accouterments that hung from his neck, ears, and ankles. He held up his *assegai*, or short stabbing spear, in royal salute, greeting me by my native name.

"Macumazana, I am Bayushtiak. The Great One has sent me to protect you."

By "Great One," I knew he was referring to Zikali, but I had no idea what he was talking about otherwise.

"Bayushtiak, thank you for your diligence," I responded in the Zulu tongue, "but please return to your master and tell him 'no thank you' as I am in no need for a bodyguard."

"Oh, that is not possible, Macumazahn, for he told me that if you were to start your expedition without me as part of your party, then I would die in a dishonorable fashion and that my spirit would live forever trapped in a turtle shell without hope of escape. So you see, Macumazahn, that, unless you wish me thus, which, as you well know, would be far worse than even wandering forever in the featureless underworld, you must allow me to take care of you as a wet nurse would her mistress's baby."

Now, clearly I was offended by this analogy, but beyond that I was confused. "Bayushtiak, did your master say why I would need a bodyguard?"

"He showed me some signs and whispered secrets into my ear, but there is nothing that he gave me leave to share—not even with you."

Now, I was in an untenable position. On one hand, I had no need for protection. It was my job, in fact, to protect the others in my charge. But if I refused the man, I knew full well that the hideous black dwarf would cause the man grief somehow, and I didn't want to be responsible for that. What matter if we had an extra member in our party, and the man looked capable enough, strong, self-confident—no doubt a good man to have with you when trouble arose.

"Well, Bayushtiak, it appears that I don't have much of a say in the matter as I well understand how Zikali keeps his word. Welcome, then. But I would appreciate a word of warning when you see this mysterious danger approaching."

"Oh, Macumazahn, do not fear on that account. The Great One heightened my sight and gave me wondrous charms and medicines that will allow me to see forward when the time comes."

"Well, then," I said, feeling manipulated, "it's all settled."

The next morning, Holmes, Scott, Huxley, Cuff, Hans, Bayushtiak, and myself boarded the *Deborah*. The ship weighed anchor, and off we headed north up the east coast of Africa.

I had a time of it explaining to the others about our new compatriot, for he was not the sort of companion that any one of them was used to, but, in the end, they all accepted this unexpected turn of events, since they, just as myself, had no real control of the situation. Thus, you are beginning to understand the power of Zikali.

The master of the ship was one Captain Endfield, and he took full and instant umbrage at having Bayushtiak come aboard. It offended his sensibilities to have a "savage" on the ship. Bayushtiak, for his part, took no notice of the man, occupying his time, once we had set sail, observing the world from the standpoint of the bow of the ship.

"Macumazahn," he would say to me, "little did I know that the world was so wet and big. I see that it goes on seemingly forever, and no matter how fast or far this vessel moves, even as day turns to night and night becomes day, over and again, there is still more water ahead, with no end in sight."

"Yes, Bayushtiak, such is the way of the world, or rather the planet, for they say the earth is a round ball. Naturally then, you can travel around it forever, and they also say that it is mainly covered with water, so you could travel thus forever surrounded by water." I noticed that whereas a civilized man would soon become bored with the monotony of the endless sea, Bayushtiak's demeanor was never less than sheer wonder. Many a time I would see him there rooted at the ship's bow, and I would think how much like a child he was.

Without prolonging this narrative longer than necessary, let me just say that we sailed up the coast—a journey of some three thousand miles and nearly two weeks time—then eventually around the Horn into the Gulf of Aden, through the narrow Strait of Bab el Mandeb comprising Yemen on the east and Somaliland on the west, thus into the Red Sea. Within a few more days, we turned hard south into Annesley Bay and finally came within sight of the two wonderful piers tipped with lighthouses that the English army engineers had built four years previously in preparation for receiving Napier's armada. These piers—marvels of engineering both—extended 900 and 700 yards into the sea from the desert shore. Beyond them, a few hundred yards further up on the shore, was the strange and anomalous sight of several derelict and rusted locomotives, which had been left behind by the army as it hurriedly left. Beyond these, some thirteen miles away due west, the

Ethiopian highlands began their precipitous climb high into green mist.

As cool and refreshing a sight as the highlands struck me just then, I knew that we would be headed south into the desert.

As we approached the piers from the east, we were very surprised to see another vessel approaching from the north. Captain Endfield was not expecting this and, as was his nature, became quite flustered. As it would have proven fruitless to even discuss or guess about the nature of this "intrusion" or "crossing of paths" or however it should be phrased, we passengers simply watched and waited. It seemed certain, though, that the other was also a British naval vessel, for we could see the colors flying in the wind through the spy glass that the captain made available to us.

The *Deborah* landed at the end of the longer of the two piers. As we unloaded our supplies, Holmes described to us what he had seen there before, comparatively recently.

"Gentlemen, just imagine four years ago, at this very spot, utilizing these very piers that he had built for the purpose, Field-Marshal Napier gathered together all his men, animals, and materiel, which included fifty elephants with which to carry the heavy guns. Once the shorter pier had been constructed, a tramway was laid along it, and the fleet began to unload.

"Can you imagine, all along the shore there was a city of tents. Thousands of Indians, Egyptians, Persians, and Ethiopians hauling supplies from the ships. Over there was the native bazaar, over there the hospital, along there the storehouses, beyond those the animal compounds with over 20,000 mules alone. Right here on this very spot on this pier and yonder on the other as well were the two condensers that produced almost 200 tons of potable water each day. You can see there where they were fastened down.

"The heat was appalling, and the flies a veritable plague. Dust stirred up by all the feet, both human and animal, billowed in the air constantly. A city popped up in the desert almost overnight. The logistics of it all were inconceivably awesome, at least to one inexperienced in such matters such as myself. The army assembled, then marched and conquered. It was hardly more complicated than that, given the anachronistic, almost barbaric, nature of the enemy.

On our return, it was all dismantled and loaded back onto the ships, everything, that is, except these piers and those locomotives. The whole affair was quite remarkable."

Hans, of course, took all of this in and then offered his own brand of wisdom. "Baas, even if the Baas with the shiny chin had not said so, I could tell he spoke truly from the tent pole holes, the droppings, and all the rest of the spoor. Even four years has not been enough to make all these things new again. Just think, Baas, it would be like all of Durban here one moment and gone the next!"

It was about this time that the other vessel reached the piers and secured itself. Captain Endfield, my clients, and myself, all stood by, our curiosity at a peak.

It was not long before some people disembarked and approached us. Of course, there were among them sundry mariners, but the central group comprised four men and a woman. One of the men was obviously the captain of the other vessel and he broke off from the group and approached our captain. He seemed quite happy. They greeted one another precisely and the new man introduced himself to Captain Endfield as Baker by name, Captain Joshua Baker.

"Captain Endfield," said Baker, "We were beginning to wonder if you would ever show up," which was an interesting manner to start the conversation. Thereafter, the two discussed numerous matters of consequence to the navy. In the end we learned that, for its own reasons, the British Admiralty had required Baker to catch up with the *Deborah,* and that Baker had found that using the new Suez Canal—which had connected the Mediterranean Sea with the Red Sea just two-years before—made this feat simplicity itself. It made entirely moot the necessity of circumnavigating the entire continent of Africa, which is precisely what the *Deborah* had been required to do, first to pick me up at Durban, and then to continue on up the east coast of Africa. The sailing of the *Granger,* which was the name of the other vessel, had been smooth and without incident. In fact, they had been waiting for us for six days, using the time to take depth measurements off the Abyssinian coast and other assorted matters of marine research.

Now it was that Huxley stepped up to Captain Baker in a not altogether cheerful mood. "Huxley's my name, sir, and I would greatly appreciate knowing the meaning of this. Leaving Britain, as we did under the strictest orders and secrecy, nothing was mentioned of collateral matters."

At that moment, the rest of Captain Baker's group joined us. It was the older of the three other men who approached Huxley. He was a man in his fifties. From his upper lip and chin grew a prodigious growth of facial hair that was part mustache and part goatee, while his cheeks and temples were smoothly shaven. He was about five inches taller than myself, seemed strong and fit, at least it appeared so due to the girth of his chest and shoulders, and subsequent events would prove me correct.

This fellow held out his hand and said, "My good man, I gather you must be Huxley, Thomas Huxley. And these others are—" At which point he nimbly attached the names of Holmes, Scott, Cuff, and myself to their correct owners while briskly shaking each of our hands in turn. When he was quite done, he said, "Now, please let me introduce myself. I am Richard Burton."

He said that in a simple manner, but I couldn't help but notice a bit of a gleam in the man's eyes.

Indeed, he no doubt had good reason for his mirth, for the umbrage that had seemed to fill Huxley now suddenly dissipated just as abruptly. There was a profound silence among our group that was broken only by the cries of the sea birds. The silence became prolonged and a kind of amazement overtook my Europeans, myself included, I must admit. Finally, like a dam bursting, we all began to talk at once. Realizing the futility of this, we all stopped and Huxley took over again.

"Mr. Richard Burton of Meccah, Harar, and Tanganyika fame?" inquired Huxley.

"I suppose that would be one way to describe me. Yes, I have visited those places and made a bit of a stir in the process."[30]

Huxley swallowed and bowed. "Please, Burton, I offer my apology. Perhaps my manner was a bit impudent, but I'm not very good at surprises. I can only assume that there is an excellent reason for all this."

"You're right there. At least the Crown seems to think so. But let me introduce the rest of my party. This charming lady is

Professor Maria (pronounced Ma-RYE-ah, Churh) Mitchell, and these two chaps are Gunnery Sergeants Daniel Dravot and Peachy Carnehan."

They both saluted smartly at the sound of their names and the one called Dravot stepped forward. "Of the Queen's own royal infantry, Indian Army under Field-Marshal Lord Napier, SIR!" he added forthrightly. An immense man with a full flaming red beard, he reminded me rather of a Viking of old. He stepped back and joined his mate Carnehan, whose own distinguishing characteristics were his bushy dark eyebrows that went clear across his forehead without a break and shoulders that were as broad as Dravot's beard was red.

Burton went on, "The Crown has loaned us these two fellows because of special knowledge that is theirs. Since the four of us are embarking on a sort of quest that was instigated at the request of Professor Mitchell, I'll let her explain."

Maria Mitchell smiled at my group and spoke with a clear American accent. "I should be happy to, but shall we first retire out of the sun to a more comfortable situation with plenty of room to spread out."

The two captains graciously offered accommodations on their respective vessels, and finally we were led to the officer's briefing room aboard the *Granger*. We were quite a group, I must say. When we were all settled—Bayushtiak choosing to stay on deck to continue his examination of the world's girth, and Hans as usual, crouching unobtrusively in a corner—there were Captains Endfield and Baker, myself, Holmes, Huxley, Cuff, Scott, Burton, Dravot, Carnehan, and, of course, Professor Mitchell. Eleven men and a woman who had mysteriously come together and assembled in this simple room on the edge of the closest thing to the middle of nowhere that I could imagine, all by the will of the British government.

Except for Professor Mitchell, who stood, and Hans, we all somehow fit around an oblong table. She appeared to be in her fifties. Her countenance was expressive but entirely severe. Her hair, which was dark and beginning to gray, was pulled back into a tight knot. Her clothing matched her countenance in both tone and style, being dark and severe with only a white lace collar to add a little diversion to the whole.

"My name, as you know, is Maria Mitchell. Some of you perhaps have heard of me. Certainly my name doesn't have the cachet of Mr. Burton's, nonetheless, in some scientific circles, my name has some meaning. For instance, Mr. Huxley and Mr. Holmes, I would be very surprised if neither of you knew of me."

The two men thus addressed rose to the occasion. Huxley cleared his throat and sat rather more tall in his chair. "Certainly, Professor Mitchell," he began, "I have the pleasure of addressing the eminent professor of astronomy at Vassar College in New York State. I believe it was in 1847 that you discovered a comet, a fact that remained newsworthy for nearly a year. I was but a lad at the time, but I remember it well."

Miss Mitchell smiled and was about to open her mouth when Holmes also took up the challenge as well. "If I recall correctly, professor," he began, "your particular fields of interest are sunspots, the surfaces of Jupiter and Saturn, and meteorites."

"Indeed," she responded, seeming pleased, "correct on every point, and it is the latter interest, that of meteorites, that brings me to Africa and to this very spot conferring with you gentlemen at this very moment. I've come in search of a phenomenon unheard of thus far in the study of meteorites. This phenomenon came to light in 1868 here in Ethiopia and was witnessed by these two men," indicating Dravot and Carnehan. "Gentlemen, please do me the honor of taking up the tale from the beginning."

The two men stood and snapped to attention just as though an officer had barked an order. It was Dravot who started.

"At the beginning, all right. Well there we were, Peachy and me, happy as could be. Stationed in Bombay we were and glad of it. We were gunnery sergeants, we were, under Field-Marshal Lord Napier in the Queen's own Indian Army. Well, next thing we know we were boarding a ship and weeks later landed at the very same God-forsaken spot where we are right now, pardon my language, Ma'am. And soon, in a matter of mere days, as I live and breathe, a whole town popped up . . . ."

Holmes took this opportunity to interrupt, a bit impatiently. "Dravot, my man, the details of the camp are well known to us and not important at the moment." Dravot looked a little abashed as though the wind had been socked right out of his sails.

Seeing that reinforcements were required, Carnehan stepped in. "Be that as it may, Danny here and me at some point considered all the problems and difficulties that lay in the direction of the general march, which was northwest up into those very mountains outside there, but which wouldn't seriously start moving for several days, and we decided to explore a bit in the opposite direction, to the south it was, which we found was truly horrible desert country, as you will soon see."

Dravot took it up. "And it was when we were out there in the desert several days, glad to be away from the hubbub yonder in the mountains—a lot of bloody shooting and such—that the miracle happened."

"Not that it was rightly a true miracle," interrupted Carnehan, "but it came with all the accessories, a great light in the sky and loud noises from heaven, as God is my witness! But I suppose it was really that we just happened to be in the right place at the right time. It was about midnight, we were bivouacked in a dry riverbed where we were toasting the Queen, bless her heart, when it exploded out of the sky and streaked toward us, scaring the stuffings out of us."

Dravot took it up again. "It was a meteor, as you live and breath, a real spectacular rock shooting from the sky. What with all the blazing and crashing and whistling and all, it was quite a show it was. Well, it hit off to the east of where we were, and not too far. So in the morning we went looking for it, and blimey, what we found was queer enough to get the whole ever-lovin' government to wondering, which explains just why Peachy and me are right back here."

"And just what did you find?" I asked, bursting with curiosity.

"Why a graveyard of meteorites, of course! Have you ever heard of the graveyard of the elephants or of the whales, well this is much the same thing, hundreds of craters each with a bit of charred rock half buried. We found the new one, all right. It was still red hot from its plunge, but otherwise it didn't seem any different than the others. They all seemed part of a family if you don't mind my conjecturing. Well, we scraped around a little and found some interesting pieces, having no notion as to the value of the things, and pocketed them."

"The wonder of it," Peachy continued, "was that when we went back the way we came and merged into the tail end of that long column the front of which was days ahead high up into those mountains, no one seems to have noticed that we'd been missing."

Dravot interrupted in a precisely timed manner. "My thinking, y' see, was that they were glad to be rid of us! After all, it wasn't as though Peachy and me didn't have a pretty thorough reputation!"

"So there we were, possessors of this most arcane knowledge," Carnehan continued. "'Danny,' I said, 'what are we to do now? You and me, we've been bloomin' witnesses to a true-blue wonder of nature. So what's next?'

"Well, there was nothing next. At least immediately. That was four years ago, and we gave up trying to figure out how to make a profit, so to speak, from our discovery, but tongues being what they are, word got 'round and bits of our rock got 'round, too, and lo! some months ago, this lovely lady here communicated with us, and here we are, loaned out by the Queen herself to help this here lady seek that very exact same spot of our bloomin' miracle."

"Thank you, gentlemen," Maria Mitchell said, continuing. "Naturally, one of the first things we attempted to do was to contact Mr. Holmes here to request his guidance and aid due to his previous experience in the area. It was then we discovered we had missed him by a matter of only a few weeks. With the aid of the Museum authorities, we were able to contact Mr. Burton, who, auspiciously for us, had only just then rejoined the world, having been entrenched for months focusing on his Zanzibar project. We proposed that, given his background in east Africa and gift of languages,[31] his companionship and guidance would be of great service, to which he kindly agreed. We, nonetheless, were firm in our belief that Mr. Holmes's services would be invaluable. In due course, we were able to compute the probable course and timing of your northerly expedition from Mr. Quatermain's home and realized it was highly likely to rendezvous with you via the Suez Canal. And, at long last, here we are, all together, by the grace of the great God Himself."

CHAPTER THREE

And Then There Were Twelve

Dravot and Carnehan told us that their "graveyard" was three or four days forced march south-south-east, which was in the same direction that Saint James had indicated he had gone, though the two adventures had been separated by some weeks, one at the beginning of the army's expedition and one at the end.

"Like it as not," Dravot volunteered, "seeing that it was just the two of us, Peachy and me made good time. We wanted to do our sightseein' and be back before we was noticed missing and in short enough a time that we could come up with a sensible excuse. But with the likes of this crowd, with a lady and without a gun in our back, so to speak, it's probable to take twice as long, at least. Six, maybe seven days." Dravot shrugged, looking for all the world like a man who, for the moment, had no control at all over his destiny.

Well, there was nothing for it now. Once the direction of travel was made clear, as well the terrain and climate we would encounter, taking into account that we wouldn't have bearers, we spent the next day choosing and packing our kit, which consisted of the following items:[32]

Nine express rifles and six hundred rounds of ammunition.

Two Winchester repeating rifles (for Hans and Maria) with two hundred rounds of cartridge.

Ten Colt revolvers and two hundred rounds of cartridge.

Eleven Cochrane's water bottles, each holding four pints.

Ten blankets (Bayushtiak eschewing such frivolities).

Ninety pounds of biltong (sun-dried game flesh).

A couple hundred small dry biscuits.

A selection of medicines and a few small surgical instruments.

Our knives, compasses, matches, a pocket-filter, some tobacco, a trowel, sundry digging tools, and the clothes we stood in completed our supplies. Later, too, I discovered that Burton had brought along his surveying equipment to which he was much attached.

In my experience, which in many African matters is substantial, this allotment of equipment was modest for the desert adventure we proposed. These were the bare necessities. Nevertheless, every ounce, I knew, would seem to double as the trek lengthened, especially when crossing a scorching desert. Even still, it was a heavy load per person. Obviously we would not allow Miss Mitchell to carry a full load, as she did not seem by nature to be an outdoors woman, and so approximately half of her kit was distributed among the others. She protested vehemently about this, but soon gave up as we men were not about to give in.

What I had no way of telling at that time was what a vital woman she could be when her back was against a wall. In a few days her mettle would be tested and she would prove to be much more than she seemed.

As we were all making these final preparations, double-checking our supplies, etc., Hans stepped up to my side. "Baas, tell me again why it is here I am going to die, cooked like an ostrich in an oven," he queried in his insolent tone. "I don't understand why these old books and old bones and rocks from the sky are worth all these fine men and that lady turning themselves into hyena food. Of course I don't count myself amongst those fine men, but unless I am mistaken, I too will join them in the hyena's belly."

"You silly fool," I whispered harshly. "If worse comes to worse, I would grab the hyena's throat and eat him, and thus we would all live."

"Baas, the blacks here call you 'Macumazahn,' which means 'Watcher by Night,' not 'Uhlanya Ngokweqile,' which means 'Mad Beyond All Reason.' I beg you to remember that if you were to grab the hyena's throat, he would try to tear out yours and in all likelihood would succeed."

Naturally I was not about to take such language, even from Hans, so it was that I said not too kindly, "How dare you waste my time with your silly nonsense," all the while as the toe of my boot strove to encounter the seat of his filthy pants, but he was too quick and jumped liked a startled rabbit. But this was more of a long-standing and time-honored ritual between us than anything else and the next time I saw him, neither of us thought to mention the matter.

We had become quite a swollen group to be sure. At first, I thought I would have to fight with Burton for my rights as safari leader, but he was perfectly happy for me to take the lead, which I was grateful for insofar as I wasn't in the mood for political nonsense at that time.

I remember that about this time I began to think wistfully about the locomotives that were just sitting there. If only one of the things would come to life and haul us away wherever we wanted to go . . . .

To the northwest, some dozen miles away, the fertile slopes of the highlands began to rise, but to the south, the desert was boundless. From the Red Sea water's edge, as with most shores, sand ruled. The difference was that the sand continued on indefinitely.

Thus, we made arrangements with the captain of the *Deborah* to return to this spot beginning in three weeks, wait a week, then return after another three weeks, and so on for four months. During the extended intervals, the vessel would be performing mapping and surveying duties for the British government. The *Granger*, we all agreed, had concluded the business that it had with its four passengers, and we discharged her Captain Baker to continue on whatever other Queen's business he was obliged to pursue.

We decided to avoid the heat of the day and to travel by moonlight. And so it was in the late afternoon, deep in shadow since the sun had dropped behind the mountains on our right, we headed directly into the heart of one of the loneliest, bleakest spots on the face of the earth, a vast area of barren wastes, broken lava flows, crumbling rock, and salt flats known as the Danakil Desert—a truly hellish place, arid, monstrously hot, torn by volcanoes, and prone to earthquakes.[33]

That first night we passed over patches of uneven gravel and greenish sand rich in copper and through fields of broken and jagged black obsidian. As hard to traverse as it was, it did have the advantage of being relatively flat.

At dawn, we entered a different realm altogether, one of torturous, steep gullies that rolled away from us like endless waves to the horizon. One notable feature of these gullies was the vibrant colors they presented—deep reds, bright yellows, translucent greens, browns and blacks, and aquatic blues, all arrayed in pleasant stripes along the gully walls. I assumed this was due to the fact that, as in many deserts, it seldom rained here, but when it did or if there was a heavy rain, however short in duration, in the mountains to the north or west, the water would rush in torrents that funneled into these gullies, vanishing afterward into shallow salt lakes that, in turn, soon evaporated. But in the wake of these floods, the sides of the gullies and ravines would appear riven, as though a giant's axe had cleaved asunder the old tired and worn walls of rock, revealing shiny new, thick layers of rock of distinctly different colors and character, minerals from distant eras, from epochs unimaginable.

Yet as fearsome as these gullies seemed at the time, it turns out they were relatively shallow and nondescript compared to the region we would soon encounter—but I'm getting ahead of myself.

We halted on the south side of an east-west oriented gully that was deep enough that it could almost be called a shallow canyon. There was some discussion that perhaps it would be better to make camp on the bluff above, for in the event of a flash flood, the water could roar down on us with the speed of an express locomotive, and also because, typically, gullies and canyons in this climate tended to be hot and stifling. But due to some trick of nature, that gully at that time enjoyed a steady and comfortable breeze coursing along its length, and, added to the relief afforded by the shady side, in the end gully won out over bluff and we settled into our first camp, which was plain and practical.

We supped on some of the provisions we'd brought, drank warm water sparingly, and fell into conversation. This was the first opportunity we'd had to actually get to know one another, and I was rather curious about this assorted lot that it was my fate to have fallen in with.

As happens when several people who are mostly strangers to one another are thrown together by chance, our group had naturally broken into little groups. Huxley and young Will Scott sat conferring quietly. Richard Holmes and Miss Mitchell were as well. Dravot and Carnehan were prowling together around the edges of the gully. Detective Cuff, Hans, and Bayushtiak stayed more or less off to themselves. So it was that Burton and I gravitated to one another, as our backgrounds had points in common.

"Quatermain, I say, I've been wanting to meet you for years," said the famous explorer.

"Well, sir, it appears that your wish has finally come true. I, too, have heard much of you. I'm actually surprised that our paths haven't crossed before."

"I believe that you haven't come this far north before now, and I haven't had the opportunity to visit your home country and in between, as they say, is the 'Dark Continent.'"

"Yes," I responded, for some accountable reason feeling chastened. "But, of course, that region is not so dark now that you have explored and surveyed so much of the central lake region. I must say that I feel I already know you through the stories passed on by travelers I've encountered and from the newspapers."

"Yes. That is the way of it, isn't it," Burton said philosophically.

Thus we chatted, neither feeling particularly comfortable, I suppose. Eventually, knowing that rest was more important than talk, I went about the posting of a guard, Dravot I believe, and the rest of us settled in, preparing as best as we could for the heat of the coming day. In my own fashion, I was asleep before you know it, it being my nature to be able to sleep under any circumstance, hard or soft, wet or dry, hot or cold, imminent danger or not.

In the late afternoon, we ate, broke camp, and set out once more. Before two hours were up, we came to some of the most desolate and forbidding territory I had ever encountered or could imagine. Suddenly, we could see in the bright moonlight a vast and frightening region comprising wide gorges and ravines and hills cut into the wasteland by wind and the action of prehistoric rivers. It was truly astonishing to see these nearly vertical five-hundred foot dips and rises, one following another like wrinkles in a titanic rumpled blanket out to the horizon as far as the eye could see.

We consulted Dravot and Carnehan and they were adamant that they had, in fact, encountered this very same landscape and had not found it necessary to traverse it. Those four years before, they veered further south and had succeeded in circumnavigating the gorges. Indeed, as we marched through the night, the treacherous terrain smoothed out somewhat.

Needless to say, from the start of our journey, Huxley and young Scott had their eyes riveted to the ground at all times—both as we marched, of course, and particularly when we stopped—searching for the bones of the human ancestors they coveted. Obviously, proof of the continued existence of neither Emperor Theodore nor of millennia-old scrolls was forthcoming quite yet, as we had only just started.

At dawn we settled into the second camp of our expedition. It was as we were preparing to sleep that detective Cuff spoke to Professor Mitchell. "Perhaps you can explain to those of us not acquainted with meteors, falling stars, and such, just what you are seeking and why. Please understand that this whole detour, so to speak, was not part of my charter, and I need to come to terms with it." Well, I must tell you that that appeared to be just the right question, for, just as though a coin had been inserted into a player piano, the lady then almost gleefully launched into what amounted to a lecture.

"Well," she began, "let's define our terms at the outset. If you see a streak of light in the sky, what you are seeing is a bit of material from outer space possibly no bigger than a grain of sand entering our atmosphere at a tremendous speed, possibly around 20,000 miles per hour. Its substance encounters the particles of air in our atmosphere, and at such a high speed, the pure friction caused by the encounter burns the material, vaporizing it out of existence. This bright streak in the sky is called a 'meteor' or, less accurately, a 'shooting star.' These flaming bits of sand constitute the vast majority of the meteors that we see.

"Larger chunks of material can also be seen as meteors as they plummet through the atmosphere, but these are far fewer than their smaller brethren. Many of these are sufficiently big that only the outermost layer burns, then some part of the original material survives the superheated furnace as they enter the atmosphere and crash to the ground. Once the surviving material hits the ground, that material is called a 'meteorite.'

"Virtually all meteorites to the naked eye of laymen look no different than ordinary rocks. Nonetheless, they can be categorized into three groups—stones, irons, and stony irons, with the stones being by far the most common."

It was left to Hans to ask the most obvious question and, of course, he directed his query to me. "But, Baas, in my head I can see a picture of rocks falling out of the sky, some burning all up, some not, but where do they come from?"

Miss Mitchell was quick to reply, "My good man, meteors and meteorites can originate almost anywhere beyond the earth—the Moon, perhaps, or the other planets, comets, asteroids. Over time, these bodies tend to jostle about and shake off the stones and irons that hurl through space for millions of years. Some eventually reach earth and, well, now you know what happens."

Hans lifted his filthy hat and scratched his scalp, his perplexed countenance not having changed. I knew that later I would need to concoct an analogy that he could understand, seeing that matters of even the simplest astronomy were excluded from his world. Dear me, in fact, I could only just grasp some of the concepts that the woman was tossing around so blithely. Twenty thousand miles an hour, indeed. Just what does "outer space" mean anyway? Then it was that I asked something that tugged at my mind.

"Professor Mitchell, just why aren't we beaned by these falling rocks on a regular basis?" The funny thing is that just at that same moment, I noticed that Huxley seemed to want to say something, but then he caught himself and continued to bite his tongue, restraining himself from saying whatever it was that was on his mind. I bring this up because a few minutes later an explanation for this odd moment presented itself.

Professor Mitchell smiled. "That is a wonderful question, Mr. Quatermain. Actually, it is estimated that only a few dozen meteors per year survive the journey. And the earth is so vast that the majority of these fall into the ocean or into the ice of the poles or into virgin territory of one sort or another. The chance of being struck by a meteorite is astronomically small." She smiled again, perhaps at her play on words.

"And now that we have the benefit of this explanation," I went on, "please tell me again why we are searching for this graveyard of yours, or rather that of our two imaginative soldiers yonder."

"That can be simply stated," she replied. "The examples of the rock that Mr. Dravot and Mr. Carnehan brought out of this desert were of the iron variety. The description of the region the men provided leads me to believe that most, if not all, of the meteorites they've seen are irons. So the principal question arises: Why do so many of these iron rocks from outer space come to earth in such a concentrated manner? Is it the region that somehow attracts them? Or is it their timing and trajectories that somehow cause their falls to be focused?"

There was a lull in the conversation, and I was about to suggest that sleep was most important just then, when Huxley chose this moment to break his silence.

"Before retiring, my dear, I must tell you that I have been most anxious to discuss with you an avocational interest of mine. You see, beyond the fields of biology and anthropology in which I have some notoriety, I also have an interest in astronomy. My particular passion is for the myriad of asteroids. I have spent much time studying their dynamics relative to the orbits of Mars and Jupiter."

"Well, that is wonderful, Mr. Huxley. Then you must be familiar with the work of my colleague Daniel Kirkwood."

"Naturally. Naturally. His demonstration of the existence of the so-called Kirkwood gaps—just six years ago, wasn't it?—has proven consequential in my own research."

"May I ask what the nature of that research is?"

"It is a qualitative mathematical analysis of various permutations of the Olbers hypothesis."

" . . . That between Mars and Jupiter there once was a planet that exploded, thereby forming the debris that we call the asteroids."

"Yes, precisely . . . ."

The two of them had been walking to the edge of the camp during this discussion and I heard no more. I could see that they would be animatedly discussing their mutual interest for a while, and that it would be pointless to try to persuade them just then to rest.

And I must tell you, personally, I wished Cuff had kept his question to himself, as I didn't like the aching in my head that followed this discourse on subjects utterly foreign to me. As I have said, I am a simple man with simple needs, and the notions that were being thrown about that dawn were such that I would have been very pleased to have avoided them altogether.

Thereafter, we left the land of gullies and canyons behind and the volcano—Mt. Erta Ale, if I haven't mentioned the name already—grew steadily more prominent in the west. Nevertheless, despite the proximity of an active volcano, the terrain became less rocky and more sandy. Indeed, most of that night the going was made all the more difficult due to the fineness of the sand and the fact that our progress was intermittently blocked by vast sand dunes. The next morning, we had again set up in the pitiful shade of one of the few prominences of solid rock still available to us. I was checking our water supply and lecturing on the subject of water rationing when suddenly we heard a distinct cry in the distance.

"What was that?" said Cuff, startled.

"It sounded like a cry for help," ventured Miss Mitchell.

"Rather like a lost soul," said Richard Holmes.

Even as we were making such queries, the cries continued unabated. The whole group—save Burton—became agitated. Even implacable Bayushtiak seemed over-awed by the sounds.

Hans plucked at my sleeve. When I looked down at him I saw a sight I have rarely seen, that of Hans with huge eyes and an expression on his face that was not insolent. He said ever so carefully in Portuguese so that no one of our party could understand, "Baas, I think that spirit is calling my name. Don't you hear it? 'Haaannnsszzz . . . Haaannsssszzz . . . Haaaannnsszzz." I was filled with mixed emotions. I wanted to tell him that he was being ridiculous, but the look of fear on his face quelled that first instinct, and also, the sound *did* sound like a voice protractedly crying my servant's name.

For myself, I doubted that the sound was human. I had begun to formulate a theory—wagering silently to myself that gas vents from the volcano were doubtlessly nearby and that the sound was some sort of escaping steam—though I had to admit I had seen nothing to back up my idea and, furthermore, I really had no idea if such a thing was possible.

In the meantime, Holmes and Miss Mitchell were walking toward the edge of camp and were continuing on. Holmes was saying, "We must help the poor wretch. I hope we make it in time" and such when Burton spoke up.

"I wouldn't bother if I were you," he said.

The two erstwhile saviors looked indignant and demanded to know if he were so unchristian as to not care when confronted with such a plaintive cry for succor.

His response was, "Of course I would . . . if the cry was genuine. But what you are hearing is not emanating from a person, or from spirits (as your manservant assumes, Quatermain [a pronouncement that startled Hans as much as I, for we both thought our conversation private]), or from jinns as the Bedouin believe. This sound is merely a variation of El Bromador, a geological condition that has been observed in the deserts of Spain (and Chile, as well, if I'm not mistaken). The distinct cries you hear are the consequence of shifting sands in large dunes such as we have been seeing. Some call them 'the singing sands.' There are even cases of brave folk who have been lured to their own deaths trying to rescue will-o-wisps. In my wanderings in Arabia, I have had the opportunity to become acquainted with the phenomenon, but only occasionally I assure you since it is really quite rare that the sound should occur when there happen to be human ears about. We should consider ourselves blessed by Allah that he has allowed us this privilege. Sit back and enjoy."

Holmes and Miss Mitchell returned to their places reluctantly. And indeed, as we sat and listened, the wailing quickly grew in intensity and then changed pitch, metamorphosing into the high notes of camel bells, then still later we could make out mournful violins and gleefully plucked harps, then the roar of a mighty organ, and the roll of drums. This turned into a successions of explosions, as though someone in the distance was setting off canon blasts. The finale was volleys of what seemed like thunder. It was really quite amazing and we all loitered around the camp in awe of the sounds and quite unable to rest. Around noon, in the absolute heat of the day, it all stopped suddenly—as inexplicably as it had begun. All at once we were left in silence and the normal quiet of the desert returned. Gratefully, we started to snatch what rest we could.

As I have explained, I have no trouble sleeping, but neither do I have trouble coming instantly awake and fully alert when necessary. The sun was still up when I woke to another sound of moaning, another cry in the wilderness. I was about to dismiss this, as I was learning much about the strange way of deserts, when something about this cry seemed distinctly different than that which we had heard earlier.

Hans, Bayushtiak, and myself were up and running toward the sound before anyone else was awake. We flew around a dip in the nearest shallow dune and there found not more singing sands, but a desiccated and dying man.

He didn't seem to have any wounds or even broken bones, so we picked up the poor fellow and brought him into camp. To say that my group was surprised would be an understatement. It wasn't long before some rather harsh words dealing with priorities were exchanged with Holmes and Miss Mitchell on one side and Burton on the other, but this blew over quickly. We spent the rest of the day and half of the next night nursing the man. He was resilient, there can be no doubt. Once we were able to finally persuade him that he had in fact been rescued and that we were not a troop of angels come to escort him to St. Peter, he was wonderfully grateful.

His name was Axel Lidenbrock, who we learned was a German geologist whose field was volcano research. Physically there was nothing about him that stood out, except perhaps that I could see that before his travails, his face and complexion must have been what you would call "cherubic," which lent him a far younger appearance than the middle age he declared himself to be.

"It has been a goal of mine for years to explore Mt. Erta Ale." he said. "My team is on the other side of the mountain. I went off on the trail of an elusive basalt when I was tempted first by this stratum and then by that metamorphic intrusion. Perhaps I was foolish to set out on my own, for soon I had no idea where I was. I think the heat affected me more adversely than I was prepared for."

By the middle of the night, he understood clearly enough that we were on our own journey and couldn't very well leave him there to die. But neither could we take the time to seek his companions. He really had no choice but to join us. By the time the moon rose over the dunes, he had gained enough strength so that we were ready to continue on our astonishing hodgepodge of missions.

Though somewhat chastened and upset by the occurrences of the day, my party mustered its will and forged ahead. In fact, nothing much had really changed, except that now our ranks had been swollen by yet one more, so that now there were twelve of us.

Before dawn, the vast quantities of sand began to dwindle and we came to an area where a series of cliffs rose steeply on our right and where the gorges had reappeared, dipping in and up and curving around randomly on our left, that is to the east, with only a barely distinguishable path between these two obstacles. We hated to have so little choice, still it was good to have any kind of path to follow in that wilderness, though I suspected that at any time the path might run into a blank wall or take us to the edge of a precipice.

Then, as the sun rose over that far off but ever-present eastward mountain range, the same that dogged Saint James's heels, as you may recall, we began our search, as we did each morning, for an appropriate place to settle for the day. At that point, Hans drew my attention southward.

"Baas, I think we had better hurry and find a roof for our poor heads, for, if I'm not mistaken, this oven of a desert has cooked up a new surprise, one that will tear the skin and flesh from our bones, then chew up the bones for good measure."

Indeed, there between us and the horizon, a great mottled sickly yellow and brown haze with swirling wispy edges had formed. You didn't need to be a true-born Bedouin to see that some sort of sirocco was fast approaching. Then it was that I heard Burton barking orders, to which I added my refrain. In a short while, we found shelter under a low rock overhang, and, piling our bags, sacks, and whatnot between ourselves and the open desert, we dug in for the duration. It didn't take long for that burning, furious wind to hit. It was fearful. It howled and bellowed around us for hours, sometimes sucking the very air out of the little makeshift cave and other times finding the gaps in our redoubt, blasting needles and knives of sand at our hunched-together bodies.

When finally it was over, providence proved to be on our side for we were unscathed for the most part. And insofar as there were a few hours of scorching daylight left, we made ourselves as comfortable as we could right where we were.

When the moon rose, we roused ourselves stiffly and slowly moved about gathering our things. I remember that I was overseeing these preparations when one of the two soldiers, Carnehan I think [as the two of them have tended to blend in my mind], began to curse, and when I went to investigate, Hans with me, the man thrust his rifle out so that both Hans and I could see it clearly.

"Whoa, Baas! What did I say of late about this desert eating first your flesh and then your bones? Oh! I must learn to keep such things to myself, as the spirits might sometimes like what they hear!"

Certainly, Hans had good reason to want to eat his words. Apparently the rifle had been protruding out from the barrier that we had hurriedly constructed and, as such, caught the full power of the wind. Its wooden stock had been sandblasted clean off! Only pitted metal remained!

The three of us, and also Dravot, who had been attracted by the cries of his comrade, could do nothing more than shake our heads at the wonder of it. Then we went about our business packing our kits and such, so that within an hour, we were off again.

Can you just picture us? Ten able men, one invalid, and a woman wandering in the desert, in the dark, at the mercy of one of the most horrible climates on earth, with no clear idea what our destination was, with only the vague hopes of a few academicians and politicians and only some uncorrelated scribblings and unauthenticated statements [probably made under duress, now that I think about it] to guide us! My poor mind boggled that I ever let myself be talked into this foolhardy venture.

Our trek for the next day and night meandered across a sere landscape not remarkably different from the drab, blistering desert we had been traversing all along. Just as we were setting up yet another camp, Huxley approached me and asked my opinion of a certain geological feature that he had noticed on a rise a bit to our south. I peered at it through my glass and offered my opinion that it seemed to be a small cave. He and Scott then determined to explore it, and I admit my curiosity was piqued so I went along. The ground there was particularly broken, not sand at all but shattered sandstone. The rise was steep and the three of us climbed hard as we aimed for the cave. Then Huxley noticed something partway up the slope. He stopped and peered at it without touching it. Scott did the same.

"That's a bit of arm from a sub-man . . . a troglodyte perhaps," Scott said.

"I think not," I said. "It's too small. It must be a monkey of some kind."

All three of us knelt to examine it. Huxley said, "I believe you're right, Will. It is nearly human, but not quite."

I looked again. "Monkey," I said with conviction.

Huxley ignored me and pointed beside my foot. "What is that, Will?" Scott carefully picked up a scrap of material and announced, "Why, it's the back of a small skull."

A few feet away was part of a femur, a thigh bone. We stood up and began to see other bits of bone on the slope: a couple of vertebrae, part of a pelvis, all of which Huxley announced were sub-human.

Scott picked up a bit of bone and stood quite still for a moment then said, "Thomas, do you think these are all part of one individual, parts of a single primitive skeleton?"

Huxley grew so excited, I was frightened for him. "I can't believe it!" he cried. "I can't believe it."

The two of them began to howl with joy, jumping up and down. They hugged one another in the hundred degree heat, but as I looked at the heat-shimmering gravel, I could see many more of the small brown fragments.

"Gentlemen," I said quietly, "don't you think that caution would be more appropriate here since that which you are celebrating is still on the ground and quite vulnerable. You may step on something."

Hans, who had been attracted by the din, came up quietly behind me and asked, "Baas, why are these grown and plainly sober men behaving like drunkards, even as I myself have been known to do, or so you tell me and I would never disbelieve anything you would have to say, even though I happen to know that it would have been quite impossible for them to have drunk anything at all because if there had been something, you know I would have sniffed it out." He said this last with a grin that exposed all of the coarse stumps that were left of his teeth and I had to wonder what his skeleton would look like if it was dried and scattered about the rocks as this other one had been.

"But, Baas," Hans added after a few moments more of witnessing the odd scene playing out before us, "watch the older one, the one with the hairy face. Does he really seem so filled with joy, or does he seem more like a man jumping up and down to impress another man's wife?"

I told him I had no idea what he was talking about. He shrugged, then grinned and shuffled off, commenting that it was none of his affair anyway.

Well the end of it was that Huxley and Scott very carefully packed up the various pieces of the skeleton in cotton and small sacks brought for the purpose. As they took measurements of the spot where they had found the bones, Burton indicated that he had with him (indeed never went anywhere without) chronometers, prismatic compasses, thermometers, a telescope, a portable sundial, sextants, barometers, and a box of mathematical instruments, the services of which he offered. Thus, with Burton's aid and his surveying instruments, the precise location of the bones was determined, the better to guide future naturalists should they wish to follow in our footsteps.

Once all had been measured and packed, young Scott remembered the cave, which had been our destination prior to their discovery of the bones. He chose to return alone up the slope and investigate its interior and, except for one small incident of the type that you would expect from exploring a new cave, he exited it before long, and thus we rested until nightfall.

CHAPTER FOUR

The Abyssinian Enterprise
(Being the First Digression)*

[Sherlock] Holmes threw down the news section of the *Daily Telegraph* in disgust and paced the floor. I looked up from the novel I was reading, it not being necessary for me to utter the obvious question that paused at my lips.

"Once again, the deficiencies of the journalistic method become only too clear," Holmes ranted. "There is an item today about a journalist in Burma who claims to have endured, and to have been rescued from, quicksand. Nonsense! The man is clearly a fraud!"

---

* Editor's note: Being curious as to the nature of the "small incident of the type you would expect from exploring a new cave" that Quatermain refers to, and finding no further reference to it in the manuscript, this editor made inquiries. In time, Mr. Gary von Tersch of Belmont, California, contacted me, confirming himself as a distant relative of Dr. Watson. He sent me a photocopy of the astonishing item included here, found amongst a trunk full of miscellany that he had acquired ("inherited" being too strong and specific a word) from a spinster aunt (whom he asked not be identified) upon her passing. The piece appears to have been Watson's first attempt at writing up Sherlock Holmes's "Adventure of the Copper Beeches, "which was written at a much later date than the transcription of Quatermain's Ethiopian adventure. That the following passage was excised from the final published version of "Beeches" was an obvious editorial decision as it is totally irrelevant to the main narrative. That Holmes's telling of the adventure in fact happened at the precise chronological point just prior to the arrival of Violet Hunter, I believe can be taken for granted as accurate. I reprint this material here in the belief that it will shed light onto a number of different aspects of the narrative presented in this book.—T.K.M.

This was too much for me, and my impatience showed, I fear. "Holmes, you have no right to accuse another man of lying until you have 'walked in his shoes,' so to speak."

"But I have, Watson!"

Then I thought I understood. "Of course, Holmes, you are referring to that horrible moment last October during the Baskerville investigation when Mrs. Stapleton and I pulled you out bodily from the great Grimpen Mire."

"Ah, my dear Watson, I commend you for your excellent recall. Indeed, sinking to my waist in that green-scummed, foul quagmire did include some moments of concern, of that there can be no doubt! Yet I speak of another incident altogether, one of a different sort, I must say, since I can testify firsthand that the sensation of being pulled down by slimy miasmatic mud is, on the whole, a different one from being consumed alive by talcum-fine sand. Another point of rather important difference, for the record, is that for the former my trusted Boswell was there, for which I will always by eternally grateful, but for the latter, I was totally alone!"

To say I was aghast by this pronouncement does not give justice to my feelings. "You were? What on earth do you mean? Where were you?"

"I can see I piqued your interest, Watson, and I suppose it would be foolish of me to hope that you could merely return to your novel without an explanation."

"That is most certainly true," I said.

"Well then, once in a foreign land, when I was a lad still in university but traveling, I had some ignominious ill-fortune. It is an embarrassing episode in its own right and is nothing I very much like to remember let alone discuss."

"Pray do nonetheless."

"Only to put the lie to this scoundrel newspaperman who is presenting fiction as fact."

Here, Holmes sat in his favorite chair, steepled his hands under his chin, closed his eyes, and reflected for several moments. I was under the distinct impression that he was putting himself into a self-induced hypnotic state. When next he spoke again, his voice was, remarkably, a higher pitch!—the voice of a mere youth! Here are his exact words as I jotted them down:

◆

"I opened my eyes [said Holmes] and was instantly aware of many impressions simultaneously. Foremost among these was the lack of sensation in my limbs. By this I mean that, with regaining consciousness, I attempted to move my arms, but found it impossible to do so. In a moment I deliberately made the effort to move my legs, with the same result. It was at this point—being totally disoriented, not remembering where I was or what I was doing there—that the seed of panic was born within me.

"I found that I could manipulate my head, twisting it around, and blink my eyes at will. Yet it had not occurred to me so great was my disorientation, that perhaps the better part of valor at that time would be to vocalize my concerns, that is, to speak up or call out, but I suppose one reason the thought had not as yet occurred to me was because there was nobody to be seen and, therefore, presumably, no one to hear my outcries.

"But it was the lack of sensation in my limbs that concerned me the most. At first I thought it was merely a case of common numbness, that my muscles had deadened for some good but temporary reason, as when circulation is restricted for a time and your leg falls asleep.

"It was then I began to fully take into account my surroundings . . . and was horrified for the effort. Once I attempted to maximize my acuity and make sense of what my limited senses perceived, the impression came to mind that I was completely within some sort of giant mouth, for I could plainly see a patch of dim light to my left around the interior perimeter of which I could see equally plainly rows of teeth, inhuman, monstrously long and malformed, but teeth nonetheless and not to be doubted with regard to their material existence.

"I suppose that everything I have so far described took place within a time span of, say, ninety seconds. For all the world I was like a disembodied head floating in the dim cavern of a gigantic maw. *And I had no idea how it happened that I had arrived at such a fate.*

"Realizing that I had best focus my energies elsewhere, I regained possession of some of my faculties—taking the tiger by the tail, so to speak—and decided to concentrate on the immediate problems. I decided that my primary concern, and the one that needed to be dealt with first and foremost, was the problem of not being able to move my limbs. I tried to ignore all sensations but the acceptance of my physical surroundings—to better understand my predicament. But the light was so dim that this availed me little. Then I tried to list that which I *did* know.

"Now let's see . . . who am I . . . ? I asked myself. And no sooner had I framed the question . . . I felt myself move *down*. Oh, my good Lord! What was happening? Then I felt a curious sensation, and experienced a plethora of emotions. For the first time I actually *felt* my body. But I felt it because there was some enormous suction pulling at it. Pulling my torso down from below. I flailed. As you can imagine, out of some pure instinct I flailed wildly and then I saw my arms and from them flew mounds of sand, and suddenly it came to me that I was buried up to my neck in sand.

"But it further came to me that I wasn't merely buried. I was being pulled down into some sort of desert quicksand. Then I remembered. It came to me that I had bogged down in the stuff and, out of pure horror, I had passed out . . . not a proud moment to be sure, but a useful one, for apparently my suddenly quiescent body attained some sort of stasis or equilibrium and the process stopped with my head still above the sand. So great had been the shock that I had lapsed into a momentary amnesia, but it all came back to me now. Just then some sensibility pierced through the panic, and I fully realized that it had been my cessation of movement that caused the descent to stop in the first place . . . and that my only hope lay in the possibility that it might work again. So I sputtered a curse, for the sand was already up to the top of my lower lip, held my breath, and resisted all instinct to move.

"And, my good man, it worked! In a moment, the suction stopped all at once with only my nose just above the level of the sand. I waited a while, breathing fitfully through my nose, as I can assume you appreciate, and slowly forced my head back to try and get my mouth clear, succeeded to some limited extent, and waited.

"For an eternity I waited thus. Able to do nothing but breathe, sort through my fears, and hope for deliverance. Of course, I dared not cry out for fear of upsetting the balance of things. My only chance lay in my mates coming back to look for me, which I knew they must, for they were one and all honorable men *(all but one as I would learn soon enough!)*, and they wouldn't tolerate my absence for long.

"And, indeed, presently I heard Quatermain's voice. 'Will! Will Scott! Will!' Yet he did not as yet appear at the opening of the gallery—for that is what the giant mouth in fact was, of course, the opening to one of the lesser caves within a cavern—and I hesitated a few moments before responding. But then I saw his silhouette and that of Richard Holmes, and I whispered, 'Here, Quatermain.' But of course it wasn't nearly forceful enough, and neither could they see me with only my face protruding above the sand. 'Quatermain, over here,' I said a bit louder. But it was no use. In a moment they disappeared from my perspective, and then I heard my brother, 'Will, are you playing some sort of game? You are much too old for that sort of thing, you know.' Then I heard Holmes's voice respond, even as it faded behind a bend in the tunnel, 'My dear Huxley, I rather doubt that your assistant would stoop to mischief under the circumstances. That would be a serious matter indeed. But there is some sort of mischief afoot; of that there can be no doubt.'

"Well then, you can imagine my circumstances. I had to make a quick decision as to whether to cry out at that moment or bide my time till they returned. Heaven only knew, however, how far down the passage they would go before retracing their steps and how long it would be before they returned. I decided that I had not a moment to lose, and I cried out, while trying to summarize my situation as succinctly as I could: 'Hallo, over here! Just past chamber. Quicksand! Quickly!' At least the last word I had intended to be 'quickly,' but the sand had covered my mouth by that point and I knew I was gone. By some survival instinct, I held my breath, shut my eyes an instant before the grit pored over them, thanked God for what modest success I had had in life up to that point, and waited to die."

Holmes roused himself and after a few moments wherein he seemed to regain his orientation, he said, "And it came to pass that my cries were heard, a strong tether touched my hand, which I had somehow forced over my head. I clung to the rope with a strength seemingly independent of my own will, grasping it with all my might, and by heavens, here I am to tell you the tale and give the lie to this infernal journalistic fool, Watson. You may title your notes of this affair 'The Abyssinian Enterprise' if you wish."

Whereupon he snatched up the *Daily Telegraph* again and turned to the advertisement sheet. He perused that section for some time, then let out a great sigh. I expected the worst and he did not disappoint me.

"My dear doctor," said he, "I fear I must ask for your most profound forgiveness. The cup of my patience is so low today as to be virtually dry and my mind is awash."

Here he seemed again to contemplate the vicissitudes and pointlessness of existence. I was beginning to believe that his general displeasure had finally vented itself, when he tossed aside the advertisement sheet and remarked, "To the man who loves art for its own sake . . . ."*

---

* Editor's note: From here on out the narrative is identical to "The Adventure of the Copper Beeches," which is readily available. However, at the end of Mr. von Tersch's photocopy, there was an additional note, a mere penciled jotting that was pregnant with possibilities, and one can only wonder if Watson ever pursued this last vagrant thought, and if he did, how Holmes responded. The scrawl at the end of the manuscript, clearly in Watson's hand, read:

"Scott, Richard Holmes, Huxley . . . and Quatermain! I have heard these names in juxtaposition before! I would ask my dear friend Q, but he has been lost to us for a half decade now. I must confront H when he is in a more amiable mood."—T.K.M.

CHAPTER FIVE

The Truth Be Told

So it was on the following morning that we gathered around a fire made of ancient camel dung we had collected near camp and conversed about our successes and our general situation.

I said, "Well, we've found Professor Huxley's bones, which proves, I suppose, that Saint James's directions were accurate enough. We've also found a stray German geologist to boot. Now all we need to do is find some meteorites, a library, a sort of new Bible, and a monarch." When I said that, I noticed that Huxley, Holmes, Scott, and Cuff exchanged glances. Unexpectedly, it was Cuff who spoke up. He had been the most taciturn of the four during the entire trip, except, as it happened, when the subject of roses came up, at which time we would all be instructed at length on the details of their cultivation, care, and feeding.

"Mr. Quatermain," began Cuff, "I'm afraid that we—that is to say Huxley, Holmes, Scott, and myself—have rather an embarrassing admission to make, an admission that will prove that we have been doing you an ill turn."

I was not exactly caught off guard by this surprising statement because my suspicions, and Hans's, had been growing for days. My response was no response at all, for I had no idea how to respond. I just stared at him.

Eventually he continued, "The problem is that this business about finding Theodore—determining if he is dead or not for the benefit of Yohannes IV, which I'm sure he is called now since the coronation was scheduled for some days ago—was pure fiction. We invented that particular goal hoping that it would give this expedition some credibility, just the sort of practical turn that it is so well known you prefer, not being one who goes off willy nilly on adventures for reasons that you perceive as impractical.

"Her Majesty's government finds that there is sufficient interest in our other goals to have sanctioned this expedition. You were an essential element, so we chose to prevaricate a bit to get our way. I hope you are not too upset."

Actually, I'm proud to say, looking back on it, that I behaved quite rationally. I said, "Let me get this straight, gentlemen, putting the ruse aside for the moment, the Crown saw political potential in Mr. Huxley's locating fossil evidence establishing the existence of some intermediary form between ape and humans, a discovery that would certainly be a boon to Mr. Charles Darwin. Is that right?"

"Quite."

"And, the government also would benefit by locating whatever surviving books may exist from the Alexandria Library, and if you were to happen to locate the adjunct volume to the synoptic gospels, as I believe you called them, that would be icing on the cake."

"Yes, again, my dear Quatermain." Cuff looked positively beatific.

I thought this over for a full minute, then said, "If this is all true, Sergeant, suddenly your role in this charade seems to have evaporated. No Theodore, then no official determination, thus your presence here is a mystery."

"Ah, but that is easily explained. I still have legal authority vested in me by our government and I possess certain important papers from the P.M. that are intended to smooth over awkward situations, should we run into that sort of trouble."

It was this moment that Hans tugged on my shirt sleeve and whispered to me in Zulu. "Baas," he said, "I have known in my life a few fellows who make their livelihoods from the sea, and who, as a result of working around fish all day, smell like fish more than the fish do themselves because the smell clings not only to their garments, but to their spirits, those very same spirits that your Predikant father never ceased speaking of. So, I tell you this man smells like fish," and here he chose to plug his nose and wave his hand in front of his face.

I responded with, "Hans, I quite agree. Your cunning has seen through the lie and through the still deeper lie."

Then I said to Cuff and the other three in his group, "Gentlemen, I am ashamed that it must certainly be true that I appear to be such a thoroughly gullible man. In fact, though, I am not stupid. There is clearly something else—so far unmentioned—that you are after. And I am here to say that I for one will not lead you another inch until I am told the whole truth."

The faces of the four of them screwed into a perfect rhapsody of guilt. They conferred in quiet tones, after which Holmes took up the narrative. "Quatermain, you are both right and wrong. Though our little group did in fact come together initially for all the reasons already discussed—less, of course, the Theodore affair and independent of the meteorite cache, which is Professor Mitchell's affair—word of our venture became common currency to those high up in our government who need to know such things (and not only ours but in other governments, as well). Very discreetly, then, representatives of the Vatican at the request of the Pope himself, asked a special favor." I must have appeared as though I intended to say something because Holmes continued brusquely, "Yes, yes, I know that the British government and the Papacy haven't got on so well since the time of Henry II and Becket and all, but the Romans explained that they had reason to believe from recently unearthed evidence that somewhere near or along our path we might stumble upon a particular Christian artifact, a relic I suppose one could say, the true and material vessel . . . that object that we have come to call the Holy Grail. They said that if we should happen to run across it, they would appreciate it if we brought it back 'home' to Saint Peters."

I was so taken aback that I was unable to talk for quite some time, and when I did it was more akin to undiluted and incoherent blustering than any sort of common communication. It was not one of my better times, that is certain.

Just then, Richard Holmes rummaged through his rucksack and withdrew a bundle that he presented to me. "This is to substantiate what Cuff's been saying," he said. "Almost two years ago some documents came to light that Church officials acquired. They tell quite an astounding tale that laid the ground for our own present quest. The manuscript in your hand is a summarization of the catalyst event. It was drawn up by His Eminence, Alberto Cardinal Cigliutti, Prefect of the Holy Office and Vatican Secretary of State. What you have there is a translation from his Italian and, though it is told in a rather reflective tone with perhaps more assumptions and leaps of faith than historians care for, it is nonetheless the reason we are where we are, sitting around a pitiful excuse for a fire in the most God-forsaken desert on the planet."

I quickly scanned the manuscript and my primary reaction was pure wonderment that such distinguished men of the realm could be so ready to believe a word of it (and I thought I was gullible!).

[Quatermain note: As it happened, Mr. Church, because this manuscript was considerably more complex than the previous pages Holmes had thrust at me, I specifically asked to hold onto it so I could take my time studying it. Thereafter circumstances changed so quickly and with such astonishing force, that I never had an opportunity to return the document let alone ask to copy it. As I still possess the very document I had been handed, I am asking Dr. Watson to have it copied along with the others and to attach it in an appropriate point.—A.Q.]

[Watson note: I have done as Mr. Quatermain requested and inserted Cardinal Cigliutti's document at this point in the story so as to maintain the continuity of the tale. —J.H.W.]

The medallion of Tomasso Masini da Peretola.

CHAPTER SIX

The Reflection
*(Being the Second Digression)**

A Reflection into the Final Moments of
Piero Lorenzina's Earthly Life
By His Eminence, Alberto Cardinal Cigliutti

Dearest God the Eternal and All-Knowing, please forgive me my presumptuousness. If I seem to be consciously taking upon myself that divinely prescient quality that you hold so close to your own breast and only share with the greatest of your prophets, I ask that

---

* Editor's note: When I, the modern editor, finished reading the manuscript that Mr. Quatermain says was presented to him at this juncture, it occurred to me that some sort of corroborative evidence would save me and other readers the necessity of taking this most unusual narrative at face value—despite my temptation to do so. As it happens, my wife's mother has an influential lay position in an important California Diocese of the Roman Catholic Church, and I was able to persuade her to field some inquiries for me. In about six months her efforts bore fruit in the information that the Vatican Secretary of State during the time frame in question, Alberto Cardinal Cigliutti, had living relatives who retained some of his personal possessions. For reasons of privacy, I am unable to divulge the names or even the nationality of this family. Let it only be said that they were kind enough to allow me to explore the cardinal's papers, where I discovered in a yellowed heavy envelope in a dusty trunk a hand-written manuscript. Though I don't read Italian, my Romance language background being French, I could see certain words that seemed to be appropriate. Indeed, when that manuscript was translated, the tale it told—while obviously not word-for-word identical due to the vicissitudes that lead different translators in different eras to different decisions and interpretations of abstractions—was the same story, point for point, as the one contained within the Watson/Quatermain manuscript, the original of which had been in the possession of Jim Turner, then editor of Arkham House.[34] The version here is based on the Watson/Quatermain manuscript.—T.K.M.

understand. I am doing so only because of my urgent need to understand better the man named Piero Lorenzina. Unknowingly, except perhaps for a moment at the very end, he was clearly the vehicle of your purpose, a tool that you wielded. In a way, he was your messenger, meant to bring back to the world the supreme joy, the ultimate wonderment, that has been lost for so many ages. I feel compelled to understand the man; I need to understand why this man was special to you. I have studied the man and his life for many weeks and have assembled a complete historical and biographical dossier that includes interviews with his few living friends and many of his students, as well as the testimony of those individuals he encountered on his last journey and who witnessed his outward behaviors. I believe I have enough now to begin the—perhaps impossible, perhaps impudent—task I have set upon myself, namely to reconstruct the last hour of his life, his thoughts, his emotions, the essence that was Piero Lorenzina those moments before you gathered him to your infinitely merciful breast.

Remember, most loving and compassionate virgin Mary, it has never been said or heard that anyone who turned to you for help was left unaided. Inspired with this conviction, I run to your protection and stand before you penitent of my wrong doings, for you are my mother and the mother of all. O Mother of the Word of God, neglect not my prayers, despise not my words of pleading, but in your mercy, please hear and answer me.

Divine Mother, I ask that you please guide my thoughts, my imagination, my assumptions, to be worthy of you. Amen.*

---

* Editor's note: The majority of the cardinal's manuscript, which follows, was written in the grammatical form called the perfect conditional tense. In this tense, in the English version, most predicates include the qualifying verb combination "would have." So, rather than writing "Piero threw out some corn," the cardinal wrote "Piero would have thrown out some corn." Instead of writing "In its place, fear arose" he wrote "In its place, fear would have arisen. "The purpose clearly was to unequivocally qualify each and every one of his extrapolated statements. Since he didn't know Piero

March 10, 1870

A score of pigeons dived and whirled around Piero Lorenzina. He scattered another handful of dried corn over the dewy pavement. In front of him, across the piazza, a rosy opalescence fanned through the thinly clouded sky over the silhouetted face of Santa Croce. With east at its back, the basilica often took on a fiery, sanctified cast as the swollen sun rose over Florence's sea of ancient, red tile housetops.

Piero studied the pigeons intently. As they bickered and pecked at the corn, a worn smile of indulgence moved across his smooth, age-spotted face. For eight years he had shared his early morning hours with Florence's pigeons—since his beloved Maria Grazia had passed on. Now, it was only a week to his eighty-seventh birthday and nearly all his friends had gone, too, each funeral giving him progressively more reason to attend to his birds.

During these last years, he had disciplined himself to rise each morning before dawn, spruce up, put on a clean suit, and patiently walk to either the open-air restaurant in the Piazza della Repubblica or to the Caffe Campana d'Oro where he liked to sip a coffee with milk and read. But he always stopped at Piazza Santa Croce, for the church had been Maria Grazia's.

Somewhere distant a horse squealed. All at once the pigeons took off with a half-hearted flapping, describing a wide half-circle above Piero's head, and fluttered back down some distance in front of him.

Come back, my fidgety little friends, thought Piero. He made a motion with his arm as though tossing a handful of corn to the ground. Instantly, the pigeons were airborne, and in one low

---

Lorenzina and was not witness to the scenario described, he felt incumbent to write no statement at all as fact but as speculation. As the entire manuscript is couched in this stilted manner, I have taken the liberty of removing the awkwardness. Though causing the cardinal's manuscript to be somewhat less precise, this has had the corollary effect of making Piero's presumed last hour eminently more readable.—T.K.M.

hop were back at Piero's feet. A few pecked at the remaining kernels and crumbs, but most peered at the ground and cocked their heads up at the old man questioningly.

"Ah, my little children are not so very smart," he said. "You are always fooled so easily by Piero's little game."

He threw out another handful, and the birds flapped around, jostling one another for the corn treats. A dusty-white dove lighted on Piero's right shoulder, cooing gently. The old man said, "So, *piccino mio*, you think to thank me." He placed a morsel between his wrinkled lips and puckered. Without hesitation, the bird snatched the tidbit, lifted its beak, and swallowed imperially.

At that instant, the entire flock, including his small companion, took off furiously. Piero followed their flight into the pale-blue sky. In a moment, he was surprised to see the sky fill with birds, countless throngs rising high from the four corners of the city, circling and converging—thousands of pigeons peppering the vault.

After the initial wonder of the spectacle, Piero's surprise quickly fled. In its place, fear arose. Living over eight decades had taught him something: animals have an unaccountable prescience about disturbances of nature. Some evil was impending. In this light, the sky full of circling specks abruptly took on the likeness of a routed army—legions running pell-mell from a marauding enemy.

But whatever the evil, Piero knew that it would be useless to run and hide from a force that frightened the pigeons from an entire city. To rush around seeking shelter from some vague terror could only be in vain.

Besides, he thought he knew what to expect.

He started to walk slowly away from the church, using his treasured Ethiopian ebony cane—an anniversary gift from Maria—as though it were a third leg. Methodically, childishly placing its tip where the cracks in the pavement intersected, he came to the fountain at the Palazzo Ferristori end of the piazza. Sitting on the ledge of the pool, he planted the cane in front of him and rested his small, weathered hands on the head. In a few moments, he felt the soothing effect of the gently splashing arcing twin streams of water. His gaze took in everything around him.

It was still too early for the morning throngs and bustle. The vias were quiet, the piazza all but deserted. He spotted a young couple slowly walking toward the basilica, and he thought of Maria Grazia. *How many times would we have walked around the earth if all our walks were added together?*

Santa Croce stood firm and spiring like a mountain. Its gray and white marble face had emerged from shadow and had begun to gleam milkily in the morning light. Piero made out, beyond and to the right of the church, the massive stone bulk of the Biblioteca Nazionale.

As always, Piero was impressed with the fact that from this one spot on the ledge of the fountain he could take in at one glance the houses of both God and the cumulative knowledge of mankind. There, in one eyeful, were two veritable vaults, one housing the classic art treasures of several centuries honoring God and His own, the other guarding some of Western Civilization's most priceless manuscripts and incunabula.

I am Alpha and Omega, the beginning and the ending, he thought. *Behold! The Father and the fruit of His children!*

He glanced again at the couple—tiny in the distance—walking arm in arm toward Santa Croce. They were very young, no more than fifteen, surely.

At that moment, all at once, he greatly longed to be fifteen again himself. The feeling lasted only seconds. He could not let himself be seduced by thoughts of the poignant impossible. Not at his age! Then, stretching his legs out, he thought of his many children. *Santa patata! The children!*

Piero and his wife had never had children of their own; nor had they adopted. Instead, they were satisfied to devote their lives to *challenging* the minds of children. Maria Grazia, through her strength of character and pure determination, had been taken on as editor of children's books for Giuseppe Berini, Publisher, and Piero had been a teacher.

Piero loved teaching. He had taught ten and eleven year olds, because *their* minds, he believed, were especially bright, inquisitive and open to new experiences. There had been nearly a thousand of them during the twenty years he had taught *scuola elementare.*

Then he left municipal education for the more lucrative private sector. During the next twenty-four years he had tutored boys and girls of substance, opening up the cosmos for them, being always conscious that he was crafting them into the kind of men and women he believed should properly populate the earth. Maria Grazia had delighted teasing him, calling him her little Dr. Frankenstein.

Piero had loved her. He had loved all the children. He had loved his work.

Now, he watched the couple stroll toward Santa Croce and sighed.

His attention was again drawn to the swarming birds ominously circling high overhead. He waited for what he knew must come.

In another minute it came.

Gently, as though a small sleeping child had rolled over, the ground shook. Some cigarette butts and a lone scrap of paper bobbed placidly in the calm at the edge of the pool. No wrenching. No thunderous tumult.

A reply to Piero's sigh.

Piero heard a dull, thudding crash behind him. He turned and saw a cloud of dust rising from the wide sidewalk across the via. A pile of broken brick and mortar lay near the corner of the old apartments adjacent to the fifteenth century Palazzo Ferristori, the "Poorman's Palace" as it was called.

Piero's curiosity was piqued, but he assumed the tremor was only a precursor of worse to come. He sat and waited, watching. He spotted the couple rushing up the church stairs, then lost them in a shadow. An ornate carriage rounded a corner behind him and ventured down Via de Benci, its single passenger engrossed in a newspaper, apparently oblivious to the geological shiftings transpiring beneath Florence.

He waited for more shocks, but there were none, and after awhile he saw that the city was coming alive. Some shopkeepers arrived at their kiosks in the piazza, flinging open plank shutters. Other merchants began opening up their shops and stalls. Cabs and carriages became more numerous. It seemed as though no one else had noticed the tremor or, for that matter, the pile of brick by the corner of the apartment. Looking up, he saw that the pigeons were descending again.

Then he spotted a knot of book-toting youths walking toward him—toward the mound. They were still two blocks away, talking among themselves, in no great hurry. Quickly, with some pain, Piero stood up and crossed the via. He peered down at the crumbled bricks. He looked up at the corner of the apartment. At first, he could make out nothing. Then, squinting, he saw the gash in the wall near the corner of the second floor.

Santa patata! A thought struck him with a weight it never had before: these buildings around the piazza were well over four hundred years old. Santa Croce itself was over six hundred years old. No wonder the building would begin to fall apart at the slightest jolt. With this last thought, Piero's first inclination was to draw back away from the moldering building, for he still feared aftershocks.

But before he could put action to the thought, he spotted a tiny anomaly. He pushed aside a piece of a brick with his cane. He thought he saw a bit of brown paper. He bent down and tried to pull it from the debris, but the piece broke off into his fingers. His breath caught. It was very old, brown and brittle. One was not born a Florentine without having an inborn sense for priceless things. He achingly got down on his knees and brushed aside some of the dust and crumbly mortar with his handkerchief. Carefully he moved some of the smaller bricks by hand and pried away the larger ones with his cane until he exposed a thick folio. Part of it looked damaged, but the cracked leather binding appeared to have protected most of it from major loss. Carefully, piece by piece, he picked up the tiny fragments of broken paper; then he warily lifted the cover slightly and inserted the pieces between the folded leaves.

The group of boys passed him by now, hardly giving him a second glance. Just another old beggar rummaging through the city's refuse. Eagerly, gently, he pulled the volume out of the pile. It was heavy. With his cane he probed the rubble. When he was sure he had picked up every scrap, he held the folio tightly against his chest with his free arm and crossed back to the piazza.

Breathing excitedly, Piero sat on the fountain ledge, carefully centering his find on his lap. He used the handkerchief to wipe away the dust from the decaying, grainy leather. Whatever else the book might be, it was certainly ancient. Piero guessed it could have been hidden in a niche in the apartment wall centuries before, then plastered or bricked over, much as it was suspected must have happened to Leonardo da Vinci's vanished wall painting *The Battle of Anghiari*. Given the age of the building, the volume could well prove to be fifteenth century. The binding appeared to be leather, perhaps pigskin, but Piero did not pretend to know much about such matters.

Set into the center of the cover was a circular, tarnished bronze medallion. He placed his right hand on the old leather to measure the medallion. It was not quite as wide as his thumb was long. Squinting, Piero could just make out the design, for the green tarnish and the embedded dust of centuries combined to dull the image—a dish or bowl of some sort over which floated an eight-pointed sun; the sun's beams were triangles with their tips truncated, the lower one of which poured into the bowl; a ring of intertwining snakes and vines encircled the whole image, breaking wherever the open beams met it; a Latin legend—VIVERE EST QUAERERE • QUAERERE EST INVENIRE • PRAEMIUM EST VITA IN PECTO DEI • MD—surrounded the wreath and formed the circumference of the medallion. Piero translated the legend: "To live is to seek; to seek is to find; the reward is life in God's breast," followed by the year, 1500. Piero smiled, for the maxim could easily have been one of his own.

An emblem with this sort of design, he knew, was related to alchemy. More than likely this was an old alchemist's text. When he realized this, he flushed with excitement. Slowly, carefully, he opened it as much as he dared and studied what he saw. The rag paper was thick, brown with age, and fragile. He ran his fingers over it. It felt coarse. A line of faded, black ink proclaimed in Latin that this was the workbook of Tomasso Masini da Peretola[35], dated in Roman numerals from 1496 through 1500. He turned slowly one by one through the pages.

Steadily, his ecstasy was joined by the rage of helplessness.

Though he had never heard of Tomasso Masini, the volume he held in his hands was clearly a work of art, a creation of genius. That filled him with joy for his good fortune at finding this masterwork.

Yet, the irreparable damage done by the long fall from the second story made his heart ache. His fury ranged out, irrationally cursing Masini for not taking proper precautions, at the uncounted tenants of the apartment for being so abysmally blind and ignorant, at the inept mechanism of pitiable Fate for delivering up a prize of this magnitude in such a manner!

He barely noticed as a breeze came up, widening the spray of mist from the sparkling arc of the fountain.

Despite this great rush of conflicting emotions, he continued to turn each leaf gingerly, allowing each page a brief inspection. Surprisingly, he found that much of the writing was intact. It was a veritable hodgepodge of Latin, Greek, Hebrew, medieval Italian, and some sort of incomprehensible cipher, all interspersed with a potpourri of ornately drawn symbols, part mythical, part mathematical. As he leafed through, Piero read many disjointed phrases, but they seemed meaninglessly jumbled. Most pages were richly illuminated with serpents, trees, and nude men and women reminiscent of Eden; or with exquisite, richly colored mandalas; or with moons, flowering plants, pointed stars, towers, and all manner of archetypal images. There were also frequent woodcuts and engravings so bizarre and grotesque that, in Piero's estimation, they rivaled Hieronymus Bosch.

The book was a colossal find! At the very least, it was an orgy of medieval design and color. And that was an assessment based solely on its visual power. There was no guessing what marvelous insights Tomasso Masini da Peretola could now share with the world.

Then turning over a page, Piero was surprised to find a ragged scrap of parchment covered with clumsy Black-Letter Latin. It was immediately plain that the parchment was centuries older than the rest of the book and had been sewn in separately. The writing was faded and filled the page into the corners so that Piero had a difficult time trying to make any of it out. Indeed, parts of it were blackened, possibly scorched. He ran his fingers over the page. It was crisp and full of what he supposed were wormholes.

Quickly, Piero flipped the parchment to see if there were any more like it. The shock of what he saw petrified him. Disbelief and wonder snapped his vision out of focus. He fought to sharpen it. This had to be a dream! Not in his wildest imaginings could he have foreseen this! He quickly looked ahead to see how many of these new sheets there were: fourteen leaves of vellum, yellow with age but of a much finer quality than the parchment. They, too, were sewn separately into the book. Piero's gaze lingered over the *familiar* style of the precision sketches, over the eccentric, backward script that only one man could have achieved so effortlessly. He touched the pages gently, reverently.

It was unbelievable, yet there could be no doubt. Whatever else this book might be, he knew that these fourteen leaves, filled on both sides with drawings and annotation, were priceless beyond knowing. He held in his hands actual pages of a Leonardo da Vinci notebook! A lost treasure of untold consequence! A new codex!

Santa Maria, Madre di Dio! What have you led me to?

Carefully, he closed the folio. A wind came up, spraying him with moisture from the splashing fountain. Suddenly afraid, he pulled off his coat and wrapped it around his find.

He must think. What should he do? Should he take it home to his little apartment and study it to his heart's content? Should he sequester it somewhere, keeping it for himself? The temptation was tremendous. At length he looked up and his eyes rested on the imposing stone vault that was the Biblioteca Nazionale. But, of course, there was only one thing he could do. The book must be put into the hands of proper scholars—authorities who could study it and disseminate their findings. He had been foolish to even consider keeping it for himself.

The excitement made him feel weak. *Maria Grazia, what should I do? If only you were alive and here to share this with me. How would you want me to handle it?* The thought of his long dead wife suddenly filled his mind. It turned his thoughts forcibly to Santa Croce, towering so grandly before him. She had been the religious one, a good Catholic attending Mass every morning. He had not thought it necessary for himself. He felt comfortable with his God and didn't feel that a daily pilgrimage would improve things any. It had hurt her at the start of their marriage and was the cause of many arguments, but Piero's temple was the human brain, where God resided at all times. He considered all works of both nature and man to be God's works. Though he thought of Santa Croce as monumental, awesome architecture; as a measure of the skill of his species; as a reflection of both the magnificence and delicacy of God; he doubted that God was any more there than He was in the cobblestones below Piero's feet or in the pigeons that were now tentatively returning to the piazza.

Nevertheless, he had often accompanied Maria Grazia to church, and many times he felt a distinct warmth rush through him as he knelt beside her and received the Sacrament. But he had always attributed this more to being close to Maria, loving her, and sharing with her something that was important to her, than to the powers of Christ.

Then, when she died, he could not bring himself to attend church alone except sometimes on their anniversary, or when he was caught up in the Christmas or Easter spirit, and even then it was only a hollow gesture. The trouble was that Maria Grazia was his only link to the Church.

And now, feeling the weight of the incalculably valuable volume on his lap and wishing that Maria Grazia was there so that he could relish the wonder on her face, that old warmth rushed over him again.

Piero Lorenzina began to sob. The memories of fifty-six years of marriage, of true love and companionship, flooded in on him.

He remembered the task ahead of him and wiped his face dry with his hands. With a fraction of his attention, he noticed that a crowd had gathered curiously around the heap of bricks behind him on the sidewalk. He stood awkwardly and began to walk the length of the piazza toward the biblioteca, clinging to the to me that somehow had opened up a link to his dead wife.

The square was buzzing with activity now. Piero, blinded to all but his self-imposed duty, was oblivious to the leatherware shops and the kiosks displaying plaster Madonnas and the maniacally hawking merchants and all the rest whose lifework was the waylaying of insatiable tourists.

As he drew near the basilica, the wind came up and Piero felt the morning chill bite through his shirt. He was not used to going without a coat at this hour. The book was heavy and bulky and he needed both hands to hold onto it. It was difficult walking with a load and not being able to use his cane, which dangled uselessly from his left hand.

He turned south onto the via toward the Piazza dei Cavalleggeri. Across from that piazza was the main entrance of the library. Suddenly, a blast of cold wind shot clear to his bones. He stopped in front of Santa Croce, trembling. He tried to get a better hold on the book. The wind blew steadily down from the dark, shop-lined via behind him. He shivered violently, grimacing. He took a few more steps, but stopped again, suddenly dizzy. He tottered, feeling a tremendous pressure push down on him. He felt as though he were carrying the world.

Abruptly, he made up his mind. The burden and the cold were unendurable, and the open doors of the vast church were too inviting. The shelter inside would rejuvenate him. Though it was critical to get his amazing find into proper hands, if he were to collapse from exhaustion halfway there, someone else finding the tome might not know what must be done.

As fast as he was able, he mounted the church stairs and, passing through the cloisters, entered the nave. Though not strictly warm, the dusty air was considerably more comfortable than the chill outside. It had been almost a year since he had entered Santa Croce, but it appeared not to have changed at all. That somehow made him feel more comfortable.

As he stood just within the cavernous Florentine-Gothic interior of the basilica, he was struck as he had always been by the wholly different quality of the sound within. Somehow, the resonance or the air pressure or both caused a definite physical sensation, contributing to a feeling of other-worldliness. Oddly, this sensation, too, was a distinct comfort to him now.

Piero moved to the right side of the church and slowly made his way down the aisle past Michelangelo's tomb and the tomb of the composer Rossini, past monuments to Dante and Macchiavelli, by a bas-relief of the *Annunciation* by Donatello, and turned into the right transept. His movements were automatic, as though time had erased nothing.

At the end of the transept, he walked straight into the Baroncelli Chapel, which had been Maria Grazia's favorite, and was grateful that it was warmer still than the nave. Nothing had changed here either. The Giotto fresco of the *Coronation of the Virgin* still watched over the chapel from above the altar exactly as it had when Maria came here every morning. He moved to the front pew, genuflected, and sat thankfully on the plain bench, placing the book carefully beside him. He made the sign of the cross and knelt painfully in the exact spot where Maria had put her knees so many times. He gazed up at the ghostly outlines that were all that remained of the Coronation after the fresco was inexcusably covered with whitewash some centuries before, and he considered the frailty of mankind. He was terribly tired; yet, in this setting he found himself waxing contemplative, weighing human artistry against human perversity. He laughed at his foolishness, then prayed for strength enough to take the fabulous volume to the biblioteca. He sighed deeply; closing his eyes, he asked, too, that Maria Grazia was well and happy. He breathed quietly, savoring his immense good fortune, feeling thoroughly content, remembering . . . .

All at once, a chill ran through him despite the comparative warmth of the chapel, and he had a strong craving for a steaming coffee. He was still on his knees and wanted to sit because his knees ached, but he couldn't summon the strength to move his legs. He tried very hard, but he only succeeded in making himself more tired. The physical exhaustion turned to sleepiness. He rested his head on the support in front of him. He closed his eyes and saw a vision of Maria as she had appeared on their wedding day, so young and dark and slender, dressed in white and blushing behind her veil. He felt his heart fill with her. The fullness pushed on his chest. He opened his eyes and the vision did not fade. She was still there holding her hands out to him. She moved into the pew and sat beside him. He was very cold, yet he knew only gladness that his Maria Grazia was beside him again. He took her outstretched hand. It, too, was cold, as though she'd just come in from the out-of-doors.

A tingle of joy swept through his body, cresting along his spine. He couldn't keep his eyes off her.

Maria, the book, the great book—it must be put into proper hands. The scholars must get it. Please, help me. I cannot tell you how important this is! It must not fall into the hands of the callous or the careless or the unthinking. It must not!

Don't worry, my Piero. It will turn out well, he heard her say; then all faded except for Maria Grazia, his cherished wife for eternity.

🐎

Thus ends, Heavenly Father, Holy Mother, my reflection on the last hour of Piero Lorenzina's life on earth. However, there is great—without doubt inspired and divine—irony here. Be it noted that I have assumed in the preceding that Piero took absolutely for granted, perfectly naturally so, that the earthquake had dropped into his safekeeping an authentic Leonardo da Vinci codex. I made this assumption because my in-depth study of this otherwise learned man has shown no strong inclination toward art history or comparative scholarship. Otherwise he would have seen what our Vatican art historians and textural scholars easily observed, namely that the journal was another of the many extant works by the able hand of Gian Giacomo Caprotti. Leonardo adopted the ten-year-old Gian, nicknamed Salai, which sobriquet underscored his devilish nature, into his household in 1490 where he seemed to have fulfilled many roles, part apprentice, part servant, part devoted companion.* In any event, it has been shown that Salai is the artist responsible for numerous paintings and drawings done in Leonardo's style, but not done by the great artist himself. In addition, and therefore conclusively, once the reverse script on the fourteen pages of vellum had been read and much of its oblique

---

* Editor's note: Salai stayed by the artist's side for 26 years until the great master's death.—T.K.M.

meaning deciphered, it became obvious that it was no less than Salai's own journal of the long, taxing journey in search of the ultimate wonderment. That he mimicked here his master's frequent tendency to secretiveness is only natural given the nature of his quest.*

Alberto Cardinal Cigliutti

---

* Editor's note: The cardinal made these statements about 1870 at a time when over-enthusiastic scholars were seeing evidence of Gian Giacomo Caprotti's work everywhere. More recent scholarship has thrown into doubt many of those findings.— T.K.M.

CHAPTER SEVEN

Bayushtiak Intervenes

"Twaddle," I said, thinking that Hans and I had been thrown into the company of lunatics. Or at least some of them were.

I quickly pulled aside Miss Mitchell and asked if she had had any notion of the true goal of Holmes, Huxley, Cuff, and Scott.

"Why no, I didn't, Mr. Quatermain. I'm as appalled as you, you can count on that. Why, the Grail is merely a Celtic myth. And I cannot account for the behavior of these otherwise notable men."

Burton, of her party, volunteered much of the same, as did Dravot and Carnehan.

Nonetheless, their falseness aside, these people had hired me, and they were dependent on me. "There's nothing for it," I said to them all, "but to turn around and return the way we came. I vow to continue to the best of my ability."

"But Quatermain," Holmes was quite firm. "I haven't shown you the final proof yet. Remember, you just read that embedded in the book Piero Lorenzina found there was a vellum notebook. That notebook tells how Leonardo da Vinci's friend Tomasso had stumbled across the final written words of a dying eleventh century crusader and that the crusader's words gave detailed directions on how to find the Holy Grail. Furthermore, because he determined to his own satisfaction that the writing was both sincere and authentic, in the year 1500, Leonardo dispatched Tomasso and another close companion named Salai off in search of the Grail. That notebook was in fact Salai's journal and describes how they traveled for months in extreme climates, all the while following the route laid out by the crusader. And according to Salai, and later vouched for by Leonardo, who added copious notes in the margins of the journal, they did in fact find the Grail. However, they chose to leave it right where they found it. Salai wrote, I'm sure parroting Leonardo's wishes, that he couldn't see any good bringing it back. It was better off where it was—away from the greed of men. And so they returned home, richer only for the experience.

"Unfortunately, just as was typical of Leonardo when he wanted to be either discreet or abstruse, his compatriot Salai did an excellent job expressing himself in an entirely oblique and cryptic manner. Much of his 'travelogue,' if you will, is meaningless to anyone but Leonardo and himself. All our attempts to glean something instructive and geographically useful from the notebook have thus far failed."

So it was only natural for me to ask, "So what good is it?"

Here Holmes positively gloated. "Don't you see. Leonardo da Vinci *said* Tomasso and Salai found the Holy Grail. If Leonardo said it, then it must be *true*. The man was a paragon and his word is not to be doubted."

Well, in fact, I didn't see. I didn't see it at all. My patience with these people had reached its uttermost limit. I remember vividly letting out an enormous sigh of helplessness. I remember this particularly because such a reaction is not typical of me. I was half embarrassed when I'd realized what I had done and was immediately grateful that nobody seemed to have noticed.

But nothing really had changed. Thus, I went on explaining things as I saw them. "Twaddle is what I said, and twaddle is what I meant. To get back to what I was saying, there's nothing for it but to turn around and return the way we came. I will do my utmost to fulfill my end of the bargain and return you all safely to our point of departure. I can do no more."

But Holmes was rushing on headlong and was not to be stopped. I'm quite sure he hadn't heard a thing that I'd said. "You just read in that manuscript about a parchment with Black-Letter writing," said he. "Well, I have the translation of that parchment here, as well." At which point, he thrust another batch of papers into my hands. "It tells the story of certain knights during the period of the First Crusade," said Holmes. "Indeed, it contains the original geographical statements that were written by an eleventh century knight and which we misstated to you, saying they derived from Yohannes IV's spies about Theodore's location."

You've heard the expression, that a last straw can break a camel's back. Well, Holmes's last remark—a frank admission of lies within lies—was frankly that last straw. I took hold of this new sheaf of papers while in a sort of daze, the feeling of betrayal and violation now so vast that it was like part of me suddenly and violently separated itself from my body and looked at the whole scene with complete objectivity, finding it all vastly comic. This separate and new me laughed and laughed, then got control of itself and harshly whispered in my ear. "Allan," it said, "what is the use of continuing this charade that life holds any value? What more could life hold for thee beyond more heartbreak and faithlessness? Leave them to die. They are not worth your succor." And the fearful thing was that I was not able to distinguish my true thoughts from those of this shadow version of me. It was like I had to struggle to breathe and I could see dimly that survival lay only in my total abandonment of these four European devils and the others as well. Let them fend for themselves. Let them know firsthand what it is like to be brutally betrayed . . . . And that was the tenor of my thoughts as I stared at these men whose lies had led me so far away from my comfortable little home in Durban.

My hatred was black indeed.

[And I am here to tell you, gentlemen, that, looking back on it, I truly believe I was on the precarious edge of insanity at that moment. No doubt I was exhausted having only just concluded one arduous journey—that being to Heu-Heu land and back—and then starting another right away. No matter the cause, I could see myself truly tossing away forever all notions of empathy and compassion and thereafter living solely for my own selfish betterment, or perhaps, as the voice suggested, giving up on life altogether.]

What saved me was at once obvious and unexpected. The warrior Bayushtiak had crept up behind me and touched my arm. He tells me that I reacted by snarling like a wolf. Though, clearly there would have been many witnesses, I was never able to glean from anyone other than the Zulu, not even Hans, whether my reaction was really such.

"Macumazana, come back," he whispered to me in Zulu. "It is I, Bayushtiak. I am here to save you just as the Great One has directed me to do. The portents and signs he shared and caused me to remember are now coming to pass, even this very moment. The world of true men is losing you and the foul witches are claiming you . . . unless you can find the fire within yourself to return to the surface world that is real."

I can tell you quite frankly that this ugly (and quite frightening . . . to this day I fear its return) side of me did not give up lightly. It fought Bayushtiak's ministrations for what seemed like hours, and all another part of me could do was watch and bear witness. I suppose it was because this drama was being played out on a stage far removed from our real world that the time seemed stretched.

Imagine the scene! Holmes had just handed me the new set of papers, and I was holding them in the air in my fist just as a kind of fearsome mask passed over my face and a kind of paralysis possessed me, only to then have the savage Zulu approach me and whisper in my ear. What could these calculating, deceitful Europeans (as I thought of them then) have thought by this little scene that was playing out before them?

Of course, I never told them what really happened, for what would they have thought?

[Quatermain note: Indeed, now that I think of it, I have never told a soul of this incident before now! —A.Q.]

[Watson note: Here, as you may recall, Church, Quatermain became very thoughtful and quiet as he stared for a time into the fire blazing in your hearth. And then he said he was in need of fresh air, thus we all moved out to that elaborate patio (I believe you called it your "Court Hall") that looked out upon the Hudson River and the Catskill Mountains beyond—at least during the day it did, as I could see for myself come the dawn. The air was fragrant and not at all uncomfortable, and so we relaxed on the benches there and Quatermain continued, first taking a slow sip from his brandy glass. —J.H.W.]

They tell me the pause in my conversation and Bayushtiak's subsequent interruption lasted only a few minutes. Be that as it may, in a moment, thanks to Zikali's foresight and the proud presence of Bayushtiak, all was back to normal. I do admit to then upbraiding with a certain forcefulness the four men who had hired me, but that is long past, and is water under the bridge now.

I then turned my attention to the papers that were still in my hand and began to read . . . .

[Quatermain note: Now, Church, though I gave you that night the essence of the knight's story that I read then, insofar as I also retained that translation of the knight's parchment, along with Cardinal Cigliutti's document, I am asking Dr. Watson to include this material as well.

−A.Q.]

[Watson note: Which I have done at this point. −J.H.W.]

CHAPTER EIGHT

The Parchment
(Being the Third Digression)

THE WRITING ON THE BLACK-LETTER PARCHMENT

Duke Stephen is dead, as are Count Albert of Clermont, William of Saint-Giles, and Fulcher of Tyre. So too 5 and 40 other fine and noble knights. By God's grace, I live. I am the last of the 50 brave men chosen by God to carry out His will. For by following his signs, Duke Stephen led us and we found the sacred vessel that was touched by the lips of our Lord Jesus Christ. We knew this was so for the archangel Gabriel, in the form of St. Andrew, came to Stephen in his sleep and made known this fact. Now this holy relic is truly safe, no longer soiled by any that is not also holy. So now I can die in peace.

This is my story: I am Bors, Count of Mainz. Following the Christmas fest of 1096 and taking to heart the spirited words of His Holiness Pope Urban, I and my comrades in arms joined Godfrey of Bouillon on the Danube at Worms, and by ways small and great passed through Hungary and Bulgaria to Constantinople at the bidding of Emperor Alexius. Here we joined with Raymond of Toulouse, Prince Bohemond of Tarentum, Hugh of Vermandois and others.

Soon we crossed the Bosphorus and laid siege for 7 weeks on Nicaea, a capital of the enemies of Christ. Our army was 600,000 strong and we marched in God's name. Following the surrender of Nicaea, we set out toward distant Antioch. Soon we who were with Godfrey heard that Bohemond's men were in need of succor, so we came to their aid and slew the Saracens all the whole day long.

Then came 500 miles of blistering, terrible desert, but finally we of Godfrey came to Antioch and laid siege for 7 months, nearly starving ourselves, but in the end, Emir Firuz betrayed his city and opened the gates. However, no sooner had our force entered the city, then we were surrounded by Keborgn of Mosul and 200,000 heathens. So we the besiegers were suddenly the besieged and what little food we found was soon consumed. After a month we despaired, and all may have been lost but for the dream of young Peter Bartholomew in which St. Bartholomew came to him and revealed the sacred, secret spot in which was buried the Lance that pierced our Lord's side, and Lo! It was Duke Stephen himself who recovered the holy blade, inspiring us with new hope. The lance was carried aloft by our mighty host and we left the city gate and vanquished the foe. It was a great and divine victory.

But I must now tell of the dream of Duke Stephen. This day alone Stephen had slew a score of Saracens in his own right. In the night, St. Andrew came to him, he who was exhausted and sleeping deeply, and said that it was he, Stephen, who was chosen by the Lord our God to recover the Holy Vessel and then revealed its location.

Duke Stephen gathered about him 9 and 40 of his most trustworthy liegemen—including I, Bors—and gathering what supplies that could be spared, we set off. Ere long, riding eastward, our journey took us to Sarras, a small village of heathens and it was there that we found the Holy Cup sequestered in a finely wrought box of ebony that was set in a vault buried under the floor tiles in the heathen mosque. Who put it there, how or why, we never learned.

That it was the Graal, there could be no doubt because upon seeing it, our entire party to the last knight beheld a vision of the archangel exclaiming with words that hung in the air and shown with gold that before us, forsooth, was the most holy of treasures.

Now, it is true that it was only at this juncture that there was disagreement among the knights. William of Saint-Giles led the faction that believed the Graal must come to Gaul, the only land with sufficient sanctity in their view. Others, led by Albert of Clermont wished the Graal taken to Rome.

But it was Stephen who, of course, won the day. It was his idea not to ride north as would seem natural, but to go south through the Holy Land into Arabia. He said he would know where the Graal belonged when he saw it. Insofar as it was our duty to follow our liege, our small party rode hard through the sandy wastes, keeping to the eastern shore of the Red Sea. In time we ran out of land at the southern tip of Yemen, but Stephen was intent on going further. We were able to cross the Strait of Babel el Mandeb on a barge that was used by the local villages for trading purposes. Once upon the land of Africa in the southern regions of the Axumite state, we found that the terrain and climate were much the same from whence we came on the farther side of the Red Sea, by which I mean the worst kind of desert and hot.

Stephen continued to lead us as a man obsessed. We knights, who had seen the angel ourselves and understood the notion of a task undertaken for God, of course, followed his lead without question. We began what would be three days of travel by horseback in a northwest direction and thence came to the twin flaming mountains. Stephen led us between these hellish—

[Watson note: Here the translation stops mid-sentence. A marginal note, perhaps scribbled by Richard Holmes, indicates that the writing of the original Black-Letter document had been deliberately and irretrievably scraped away beginning at this point, continuing for approximately thirty-five lines. The author of the note poses the likelihood that some combination of Salai or Leonardo or Tomasso were the guilty parties and that their intent was to obliterate the detailed instructions that led them to their destination. —J.H.W.]

—rode right up to a high, vertical cliff where he looked disappointed. He ordered us to spread out and look for a way beyond the cliff. It was Thomas of Arc who spotted the cleft, which was forever in shadow and darkness and hidden from view due to the arrangement of the terrain there. We quickly entered and came out the other side of the cliff—

[Watson note: The translation again stops mid-sentence. Another note explains that the parchment had been exposed to fire at some point centuries past and that the writing for several inches was scorched and hopelessly lost. Nevertheless, the ending of Bors's tale remained.—J.H.W.]

—we all then were intent on returning home to our families and homes. Crossing back to Yemen we rode north and soon enough recrossed the Bosphorus with the intent of making our way to our Holy Roman Emperor to tell of our deeds waged against the heathen Saracens and also of our sacred charge fulfilled. Riding hard through Hungary, our small band, which, praise God, still numbered 50, found that the way west was blocked by furious bands of murdering peasants determined to destroy any man who wore the red cross.

We headed north with the hope of by-passing these misguided peasants and passed through the Transylvanian Alps, whereupon we stumbled unknowingly onto a great plain on either side of which thousands of men had gathered in preparation for war. We soon garnered that these were yet more of those mad Hungarians in a dispute with the local Poles, and seeing that there was no passing through or around these great armies, Duke Stephen prayed on it and in the end chose to lend our swords on the Polish side, believing their Christianity to be the stronger of the two. Soon the two armies were in pitched battle and we fought well, dying one by one for the greater glory of God so that at the battle's end, only I am left, but it is clear not for long.

I have, therefore, taken up the quill and feel the responsibility to record these events for all time so that those who follow will know the Graal is safe in Ethiopia.

In God's name.
Bors, Count of Mainz

CHAPTER NINE

The Gathering of Heaven's Dead

By the time I had finished this fairy tale for children, I felt so abused, so exhausted, and so terribly out of control, that I did what I always do in such situations. I excused myself and went to sleep.

The next evening, we found that the natural path we were following led to the base of an exceedingly steep but not unclimbable hill.

Carnehan suddenly got excited. "I know this place," he said. "We're very close. Danny, what do you think? Ain't we made a bulls-eye? The devil take it if we didn't."

Dravot looked about and said, "I believe you're right, Peachy, my man. I'd venture that it was at the top of this hill and yonder a bit."

Naturally, at this news Professor Mitchell became quite animated and attacked the hill, Holmes with her, only to find that more was required than just spirit and enthusiasm. Undaunted, most of my party all began to claw up the side of what was a monstrous drift. Cuff and I hung back to help Lidenbrock up the slope. He seemed depressed that he could not manage on his own and I needed to encourage him repeatedly to keep him moving. In the end, whether burdened with an injured man or not, we Europeans had to rest several times. On the other hand, Hans and Bayushtiak were waiting for us at the top when we arrived and had been for quite some time.

The moon had just set and there was nothing at all to see, as excited as we were to see something of this particular goal after having given so much of ourselves to the quest these last days. But, nonetheless, there was something about that particular night, I remember. The sky was the deepest black with the stars shining particularly bright, sharp, and unwavering—a sight even unusual for one who has spent the better part of his career out in the open on the deserts, savannas, and veldts of southern Africa.

Hans, who was never far from me, was even prompted to whisper in my ear, "Baas, the sky is ablaze as though Shaka's battalions were cooking a wedding feast over fires covering a field stretching from one horizon to the other."

Frankly this observation was quite accurate and I responded with, "Let's hope it is the fires of a happy wedding rather than the blazes of warriors tempering and sharpening their blades in preparation for a glorious battle, which, frankly, doesn't interest me overly much at the moment."

"No, Baas! Don't mention such battles, lest you put a curse on us all." And he made the Hottentot sign that was meant to ward off evil. Unfortunately, his effort was in vain, as will soon be seen.

Not being able to proceed further, we set up camp rather precariously on the hill's summit and slept an unsound sleep.

That morning we awoke and saw that we had, in fact, climbed to the top of a rolling plateau constituting a mixture of sand and broken volcanic rock, and from our vantage point we could see miles in every direction. As would be expected, the entire face of the desert to our left was a rolling profusion of gullies and ugly ravines. Ahead of us, along the horizon, a series of massive symmetrical cones were lined up like titanic cauldrons simmering some monstrous witches brew, proving that we were still in the midst of volcano country.

It was here, and it was only natural, I suppose, that Lidenbrock rallied somewhat, bearing in mind that the man was never totally coherent during the brief time we knew him. One glance at those blackened and eerie mounds, and he found strength from who knows where, pulled away from our group with the intent, I suppose, of marching across the desert to investigate those mounds more closely. He was muttering something about "tuffs this" and "igneous that," and "plugs and dikes," and heaven knows what else, which I assumed were all related to volcanism. There was one particular thing he said, though, that has stuck in my mind all these years. Perhaps that is because he slipped into his native German just then, and Burton who happened to be near, translated for me. As

Lidenbrock went stumbling ahead of us, he cried out, "See, the shadow of Scartaris, it moves slowly with the radiant star of day." And then he started calling out for his uncle. I was never able to make anything out of it because we had enough to do without being diverted and had to keep the poor raving man from chasing his beloved and, admittedly, awesome cinder cones.

I felt it was necessary to take advantage of the cool of the morning and I insisted we continue steadfastly on. Within an hour, we heard Dravot shouting, "I see it! There, beyond that rise. Do you see the black patch. That's the beginning of it."

He and Carnehan threw down their gear and loped ahead to the spot Dravot had indicated. They were quickly at the top of that rise jumping and waving their arms and shouting.

Well, the end of it was that soon our entire party had joined them, and there below us was one of the most astonishing sights I had ever seen, notwithstanding several days of concentrated astounding sights.

The two soldiers had not been making up a story, as I had more than half believed. The proof was before me—a veritable blasted valley, a scorched bowl about as wide as a racetrack and as big around. And the whole of it was filled with craters, some new, some old, most overlapping older ones, and older ones still, and each crater awash in shattered black stone.

"Baas!" cried Hans. "Am I dead that I have come here to the gates of that very underworld that your Predikant father so often warned me about when he caught me sampling square face."

The poor fellow was clearly upset. But who could blame him really, for this description was certainly quite accurate, just as his description the previous night of the stars had been. I bethought me that Hans was developing a poetic, or perhaps "dramatic" would be a better word, streak that I had not experienced before.

Still, call it the gates of underworld, or a graveyard of meteorites, or the very pit of Hell itself, whatever it was, there it was before us . . . daring us to stay away.

There was no rhyme or reason to how we behaved. We all dispersed at random through that amazing field of mysterious stones from the starry reaches outside and above the earth and we wandered aimlessly as though through a maze, around the bigger stones, stepping over the smaller ones, circling the craters, kneeling and stooping and behaving like tourists at Kensington Gardens.

I heard Professor Mitchell exclaim, "Why, just as I suspected, they're almost all irons and some stony-irons, but I can't see any stones—none at all!" Then a little later I heard Holmes exclaim, "My word! There are some green ones and some with shiny bubbles that shine with tiny rainbows!"[36]

Bayushtiak approached me then and asked, "What is this place, Macumazahn? It is like a dream world. Such rocks I've never seen in my life and have never been told about by my fathers or my fathers's fathers." You see, in the course of Maria Mitchell explaining to us the scientific background that underlay her quest, I saw no reason to translate her lecture for Bayushtiak's benefit. So, of all of us, he was the only one who arrived at this place with no preconceptions at all.

I then took a few moments to condense for him what little I understood. When I was done, his face was stern and his eyes hard as ebony crystal. He swept his arm around in a wide gesture and said, "Then these are the corpses of the stars. As I think you know now, The Great One warned me of conditions for which I must be wary. One such event has in fact happened just as he said. "Here he looked at me with wide open eyes, indicating I suppose, secret knowledge, but I was too proud to respond in kind. He ignored my stubbornness and continued. "Yet here is another. 'Beware,' he said, 'of the gathering of heaven's dead.'"

My response was calculated, of course. "Bayushtiak, my new friend, I have known you only for a few days but already I know that you are strong and stalwart and would be a great ally in time of trouble, but I don't anticipate—regardless of what your master says—that I will have much to fear from a pile of blasted rocks strewn across the plain."

His response came slowly. "Macumazahn, I don't believe that is what The Great One meant." At that, he only stood tall and proud, gazing at the cosmic field and said nothing more for a time.

When we were all sated with this new experience and Professor Mitchell had collected a number of canvas sacks full of samples, we set up camp before the sun beat down too harshly. We started a fire to heat water and prepare our meals. After we had all settled down, naturally we began to speak of what we had just seen.

Richard Burton seemed to be bursting with his desire to share his thoughts. "It occurs to me that this spot is not that far distant from Mecca, where, of course, can be found the Black Stone embedded in the north-east corner of the Kaaba. Now this stone is thought to be the only remaining relic of the shrine used by Abraham and his son Ishmael for the worship of God, and is, therefore, considered to be the very right hand of God. But in actuality it is a common enough metallic aerolite—a meteorite. I know because I have studied it with my own eyes and touched it with my own hands, and even have kissed it, all this for a full ten minutes, more than most Muslims (who are typically pressed from behind by thousands of their brethren wishing likewise to venerate it) and certainly more than any European. As most of you know, I am one of the few Europeans who have entered Mecca in the last half of a millennium—and lived!"

As Burton spoke, his eyes shown, and his chest puffed out. He was definitely a man of accomplishments, I will say that for him.

"In fact, Dr. Wilson, of Bombay showed me a similar specimen which externally appeared to be a black slag but the interior of which was a bright, sparkling grayish-white which he assured me was the result of combining nickel with iron. The point I'm trying to make here is that it is possible that the Black Stone was no different from one of those yonder and that it merely missed the mark, so to speak, and fell in Arabia, which is only a bit north of here."

Burton stopped speaking, and I have to admit that this information of his gave me much food for thought, and perhaps it did the same for the others, for we were all quiet for a time.

Richard Holmes then spoke. "You know, it is sometimes said that the Grail we are after is actually a fantastic black stone, possibly a meteorite . . . at least that's the way von Eschenbach would have it."[37] He looked around expectantly at each of us, but as no one seemed inclined to pursue this line of thinking, he let it drop, I believe a little disgruntled if I read him right.

Professor Mitchell chose that moment to offer us some of her thoughts. "My theory is that this spot is particularly magnetic, in fact possibly a titanic lodestone if you like. If that can be proven, then the research possibilities are almost endless—between the region's natural magnetic quality and the nature of the meteorites themselves!"

Holmes spoke next. "Do you mean that as debris enters the atmosphere, those stones that are chiefly iron would have a tendency to be deflected to this spot due to the presumed extraordinary magnetism here?"

"Yes, that's precisely what I mean. Mr. Quatermain, do you have your compass available?"

Within moments, we were all peering at our assorted compasses. None of them were pointing north. They all behaved strangely. Mine, in particular, moved around in circles. Burton's merely wobbled up and down like a seesaw.

At this point Holmes and Miss Mitchell conferred, then announced that, as Miss Mitchell had indicated, this was an unprecedented phenomenon and that this area required a team of specialists to follow and take detailed readings. What was required were trained mineralogists, chemists, physicists, and the like. Burton then lent a hand surveying the place with his instruments and nailing its precise location for any future visit.

Then Miss Mitchell opened her mouth to say her peace, stopped in mid-utterance, and, to my surprise, peered at each and every one of us minutely, and even looked over her shoulder! When she was apparently satisfied, she voiced her thought: "There are even those naturalists who wonder quietly if life itself may have arisen not on earth as we all suppose, but was translated to the earth via a meteoric infection, if you will."[38]

I believe she intended to elaborate on this notion, but I'm afraid we never heard her ideas because at that moment we were attacked.

CHAPTER TEN

Attacked!

[But at this point, my dear sirs, I must get off the subject for just a moment. The native inhabitants of the area we were traversing are a tough, hostile people that the Arabs called the Danakil. Indeed, the very desert we were crossing was known as the Danakil Desert.[89] These people are all muscle and unusually thin and tall. Their faces are hard and chiseled, and they keep their wiry mops of black hair groomed with melted butter. Strength and courage are all important to them. There is nothing more prestigious than for a man to kill his enemy, who he then castrates for the grisly trophy. For each man and boy a Danakil has killed, he adds a leather thong to the large, curved blade that he wears forever across his stomach. They even castrate the dead, dying, and prisoners as proof of strength, which prizes are then offered to their women. Indeed, a Danakil woman would not even consider marrying a man who had not proven his mettle, so to speak, by killing at least one man and harvesting the appropriate trophy.

[I can say all this with confidence because since the events I am about to describe, I have looked into the history of these people, which accounts record several incidents where they massacred armed parties of explorers.]

To get back, then, our group, that is, my charges, were discussing the ramifications of the meteorites and had just heard Miss Mitchell's pregnant pronouncement—when Danakil tribesmen intent on butchering us swooped into the graveyard. We were rushed on all sides. With banshee screams, they pounced on us with their spears, daggers, and occasional guns.

I am quite certain that we would all have been killed in short order if it had not been for the instant leopard-like reaction of Bayushtiak, who, if I haven't mentioned it before, was also called "Umoya Oshisayo Womphefumulo Wengwe Emnyama Elindile," which means, in fact, "The Steaming Breath of the Crouching Black Leopard" and was a special title of nobility—hence, invincibility — amongst his people.

Two questions begged to be answered: Why were Hans and Bayushtiak not aware of the presence of the attackers? Also, given the latter's clearly stated concern about the area, how on earth did Bayushtiak fail to see them coming? I've thought about this often and my only explanation is that though my two native friends were wise in the ways and particulars of southern Africa, the Danakil had the advantage, for we were smack in the middle of their home desert and also, we were jubilant and naturally distracted. For his part, Hans refused to accept this and insisted ever after that their approach must have been camouflaged by some sort of supernatural agent. "Baas, how could it be otherwise?" was his defense." How could thirty or forty men sneak up on us, with me by your side—with me whose eyes are like the eagle's and whose nose and ears are like the wolf's, and who swore an oath to your Predikant father as he died that I would care for you always, as long as I lived."

In any case, though Bayushtiak had been unaware of their coming, the very instant of the Danakil attack he was suddenly everywhere at once slashing and stabbing with his assegai, eerily silent as he went about his bloody business. His instant single-handed defense so confused the attackers that they retreated, giving me time to disperse our guns and form the group into a defensive circle behind Bayushtiak. This had hardly been completed when the Danakil, who must have realized the error of their strategy, rushed back with murderous intent. The next few minutes were a blur of anguished screams, of dodging and thrusting, punctuated by explosions of scarlet. And in the mad confusion, somehow Hans, Sergeant Cuff, and I got separated from the others, which charges I could hardly stay focused on!, and found ourselves backing deeper into the meteorite graveyard where Bayushtiak had already led many of his attackers.

At some point, I looked and saw Bayushtiak atop a huge pointed, obsidian-like meteorite chopping and slicing at what seemed a never-ending torrent of Danakil savages. Hans was to my right and Cuff was at my back, and the three of us moved to protect Bayushtiak's rear. It was fearsome, finding ourselves surrounded by savages, dodging whirling daggers and razor-like spears.

It was deadly clear that our small defending force was severely outmanned, and I had already given up hope, I must admit. I knew as clearly as I have ever known anything that I was about to die. While one part of me mechanically continued to blast and chop at the enemy, another part was preparing to meet my Maker, listing my many transgressions over the years and hoping I could talk my way past the Pearly Gates.

Then it was that a great wonder happened that turned the tide permanently. At one point, two warriors broke through the circle that some of our men had formed around Miss Mitchell. But she was not a woman to be intimidated or killed so easily. She had somehow grabbed a long dagger, almost a sword, from one of the warriors and at once stepped into the fray unmindful of danger and with a perfunctory hacking of the blade sent the head of one of the Danakil rolling. Ten yards along the ground it rolled and off the edge of a nearby gully, falling fifteen feet or so into the sand below.

At this, the fellow's confederates ceased fighting to a man, turned on their heels, and retreated. So startled was Cuff by this rapid turnabout that for one instant he was caught off guard-time enough for one quick-witted tribesman to thrust his jagged dagger deep into Cuff's loins. The next instant the Danakil was shot dead by a bullet from Hans's Winchester.

A good shot, but too late, for the damage had been done. I dashed to where Cuff had fallen, ripped open his shirt, and evaluated his wound. When I had determined that he was alive, Dravot and Carnehan lifted him and carried him back to our camp.

Of course, our first reaction was to feel confusion mingled with relief. We were not then, or ever to be made, certain as to why the attack turned so fast. Hans, I think, had the best thought on the subject. He said, "Baas, what I think happened is that the warriors saw a woman behave like a man and not only defend but attack and kill. After all, it is their job to impress the women. I think that the lady's attack was something they could not understand and therefore they grew afraid, perhaps of witchcraft for all I know, and left as quickly as they had arrived."

As he happened to say this in English, he was overheard by Miss Mitchell, who, though exhausted, laughed heartily. She said, "Mr. Quatermain, your man may have a point. All I can say for certain is that I may be a woman who men are inclined to coddle and protect, but I'm not about to stand back and let myself be killed when there is still so much to learn. The stars in the heavens above and all their brethren in all the spaces in between are my domain and I have promised the almighty God himself that I will not die until I chart their courses and know their secrets to the very best of my ability." She became thoughtful for a moment, then declared, "But all that notwithstanding, there was something else. During that time when I was so surrounded, I felt infused with some special power, something radiating from within and from without . . . something I've never felt—"

But just then, there came a yell. It was Carnehan. He was waving his arms some distance off. "Over there!" he called out pointing toward a wide, jagged prominence of meteorite stone. We rushed to and around the spot and found Lidenbrock on the far side crumpled in the center of a crater in the shade of the outcropping. I was the first to arrive, rolled the geologist on his back, and could see easily enough that the poor fellow had been killed. Blood was oozing from a long wide slash across his breast easily seen through his sliced shirt.

"He's dead," I said. But then I added, half to myself, "But this isn't right." I motioned Holmes to my side. "Look at this wound. It wasn't made by a savage's blade. It's much too clean a job. This was done with a precision instrument . . . like a doctor's scalpel, say, or a keen blade, even a razor."

Huxley ventured, "Perhaps it was an obsidian blade finer than the others."

"Perhaps," I replied, "but compare it to Cuff's. This is undeniably different. I've seen many a blade wound, and this one seems more 'civilized,' if that isn't an odd word to use, than anything any native could have accomplished."

Then there began a discussion between Burton and myself where the tribesmen could have acquired such a blade, deciding that it was probably from a looted caravan.

Obviously all the others reacted in manners according to their personalities. After all, we hardly knew the man. His exposure and exhaustion prevented him from communicating much, and what little he did say was mostly ravings of one sort or another. Holmes, Miss Mitchell, and Huxley were, for example, solicitous, worried about his next of kin, what to do with his mortal remains, etc., while the two soldiers seemed stoic enough or even unconcerned.

It was young Will Scott who had the most interesting reaction. As I was hovering over Lidenbrock's body, Scott forcefully injected himself into the scene, nearly pushing me to the side. He pulled a magnifying glass from out of a pocket, fell to his knees and began examining the ground, all the while grumbling. I would have been appalled, but the oddness of his subsequent behaviors quickly eclipsed all else. As far as I could make out, his grumbles seemed to consist mainly of the words "trampling" and "fools" in all sorts of permutations. When he was finished with the ground, he held his glass close to poor Lidenbrock and looked minutely at every aspect of the body, in particular the wound. When this had been going on for some little while, the novelty had worn off enough that the attention of the others wandered, and eventually only myself, Hans, and Huxley seemed to pay him any mind.

"Baas," Hans spoke quietly without taking his eyes off Scott, "what is this pup doing? What is so interesting about a man's bones and dead flesh. I have never heard that you can flush out a witch with a glass, but maybe I am wrong . . . or perhaps the pup is a witch."

"I think he is trying to find out how the man died."

"But that is clear enough. One of those savages was handed a kill on a platter and he didn't ask any questions."

All I could do was shrug for Scott's behavior was peculiar to be sure. Then all at once, he saw something that seemed to startle him. He glanced over at Huxley, then redoubled his observations over a certain area. Finally he stood tall, pocketed the glass, and strode with purpose to his mentor. They moved apart and spoke far enough away that I could not hear them. In a few moments, Scott became agitated at Huxley, who seemed completely unperturbed. Then in another moment Scott came close to shouting. But he was able to restrain himself and neither Hans nor I could ever piece together the fragments that we could make out. I heard individual words that sounded like "university" and "saber." Hans thought he heard "brother" and "villain." The oddest thing is that, more than any other reaction, Huxley seemed almost amused by all the fuss Scott was making, going so far as to break into a broad grin.

In the end, I decided it was nothing of my concern, but the upshot of the affair was that beginning then the easy rapport the two had shared—of wise teacher and willing student—vanished completely, and for the duration of our expedition, they avoided one another—as much as one could in our circumstances.*

I then assessed our condition. Aside from Lidenbrock and Cuff, my group had accounted for themselves well, and by the grace of God, we were largely unharmed.

---

* Editor's note: By this point in Quatermain's memoir, due to our advantage of perspective almost a century and a half afterwards, it is obvious from Quatermain's descriptions that "Will Scott" was in reality the great detective Sherlock Holmes traveling under an assumed name. It is sadly ironic that Quatermain would never know that his encounter with the gangly teenager was, in a sense, historic, but, of course, it would be another 15 years before the world began to take notice of Holmes. While Quatermain's observations do not really give justice to Holmes' deductive prowess, a circumstance clearly due to both young "Will Scott's" low-key investigatory technique and Quatermain's understandable ignorance, Holmes' genius was nonetheless on display for all the initiated to see. Regardless, I became bound and determined to somehow buttress Holmes' forensic examination of Lidenbrock—over and beyond Quatermain's few remarks. I reached out again—just as I had done to obtain much of the other supplementary material in this book—and put forth inquiries, and then patiently waited. In the meantime, the first (mediocre) and second (preferred movie tie-in) editions had been released. Naturally, I was disappointed that the book was published without a proper Holmsian resolution to the mystery of Lidenbrock's death. However, my waiting was not in vain as now we are all enriched because a response did wind its way slowly over four continents so that, in the end, one day I opened a tattered box that had come in the mail and beheld, lo and behold!, Dr. Watson's original manuscript, in the same round hand as his rendering of Quatermain's memoir, of "The 'Gloria Scott'"—a manuscript that was deemed irretrievably lost by Holmsian authorities. Of course, "The 'Gloria Scott'" is the one adventure of the Canon (that is,

Watson's original chronicles) that not only describes Holmes as a teenager, but wherein we are told Holmes became inspired to turn what was then merely a hobby into a career. Yet, as wonderful and utterly invaluable as this find is in the wider scholarly sense, for the purposes of this volume, it was not that original manuscript (which I eventually donated to the Parker Family Collection, Special Collections Library, at the University of Michigan) that is of interest, but rather the bit of paper torn and ragged on all four edges that was tucked between the manuscript pages. The context of the piece of paper is unknown. We know not why it was written, why it was apparently torn from a longer work, what that longer work might have been (it might have been a journal or even an affidavit), or why it was placed within the manuscript. Of course, one natural conjecture is that since the paper seemed to reference an incident that occurred in 1872, an incident only approximately two years before "The 'Gloria Scott,'" it seems only natural that the two records would gravitate together for the sake of orderliness and safekeeping if for no other reasons, though, of course, the actual writing of the *Gloria Scott* affair must have happened in the early 1890s soon after Holmes brought the earlier encounter to Watson's attention. In any case, this new revelatory material clearly warranted a new and revised third edition. Now, not to draw out this explanation any longer than necessary, here is the content of that scrap of paper:

"—and again my thoughts return to that dreadful day. Lidenbrock was the first dead man I had ever seen (other than in the occasional morgue or audited class at St. B's. It was appalling, devastating, but I knew that if I could be of any use, I needed to put my skills to work right away before the evidence of the ground could be trampled further, and before the body had been pushed and shoved and hauled and lifted and all the rest. At first I despaired that the ground would have been mercilessly trampled and scattered during the battle and that Lidenbrock may as well have been stabbed by a ghost, for all the evidence that the ground would reveal. (Looking back I cannot help but imagine how useful the dog Toby would have been then!) It was bad enough that Q. felt the need to turn the body over, but there was little enough harm, thank goodness. Still I had never dealt with such quantities of human blood, so I steeled myself and examined the sand and rocks and discovered that my earlier despair had been premature. I found the marks of a shoe that had been impressed into the sand *after* the general melee had stirred up the ground but *before* Quatermain's shoe-prints had registered, thereby suggesting that the print that was sandwiched between the others was from the shoe of the man who had entered and then left the arena during the mere minute between the routing of the savages and Carnehan's call. That, from the markings, the battle appeared less intense there, probably due to the projection of sharp stone, merely aided my observations. From the impress of the shoe, its size was immediately determined and from an examination of the entry point of the weapon and various associated measurements I determined the angle of the thrust (bearing in mind L.'s sagging posture and his probable physical predisposition during the battle), the force behind it, the distance above the ground of the hand that wielded the weapon, the height and weight and general build of the killer, the hand used, and verified Quatermain's conclusion that L. had been stabbed with a sharp precision instrument of a different order than an obsidian flint.. The method was clear. The only question that remained really was, if you eliminate the Danakil (who did not wear Western shoes, of course), who could be a murderer? I did a mental inventory of our odd assortment of individuals, discounting first one and then another until no soul there could have been responsible for L.'s wound. Furthermore I convinced myself that there could not have been any motive, at least among our company, as we had all just met L. But then I saw the nearly invisible thread that clung to the top button of L.'s coat, clung because of static electricity. I picked it up with tweezers and examined it with my glass. It was silk, red, and of the finest South Indian variety, which is much sought after. There was only one man in our company whose apparel included silk. A man whose build, etc., also perfectly conformed to my conclusions. I glanced over at my brother but he affected interest in Miss Mitchell. No. That was not possible. Not to be baffled, I started all over again and reevaluated the corpse and the scene with my glass and tweezers and measuring tape with every skill at my disposal, and I finally realized that there could be no doubt. I girded myself and repeated over and over: 'If we eliminate all possibilities, that which remains must be the solution, however improbable it may seem.' I looked again at my bother and he was looking at me in an unconcerned fashion. I went over to him laid out the evidence and my conclusion and he merely looked at me, seeming like a complete stranger. I remember being afraid, not for my safety but for my loss. There was no doubt that my brother was a villain and a vain one at that. He remained completely unperturbed. I was in unfamiliar territory and could only draw back—" —T.K.M.

CHAPTER ELEVEN

Once Upon a Time!
(Being the Fourth and Last Digression)*

[My! Mr. Holmes is quite cantankerous today. For all intents and purposes he is ordering me to take dictation, and I have half a mind to remind him that I'm not his secretary, but his old landlady paying a pleasant country visit to her eccentric former tenant. I suppose he is cranky because he has just returned from a trip abroad on who knows what business, and has taken to bed with influenza for his trouble. I was rearranging his provisions in the pantry into some sort of order, with a shelf devoted to jars of different varieties of honey, when he called out, "Mrs.

---

* Editor's note: Once it became obvious that Will Scott was in reality Sherlock Holmes, I enjoyed witnessing vicariously the teenager's immerging detective skills, It was also instructive knowing that the young man must have comported himself well during a merciless and bloodthirsty attack from the indigenous peoples of an exotic and awesome land—at the *beginning* of his career. I then became curious about the *end* of his career. Searching the Internet, I followed links deep into what must be a kind of digital catacombs of the Net. Eventually, something fleetingly crossed my vision as my mouse clicked away. I backed up and saw a black and white photograph of a faded old piece of stationary with the letterhead "John H. Watson, M.D." and a salutation that read "My Dear Holmes:" My heart raced as I counted 31 pages total. All four margins of the sheets were crammed with copious comments in a crabbed hand much different than Watson's now familiar round script. Those pages connected Holmes uncannily to an age-old myth cycle and to a lost world. That document included here—juxtaposed with Quatermain's memoir—sheds considerable light on Holmes' methods at the two extremes of his life. On the first page, in a tiny script above Watson's letterhead and running into both side margins to the bottom of the sheet, is the text that begins above.—T.K.M.

Hudson, may I have your assistance, please? I am happy to see that our Dr. Watson has taken a few moments out of his hectic schedule to correspond. I do hate to trouble you, but I've tried to read these letters, and between our friend's declining script and a weepy eye from this damnable flu, I am having some difficulty. Might I ask you to pull over that chair to make yourself comfortable and read aloud to me these missives? They are rather lengthy as these things go." Of course, I assented. "And, also," he continued, "if you will please take down any extemporaneous comments that I may make during your reading, I would be obliged. My memory is not as keen as it used to be, I don't want to lose the thread of my own thoughts later on should I ever need to refer back to them and when they are no longer conveniently cached in my head."] [To help keep Mr. Holmes's records straight, I should say that the envelope of this first letter was stamped on June 15th and must have arrived about ten days ago, for it is today June 28th.]

John H. Watson, M.D.

13th June 1924
My Dear Holmes:

It's difficult to believe that it was only six weeks ago that I paid my lovely visit with you at your little farm on Sussex Downs. Though on some level I always understood that beekeeping was unique in its own way and hugely satisfactory for those with a love for the insects, I dare say that you have made that avocation into an art form. Your hives are veritable cities, complete with upper classes and lower classes. I find this wonderful no matter how many times I visit! And the honey we enjoyed on our toast for breakfast—was nothing less than divine. I wished that I could have stayed longer than a week, but my work, even at this point in my life has its many responsibilities, and I, unlike you, am not quite ready for retirement.

The irony is, however, that I had no sooner returned to my lodgings and practice than I received a wire I from an old college classmate, whom I may have mentioned once or twice in our Baker Street rooms, Lynwood Reginald McCabe, that necessitated precipitous action. At the point when I began the serious study of medicine, he was studying mathematics and later went into architecture, developing quite a name for himself and opening his own offices. His strength, as is my understanding, was his emphasis on function, and his designs included grocery markets and barber shops, as I recall, and eventually banks and centers of finance. He has long since retired and bought a sheep ranch in southern Ireland. I had not thought of him in years, and here was this note nearly begging me to drop everything and come to his aid—in Ireland of all places! I packed, arranged yet again for two of my long-suffering colleagues, to whom I'm greatly indebted, to divide my patients between them for the duration, and found myself before dawn standing in the swirling mist trackside at Victoria Station. There followed multiple rail connections, two ferries, more rail connections, at least one omnibus, and cabs to the extent that I've lost count, I finally arrived at the Bottle Hill Hotel on the main street of the tiny town of the same name some 45 miles north of Cork.

The proprietor sent word of my arrival to McCabe who dispatched a car and by seven p.m., when it was still warm and light, I was sitting on the porch of my old friend's villa overlooking a long stretch of hilly green pasture that was thick with grazing sheep and lambs, who filled the atmosphere with their plaintive "baahs" as the shepherds and their dogs coaxed them to other ranging areas.

As of yet, despite my vigorous enquiries, McCabe would not come immediately to the point to explain either the reason he sent for me or the apparent urgency of his letter. From where I sat, he seemed as fit as a fiddle, and all seemed placid enough. It was over a simple but plentiful supper prepared and served by his staff that he finally explained the purpose of my rushed visit.

"Watson," he began with a forkful of lamb and carrot casserole paused halfway to his mouth, "I asked you to come because I have a bit of a mystery on my hands."

"Well, then, McCabe, I am flattered by your faith in my prowess, but I fear that over the years, despite my best efforts, I am not in the same league as my friend Sherlock Holmes, and he, as you may know is in retirement and seclusion, not to be disturbed under any circumstance."

"Oh, I had no idea. But I did not ask for Mr. Holmes, I asked for you—because my mystery seems to have a medical basis, and naturally your reputation as a physician is known far and wide."

I must say I could feel myself blush at this remark.

"Watson, before I explain the problem, I must preface it by relating some of its circumstances. My ranch manager is a man named Donald O'Neary. He's been with me for many years. All my crops, sheep, other livestock, and land are under his supervision. Some days ago, he mentioned in passing to me that he'd noticed a hedge of blackthorn bushes had sprung up near one of the stream crossings."

> [Ah! Blackthorn! Fascinating stuff! I could and should write a monograph solely on this bush and its berries. It's said that Christ's crown of thorns was made from it. And blackthorn is used to make magic wands! In fact, Little People are supposed to live in its branches! Heinous crimes, even village genocide, are known to have had at their heart assumptions and presumed knowledge about blackthorn! This is not a bush to be trifled with, Mrs. Hudson!]

McCabe continued: "Donald shouldered a shovel, rake, and shears and began to march across the pasture. I suggested that he take his son, Tieg, along or another man, but he can be obstinate and said they had their own work to do and there was no reason, in any case, as he was perfectly capable of handling the task himself. Altogether he seemed happy and in good health. That was in the morning, and when he wasn't present to supervise moving the flocks in the afternoon, Tieg went looking for him. About an hour later one of the shepherds rushed in and said that they had found Donald sound asleep near the stream, but they couldn't get him to awaken. They were bringing him in, and I sent for the doctor. We tried to make Donald comfortable in his own bed in his own house behind this one. It was then we discovered that there was a small circle of fungus growing on his chest. The local doctor, Dr. Abernathy, who is about half our age, mind you, confirmed that Donald was unconscious and confirmed that there was a fungus growing on his chest, but all he could prescribe was castor oil. Otherwise there was nothing he can do because Donald clearly had been tampering with the fairies."

I jumped up and exclaimed, "Unconscious! Fairies! Why are we sitting around? Show him to me!"

"There's no hurry, Watson. You see, all this happened a week ago, and he seems not to have changed at all."

"A coma?" I asked.

"I don't know. That's why I asked for you."

Fairies! Holmes, can you believe it? I was in for one rude awakening after another!

"You say that the local physician cannot help the man because your man is under a fairy's curse?"

"I fear that is accurate enough. But you see, the doctor is a child of this land. He grew up here, went to Dublin and then London to receive his medical training and returned to be of use to his own people. As a result, it seems the community's folklore is as alive to him as it was in his ancestors."

"Enough of this. Show me your man."

I grabbed my bag and we went out the door. McCabe led me to an outbuilding that lay near his home. Before we reached the door, a young man exited and came towards us. He was 20 years old or so, possessed a strong, dark body that was covered by a pair of baggy, brown trousers and a long-sleeved, red-plaid, woolen shirt. His pants were held up by a pair of yellow suspenders.

"Dr. Watson, this is Tieg O'Neary, Donald's son."

We perfunctorily shook hands. It was difficult to get out of the boy any information that could help me. His principal communication were words to the affect of "It doesn't seem right. I don't know what to think. Do you think you can do something? It just couldn't be fairies!"

I finally pushed past the boy, saying, "Let me be the judge of that!"

Inside the cabin, I found in his bed an older man of the same sort as the boy. I began my examination. His pulse, temperature, skin tone were all consistent with a man who was sound asleep. I could see his eyes moving under his closed lids in the manner of a man who was dreaming intensely. I pulled down the blanket to reveal his chest, and yes, there was a circle of lichenous fungus about five inches in diameter encircling a patch of greasy, blistered and bubbling, greenish brown mold. I had never seen anything quite like this, and I had to force myself from turning my eyes away!

McCabe touched my arm and said quietly, "It has grown. It was only a small patch when we found him a week ago, perhaps an inch across."

Young Tieg O'Neary said then, "I remember he laughed as he was leaving. He jokingly said he hoped that they weren't fairy bushes, those he was planning to pull out! My father never took that sort of thing seriously. Usually, he would play along when the subject of fairies came up among our staff and the villagers, but he always told me that the folks around here were ignorant and knew no better and would even go so far as to hallucinate music that they claimed was fairy music when he knew perfectly well that there was no music at all."

Tieg went on to explain that it was common enough for some of their neighbors to leave lights on or candles lit in the windows at night to ward off the beings. On the other hand, he's heard of some in other districts who left whiskey out at night for the benefit of the fairies.

What am I to make of all this nonsense. Well one thing is for certain: I have an extremely ill patient, and I had better find out what what's ailing him. I saw to the comfort of Donald O'Neary and McCabe arranged to have one of the less nervous neighbors stay with him all night, and then we adjourned to the main house.

As we smoked around the fire, I realized that I hadn't seen O'Neary's wife, the mother of Tieg. Approaching the subject indirectly, I could see that Tieg, as well as McCabe, was reticent to discuss the subject, but eventually I learned that some 15 years before, when Tieg was but a boy and McCabe had not yet even come to the area, Tieg's mother was kidnapped from her own house, or presumed so, and was never seen again—though, of course, there were rumors for a time that she had been spotted in Dublin and London and even Paris. The majority opinion in the neighborhood was that she was "taken by fairies"! Frankly, I'm sorry I brought it up as all I did was dredge up bad memories.

They also explained how the morning following Tieg's finding O'Neary, McCabe took a party out to see what they could see. In fact, there was a hedge of blackthorn bushes near the stream, and one of them had been hacked down and lay broken on the ground. Tieg showed McCabe the spot where he had found his father laying on his back motionless. They saw nothing else at all that suggested wrong doing or mischief of any sort. It was just as though the man had had a stroke and fell where he was standing.

Before I retired I made clear that if I was to help, I had to see the spot myself and interview the doctor, and that was arranged for the next morning. McCabe showed me the room that would be at my convenience during my stay. It is quite comfortable and has three lamps, a four-poster bed, a closet, and a sturdy oak secretary where I am sitting and composing this note to you. I hope to add the sequel with more data tomorrow before I post it to you.

14th June 1924
To Continue, Holmes:
Before dawn this morning, I was introduced to Dr. Abernathy (which to his credit seemed unperturbed by the early hour), and we discussed the matter over breakfast. I questioned him quite firmly without stating outright that I believed him to be incompetent. Nevertheless, here follows an approximation of our conversation:

"Dr. Abernathy," I began, "I have examined O'Neary and, while his symptoms are indeed curious, I'm told that without benefit of a thorough examination, you have decreed the case hopeless and the work of fairies, and, furthermore, you've declared castor oil—castor oil!—is some sort of universal cure that will eradicate the fungus growth!"

"Dr. Watson, I would hesitate to put any of the facts in exactly those words, but my examination was not as perfunctory as you've been led to believe, and, furthermore, I am expert on the maladies of these parts, of its culture and peoples. And I in no way suggested that Donald O'Neary's case was hopeless. Please take it as fact that I pride myself in knowing how to speak to my patients in language they understand. For example, under normal circumstances would you explain to the parents of an injured girl that because her patellar tendon attaches to the tibial tubercle on the front of the tibia and because that tendon is also attached to the bottom of the patella where the quadriceps tendon is attached, when the patellar tendon ruptures, the patella therefore loses its anchoring support to the tibia? Or would you simply say that she has injured her knee?

"In that same vein," he continued, "it is sometimes necessary for me to simply tell my patients that they have been visited by fairies."

Here, regardless of his stated rationale, I was shocked and must have looked every inch of it.

"Though, I admit," he went on after a pause, "in fairness and in thinking it over, I was surely wrong to make such a suggestion to McCabe, who is a thoroughly educated man. In my enthusiasm, I suppose I sometimes fail to separate one order of patient from another. But, tell me, doctor, how would you describe a fairy?"

"Me? Why I wouldn't have a reason to try!"

"Humor me."

"Well, I suppose a fairy is defined as a tiny humanoid only a few inches tall with wings and lives among the flowers." Then I was hit with an inspiration. "Like Tinker Bell in *Peter Pan*!"

"Well, it is true that the popular magazines and the arts generally have encouraged that image and fanned it to the point where it is now pervasive and utterly taken for granted. To the degree even that Sir Arthur Conan Doyle was fooled by the Cottingley fairy photographs, which were clumsily contrived by two children."

"I don't understand what you're trying to say," I ventured. "It sounds as though you have no more patience for fairies than I do."

"Those tiny fairies that you just described, doctor, are the product of the fertile imaginations of elitist town dwellers and city folk, of poets and playwrights, of painters and artists and illustrators who set themselves above country folk and who have perceived themselves as sophisticated and modern, especially at the close of the nineteenth century. The fairies of rural Ireland, however, are a different matter entirely."

I was about to interrupt, but he would have none of it.

"The Celtic people have passed down tried and true information about fairies for some two millennia. Stop, doctor, and contemplate what a gulf of time two thousand years is! Mind you, these people couldn't read or write so they kept their culture alive and protected the well-being of their families and communities through oral tradition. If you build your house over a fairy path, keep the doors open at night to allow the fairies free passage, otherwise your livestock will sicken and die. Keep your eye on newborn babes, as the fairies will substitute one of their own if you aren't careful. Do not disturb a heap of stones in a field, as the fairies who live inside the pile will cause you no end of trouble. Calling them 'the gentry' or 'the good folk' or 'the fair family' or suchlike terms will ease their tempers and divert their malice. There are thousands of such directives—changing surprisingly little over time—and surprisingly specific to regions. The rules and perceptions can change radically from village to village, from county to county, even from nation to nation. For instance, there are the *pobel vean* in Cornwall, the *brownies* in Scotland, the *corrigans* in Brittany, the *tylwyth teg* in Wales, and countless others. And, of course, here in Ireland, we have the *sidhe*. All remarkably similar in some ways and yet distinct in others. And from thence derive all the leprechauns and elves and most of the other wee folk that haunt these lands!"

I was aghast that this doctor had the temerity to avoid my questions as thoroughly as a politician! I tried to steer the conversation back toward subjects that I understand. "What do you say is the nature of the fungus?"

"It is a simple *mycelium* fungus," Abernathy answered, "which is the root cause of fairy rings in soil and circles of mushrooms in fields and forests. These fungi can grow quite enormous if not eradicated, you know. In O'Neary's case, it is obvious that the fungus has somehow transferred itself to his skin. Though not common, this is not unheard of either, and a distillate made from boiled castor oil will prove quite effective if rubbed into the contaminated area."

Fairy rings! Fairy traditions! Fairy curses! I'm sick to death of hearing such nonsense!

After breakfast and after that so-called doctor exited, Tieg and McCabe took me to the spot where O'Neary had been found unconscious. It was a good hike, and as neither McCabe nor I are as agile as we once were in our younger days, it was slow going. We aimed toward Bottle Hill (the tor, not the town) and which is also called Knock Magh, and Tieg volunteered that local legends held that there was a fairy city deep under the hill and that it was honeycombed with passages and tunnels of pure gold.

"But, doctor, I don't believe anybody has ever chosen to investigate, as everyone believes the legends—more or less," Tieg said. "Even father, choosing not to incite the distrust of our neighbors, has always respected the ban and has prevented the sheep from grazing anywhere near it. All this acreage has lain fallow for years."

It was close to midday when we crossed a stream by way of a tranquil bridge and soon afterward had crossed the pasture and came within sight of an enormous rough column of stone with a more-or-less pointed top. It was a single stone about the height of three men and alone in the midst of the field. You can see it in your mind's eye, I'm sure, Holmes, as it reminded me of those monuments of stone that you and I encountered in Cornwall.

"What is this?" I asked pointing to the column.

McCabe said, "Oh, that is just an old standing stone. They are common in this land. Legend has it, of course, that they are some sort of fairy signpost that marked some crossroads on a fairy path. Others say that they are prehistoric, built by long forgotten peoples."

I was so exasperated at all this fairy talk I had to keep my temper. I couldn't help but imagine how you would react to all this nonsense and remembered how you proved that whole Baskervilles business with all its legends to be fraudulent.

[Ha! Watson! You assume too much. Fairy bushes and fairy paths are very real to people who seldom travel more than twenty miles from their villages.

Fairy wisdom has lived for good reason through time immemorial. As to that other matter, all I did was show that an unscrupulous man had used the Baskerville legend for murder. I did nothing to prove or disprove the legend one way or another!]

Nearby, perhaps twenty yards away, there was the hedge that was the center of so much trouble. There were about fifteen of the plants growing close together. At the end of the hedge was a weathered hole about three feet across and the dead and dried bush that had been cast aside.

"You say the stone marked a path," I said. "Is there a real path, and where exactly is it?"

"Over here, Dr. Watson," McCabe said, and in a few moments we came to a worn pebbly path. I asked the two men to stay just where they were for the time being as I wanted to look around, and I am proud to say that I began my investigation in emulation of you, Holmes. I had even troubled to bring a small magnifying glass. The ground was covered with footprints and shoeprints, some old, some brand new its seemed. There were also some marks that, I thought, a large snake might have made.

When I rejoined them, I jokingly wondered aloud what kind of curse the fairies would put on me. And I was surprised to see that both went white as their own sheep and didn't respond in any manner.

With this realization that my hosts were not immune to the power of the local myths, I decided to change tactics. I wandered casually over to the standing stone, or the fairies' road sign, as it were, and began to examine its design and substance. I used the glass to examine minutely the areas of it surface that I could easily reach. I am no geologist, but it looked to me to be ordinary black basalt that had been exposed to the elements for centuries and much weathered. As I did so my shoe must have knocked or kicked into its base, so that when I stepped back I found that a fragment of stone as big as my fist lay at the foot of the standing stone. At first I thought that the larger rock must have been cracked somehow at some point in time, and I clearly jarred this small piece loose with my shoe. Even from where I stood, I could see that the sharp edges of the small fragment exactly matched the new cavity in the bigger stone. I picked up the piece and examined it with the glass I still had in my hand. The first thing I noticed was that it was shiny, more like volcanic glass than basalt, black and oddly slippery. Furthermore it was marked on the inward facing side with what looked like organized scratches. I found this most interesting and slipped the piece into my jacket pocket. All this happened on the side of the standing stone the faced away from my two guides, thus they did not know, and do not now know of any of this circumstance. I'm not sure what exactly I was thinking just then, but it has proven convenient to examine the piece without being subjected to superstitious outcries.

We returned without incident and I quickly retired to my room where I have been looking at the stone through the glass most minutely and can say with certainty that the scratches are definitely hieroglyphics or runes of some sort, about five dozen in number. The resultant conclusion is that at some point in antiquity the piece had been somehow broken from the larger rock, inscribed, and then replaced to fit perfectly into its spot of origin so that it was impossible to know that such a subtle graffiti had ever been perpetrated—unless one knew the secret. What it all means is another matter. It is an interesting curio, and I think I will use it as a paperweight. Knowing your interest in philology and ancient languages, I've just made a rubbing of the marks with the side of a pencil on some of my note paper. I include that rubbing here for you inspection. I will send any sequel when and if there is one. I am

Honored to by your friend and colleague,
And conclude this note with warm regards.
John Watson

[Since I was holding all the letters in my hand as I read, Mr. Holmes asked to see again the page with the markings that Dr. Watson had described. He looked it over most carefully, checking the reverse side, and then he shivered, ripped the paper in half and in half again, over and over until the paper had been torn into minute pieces. Then he placed all the torn paper onto a saucer, lit the pile with a match, and when it had all burned, he crushed the ashes, stirred them, and crushed them again several times. Then he said, "Mrs. Hudson, I must now decide what to do with these ashes as I don't want them proximal to this house." Of course, I knew better than to inquire what the fuss was about and I suggested that he mix the ashes with a bowl of birdseed for the birds to consume and disperse to the four winds as fate decreed. "Capital idea, Mrs. Hudson! I will not waste a moment!" He then put action to word, and returned to his seat. Then he said, "By the same token, Mrs. Hudson, we must take possession of the good doctor's paperweight as soon as possible and dispose of it in an equivalent manner." Then he bid me continue with the next letter.]

John H. Watson, M.D.

17th June 1924
My Dear Holmes:

I apologize that my last note must have arrived long ago, and that there has been no further sequel until now, and it's not of much consequence. The last days I have been recuperating from my long hike to the standing stone and blackthorn hedge. Because I have a strong intuition that the cause, and perhaps the solution, to O'Neary's strange malady lay beyond those two landmarks in a little-visited valley or gulch at the further end of McCabe's land, I've arranged with him to explore the area this coming Saturday, 21 June. The region it seems has points of interest, but I was astonished to hear that neither McCabe nor the O'Nearys has ever traveled much beyond the location of the standing stone despite their living so close to it. (It is truism, I suppose, that residents of an area are the last people to visit the attractions of that area, as I for one, have never been *inside* the Tower of London.) In the meantime, I am caring for the elder O'Neary and applying the ointment derived from boiled castor oil as Abernathy directed. It certainly can't do any harm. The nearest medical facility is far off in Cork, and as I don't want to risk the rough travel, I am caring for him here, and he appears to be no worse off for the attention he is receiving.

Your loyal friend, as always,

Watson

> [Here Mr. Holmes burst out: "Watson, Watson, Watson, beware! You should not be meddling with things you don't understand! I'm really far too old to have to bolt up and rescue you, old friend. I simply don't do all that well traveling any more." He heaved a great sigh, then asked me to retrieve three of his commonplace books, which he then spent some time meticulously amending. Quite a while later, he asked me to replace them, and he simply said, "Mrs. Watson, pray continue."]

John H. Watson, M.D.

23rd June 1924

I don't know where to begin. Two days ago I experienced Hell! How does one describe literal Hell after one has actually been there?

The day before yesterday, early in the morning I loaded and pocketed my pistol just to be on the safe side, and we packed some things, including Hubert electric torches and shotguns into McCabe's farm lorry and slowly bumped our way over the pasture and stopped to get our bearings at the standing stone—the so-called fairy's road marker. I scoffed then, but not now! If only we three babes in the wood could have known then what we'd endure in just a matter of hours! We followed the fairy path down into creek beds and up and down gullies, around hedges and still more hedges, all of which were mature plants and already in place when he bought the land. For now they served to separate various unused parcels near to Bottle Hill.

In due course, I could see in the distance the wide mouth of the gorge that was our destination. Upon arriving, McCabe drove a short distance into the opening, but it fast became obvious that the narrowing of the passage prevented further progress by vehicle.

We grabbed our guns, torches, and water bottles, and marched forward into what proved to be an unexpectedly convoluted defile with sharp bends and rough rocky walls. It was noticeably cooler due to the abundance of shade. I suppose we hiked thus for half a mile or so. Then we rounded one sharp bend, and stopped dead at the sight we saw!

Now Holmes, everything I have described in my letters from Bottle Hill up to this point was commonplace enough, but at this moment, as we made that turn in that deeply shadowed gorge, it seemed we were all dropped into a hashish dream or into Alice's Wonderland. From that moment, all the laws of reality ceased to exist, and, frankly, looking back on it, I don't honestly know what was real or not. We rounded that turn—and beheld a small elderly deformed man about four feet tall pacing in front of a small cave entrance with his short arms clasped behind his back. Under his cocked green hat (with a feather in its band) that seemed too big for his big head, he had long unkempt white hair, a grey terribly wrinkled face with large lips and red piercing moving eyes, that never seemed to stop moving, and a sharp pointed nose. Despite his extraordinary appearance, my impression was that he was worried, and thus his pacing. His heavy green fur great coat sported a wide bright red color and was draped over his entire body like a tent so that it was impossible to see his torso, legs, ankles, or feet. In addition, he had a pronounced hump that instantly reminded me of Lon Chaney's hunchback in "The Hunchback of Notre Dame." This hump caused the fellow to bend in a distorted and apparently uncomfortable manner during our entire interview. And before we could in any way wonder aloud at his sudden appearance, the little man spoke in a loud raspy, angry voice:

"There you finally are. I've been hearing you for a devilish long time. You've made enough noise to wake the dead." We were still so shocked that none of us knew how to respond. Then the little man demanded, "Where do you think you're going?"

"We are doing an inspection within the boundaries of my own property," McCabe answered gathering his wits about him, "and just who are you?"

The little man broke into howls of laughter. "*Your* property!" he gasped through his laughter. "Why, man, this and everything that you can see in any direction from the top of that hill" (he pointed in the direction of Bottle Hill, which, when all was said and done, was our real destination) "is *my* land and you are the ones who are trespassing!" McCabe could hardly contain himself he was so outraged by both the creature and his utterances.

"Your land! I suppose you will tell me next that you are a fairy and this is all fairyland."

"As a matter of fact, I am one of the fair people—I am Brian of Knock Magh, honorary possessor and guardian of this enchanted land." He pulled at his red collar proudly and added, "I am an important leprechaun."

I tell you, Holmes, I didn't know what to think.

"Don't be absurd," said McCabe. "You are a dwarf who is either having a great time wasting our time, or you should be institutionalized! Where are you from?"

The fellow who called himself Brian of Knock Magh pointed to the cave behind him and shrugged. "Didn't I just tell you? Here is my home, and all the surrounding land."

"And just why do you claim that?"

"Because the custom is age-old, of course! Who is it that asks such a stupid question?!"

"I already stated clearly, I am the owner of this property—Lynwood Reginald McCabe, by name!"

"Regardless, Lynwood Reginald McCabe, I cannot allow you to proceed!"

Well you can imagine that McCabe didn't take that announcement very well. "Get out of my way, stranger!" he bellowed and took a step. But the little man leaped in front of him gesticulating—flailing his arms with the loose material of his fur coat flapping like a great stork protecting its young.

When McCabe saw that unless he physically injured the little man, they were at a stalemate, Brian of Knock Magh continued. "I wish no malice, and I am not nearly as mischievous as some would believe. Admittedly, some of my kin can rationalize any sort of behavior, but I am of royal blood. I merely wish to warn you to turn back, for there is nothing for you ahead, nothing at all. But I can see that it will be difficult to persuade you. So can't you three gentlemen at least tarry for a moment to keep a lonely leprechaun company for a few moments."

The little man turned toward the cave mouth, and reached for a kind of pot that steamed over a small wood fire there. "Have some refreshment, please. When I heard you coming I heated a traditional drink made from milk, fermented honey, and herbs."

Naturally there was some argument from McCabe, and he looked at me with a look that merged anger and hopelessness. But Brian was very persuasive and Tieg and McCabe and I each accepted from a small platter a tiny cup hardly bigger than a thimble containing some fluid. Under the circumstances, however, none of us went so far as to actually sip the drink that had been offered us by one who was likely a lunatic. The aroma, I will say, was not unpleasant—you will appreciate that honey was the predominant smell.

But this moment of respite didn't last long. McCabe in his impatience, pushed his cup back into the man's grubby hand and motioned us to follow him.

"You cannot go on!" rasped the little man. "I cannot answer for the consequences that will result from your continuing! I warn you! Bottle Hill is not for the likes of you mere mortals. Your lives and many others hang in the balance!"

"Get out of my way, stranger. Not even for your proverbial pot of gold could you dissuade me from my purpose." Brian tried once more to block McCabe. "Get out of my way, I said!" McCabe cried, and the little man in flamboyant green and red finally acquiesced and allowed us passage.

"Do not progress for there is only danger ahead. I beg you! Danger, death and destruction. Fairyland is not for you. Never for humans at all. I cannot answer for what will happen from here on out."

Naturally, we ignored him. Little did any one of us know how right he was!

"Don't say that I didn't warn you!" cried Brian as we rounded another bend.

In consequence of this peculiar episode, I suppose, Tieg picked up a stout stick he found on the trail, which I supposed could be used for as a weapon. His staff ground noisily into the earth. It was the only sound except for our own breathing and of our footsteps, as Brian's cries faded into the distance. The air was preternaturally quiet with no breeze at all. And there was no trace of movement anywhere."

McCabe was especially quiet and seemed lost in thought, and, as the quiet was beginning to trouble me and as I was lagging behind, I quickened my step. It was only about 30 minutes later that the gorge seemed to end abruptly and suddenly we were facing a lofty vertical rock crag at the foot of which was a moraine of boulders, the residue of some ancient landslide.

We moved to examine the cliff which was deep in shadow. It didn't make a lot of sense that a trail, made by fairies of anyone else, would just stop at a wall. Before too long, of course, we found a cave entrance that was thoroughly camouflaged by shadows, jutting rocks, and various seams of colored minerals blending in peculiar manners. If you weren't looking for it, it would have been totally invisible from any angle. In that sense the entrance was expertly veiled. Tieg reached into his pack and pulled out the three electric torches and passed two of them to us. I made sure my revolver was safe in my pocket, and we loosened the straps by which we carried the shot guns. We stepped into the cave and I for one was full of curiosity!

We were still within sight of the light from the tunnel entrance when we came to a crossroads. To both the left and right, glimmering in our lights were veins of red marble, violet limestone, and pink quartz. We could see just within range of the light beam that the left hand tunnel seemed to end in cavern—large or small I could not know—resplendent with pointed and sharp stalagmites meeting stalactites. We could see all this from where we stood, but right then and there we needed to decide which road to take. There was bit of a breeze issuing from the right tunnel, so it was decided that we would turn right.

Just then McCabe reached into his pack and pulled out a ball of twine and smiled. "I was supposing we would find a cave for our trouble, and thought that marking our trail would save us from getting lost. Rather like Hansel and Gretel." He grinned at his joke as he anchored the end of the string under some stones, and we went on. I must admit that we slipped and fell on loose rock several times until we got the hang of it. McCabe stopped every now and again to wrap the string around some protrusion or another. And then, as another challenge, we learned to watch our step for the ground had changed from loose rock to a wet and slippery slimy substance, some sort of moss I suppose. We had not yet entered the world of fungus!

Finally, we reached the end of the tunnel and we were fortunate that we weren't rushing, because the tunnel unexpectedly opened onto a vast grotto with great thick boles of calcium reaching from floor to ceiling, titanic green, yellow, and black pillars that looked for all the world like they were supporting the vast domed vault that itself sparkled nearly miraculously with the reflected lights of thousands of crystals of every imaginable color! Across the floor, far below, we could see a stream meandering through a forest of stalagmites.

In a few minutes, we found a natural and easy enough road that led all the way down to the stream. From the perspective of the cavern floor, we became aware that at several places in the walls were fissures and holes that were doubtlessly entrances into other caverns. Tieg had been ahead of McCabe and me, and now we saw him bending down by the stream. His whole body was aglow with orange light from his electric torch reflecting from the naturally polished surfaces all around us. McCabe knelt too and stared in the direction Tieg was pointing. In a second I too was looking and saw that they were inspecting a small object near the flowing water. Tieg held his torch down and, falling to his knees, he picked the object from the ground and held it up, a small grey mushroom hardly bigger than his thumbnail. Then we saw that there were dozens of them lining the edge of the stream.

McCabe scratched his head and said. "Who would ever think that anything could grow in this cold and pitch-darkness. Maybe, before now, no light has entered this region for millions of years." He wrapped the string around a nearby column as he talked and we then again began following the breeze that fate had made our guide. The vast cavern we were in could be envisioned as a great bubble in Bottle Hill, but it didn't take long to pick our way over the floor to find a tunnel at the far wall. By now we were pretty inured to all the varied material over and through which we marched. Except for the lights that we brought, we were in a world without light, which was a truly frightening thought. We followed the draft for some time and then realized that it was growing stronger. At the same time we became aware that there was light entering the tunnel from some point ahead. Finally we saw the tunnel's end, but unexpectedly I felt a strange pulsation in my ears. We approached the end of the tunnel cautiously, wondering what could possibly be the source of light and air. As we quietly approached, all at once we became aware of furtive movements in the darkness behind us beyond the bends we had just traversed where our light could not penetrate.

These sounds were unexpected and terrifying, but we had few choices. We moved ahead until we came to the end of the road. The tunnel simply stopped dead at the edge of a ledge that overlooked a great canyon deep in the bowels of the earth, far deeper and larger than the great cavern we had left behind. And what we saw there and experienced from that moment on will forever haunt me and plague my dreams forever more! There must be some way to purge my brain of those images and experiences! At least the hideous visions that nearly killed us when exposed to the devil's foot were inside our own heads. Now I don't have that consolation!

In the middle of this new canyon, on the floor, was the source of the light that had attracted us. It was an undulating glowing mass like a living hill. It pulsed and rippled, and waves moved over its jelly-like surface. We stood stunned and stared in horror, not only because of that gargantuan protoplasm-like thing, but because of what we saw surrounding it.

There were hordes of creatures dancing to some impossible tune that we could not hear but pulsed in our ears nonetheless. They danced in a circle around that monstrous mass. There must have been five hundred yellow-green bulbous things, part fungus and part insect, like sponges with spidery legs and huge multifaceted eyes that reflected our lights. It was as though we were hypnotized and commanded not to look away.

The dance never slowed, but suddenly there was a transformation in the rippling mass. Before our eyes, the top half of it began to metamorphose into something else. It began to grow in a vertical direction, like an unheard of yeast was causing it to rise. As it grew taller, it also grew more narrow and began to take on recognizable form almost as though an invisible hand were sculpting clay, but clay whose mass must have been equivalent to an ocean liner! And then it all coalesced into the shape of a stunningly beautiful woman. What we could see was entirely nude but giant, as giant as an oak tree, with a jutting posture something like the figurehead on the bow of a ship.

Then Tieg gasped and screamed, covered his eyes and fell to his knees.

I looked away from this distraction and back at the woman thing. Though my brain told me that she must be something utterly alien, I could feel that she had some power over me and I was mesmerized by her beauty. Part of my mind resisted; it was like a tug-of-war of minds.

Then I forced myself to look down at the lower half of the still undulating mass. Even as I looked on, I could see it change shape too and elongate and turn into a long narrow tube—like a gargantuan grey bladder of a termite queen—out of which flowed a continuous stream of gelatinous infant creatures, smaller versions of those dancing around her!

[My Dear Watson, shame on you for disparaging the egg-dispensing mechanism of our insect friends! But, given the circumstance, I'll not fault you overly, old friend!]

I tried to look away in disgust, but I couldn't and was forced to witness her smile change into a demonic grin, a grin that spread literally from ear to ear across her gigantic face and then fill with a myriad of horrible teeth, so that her head came to resemble some hideous cross between a shark and an alligator.

I must have gone insane then.

All this happened and I was not even aware of the presence of McCabe and, except for his scream, of Tieg. But somehow our senses came back and, as one, we turned around with the goal of running and escaping. We retraced our steps, but we only got perhaps fifty yards when a creature like we had seen dancing move into our path from some unseen cavity in the tunnel wall. This had been the source of the furtive sounds that had caused us some concern earlier. It moved toward us slowly, for it had the equivalent of legs, but its mandibles or talons were stretched out toward us threateningly and in the middle of each was a deadly stinger from which dripped a milky liquid that must have been some sort of venom. It was Tieg who came to his senses first, raised his shotgun, and blasted the thing at point-blank range. But it was immediately replaced with a dozen more. I cannot begin to describe the loathsomeness of these creatures. I said they were like sponges for their bodies were covered with holes an inch and more in diameter, each one of which seemed to open and close rhythmically like fish gills. Its head was on a stalk and reminded me of the head of a praying mantis. And its eyes were more akin to the things that a spider views the world with than anything sane. And I noticed that these things were making sounds! Ponderous popping sounds like huge gelatinous bubbles would make followed by slow sucking sounds. It was then that I saw a yellow mucus or slime extrude from their pores or gills or whatever the holes all over their bodies were.

By now we all had out our guns and were shooting and loading as fast as we could, but it seemed that six or ten replaced every one we slaughtered. All the while I kept trying to tell myself that there were perfectly obvious scientific reasons for everything we were experiencing. But somehow we managed to press forward. I thanked the good Lord that we still clung to our electric torches and that they had lasted all this time. But no sooner had that sentiment entered my mind, of course, one of them began to flicker and I feared that we would soon be fighting these creatures in the pitch dark, which clearly was to their advantage.

Still to my surprise we managed to advance until we were at the cavern with the meandering creek. We had emerged from the tunnel, but all that did was allow the creatures to come at us from still more angles. From everywhere I heard their slobbering, jabbering, bubbling noises. They surrounded us, arms extended, stingers dripping, and we were running out of ammunition!

We were surrounded and doomed!

And then, amazingly, unexpectedly, unbelievably, the strange little man named Brian of Knock Magh, the dwarf who believed he was a leprechaun, simply appeared out of nowhere and, as strange and impossible as this sounds, he bore in his hands a compact submachine gun that chattered and poured bullets seemingly endlessly—in fact, in excess of 600 rounds per minute, I've learned—into the torsos and heads of the creatures attacking us!

The noise must have been deafening in the closed space of the cavern, but we took no notice.

I heard Brian say, "This will only stun them, as they are comprised of mainly holes in the first place. But now you have time to escape. Go left and right and left and left. Then you will see the light of the moon!"

For a time, Brian slowly preceded us shooting a path through the tide of creatures. But at some point he was no longer with us, though we could hear his weapon off in the distance. Then the next thing I remember, I was in the open air with the moon and stars shining in the sky above us. The creatures were not following us. We did not know why, nor did we care. Then I collapsed into a dead heap.

When I woke with the rising of the sun, I saw that McCabe was nearby, sitting up and looking dazed. Tieg was right next to me and rousing much as I. But then his eyes opened and he began screaming and screaming, so that McCabe and I had to hold him down. Not then, but eventually I learned to my horror that the female creature resembled his lost mother as he last remembered her. Poor Boy!

Mechanically, we moved in the direction of McCabe's villa and at one point crossed paths with a party that was searching for us. Back at the house, we placed ourselves in front of a huge fire and curled up into fetal positions, not daring to sleep. We could only quake and gasp for air.

Holmes, I know you will not believe a word of this. I can hardly believe it myself.

Though of course, my first impulse was to get away from that land as fast as humanly possible, I remembered that I had a patient. When I looked in on him, I was astonished and gratified to see that he was conscious, sitting up, eating a little—and that the fungus ring on his chest had noticeably reduced in diameter. I've stayed with McCabe and the O'Nearys for a few more days and continued to administer the castor oil salve, which in fact seems to be just the ticket. Nobody knows for sure of course, but we speculated that there must indeed be some kind of hypnotic connection between the creatures, particularly the hideous mother creature, and some of the things and conditions that folklore has always insisted were subject to the supernatural whims of the Little People and fairies. And Donald O'Neary owes his recovery to that connection being severed when we unexpectedly disrupted the daily routines and habits of the creatures. McCabe and the two O'Nearys tell me that they cannot continue living here and will relocate as soon as they are able. That determination is blunted severely, however, by the knowledge that wherever we go on this planet, there must be more such "cities of gold" where reside the "fair family"! Certainly, the Celtic nations, at the very least, are rife with the things. When McCabe, Tieg, and I compared our experiences, it was manifest that we all experienced the same horror, unaccountably bookended first and last by Brian the leprechaun! I believe that it was me who broached the idea that it may have all been a soul-altering hallucination, but none of us really believe that.

I will post this as soon as I get to the hotel and begin my return journey, which promises to be just as complex and arduous as the journey here.

Your lifelong friend,
John Watson

[Mrs. Hudson—May I impose on you one further secretarial task. Please send a note to the Birmingham Small Arms Company letting them know that I found that their Thompson automatic model BSA 1926 (with ammunition belts) is a triumph of efficiency. Please thank them for their kindness, but also explain that I found it necessary to leave the equipment behind. I am exhausted now. Travel does not suit me any more. I never got so sick and so weary so easily in the past. This damn virus! Oh, one last thing, Mrs. Hudson. You remember that long fox fur coat that you left behind during your last visit because you couldn't fit it in your luggage. I hope it wasn't of sentimental value for I fear it is hopelessly ruined. I'll buy you a new one.]*

---

*Editor's note: The juxtaposition of the foregoing incredible episode with the incident that readers will encounter in the next chapters of this book is provocative. My findings have shown clearly enough that Sherlock Holmes physically descended into a kind of Hell at the very *end* of his career, while, as the reader will see, he seems of have experienced a kind of Heaven at the outset, or *beginning*, of his career. If one were to choose to look at this in the context of the Apostles' Creed—that centuries' old tradition that says Jesus "was crucified, dead, and buried; descended into hell; rose from the dead; and ascended into heaven"—and if one was inclined to take such a comparison seriously, then it is not difficult to imagine that Holmes experienced a kind of upside down variant of Jesus' last days, which could serve to validate the school of thought that suggests time may not necessarily be linear and that effects can precede causes, a theme touched on by both Arthur C. Clarke (especially *Childhood's End*) and Carl Jung in their writings.—T.K.M.

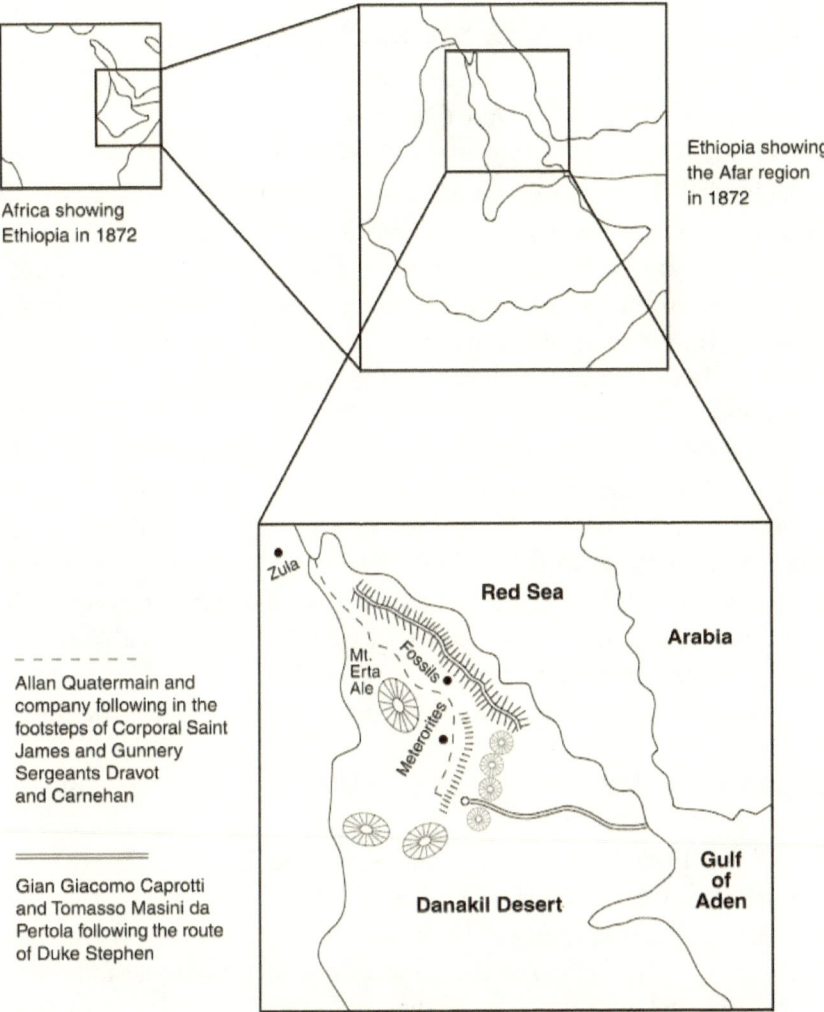

Africa showing
Ethiopia in 1872

Ethiopia showing
the Afar region
in 1872

Zula

Red Sea

Arabia

Mt.
Erta
Ale

Fossils

Meteorites

Gulf
of
Aden

Danakil Desert

Allan Quatermain and
company following in the
footsteps of Corporal Saint
James and Gunnery
Sergeants Dravot
and Carnehan

Gian Giacomo Caprotti
and Tomasso Masini da
Pertola following the route
of Duke Stephen

This simplified map is the result of analyzing data derived from
the Black-Letter parchment of Bors, Count of Mainz; fragments
gleaned from Tomasso's Zoroastro Codex; the account of Corporal
Saint James; the accounts of Gunnery Sergeants Dravot and
Carnehan; and the verbal record of events as set down by Dr.
John Watson.

TKM 2005

CHAPTER TWELVE

The Chapel

We buried Lidenbrock in view of his beloved volcanoes and Burton took exact bearings to provide to the next of kin. In addition, we fashioned a sort of stretcher for Cuff that we would take turns carrying, then gathered our supplies and marched on despite the heat of the day with the purpose of finding some spot where we could find shelter and which we could defend in the event of a renewed attack.

But that was easier said than done in that hellish landscape. We left behind the meteorite field and all the rest of that day dragged ourselves across the shifting, whispering sands. Slowly, the undulating crevasses and washes flattened out and we found ourselves on flat desert again, which just as abruptly ended at the vertical edge of a plateau. We saw that the cliff ran to both our left and right for as far as we could see. The descent was at least two hundred feet, and not even Hans was disposed to attempt the climb down.

Despairingly, we headed southwest along the edge of the plateau, all the time keeping an eye over our shoulders, half expecting the Danakil to strike again, and also looking ahead for a passage down. Our march was made a little easier at this point because the plateau sloped gently in our direction of travel with the result that the vertical drop to the desert floor steadily lessened.

It was toward nightfall, then, that we saw a tiny gleam of light ahead of us. It was the setting sun reflecting off a polished surface such as metal or glass.

Hans, who tended to act as our scout and was some distance ahead of us, saw it too. He ran ahead and investigated, peering over the edge of the cliff. Then all at once, he began to shout for our attention and jump around like a monkey, pointing down and jabbing with a finger. When we arrived by him and looked down where he pointed, we were amazed by the most incongruous and oddest of sights. Down below, out there in the middle of the desert, built on the edge of a wind-swept ravine, there was a sort of church or monastery mounted with a lacy delicate-looking orthodox Christian cross, the point of which rose just far enough above the cliff to catch the sun and thus attract our attention.

There were steep stairs—about ten feet wide from edge to edge—hewn into the yellow sandstone cliff face. I noticed that they were smooth and worn down in the center, as though they had been in use for centuries. Having no choice, we clambered down. The reasons were simple enough: first of all because there was no where else to go, and second, Sergeant Cuff was clearly in need of more medical attention than we could provide in the wild, and perhaps this place would be able to help. Indeed, perhaps the residents of this place would know something of the other matters we sought. Also, to be honest, we went because we were all, every one of us, full of curiosity. I suppose we made a great deal of noise as we descended. Certainly, it was a cumbersome business hauling Cuff's stretcher down.

It was only natural then that when we touched the floor of the ravine, there were waiting for us four very formal looking fellows. All were quite black, but three were older, sporting trimmed beards like white, curly wool, wearing long purple robes and matching caps that were perfectly flat on top. The younger, but nonetheless middle-aged, man was beardless but otherwise dressed the same. They all grinned from ear to ear and seemed quite happy to see us. They were standing before the gate of a tall wall that enclosed the monastery.

As our two groups stood facing one another, taking stock of one another, I could see inside through the gate, that is to say into the further side of the wall, a most wonderful little garden filled with roses of every imaginable color.

"Well, Quatermain, aren't you going to speak to them," Richard Holmes ventured in a manner that I considered brusque.

In fact, though, at that very moment I was wondering to myself which language would be best suited when the younger man spoke first. He held out his hand to me in the Western fashion and spoke in English. Utterly amazed, I took his hand, and he said, "Gentlemen, welcome to the Chapel of the Immaculate Heart. I am Tabot Haile Mariam, and these are my brother priests. We are of the Order of Sainte Mariam the Divine. We have been aware of your coming for some days and are full of questions as to what would bring you here to us in the desert, which I daresay is, and I can say this with some authority, without doubt the most terrible spot on earth. Welcome."

"You are most kind," I responded, seeing that the Englishmen and the American woman in my party were all grinning with relief (as I myself felt, though mystified) at hearing our own language spoken.

"Ah, you are wondering how it is that I speak English well. That is simple. When I was a child, some other Englishmen much like yourselves were seeking the source of the Nile and stumbled on my village, which was on the northern shore of Lake Tana. They tarried there for two years studying our way of life and religion and, being a quick study and nimble, I became their go-between or messenger."

This exchange had taken only a moment, and I thought that his explanation seemed reasonable enough. He was about to say something more when it seemed they all noticed the wounded Cuff on the stretcher for the first time. Two of the older men suddenly became totally solicitous and began to minister to him at once without saying a word. Cuff, who was conscious, tried to say something, but one of these priests hushed him by placing a finger over his parched lips. They lifted the stretcher and gingerly carried Cuff through the gate.

It was then that a most unexpected and, thinking back on it, a most wondrous, though predictable, thing happened. The two priests had only gotten about halfway across the rose garden, when suddenly their patient managed to cry out. "Stop!" he called. "Stop, I say. I must see this place!" You can imagine how startled the priests were. In fact, they almost dropped the stretcher, I think. But Tabot quickly translated, and they set the stretcher gently enough on a sort of rock bench that happened to be there.

Cuff was struggling to lift his head and look all around. His face seemed to glow, which was odd given the circumstances, and then he started to rave: "What a rosery!* A rosery fit for a god. Just the right exposure, yes, south and sou'-west. How do you achieve

---

* Editor's note: That is, a rose garden.—T.K.M.

adequate water in this hellish place? I must commend the gardener." He craned his head up and around, and even though the struggle was apparent and you could almost feel his pain, he ignored all protestations and peered around in as much of a circle as he could. "Ah. Even here, there is clear sign of advanced civilization. See the shape of this rosery—it's a circle set in a square. That is a fine design. And the paths between the beds . . . . Oh, I see they are crushed rock . . . well, I suppose that must do in this region, but beware! Roses do not like being surrounded by rock. It is hard on them."

Thus he waxed about the infrastructure of the rosery for a time, and then fell silent. It was just as the priests were about to pick up his stretcher again that he blurted out once more. "See the colors, whites and reds and yellows. And, oh, there are the blush roses. They mix so well together, don't they?"

At that he seemed to drift off, and the priests were able to continue with their task of moving Sergeant Cuff indoors.

My emotions were many, I must say. Perhaps it was not too late to save the man. But I put all that aside for the time being and turned my attention to Tabot. "Yes, Tabot, your desert does test the most hardened and intrepid. Of that there can be no doubt. In fact, we have only a few hours ago been battling for our lives, even burying one of our own, and some of us have wounds that need to be tended to, though I daresay that the one you have already taken in, Sergeant Cuff by name, is already being helped by your doctors."

"True enough," said Tabot. "We will help him as well as we can, though I cannot promise anything. Now, tell me. What on earth brings you here?"

"That is a very long story, I fear," was my reply. "I don't mean to seem rude, but the telling of it should wait until we are rested. For now, let me just say that we are explorers seeking knowledge."

Tabot chuckled at this and said, "There is a saying in your world, I think, something about getting blood from a turnip. That, I think, is the amount of knowledge you can get from these sands," gesturing out across the desert. He said something to the remaining priest and they shared a good laugh. "Do come in and refresh yourselves, rest from your weariness. Our water is your water. I can't speak for turnips and blood—" (here he broke into a wide smile)

"—but, by the grace of God, water is abundant here in this spot—a true miracle from the Blessed Mother. You will find that we are rich, therefore, rich with fruitful crops and numerous sheep and goats."

Hans had skulked up during this interchange and he whispered to in my ear in the Dutch-based Afrikaner language. "Baas, remember the story of the spider and the fly. This is a pretty mirage complete with four smiling spiders."

Really, I was becoming impatient with his ceaseless negativity, but I said, "And what do you propose I do, be still more rude and refuse their hospitality? Besides, we are grown men and well armed and we will be able to protect ourselves if there is trouble."

"Baas, you are no doubt right and far be it from me to suspect your judgment, but still a little voice inside me worries that our gateway to the Big Baas's house in the sky may be through the belly of a cannibal."

At this point I chose to ignore my servant, whose protestations had attracted the curiosity of our hosts. I sidestepped the issue by happily accepting the invitation to enter and refresh ourselves.

The priests turned and entered their grounds, and the ten of us gratefully followed, though I must admit that a verse from the Scriptures popped into my brain at that moment, "Enter ye in at the strait gate: For wide is the gate, and broad is the way, that leadeth to destruction . . . ."[40]

In any event, of course, having no foreknowledge of the astonishing things that would befall us, we entered and found that the rosery included a most delightful well, from which we drank our fill of clean, fresh water. Thus we rested for a while longer in that wonderful little garden with the fragrance of roses filling the air.

Once situated thus, I noticed that the monastery structure was actually two structures. The building to the left as we faced them was the smaller and was in fact the priests's living quarters. The larger, on the right, was the chapel, or church.

Eventually we were led into the spare interior of the former, where we gratefully doffed our kits and sat on the crude benches that surrounded an equally crude table.

Young Will Scott then asked Tabot a question: "Sir, when was this church constructed? It seems so odd to have a church isolated so, in the middle of the desert."

"As a matter of fact, construction began in the year 1500—a nice round year, don't you think? Our order is one that sought isolation, the better to meditate and seek revelations from God—away from the distractions of the world."

Huxley spoke: "My good man, if that is the case, we are sorry that we have arrived on the scene and disrupted your meditative way of life."

"Think nothing of it. We also consider ourselves a holy oasis for weary travelers. Though, of course, we have few enough of those!"

"Tabot," I inquired. "You said that you were informed of our arrival. By whom?"

"Oh! By the Afar—or the Danakil, as they are known outside this land, but Afar is what they call themselves. They have been monitoring your movements since your ship arrived at Annesley Bay. A hardy but terribly mean-spirited people, as I'm afraid you have found out the hard way. They had promised us that they would leave you undisturbed, but I suppose the temptation to raid and perhaps acquire a few trophies—" here he couldn't help but smile sardonically "—were more than they could bear."

"I suppose entertainment options are limited here," Huxley responded. "Still, we did lose a man, as Quatermain said, and had to bury him yonder."

"We regret their behavior terribly and apologize most profusely," Tabot went on. "I am glad that there was no other loss of life among your party." Then he hesitated. "I fear for your friend Cuff, though."

Richard Burton ventured a question at that time. "Tabot, how do you and your priest colleagues manage to avoid becoming, yourselves, souvenirs of your spies?"

"For centuries there has been an agreement, a time-honored agreement. They serve as our eyes and ears and we pave the way for them to a higher world, as we have touched some of them a bit with matters of the spirit. But, I'm afraid that this breach in our agreement causes us some concern. My brothers and I will deliberate on that and decide how we will respond." Whereupon he left us to ourselves for a time.

Then young Scott, who, if I haven't said so already, was by far the most restless of our party, stood and paced about the table. All the while he was muttering to himself, then finally he left, nearly launching himself out of the room, in the direction that Tabot had gone.

Before long he returned with the priest in tow. I was frankly amazed that young Scott would have the gall to behave in such a manner in the establishment of those who were even then giving us succor. Nevertheless, he spoke, "I'm sorry, but I am filled to the brim with curiosity about the chapel and I have asked Tabot to allow us to enter it and observe its special features."

For his part, Tabot seemed unperturbed about this further imposition into his life and life style. He began to lead us to the chapel, or church, proper, and suddenly all seven of my charges rose at once and all but marched after the priest, with Hans, Bayushtiak, and myself following. How and when, I wondered, had I lost control?

The church was circular, and in a moment we found ourselves on a walkway that circled it. This walkway was open at the sides but covered by an awning of thatch. Tabot walked us around this path explaining that he and his brother priests used this area in particular to sing hymns to God as they walked in endless circles around the building. We came to an opening in the outside wall and entered. For a brief moment I became disoriented. It was as though I had stepped into an art gallery of the British Museum. This was an enclosed inner circuit or walkway (the *k'ane mahlet*), which in turn circled an interior chamber. What had taken me aback was that the walls of the *k'ane mahlet* were literally covered with paintings of the Virgin Mary in every conceivable pose. There she was alone in the desert, alone in the jungle, surrounded by handmaidens in the desert, surrounded by handmaidens in the jungle, adored in the city, adored by animals, bathing under waterfalls, with the baby Jesus and without, with angels and without, clothed and unclothed. Some were portraits that reminded me of Leonardo's *Mona Lisa* (at which I began to wonder . . . .), and some were landscapes both barren and verdant. There were hundreds of these, and I can say with confidence that all the members of my party were clearly as amazed as I was. Perhaps the most amazing thing of all was the outstanding *quality* of many of these works.

One painting in particular captured the attention of Richard Holmes. I was standing next to him, so I can relate that he was gazing at each of the paintings with great interest, but when his eyes came to this one, I could hear him gasp. His attention was riveted to the piece. He leaned over and examined it and whispered, "My God, Quatermain, it's a da Vinci original. I'm sure of it. An unknown, uncataloged da Vinci painting. It's astonishing. This is not simply a style similar to da Vinci's, I'm sure. It's authentic. It must be! How on earth did it get here?"

The picture in question showed a beatific image of a standing child-like Mary, her head surrounded with a lacy halo. She had on a kind of shawl, black in color, closed at her bosom with a broach in the shape of a rose. In her outstretched right hand there was a scroll tied with a red ribbon. And in her left hand was a chalice, which I supposed was some sort of rendition of the Holy Grail or some such.

"But that's not all, Quatermain! Look *where* she is standing!" I observed that the artist had chosen to place his Mary in the middle of what was obviously a large and luxuriously appointed library, but one that housed scrolls rather than books. These scrolls were piled in cubbies of which there were three or four dozen or so visible in the background. Holmes's excitement, of course, drew all the others closer and each of them in turn became excited at the genius so evident in the piece—a piece hanging on a wall in an unknown monastery in the middle of an awful desert in a country that Europeans for the most part were barely aware of.

Holmes turned to Tabot. "Please, can you tell me the provenance of these paintings, and in particular this one."

Tabot hesitated. It seemed he was taken off guard by the question. "Please forgive me if I don't have an immediate response. We do, you understand, live with these renderings every day and don't often think about their origins, merely grateful that we have been chosen by God to be their caretakers."

He paused to reflect for a few moments, then continued. "This church began construction in the year 1500 and was finished shortly afterward. As soon as it was completed, all the Christian churches of Ethiopia and, in particular, one of the churches in Axum, St. Mary of Zion far to the north, presented to us, or to this chapel, much of this collection for the glory of Jesus and of his mother, Mariam, daughter of God. The remainder have made their way here over the years, as our existence is not unknown to the other orthodox churches of the land."

Holmes was persistent, however. "This painting showing a collection of scrolls, I was wondering what could have been the model."

Tabot hesitated for the briefest of moments, then shrugged. "No doubt it was inspired by God in the highest."

"I'm sure," muttered Holmes.

Certainly all these paintings triggered a number of thoughts and emotions in the various members of my party, but the upshot of it was that we were still in the dark as much as before.

In any event, we elected to continue our little tour of the church. We came to another opening—this one in the innermost wall of the *k'ane mahlet*—and entered yet another interior chamber. This proved to be still another walkway surrounding yet another interior chamber. This walkway was called the *keddest*, which Tabot explained was a place dedicated to prayer and communion. The central chamber beyond we learned was called the *mak'das*, and it was there that the Holy of Holies was located.

The Holy of Holies was exactly what it sounds like. Only the most senior priests ever could enter the area. This is where something immensely holy called *tabots* were kept. I couldn't help but note the similarity to our host's name, but Tabot avoided answering my questions and it was only after subsequent determined effort that I got him to explain that he was named after the *tabots*, and that they were replicas of the tablets God presented to Moses— that is to say, the stone tablets on which God wrote the Ten Commandments. He also explained that every Ethiopian church was constructed in the same manner, and it had been so since time immemorial—the most holy *tabots* housed within a central Holy of

Holies surrounded by concentric circular walkways, so that if seen from above, the whole arrangement would look like a target with the Holy of Holies as the bull's-eye.

We wound back around through the circuits and exited the church and soon were back at our living quarters. As soon as we were left alone, we jumped at the chance to compare notes, to theorize, and the like. I even caught sight of Hans and Bayushtiak off in a corner speaking quietly between themselves (Hans seldom deigned to share his opinions with anyone but me).

In due course, a simple but filling meal made up of honey-sweetened flat bread, onions, and goat's milk cheese was brought in, and eventually we tired of talk and rested for the duration of the night. Cuff, in the meantime, was still being tended to, or nursed, by the priests in an area reserved for such medical requirements.

CHAPTER THIRTEEN

The Cleft in the Cliff

The next morning, after we had freshened ourselves, a messenger arrived saying that Tabot wanted to see us immediately. In time, we had congregated outside in the rosery since our group was rather large and all the rooms large enough to accommodate us were in use by the monks and priests.

Tabot arrived and greeted us. Then he said the most extraordinary things. "Gentlemen and my lady," he began. "While the Afar had alerted us to your coming, and while we are bound to aid you as necessary, to be frank, your presence here—especially the number of you—is creating a larger problem than expected, as it imposes on our way of life. Last night I prayed upon the problem and in a dream three angels came to me in the form of the Three Kings. Gaspar was the head angel in the dream and he said that my guests were very special and that I should ask them (that is to say, you) for a token, simple as it may be, and that if you had the correct token, then you were to be escorted into the presence of the Holy Mother herself, which is a very rare honor indeed." As you can imagine, at the mention of the name Gaspar, Holmes's and my eyes locked meaningfully.

Someone, I think it was Burton, asked what he meant by a "token" and also, in an uncharacteristically rude fashion, to my mind, what he meant by "escorted into the presence of the Holy Mother," and just who was she?

Unperturbed, Tabot responded, "Why, the token is the key by which you will see the Holy Mother, and the Holy Mother is the mother of God, of course, and you will see her because it is her wish, should you have the token. Are there any more questions?" And then he waited.

Hans whispered about then, "Baas, what is this? It was so simple before—hello and good-bye, have some food, rest a while, but now he is talking about a holy sign, which is different. Even your Predikant father wouldn't talk the way that this priest with a face like granite is doing. And certainly I would rather not see any Holy Mother for fear she might be real."

I for one wasn't concerned whether this mysterious mother was real or not. I was more concerned that it sounded suspiciously as though we were about to be taken somewhere against our own free will. I was about to say as much when the priest held out his hand palm up. This was enough to quiet me.

We all started looking at one another muttering, "A token, what could be a token?" I was thinking that it could be just about anything, from one of Miss Mitchell's hair combs to the cork from Hans's beloved square-face that he liked to sniff and that he kept in lieu of the actual bottle, when that self-same Miss Mitchell inquired, "Perhaps your angels were referring to one of my rocks from the sky?" Tabot merely continued to stand with his hand out. She then inquired in an impatient tone, "Well then, can you please give us an idea of what we are supposed to show you?" Tabot was still silent. Then Peachy Carnehan spoke, "Say, Huxley, I have a notion. More 'an likely what he's lookin' for is something out of the ordinary. Anyone could show a bullet or, say, a compass or handkerchief. What about one of those remarkable bits of bone you found out there in the desert by that cave. Give that a try."

Frowning, Thomas Huxley then unpacked some of the rolls of cotton he had used to store his fossils and unrolled one very carefully. As he was doing this, Will Scott came close, and, forgoing their estrangement for the moment, helped him. In due course, a finger bone became visible and Scott carefully picked it up and showed it to Tabot, who reached for it. But Scott moved it out of harms way. "Look," he said, "but don't touch." At first Tabot was taken aback, but he settled down and bent forward to peer at the bone. Then he grinned and turned smartly around and started walking away from us through the rose bushes, heading toward the entrance of the wall that surrounded the church. When he got there, he motioned for us to follow.

Hans and I looked at one another and shrugged. It appeared that the bone was the key, though at the time I could not fathom why. Later on, I realized that it made sense.

We were soon escorted once more to the open walkway that surrounded the church and where the priests even then were walking in endless circles around the perimeter of the church. From there we were taken into the *k'ane mahlet* where we had seen all the beautiful Madonna paintings housed. It was here that I first became aware of an extremely pungent incense (that later I was to learn was frankincense) and from there into the inner communion circuit, the *keddest.* In the *keddest,* Tabot paused and waited till he had all our attentions.

He pointed to a curtain that clearly entered into another chamber. "This," he said, "is as far as any uninitiated has ever gotten, for beyond this is the *mak'das,* the Holy of Holies where the *tabots* rest, the tablets of Moses." At this moment, several more priests joined us, and Tabot very dramatically and deliberately thrust aside the curtain and bade us enter. I wish I could tell you with some certainty what I saw in that small chamber, but in fact, the incense was so heavy that vision was impaired. Having been told several times that this was the Holy of Holies itself where the *tabots* were kept, I strained to get a glimpse of the sacred objects or their container, but I could see nothing. Whether they were obscured or even removed I never learned. When we were all inside, Tabot motioned to one of the priests who pushed aside another curtain revealing a space no larger than a closet. The priest then pulled aside the rug that was there, thus revealing a wooden door in the floor, which door proved to be heavy if the man's struggles to open it were warranted. This, in turn, exposed stairs leading down. Some of us expressed considerable concern about what this was all about, but we nonetheless let ourselves be led docilely down the stairs, through a short tunnel and then up again, where we emerged into a sort of cave.

That cave opened into what I immediately understood was a cleft in the cliff wall beside which the church had been built. I was already familiar with something of the sort since the horrible Black Kloof, the home of Zikali, "The Opener of Roads," was entered by way of a similar breach in the face of a precipice.

Light poured down from the sun above into what would have appeared to be a crevasse from above, and a well-worn earth path lay before us. With Tabot leading the way, we ten remaining explorers marched forward. We rounded a bend in the path, and the wall suddenly flowered with decorative murals—paintings, carvings, and friezes—depicting various aspects of the Madonna similar to those we had seen in the *k'ane mahlet.*

Holmes was again and quickly beside himself in ecstasy. He reached out to touch one of the figures. But before his hand had moved a foot in the direction of the wall, one of the priests had quickly moved and grabbed his elbow. The normally congenial-appearing priest suddenly wore an ugly scowl, startling Holmes and myself—for I was next to Holmes and was able to observe the priest's expression—so that we both caught our breath. The man's visage was positively horrific!

Thus warned off, we proceeded along the path keeping our hands to ourselves. For perhaps half an hour we moved along the path. Sometimes it was extremely narrow so that we could only progress by removing our kits and sidling along sidewise. Hans, Will Scott, Miss Mitchell, Carnehan and myself had no problem, being either small or thin in stature. Burton, Huxley, Holmes, Dravot, and Bayushtiak found these intervals rather tight going. Other times the path opened up so that the distance between vertical walls might have been as much as ten yards. Above, I was happy to see that the sky still shown clearly through the crevasse.

I couldn't help but wonder what our fates would be if an earthquake happened to hit just then. Would the walls move in and flatten us, or would they come crumbling down—with the same effect but from a different direction?

Finally, we saw light ahead of us and I could see that we were approaching the end of the crack in the plateau. A moment later I saw that it opened up into a kind of wide gorge. A bit more and I stepped into the open and I was so overwhelmed with images that I hardly know where to begin describing them.

CHAPTER FOURTEEN

The Fountain

Totally unexpectedly I saw a crowd of people, perhaps thirty in number, dressed as from another era—my first thought was of Biblical times. Women mainly, with some men and children, most wearing brightly colored striped robes or ankle-length skirts. They were standing, talking or strolling in a kind of village square with a pool and fountain in the center. From the center of the pool rose a statue of a young woman with a great jar in her arms, and from the jar water poured into the pool, splashing noisily. There was something joy-filled and mysterious about the statue and something else, too, but all this was quickly swept from my mind as events unfolded.

Beyond the square, I saw a compact community with connected buildings built of stone. From our vantage point, we could see a main thoroughfare made of rough flagstones held together with mortar leading from the square down, around, and past countless functional stone edifices until it disappeared into the distance.

All this I saw in an instant, and the next instant, the normal harmony of the place was disturbed as you would expect when the priests from the cleft appeared with ten strangers—eight of European origin (one of which was a woman), a Zulu, and Hans.

A woman with authority in her bearing was approaching us. She walked right up to Tabot and they spoke, using what I assumed was the region's Coptic tongue. She was perhaps middle aged, with a cragged but thoroughly noble face. Over her head—which I could see was crowned with the richest of chestnut colored hair—she wore a loosely fitting covering of the deepest blue. The overall effect was quite wonderful. She had been sitting on the edge of the pool in quiet discussion with a group of other younger women when her attention had been drawn to the passage opening where we emerged.

This woman and Tabot had stepped aside some distance and continued to confer. There was much gesticulation with their faces

The first sight of the fountain from the mountain cleft:
"From the center of the pool rose a statue of a young woman with a great
jar in her arms, and from the jar water poured into the pool."

turning in our direction numerous times and all manner of other signs to indicate that our sudden appearance was not altogether welcome.

Eventually they both approached us—or rather me. The priest introduced the woman as Ruth, who was a teacher, and told us that the roles of himself and his fellow priests had been satisfied according to the laws of the matter that had been set down more than four centuries before at the time the church had been established. And without further ado, that whole bunch turned and returned the way we had come, and we wouldn't see them again for some time.

Ruth then faced me and spoke. Her language was quite incomprehensible to any of us, even to the inexhaustible Burton. Then approaching it rather academically, Holmes and Burton conferred between themselves and decided it must be a form of Coyne, the ancient popular form of Greek that long since had faded from the planet—thereby putting to rest my own rather humble speculations as to the nature of the language. In lieu of using her language, between us we tried English, French, Zulu, Dutch (that is to say Afrikaans), and several others to no avail, and all to the clear frustration of all involved.

There came a moment when all the reasonable options seemed to have been used up, and we sunk into a long silence, our collective mood being that of defeat.

Then Burton snapped his fingers! Facing Ruth, he launched into another language that was vaguely familiar to me, probably one of the Romance languages. Suddenly Ruth's face lit up. She took Burton by the hand and took him aside where they whispered together and it was perfectly clear that they were in fact communicating quite well.

When Burton returned to our group, he was grinning ear to ear. "Holmes," he said, "you told us that Salai and Tomasso ventured into these parts in the past. Suddenly I realized that it wouldn't be out of the question if Italian had some currency here."

When Ruth rejoined us, she, too, seemed quite pleased. This time she addressed our group while focusing on Burton. She opened her mouth and out emerged a slow and guttural, yet perfectly recognizable (so Burton affirmed) and passable Italian! Then Holmes himself made inquiries in the modern form of the language, which he had a passing knowledge of, and, eventually, a sort of general conversation was established.

During this interlude, one of the first questions put to her, by me, if I recall correctly, through Burton, was one which had the goal of affirming the assumptions that some of my little group seemed to prize so highly: Why could she speak Italian?*

She replied that centuries before, they had been visited by two great men who spoke in this manner and these men had tarried among them for months and spent some of that time sharing their language. Even after they left, by instruction from the Holy Mother—who at the time I took to be some sort of priestess—Ruth's people had handed the language down from novice to novice in preparation for the great day when it would be needed again. In fact, she was extremely disappointed in herself for not immediately recalling the age-old writ that required her people to use the Tongue of the Messengers, as she called it, when confronted by strangers. That we were the first such strangers in some 400 years did not seem to matter.

Nonetheless, she seemed to quickly get over her lapse, then gestured at us in our well-traveled and unfamiliar clothes and giggled. Holmes extracted from her that in her mind's eye she had always envisioned that if she ever needed to use the Tongue of the Messengers in her lifetime, it would be to individuals resembling the great prophets, not to a ragtag group of heathens!

We Europeans smiled at this and I asked Holmes to convey our gratitude and other various courtesies that I had learned over the years after much travel were always well regarded regardless of the culture or level of civilization.

She accepted the compliments and bowed slightly, gesturing with her arm to follow her.

It was at this point that Hans, who had been unnaturally quiet during this whole interchange, chose to speak, this time in Dutch.

---

* Editor's note: The necessity of Ruth and her people knowing Italian obviously preceded the Italian occupation of Ethiopia from 1936 to 1941 by centuries.—T.K.M.

"Baas! Mayhap I have been thinking that we are even now within a great hole in the rock, a hole much like the holes made by worms in apples, and just as the worm is in the power of the great beast that presses the apple within its jaws, we are likely to be flattened if the rocks come tumbling down or if the crowds choose to rise up."

"Old fool!" was my response. "Do you think I have not thought of these things? But what can we do? We are here now, and do I need remind you that we are here largely because of your proddings yonder, back in Durban? Nevertheless, though this is all very strange, in its own way it is wondrous and I for one am interested to know what happens next."

Hans appeared to be somewhat chastened by my retort, though, as usual, he needed to have the final word: "Ah, Baas, that may be so, but please don't forget that an apple infested with worms is a rotten apple!"

I suppose I must have looked at him particularly fiercely for he turned on his heels and I lost sight of him, though, of course, I knew in my heart that drunk or sober, angry or not, he would never be far from my side.

Ruth ignored this small drama and motioned for us to follow her. She took us through the throng of people, who parted before us, chattering, much as I suppose the waters parted before Moses. She led us out of the town square and onto the road (which was the only one I ever noted aside from a few paths). This road was bounded on both sides as far as one could see with buildings, that is to say dwellings, and as we passed I saw many women and children poking their heads out of the small windows or watching us from the roofs, on either side. These were one-story structures made of slabs of rock mortared together. Doors were not prominent I noticed but I saw that between every two or three houses there was a narrow alley, which led me to believe that the doors were on the side of the house opposite the street, that is to say in the backs of the houses, which I learned later was a correct assumption.

We walked thus down the main road, which twisted and turned down the middle of what amounted to a great gorge cut through the mountain, for perhaps somewhat more than a mile. Though the gorge was clearly mostly of natural design, there were many indications that certain areas were enlarged or shaped by the hand of man. Perhaps such areas were the quarries from which the towns people acquired their housing materials. I never did ask. Accompanying us the whole length were the homes and structures that made up the village, or perhaps town would be a better word, and of course most of the population, which we learned comprised some two thousand individuals, turned out to get the best view of us.

[And, gentlemen, now that I'm recalling all this for the first time in years, I'm remembering that it was while we were marching along this route that a strange thing happened.] Will Scott, who had remained perfectly nondescript since entering the gorge, suddenly took off and began running around in a most comical manner, darting off to this side, and then over to the other. The children in the crowds on either side laughed merrily to see him so, but he didn't seem to notice or mind. Whatever he was doing, he was totally absorbed. I kept an eye on him as we walked along, trying to understand his actions, but the more I watched, the more perplexed I became. This lasted perhaps five to seven minutes, then ceased as quickly as it had begun, when he rejoined our group and seemed as placid as ever. Naturally, it was Hans who solved the mystery.

"Yes, Baas, for a time I thought for sure the beardless one had somehow become possessed by a witch and that he was sniffing out the ghosts that must haunt this place. As you know, for we have known many such, these great caverns that have no roofs are full of ghosts, for spirits are easily confused and it is hard for them to find their way out. I watched and listened closely and finally began to hear the voices of these ghosts. Baas! They didn't cry out or moan or shriek as ghosts do. They buzzed. Whoever heard of buzzing ghosts? So I stayed close to him, as close as I could, trying to see with his eyes. Then, squinting, I chanced to see one of the ghosts, and then another, and another. But they weren't ghosts, Baas! They were bees. The pup was chasing bees!"

I must tell you, the expression on Hans's face as he announced his conclusion was perfectly priceless. My poor Hottentot servant simply could not imagine what would prompt an otherwise sound human being to behave thus. And, frankly, I couldn't either! Nonetheless, once I had put two and two together, it was clear that Hans had gotten to the root of the problem. Indeed, now that it was called to my attention, I saw that the gorge was in fact more than ordinarily full of the little creatures, intent at their busy tasks and minding their own businesses. Still, I had my own pride, so I pretended to mull over Hans's findings as we walked, then made a great show of agreeing with him. Of course, I intended to ask Scott about it later, but thereafter so much happened so fast that the incident entirely slipped my mind . . . until now all these years later! One thing I can say for certain, though, thinking back on the man, is that Scott was, all in all, a most curious fellow!

Be that as it may, at the end of the road, Ruth finally stopped before a temple-like structure that was built on a gentle slope so that it rose in tiered gardens up from the street. I could see through the gate and beyond and saw that encircling the structure was a small courtyard comprising still more gardens with convenient stone benches to rest upon, not unlike the monastery rosery that had so affected poor Cuff. However, Ruth bade us not to enter the interior.

Instead, she asked us to follow her a bit more and she took us a little distance off to the right and up a ramp to a separate building, which proved to be a sort of community building. We were led into an open central court, where we were met by attendants who took charge of us as Ruth went her own way and disappeared. The robed attendants led us to rooms that were distributed among us as follows: young Will Scott and I shared one room, Holmes and Huxley another, and Hans and Bayushtiak another. Miss Mitchell was allocated a room to herself and Burton and the two soldiers shared another. In addition we were shown where we could bathe.

Not that this distribution really mattered at all, for as soon as we were left alone, we all gathered in one of the rooms, that of Burton and the soldiers, as it was somewhat larger than the others, to discuss this totally unexpected turn of events.

Oh! I may have forgotten to mention that as we followed Ruth through the gorge, we learned that this community—hidden away behind the Holy of Holies of the Chapel of the Immaculate Heart and secreted within a great chasm visible only to the birds in the sky—bore the name Sinai.

CHAPTER FIFTEEN

The Girl

You can imagine our riot of talking when finally we were alone. Our experiences were astounding. Burton was certain we had discovered a hidden city of Hebrews who had been cut off from advancing civilization perhaps two thousand years ago. He and Holmes discussed and argued about these people's language, their architecture, their manner of dress, where they could have obtained the bright dyes and materials for their clothes, and any other detail that entered their minds. There were, however, two observations that troubled them deeply. They could not understand the apparent matriarchal tenor of the culture—whereas Hebrews were supposed to be typically and steadfastly patriarchal. Also, they were baffled by the presence of a statue of a young woman in the village square. Old Hebrews, they said, would not have—indeed, could not have—allowed such a "graven image" in their midst.

Finally, in the evening, a messenger came and bade us follow her, and we were are all escorted to a hall in the council building. We had no choice but to stand as there was no place to sit in the spare surroundings. In time, there came the low throbbing of a bell, ringing over and over again. After nearly fifty interminable rings, it ceased and a procession of thirteen women, one of whom was Ruth, marched in—or to be more accurate, twelve women and a girl, and the girl was being held aloft in a kind of litter carried by half of the women. The procession was well practiced and I felt I was watching a performance at the theater or even one of the well-choreographed ceremonies of the Zulu kings.

The women who were not carrying the litter moved to positions around a kind of raised dais. The others set the litter gently before the ramp that led to the dais, then joined their sisters and arranged themselves in the manner of a royal guard. The girl moved quickly up to the bench, sat primly down, turned, and looked out over us all. The entire retinue turned to face the girl with looks of obvious reverence and a great hush fell over the hall. The girl continued to look at us curiously for a time, and I tried to spot some sort of shyness or nervousness as you would expect to see in a young girl in similar circumstances, but in vain for she seemed totally poised. When she had her fill of looking at us, she stood and we were able to get our first really good look at her.

I could hardly believe it: There was before us just a bit of a girl barely four feet tall with a complexion like fresh cream, standing quite calmly. She wore a simple white cloth robe with a belt of golden fabric, and over her shoulders was a blue shawl. I could see ringlets of black lustrous hair falling from under the white scarf-like cloth, or veil, that covered her head. In her hands she held roses, the fragrance of which I perceived even though we were some distance from her. Was she some sort of leader? I thought of India's Dalai Lama* who, I had heard, always began his rule as a child.

Our group stood respectfully before and below her. Then she opened her mouth and spoke. And the voice that emerged from her mouth was the purest most crystalline expression of a human voice that I had ever heard. The voice was a girl's to be sure, but it was also a woman's. It sounded as though it came from above and beyond the firmament and from below our feet from some sort of vast hidden cavern at the same time. It sounded like all these things at once, and what it said was, "My good people, thank you for coming" in English! "I have been expecting you for quite some time."

[At this juncture, gentlemen, note that Bayushtiak, who had been a participant in all this only in the most peripheral manner and who had been watching it all with a jaundiced eye, was clearly taken aback by the ethereal voice emanating from the girl *in what I was to learn later was his own language!*]

The girl smiled at each of us and her smile was truly like sunlight radiating upon us. "I am Mariam," she said. Then she gestured around her saying, "And these are my people. I have brought you here to Sinai from your far off homes [hearing this, several of us

---

* Editor's note: [sic] Quatermain was geographically close. The Dalai Lama is the spiritual leader of Tibet, who, as it happens, is at the center of the first memoir in this volume presented as *Sherlock Holmes on the Roof of the World*—T.K.M.

looked quizzically at one another with raised eyebrows] to share with you, and through you to the rest of the world, knowledge of *the holiest place on earth!* I say again, *the holiest place on earth!*

"Long have men sought treasures such as the cup from which they believed Christ drank, which is what I caused you to believe was the object of your quest; or the Ark of the Covenant; or for the true mountain called Sinai; or fragments from my son's tree; and so much more.

"Well, I, of all people, know well what is holy and what is not and what is more holy or less holy, for I am the mother of God, and you have come to this remote spot at my bidding though you knew it not. You, each of you, came now rather than before or later because the time is soon coming when the people of this world must learn the truth of their own existence."

Here she paused, probably aware that her each and every utterance was potent, ripe with astonishing concepts, and pregnant with controversy. My impression was that she stopped to allow us to take in and digest the vastness of her brief speech. In a minute, she continued.

"They say that God created man in His own image. There is truth to that, not in the material sense, for the material aspect of God can be better thought of as the entire world on which we stand, and, by extension, perhaps the Universe without as well. No, man is created in God's image in the sense of 'mind' and spirit. Of all the creatures on earth, man is the only one that can seek God consciously, or who can arrive at God's door through attainment of merit, for God created man to join with and become God—and the destiny of each man, woman, and child is to attain God, whether he knows it or not, wants it or not, needs it or not. And though some men may not consciously strive for this, in time they will arrive there in any case.

"Of all of God's creatures on earth, man is the holiest by virtue that only man becomes God, as a child becomes an adult at childhood's end.

"Have you never gone back to the spot of your birth and wondered at the fact that it was there in that precise midwife's home or there in that very room or there in that exact glade that you came into existence, where you were born into this world? Now I bid you think. At such moments, are you not full of wonder for your very existence, for the miracle of your life?"

Her pause this time seemed especially prolonged. Then she said, "Well, I have brought you here to make it clear that mankind likewise has a place where it came into existence, where it was born, and it is time that all of mankind learn of that place so that all may feel that self-same wonder.

"The Holy Scriptures tell of the creation of the world and a place that is called Eden . . . ."

Suddenly the girl sagged, and Ruth and some of the other women jumped to her aid in a practiced manner and helped her sit back down on the dais. The girl became quiet as the women fussed over her, and I think we all used the opportunity to reflect further on what we had just heard. I certainly did. And I must say that my conclusions were not very flattering to our hosts. From first to last, this entire trek from Durban to the place called Sinai seemed to have been predicated on lies, deceit, and deception of one sort or another, and the current elaborate charade seemed to fit perfectly in line with all the rest.

When the girl regained some of her strength, she whispered to Ruth, who clearly wanted Mariam to return to the litter, but she held fast and got a set expression on her face. Her attendants moved away and stood at reverent attention as they had before. Mariam faced us again and continued in her mystical voice.

"But first, before I discuss the realm that is the real Eden of the real world, you need to know more of myself. There is skepticism among you, and that is good, for what good would you be as my messengers if you were to believe all that you heard from whomever you heard it. So I will explain somewhat. As all the world knows well, Jesus asked his beloved disciple to care for his mother. That person is myself."

It was, unexpectedly, Carnehan who first reacted to this preposterous announcement. "God A'mighty! Just how are we supposed to believe *that!* I've heard some bloomin' tall tales in my life—" Also, unexpectedly, it was a glare from Bayushtiak that stopped him in mid-sentence.

Mariam continued as though nothing had happened. "Thus, John and I headed north and resided in Ephaesus in Turkey for a time. However, we chose to continue our journey north and settled in what is now the countries you call France and England, but that did not suit our purposes either. We continued our search for a permanent home and then returned south. When we eventually came to this land, which was far more fertile two thousand years ago, the angel Gabriel came to me as he had before and declared that our journeying was finished and that this spot was to be our home. He split asunder the rock cliff, creating this hidden valley, and bade John and me enter. Over the years, mainly by sending dispatches to Galilee, we gathered around ourselves the people who were to become our community.

"I was ninety-seven years old when the great miracle happened. Death came to claim me as it does everyone, and, Lo!, Gabriel was there for me one more time. He told me that our Father wished me to tarry for there was more for me to do on Earth. Thus, at the point of my bodily death my spirit entered the body of a certain twelve-year-old girl and that child became Mariam for a year, that is, my soul, my personality, all that is invisible that was Mariam the mother of Jesus entered that girl and the girl became me. Following that, every year the woman who was Mariam moved from twelve-year-old to twelve-year-old so that the Mother of God is always within the body of a living girl. Through the mind and bodies of these girls, I have lived on."

Here, Ruth interjected: "The blessed Mother of God lives on eternally!" The girl paused again then, and I dared to break the mood by asking a question.

"If what you say is true, why does the Virgin, that is you, trouble twelve year olds?"

Mariam looked at Ruth, who responded for her, "Because that was the age of Mariam when the Angel of the Lord came to her and explained that she would in time to come conceive Jesus through the Holy Spirit, for in those days, and still in our land, that is the age of promise for a girl."[41]

Some of our party looked at one another in dismay at this statement. It was Burton who merely shrugged and reminded us that cultures the world over have different standards.

As Mariam sat quietly gazing over us, Ruth then went into more detail concerning the "possession" of the girls. In brief what she explained is as follows: When a girl ceases to be Mariam, she has no memory of that whole year. It is as though she made the transition from eleven to thirteen with no year between. Sometimes it happened that, when it was time for Mariam to move out of her body, there was no twelve-year old girl to act as her vessel.

It is at those times, as Mariam waits for an eleven-year-old to come of age, that she appears as an apparition in various places around the world for a little time, Guadalupe, Mexico, for one, and more recently in La Salette and Lourdes, both in France, where she shared some of her insights with some chosen children or others in whom innocence abounded.

[Quatermain note: As I was not altogether familiar with the particulars of these incidents, later, when I happened to think of it in Durban, I looked them up. Their respective dates were 1531, 1846, and 1858.]

Naturally, Ruth went on, there are all sorts of ceremonies built up around the miracle, with parents vying for their daughters to be "the One." The only time when it is guaranteed that a particular girl becomes Mariam is when there is only one twelve-year old girl in the town.

Then Ruth went into the history of the place, noting that when Mariam and John left the Middle East for Europe, they rendezvoused with Joseph of Arimethea who had already obtained custody of the Holy Vessel. When eventually John and Mariam decided to continue looking for a home to the south, they had by then possession of that item. Unfortunately, as they were passing through the land that would eventually include Antioch, they were robbed by brigands, and Mariam lost track of that particular object for about 1,100 years.

In the meantime, in the 4th century, when the Library of Alexandria was threatened, many of its greatest volumes were secretly shipped to this community, since its existence and location were known to the great librarians of the time. Thus, the town of Sinai held close to its bosom the wisdom of millennia.

Then, some eight centuries later, another miracle happened, of which we already knew something. For in the "fullness of time" (an expression Ruth was to use often), following their adventures in the Holy Land, Duke Stephen and his men were able to retrieve their Holy Cup. They took a wide detour and, in the end, came to Ethiopia and, being directed by an angel, sought shelter in this very valley. Of course, once being interviewed, they left the treasure here in the care of Christ's mother before they left.

Then all at once, the girl's posture slumped and her eyes rolled back. At that her entire retinue, including Ruth, went into motion, swooping her into the litter and hurrying her into another room.

Ruth returned quickly to explain that our interview would continue another day, and then she led us some distance to a dining room where we were treated as honored guests, and we enjoyed more of the simple fare of these people. Afterward, we were taken again to our rooms. For some peculiar reason, we did not converse much when left to ourselves. It was as though we were all spiritually fatigued. I do remember that Holmes was irate about something and that Huxley was particularly subdued.

Frankly I cared little about anything just then. I was confused. Nothing I had heard had made any sense, though I could not deny the sincerity of these people. I lay down with my sleeping roll, and the last thing I remembered was that Hans was curled up next to me snoring.

CHAPTER SIXTEEN

Allan's Charge

The following morning our meal consisted of cakes and honey, apples, and raisins, with cool goat's milk to quench our thirst. The woman we had come to know as the messenger came and indicated that I was to follow her. Then she indicated Will Scott and made clear he was also to come. All the others were to stay behind. She took us through a veritable labyrinth of passages when finally she stopped and indicated that we were to enter a particular room and wait.

The room was Spartan as all things were in this land. These people did not seem to have much heart for decorating or for jewelry, bangles, and the like. We did as she bade, making ourselves as comfortable as we could on some cushions that were on the floor. I was wondering why Will Scott and I had been singled out, and he and I whispered about this for about twenty minutes when finally Ruth and some other women entered solemnly, walking slowly. Once again, in the middle of this procession was Mariam, walking this time on her own power. She came to a simple enough chair and sat facing us, her matrons standing in an arc behind her.

"Allan and you who are pleased to call yourself Will Scott—for that is your name, isn't it?" she began mysteriously in that fragile voice, "I have asked to see you two now because, of your party, you two and you two alone are destined to live through the ages, not as I who do here secretly in the desert, but in the minds of men for all time . . . as I survive in the hearts of men who know not my real situation. I wished to see you in order to finish what I began to say yesterday."

Here I had to protest. "But what about Mr. Huxley and Mr. Burton and Miss Mitchell? Surely they are, all three, far greater than I and—" [and then I realized that Scott was a mere boy and heaven only knew how he would turn out].

"Yes, Allan, in an ideal world, Maria Mitchell and Richard Burton should and would enjoy renown through all time, but the people of earth have short memories or are fickle and, sad to say, the time is not far off when these two names will be lost, save for those few historians and practitioners in their fields who may remember."

"But what of Mr. Huxley?" I asked. At that moment, I saw Scott clearly wince.

Mariam continued: "Ah, the man who here identifies himself as such has no true right to that name and is determined to travel a most wayward path. The authentic Mr. Huxley will always, with certainty, be mentioned in the same breath with his mentor. Have no fear of that."

"But then you contradict yourself," Scott insisted.

"No. Your traveling companion's destiny without question will be an infamous one. In fact, in various guises, he will be remembered perhaps as long as yourself. But his fate in the balance ledgers of God is quite another one entirely, as perhaps you already suspect."

She paused here. I had the impression that she wanted her last words to sink into Scott's mind. Then she addressed him directly again. "But all that is neither here nor there. Hearken to my next words! When you return, tell your masters what you have heard and what you will hear. The bones you have will bear witness to the truth of your statements. Now listen carefully, for one asset I do not have is strength.

"The Holy Scriptures tell of the creation of the world . . . and they tell of God creating man in the land of Eden and that the act of creation took mere moments. These statements are of course true, but who is to determine what is a moment in the eyes of God, who measures time in billions of years? Indeed, God created man in a moment, a mere few million years, and he did this feat in a place that you can call Eden for want of a better name. I have brought you here to identify that real place to you and thus to all men.

"After John and I left Gaul and journeyed south, there came a time when the Angel of the Lord came to me. It was Gabriel, the same who had revealed himself to me at so many other crossroads in my life. He made me see in my mind a place on the far side of the Red Sea, a spot where I was to reside, and where I was to wait. 'Verily, the spot that I am showing you is holy,' he said, 'more so than Ur was where the Lord spoke to Abraham or the Mountain of

Sinai where the Lord spoke to Moses. Though these are surely holy places, the spot I show you is holier still, for it is the holiest spot on earth. And verily, you who are the Mother of God, you are bid to attend this veritable womb of mankind, for are you not the holiest person of the world? Thus is it not right that you should live by and in and protect the holiest place? Are you not also the mother of man? Then it is fitting that you reside by and in and protect the womb of man. Verily, I say to you, the spot I show you is the most holy in the eyes and mind of God.'

"So Allan and Will Scott, the place the angel showed me was a vast valley that ran the whole length of Africa from north to south, a tremendous valley with many lakes. The angel bade John and I to come to this very spot that is under our feet now, which is the northernmost gateway both into and out of the great valley.

"Oh, Allan and Will, let me tell you a wonderful truth. Remember, thee, how the Lord through the burning bush told Moses that he stood on holy ground? Well I say to you that the ground on which you stand is holier still." As she said this last, her eyes grew large and she smiled for the first time, as though savoring her words.

"I am growing weak, for the girl who is my vessel was never strong, but I must share with you the secret that makes this place so holy.

"That spot, which is under your feet, continues south, making up the great valley of eastern Africa, the bowl out of which sprang man, the crucible where the embryonic spirit, or God-in-the-making called mankind, was forged. Will Scott, return to your mentors, to Mr. Darwin and your true Mr. Huxley, and tell them they are quite correct in the long view that humans came into being, not all at once, but in stages over time, for that is the way that God performs his miracles, building from the blocks that are available, the stuff of life."

Just then, some women emerged from a door carrying great censers dangling from golden chains and filled with burning incense. Great clouds of the stuff very quickly filled the room and suddenly, I felt as though I had been absorbed into a dream. But just before I went under, I suddenly understood. Like a bright light, it came to me. The girl, albeit very small and very young, was just another wizard of the Zikali ilk! Just another Old Cheat with more of that horrid magical smoke!

In the dream I was out of doors surrounded by lofty trees of a kind I didn't recognize. The temperature had risen and the air was steamy. Then I began to rise, float upward at an incredible speed until I saw clearly that I had been in a jungle and that the jungle spread over a vast area butting up right onto the sea. Then I saw the forest shrink, not because I was still rising, which I was, but because it was really shrinking and much of it quickly disappeared altogether and turned into savanna.

Then, all at once, I realized I was seeing what is now the east coast of Africa, but twenty million years ago. Don't ask me how I knew that, I just did. That forest that I had seen was the home of the ape. Apes of every kind, gibbons and monkeys, bush babies and lemurs, even a variety of gorilla.

At that time, the highlands of Kenya and Ethiopia did not exist. But geological forces of astronomical magnitude were beginning to split the continent. Over the next millions of years this splitting from Ethiopia through two-thirds of the eastern length of the continent gouged and tore the earth, shifted rivers and made rivers where they never existed before. Lakes like a string of pearls formed down the rift, lakes that provided in abundance much of what the apes and all the other creatures of that time needed—water and food. In fact, east Africa became a veritable jigsaw puzzle of forest, jungle, desert, grasslands, and meadows. This great variety was a boon to the apes, who multiplied and spread and filled every niche with variations of themselves.

Then I saw that some of the apes were moving unlike apes. These apes were not loping and lunging around using both hands and feet as apes move, but were standing upright, standing tall and walking on their feet hardly different than you or me. This I somehow knew was perhaps four million years ago. There was no doubt that they were animals—just apes of a different sort—and for a million years and more these creatures lived lives not that much different than their cousins, and like their cousins communicating amongst themselves with various noises and hand and arm gestures, a vocabulary of up to five hundred words or more.

I saw that some groups of these walking apes, as all creatures do, met adversity, time and again, droughts, floods, predatory animals, great cold, blistering heat, and millennia of geographical separation from their own kind. And slowly, it became apparent to me that their having the advantage of being able to walk and run solely on their feet had certain side effects. For one thing, having their hands free to manipulate objects allowed a certain facility of invention denied their cousins. Another was that possessing a vertical posture, as opposed to the horizontal posture of four-legged animals, or even the diagonal aspect of typical apes, seemed superior for reasons of safety and stealth. And, in the long-run, these changes proved so advantageous that the creatures were able to overcome many of their adversities.

But adversity is eternal, and for eons these creatures lived as part of the animal kingdom. Because of their small size and slight strength compared to many of the carnivores with whom they were surrounded, these new apes were largely scavengers, competing with hyenas and vultures. Yet, about two and a half million years ago, some of these creatures somehow determined that they could partially conquer hunger through the use of tools—for instance, using specialized bits of stone to crush already scavenged bones to retrieve the marrow and slice the flesh off secondhand carcasses—thus the earliest men came into existence. Crude without a doubt, more naked than not, sometimes cowering and afraid, other times bold to the point of foolishness.

I came to the realization that human beings had thus come into the world (at least as presented in this vision).

It was only then that I began to fall back to the earth; and then I stopped dropping, floating in the air a few hundred feet above the ground. I could see the Red Sea to the east and the jungle to the northwest. Then there emerged from a blowing dust cloud a small group of people, travelers dressed in the Hebrew manner that I had observed in Sinai, men and women, and I knew that two of them were John, the beloved disciple in whose care Jesus had placed his mother, and Mariam, that very mother. I saw the small caravan approach a cliff that opened before them, and they came to a place of safety, a good valley with a stream running through it, and they were comfortable. Thus they stayed, naming their new home Sinai, for it was holy ground.

For 1,100 years, the people of Sinai lived quietly, being bothered by none and bothering no one. It was then that Duke Stephen and his men appeared, being drawn by their own angel and returning to the Mother that which was her Son's. They tarried but a while, then left again. Then one day 400 years later, two men stumbled out of what had become a barren desert and found their valley, having followed those instructions that had been left behind by the crusaders. These two men were Gian Giacomo Caprotti and Tomasso Masini da Peretola, called Zoroastro, who were welcomed, and I saw Salai draw sketches of Mariam, whom they met in much the same manner as we. After the two Italians left, a church was quickly put up hiding the entrance to the valley.

Then, finally, I drifted down and touched the ground, and I was aware of Will Scott beside me. I turned to Will to ask him something, then everything seemed to shift and the next thing I remembered was the sensation of coming out of a deep sleep and regaining awareness of my surroundings—of Will Scott and the slim twelve-year-old girl before me.

By degrees I regained my composure. I noted also that the more awake Scott became, the more elated and proud he became. Finally, he couldn't hold it back any longer. "Everything I just experienced seemed to back up Charles's theories—if only he had been here as well. How will I ever be able to explain it to him?" Then a thought came to him. "But it was only a dream, nothing concrete, nothing at all that I can tell Charles except that I had had a dream." His excitement trailed off and he frowned.

He addressed Mariam. "Dear Lady, that was quite a trick. Certainly I saw just what I would have liked to have seen, painted in vivid color and with the broadest of strokes, Charles Darwin's theory of the descent of man. Yet, how can I trust what I have seen and heard?"

"That is a matter of choice," replied the girl. "You may trust or not trust as you desire. I can only remind you that I brought you here from far-off England to show you that which you have now seen. My purpose was to share the truth of man's origin with those most able to divine it and appreciate its meaning. After all, we"—and here she made an all—encompassing sweep of her arms—"are all the children of God, and God wants his children to grow beyond the quaint stories they tell amongst themselves and to hearken to things as they really are.

"I did this in the only manner I can. What you choose to think of it, that I cannot help. For my part, I am only showing you two chosen ones the earth's most divine truth. All of what you witnessed happened right here and yonder as well." Here she indicated south.

"Listen to me now!"

At this point, her normal ethereal, but nonetheless calm, voice changed, indeed, her whole demeanor suddenly took on a fiery passion.

"If God is as real as, for instance, me, and is by definition divine, and if through the use of the tool called Time, he crafted people in his own image, then it would follow that people are also divine and that the spot where He did his crafting must be holy ground—the holiest of ground.

"I have drawn you here from afar to tell you my wishes. During my incarnations in Guadeloupe, Lourdes, Fatima, and such, I have asked, or otherwise let it be known, only two things of consequence. First, that all mankind turn away from sin, chiefly your disregard for God and, too, the lust for war. Second, that a chapel be built on the spot of my appearance in my honor. Well, now I ask something similar of you. I ask that all the terrain from where you stand to the southern-most reach of the great valley—the vast bowl that is birthplace of the human race—be designated holy ground and be set aside so all people can come and contemplate their existence, to perceive with their own eyes the spot where God's greatest miracle occurred, and this will make them more mindful of one another and of God, as well."

I couldn't help but interject here. "Excuse me, miss, but are you saying that you drew Mr. Scott here from England and myself from Durban and perhaps the others as well, and that you did this with powers unknown to us, for the sole purpose of telling us that you want this barren desert and lands beyond turned into a place of worship.

"Yes, a natural cathedral."

Her words struck me dumb. Finally I was able to gather the resources to say, "My dear lady, what you are asking is preposterous. What you have described is perhaps one-fifth of the African continent, making up the national territories of numerous nations. Even if every leader of every one of those countries could see the same vision we have been graced with, there is no way they could all agree to turn large parts of their countries into contiguous reserves for your so-called holy ground, or whatever you want to call it."

Mariam did not deign to comment, nor change her expression from the beatific smile that she seemed to wear forever. She merely gestured to her hand maidens and prepared to leave. However, just as she was about to disappear behind a curtain, she stopped and turned and said, "Allan, rest assured that in the fullness of time all these things are possible and will be fulfilled! For you are my tool and, therefore, blessed by God!"

Then she focused her attention on Scott and said, "And as for you who today call yourself Will, though it is true that your role in honoring these requests of mine is slight, it is nonetheless also true that your hearing me today has given you much pause. For years to come, you will think on these events and hold them close to your heart. And I say to you now that there will come a time—a score of years hence—when you will be called upon to fulfill a divine obligation for the sake of my son, and thus for me as well. You will remember both my person and my words this day, and you will know how to proceed. For you, too, are my tool and, therefore, blessed by God!"[42]

Then she was gone.

CHAPTER SEVENTEEN

The Return

Will Scott and I returned to our quarters in a daze, as one can easily imagine. The entire interview from beginning to end was outrageous, and I felt insulted that the inhabitants of this valley would assume that I would swallow any part of this pretense. They actually thought I would believe we'd been interviewed by the Virgin Mary Mother of God. Then to make matters worse, they drugged us with some toxic substance and wanted us to believe the further nonsense that there had once been a totally unknown and new upright ape that mankind was related to. And finally, the last straw, so to speak, was this astonishing attempt to reveal their desire to turn one-fifth of Africa into some sort of continental preserve.

My attempts to draw Scott out so as to affirm my own feelings ended in failure. I supposed that what he had seen that seemed to vindicate his mentors's theories was not to be criticized, for the moment at least. That the source of this information might be suspect didn't seem to occur to him. I wrote it off as a lingering affect of the incense.

Indeed, I found that even I did not feel compelled to discuss any of this with the others of our expedition, much to their chagrin. The exception was Huxley who pulled Scott aside, and they conferred briefly. Though I couldn't hear them, I could see them well enough, and it seemed to me that Scott was absolutely resolute in whatever had changed his demeanor toward the older man from one of student toward a respected mentor to animosity of an intense order. What this change of attitude meant I had no idea, and, as it happened, I never learned the cause of it nor the end of it.

In the meantime, some of the others tried to draw me out, but I would have none of it, and the day ended quietly enough.

The next morning, the messenger came and fetched Richard Holmes, who, it turned out would be gone for days. We were all concerned about this but were continually reassured that he was well, and that, in fact, he was probably never better.

It was during this interval that Cuff passed from us. The priests kindly sent word to us from the chapel. They said there was nothing more they could have done for him except make him comfortable. At this news, some of us remembered his principal passion in life and then put our heads together. We sent back a message asking if Cuff could be laid to rest in a corner of that rosery, or rose garden, he had taken such a shine to. The priests, who had, for some days, patiently weathered the brunt of his delirium and his preoccupation with their garden, said they understood and agreed. They buried him with ceremony, or so we understood, as we were a long way off in Sinai at the time. We all agreed that Cuff would have liked this. I, for one, knew in my heart that he would have liked it very much.[43] I was greatly saddened at his loss, but greatly heartened by the fact that, however briefly, I could say I had known him.

Holmes returned in the afternoon of the fourth day of his disappearance. He merely joined us at meal, walking as in a mesmeric state.

Toward the evening, he became more responsive and slowly we got from him the broad strokes. He too met with Mariam, but as his reasons for being there were of a different character altogether than mine or Scott's, Mariam spoke to him of the Great Library of Alexandria and of the Holy Grail. Apparently, she described in some detail the former and explained the provenance of the latter. Despite all our efforts, though, he remained taciturn about the details of his interview.

After another day, the priest Tabot reappeared and announced that our visit had ended and that we needed to pack and prepare to leave Sinai. The following morning, he and Ruth escorted us through the valley and back to the cleft by the fountain. As before, the townspeople came out in throngs, this time to see us off. All concerned seemed happy that we were at this juncture. Our hosts seemed grateful to be rid of us, and we were grateful to be returning to our homes.

One thing, though. We had to give our solemn oaths that we would never reveal the location of Sinai—the home of Mariam for all those many centuries. [I have kept this oath since I have never brought up this adventure at any time until now, and even so, I have changed a few landmarks here and there so as to muddy the waters; I hope you don't mind.]

Each member of the remainder of my expedition—Miss Mitchell, Burton, Dravot, Carnehan, Huxley, Scott, Holmes, and even Hans and the Zulu Bayushtiak—chose this moment to wish the community well and promised to keep their silence.

But it is the words of Miss Mitchell and Bayushtiak that I recall best. Our learned astronomer asked Ruth to convey a message to Mariam. "Please tell your mistress that now I understand that it was she who instilled in me the strength and determination to fight off the Danakil. Please tell her of my gratitude and say that I will keep her with me always."

Bayushtiak spoke in Zulu, which I translated: "My master, the Great One, the Opener of Roads, sent me to protect the white man, Macumazahn, from various and sundry threats, and I believe that I have fulfilled my obligation well. Therefore, I leave this spot with a sense of accomplishment, yet there is much more also. I feel that I have been in the presence of the One who is the maker of the very air that I breath and the sunlight that warms my face. Never have I felt so much energy as I have felt here, but an energy, indeed a passion, bent on nurturing rather than the fighting for which I was bred. I know full well that it is your mistress who is the font of all these feelings and blessings, and I will remember her in kind as well as I can, evermore."

Once we all had a chance to say our mind, Ruth closed her eyes and responded, mysteriously, as seemed to be the coin of the realm in that far-off hidden spot, with Mariam's voice: "Thank you for your kind prayers, my children. Now go and forge the changes that I have asked in secret ways of each of you. Go in peace, and believe in your uttermost hearts that all my requests will bear fruit: this is not only possible, but inescapable."

And then we were ushered out and we retraced our steps through the narrow cleft to Tabot's chapel. After more farewells, and a promise that we would not be troubled again by the Danakil on our return trek, we once again entered that horrible desert.

Thus, this story ends. At that time I didn't know this wouldn't be my only journey to the Red Sea. There was to be another, one that would be forever connected to one of the saddest memories of my life.[44]

Our return to the bay where we would find the *Deborah*, the naval vessel that had carried us to Ethiopia, which was then patrolling the coast of the Red Sea while waiting for us, was indeed uneventful. It took about the same amount of time and effort to get back to the pier as it taken to get to the hidden town called Sinai.

The only aspect of the return journey that proved of interest was that we were finally able to get Holmes to open up somewhat about his experience. According to him, Mariam asked Ruth to take him into another part of the temple where she showed him into a room with eight sides, and in a nook in a wall surrounded by torches that somehow he knew never went out, was the Grail. The look on Holmes's face as he described these events was joyful. He said he actually held it in his hands. However, his description of the object left much to be desired. I simply could not pin the man down as to the description of the cup or chalice or platter, as some say. Yet, despite his peculiar vagueness, he did not doubt for an instant that what he was shown was the real object of so many quests.

From the room of the Grail, he was led down a narrow passageway hewn from solid stone and entered a natural cavern. He was instantly aware of the drop in temperature. It was significantly cooler in the cavern, where he saw numerous tall cases set up and rows and rows of shelves that were crammed with ancient scrolls.

At some point on our shared journey, Holmes had told me that it is said that the Alexandrian Library once contained the secret method of extracting awesome amounts of energy from minute sources or how to light vast halls without the aid of fire or gas of any sort. And who's to say if those very scrolls weren't there in front of him.

Ruth confirmed that several thousand of the volumes from the Great Alexandrian Library had in fact made their way to her valley some 1,500 years ago and that there was a certain number of their population whose business it was to copy and recopy the scrolls to preserve their content against the passage of time.

Unfortunately, however, Ruth explained that despite his need to study the works, Holmes would have no chance other than the moment at hand. You can imagine his infinite disappointment, as he would have given up everything to stay, or better, to haul away much of what he found there. Ruth made it clear, though, that he and all the rest of our expedition would be leaving in due course. She did ask him if there was anything in particular he would like to see. And he responded immediately by querying about the gospel that seemed to be the source, other than Mark's, of Matthew and Luke. To Holmes's great relief and joy, she showed him the entirety of the memoir written by the magus Gaspar, the very writings that had so excited his hopes and which he had shared with me at the beginning of our journeying.

Whereupon he busied himself copying these pages, furiously scribbling, a task that utterly consumed him. When pressed, his only response was, "I cannot say. It is for the good of my country."

[Quatermain note: At this point, my dear Church, I interject myself again. Here we bid farewell to the Danakil Desert with all its terrible volcanoes and infinite sands, and we jump ahead in time.

[After Holmes's return to England and his museum, now and again I would hear a rumor or some other tantalizing word that the translation of Gaspar's thoughts from ancient Ethiopian into English was a continuing project for Holmes and his colleagues. I often wondered during the subsequent decade about the results of that effort and now, prompted and inspired by John's, that is, Dr. Watson's, desire to conclude this memoir with no strings untied, I have only just visited with Holmes again.

[After reminiscing at length, as you can imagine, I posed the question that was on my mind and he was kind enough to present me with a sort of abstract or "precise" of Gaspar's tract. Once again I take this opportunity to ask Dr. Watson to include here in a logical spot in this narrative that summary of the continuation of Gaspar's statements. *

---

* Editor's note: To review the introductory section, please refer back to page 17. These tracts have not yet been recognized by Biblical scholars.—T.K.M.

[And Gaspar said:

[Where is the word that tells us how to listen to God, that tells us that God speaks in a special language. When you see clouds in the west, you know that rain will come. You know that wind blowing from the south is always followed by blistering heat. So why can't you understand the signs that God brings you?

[God doesn't use words like fig or tree or wall or camel. Instead, he uses symbols. For instance, if he shows you a circle, you know from common sense that a circle has no beginning or middle or end. It is whole unto itself; therefore, if God shows you a circle, you know that he is gracing you with wholeness and completion.

[In the same way, a home or house is where you live your life, where you are aware, and where it is that you know all that you know. So if God shows you a house, you know he is showing you your very awareness, or if he shows you an underground vault or perhaps the depths of the sea, you know these places are lightless and the realm of dark and he has graced you with a warning saying you need to beware of something that you cannot see, of that which is below your awareness.

[God communicates to you in two ways. One is obvious and the other is less so. Both are common but only one is spoken of, though even then rarely understood. Through all time, people have spoken about God talking to people in dreams. But what is not said is that, even in dreams, God does not talk in an ordinary way using the dreamer's ordinary language. Dreams are full of symbols that mean something personal from God to the dreamer; it is the dreamer's duty to discover what is being said.

[The other less obvious way that God communicates, the way that people seldom speak of, is his placing symbols in our paths during our waking hours. Most such symbols are ordinary and self-evident. So you ask, how is a person to recognize that this or that ordinary thing is a message from God?

[It is not difficult. God causes us to notice such symbols by having them occur in the same space or time as other symbols so that two or more ordinary things happening together is not ordinary at all. When this happens, we feel a jolt of wonder or awe or even love. We all have these experiences, but I tell you, as sure as I am talking to you, that God is thus trying to get your attention, to speak to you. If in your heart you feel such a crossing of paths is wonderful, then I promise God is talking to you.

[Therefore, fortunate are you to see what you see, for these are the visions of the prophets, and many are the kings who wish to see what you see, or hear what you hear. But they never do, for they seek too hard and are not pure of heart.

[In this way, there can be nothing that is covered up or nothing that is secret between you and God. The secrets of your mind are held up to God, and God whispers back, or sometimes shouts, as the occasion deserves.

[But again, it is your duty to understand God's words to you, of what he is saying especially to you! Whether it's easy or hard, God rewards the trying.

[*Now think! There are many people in your towns, in your nations, in the whole world. Think of all the people of all the many ages who lived in all those nations. Now ask yourself this: why would God trouble to speak so to you, who is but one person among so many? Why would he send you a sign, or speak to you in your dreams? Why would he trouble himself with you? It is because you are his child!*

[He does so because you are holy as all his children are holy. But few listen. But few heed. Few trust. Few love God as he loves them. Instead they choose to be blind. They choose to be deaf. They choose to be mute. God speaks all the time, but he is ignored by so many. His signs and dreams are ignored. His messages are ignored.

[Where is the voice of Jesus that explains how the world works and how it should be observed? Where does it say that God approaches and needs to be approached with a serious heart fully open, that this is how God and man come together and that life ceases to be a mystery?

[Happy are those who show mercy, for, in this life or the next, God will be merciful.

[Happy are those who have open hearts, for, in this life or the next, they will see the face of God.

[Great are the keepers of the peace, for, in this life or the next, they will be called the children of God.

[But where is the voice of Jesus, the voice who held all these wondrous truths? Where are these truths? I do not hear of them from the caravans.] —A.Q.

We reached the *Deborah* without incident, and within a few more days, we all went our separate ways, returning to the lives we were leading before, perhaps richer for the experience, perhaps not. Burton retired to Trieste, as was his plan. Professor Mitchell returned to Vassar College with her precious bits of meteorite. However, I am happy to say that it was not long before our paths crossed again, but that is a whole 'nother tale[45] and this is not the time for its telling. Huxley and Will Scott, bitterly estranged by now for no reason that I ever saw, took away their equally precious bits of bone. The soldiers Danny Dravot and Peachy Carnehan, for all I know, disappeared off the face of the earth.[46] And, of course, Bayushtiak went to report to his master, that horrible dwarf wizard—"the thing that should never have been born"—who, nonetheless, for reasons I can never be sure of, I count among my friends.

[Quatermain note: Finally, Mr. Church, as I look over this manuscript that Dr. Watson has so kindly prepared I see that I have not made clear just why it was that your painting of Constantinople and the fountain in part inspired in me the memory that has become what I fear is a rather self-indulgent tale.

[You see, as I have looked back on all these events over these many years, I have often wondered how much of what Mariam said about the Great Valley was true and how much of my vision then could be relied on. And it has occurred to me over and again, that if there is any kernel of truth in the notion of that long, long valley being the very place where human life came into being, then it

follows that the valley can be thought of as the fountain of life, or at least human life, on this earth.

[But something that I don't understand is why Mariam asked Will Scott and myself to take on that task of bringing her natural cathedral or her impossible park into being. I can't speak for Scott, but I have been fearfully busy merely surviving since then, and besides, the whole idea was simply too far-fetched to take seriously. I sometimes feel an attack of conscience about this. Still, on balance, I believe that I will be able to meet St. Peter when my time comes with my head held high! —A.Q.][47]

Afterword

When I read Quatermain's memoir for the first time and came to the last page, my primary emotion was that of thankfulness that, with regard to Allan himself, none of Hans's evil omens came to anything.[48] Of course, poor Cuff and Lidenbrock might have thought otherwise. In addition, it seems a good thing that Bayushtiak came along, for he proved quite effective at least twice as described in this narrative.

Beyond these visceral first reactions, other thoughts come to mind. Despite Quatermain's and Watson's desire to tie up all the loose ends, clearly there were many more such ends than they ever knew, and which we can see now through the gift of hindsight.

For one thing, we never learn why Sherlock Holmes was using an assumed name in Ethiopia. While technically "Will Scott" comprises two of his actual names, they are two that few are familiar with.

We can, nonetheless, use the little that we know to delve into the matter a bit more. For example, we know enough now, through the celebrated efforts of both Watson and Baring-Gould, to make the fair assumption that the "British Government" referred to so often in the memoir may be simply the person of Sherlock Holmes's older brother Mycroft, who we have met in "The Greek Interpreter" and subsequently learn in "The Bruce-Partington Plans," that, in Holmes's words, he "occasionally *is* the British government."

Which brings us to the conundrum that we meet in the manuscript as "Thomas Huxley." Despite the fact that Quatermain diligently reports numerous inferences, instances, and clues that should have raised "red flags" for him and given him much pause, he never really addresses the mystery of the man. Personally, I give Quatermain the benefit of the doubt and believe that he was in such spiritual and sensory overload during this adventure that many nuances just went over his head. Or perhaps, in relating the story to Watson and Church, he was merely being circumspect.

Again, both with that marvelous gift of hindsight and Sherlock Holmes' own words (see Chapter Ten), we know now that the man identified as "Thomas Huxley" was nothing of the sort.

Beginning with Quatermain's casual observation that Huxley and Will Scott bore an odd resemblance to one another, and later with his observations of the familiar ease with which they could squabble in public, we can assume that Huxley is Holmes's older brother. Yet we know from "The Greek Interpreter" that no force on earth would move Mycroft out of his comfortable surroundings.

Thus, using Sherlock Holmes's own methods, if we eliminate all possibilities, even as Holmes' himself did, that which remains must be the solution, however improbable it may seem. Hence, we are left with the conclusion that "Huxley" must in actuality be Holmes's *other* older brother, Sherrinford, and that he, as Sherlock himself often did, was participating in this game in disguise and under cover.

From all this, we can conclude that for reasons unknown to us, Mycroft Holmes, with the full authority of the British government, dispatched his two brothers off to Ethiopia for some secret purpose, the nature of which we never properly learn. Despite all their stated goals, even that of locating the Holy Grail, we sense that there was something more.

Still, this does not get down to the bottom of the man we have identified as Sherrinford Holmes.

There is much more to it.

When discussing astronomical phenomena with Professor Mitchell, we note that "Huxley" suddenly waxed passionately about asteroids and their dynamics. From this alone, we can easily deduce that "Huxley" must be none other than the criminal genius Professor James Moriarty, whom Holmes identified in "The Final Problem" as "the Napoleon of crime" and who three years after this Ethiopian adventure would publish *The Dynamics of an Asteroid*, a work we are told in *The Valley of Fear* ascended to "such rarified heights that no man in the scientific press was capable of criticizing it."

Therefore, it is impossible to escape the conclusion that Sherrinford Holmes and Professor Moriarty are the same man.

That Sherrinford/Moriarty and Sherlock were not yet, at least at the start of Quatermain's memoir, the bitter enemies they would become, is quite clear. The relationship between the two is described in the most cordial terms, even that of a student revering his mentor. Indeed, this makes perfect sense since Baring-Gould tells us that Moriarty was once Holmes's tutor. This fits in the context of the story, for despite what else they claimed to be, they would have still been student and mentor. Yet, couldn't that relationship also be interpreted as that of a younger brother worshipping his older brother? I believe so.

Nonetheless, we are now beginning to see that Sherrinford Holmes was a "bad seed" and that he took the path opposite of his two siblings.

Case in point: All the information we have surrounding the death of Axel Lidenbrock leads us to the conclusion that he was murdered, as opposed to being the victim of the Danakil sortie.

With only this to go on, I will make a leap of deduction. I conclude that Sherrinford killed Axel. For what reason, you ask? Simply because Lidenbrock's unexpected arrival was not part of the equation and, beyond that, he was completely expendable. I conclude that Sherrinford murdered the man for the pure fun of it—which is no doubt the same conclusion that Sherlock had come to.

Furthermore, I think Sherlock quickly came to the same conclusion and confronted his brother, who could muster no remorse. This then was the beginning of the rift that would become legendary[49] and which would end at their famous encounter at the falls of Reichenbach.

T.K.M

Notes

1. Michael Crichton's 1980 novel *Congo* is a clear pastiche of Haggard's *King Solomon's Mines,* even to the extent that the last sentence in Congo reads thus: "The projected intersection point now marked a field of black quatermain lava with an average depth of eight hundred meters—nearly half a mile—over the Lost City of Zinj." The name "Quatermain" is sufficiently close to the geological term "Quaternary" that some readers, to be sure, would have missed the *homage.*

2. Judy-Lynn Del Rey, with her husband Lester, took over the editorship of Ballantine Books' science-fiction and fantasy lines in the mid-1970s—shortly after Ian and Betty Ballantine sold to Random House the publishing house that bore their name and which they started in 1952.

3. Indeed, Haggard went so far as to write in his autobiography *The Days of My Life:* " . . . I always find it easy to write of Allan Quatermain, who, after all, is only myself set in a variety of imagined situations, thinking my thoughts and looking at life through my eyes."

4. During the three decades before the popularization of television, and serving much the same purpose that TV does today, a profusion of magazines full of colorful stories with vivid, even lurid, covers flourished. These were what we call today the pulp magazines because of the poor-quality paper they were printed on. Whatever your taste, there was a pulp magazine for you, including *Detective Story Magazine, Western Roundup, War Stories, Pirate Stories, Railroad Stories, Amazing Stories, Love Story, New York Stories, Racketeer Stories, Fight Stories, Baseball Stories,* and countless others. One of the most enduring was *Weird Tales,* a magazine of horror and supernatural stories that began publication in 1926. (Indeed, an incarnation of it is still being published today.) Whereas most of the stories and authors published in all those other

magazines have long faded from both popular and critical consciousness, some of the *Weird Tales* writers still have fervent followings, foremost among these being H.P. Lovecraft, who died in 1937 at the age of 47. Lovecraft is remembered today principally because of the efforts of two of his young protégés, August Derleth and Donald Wandrei. These young men started a publishing company in Sauk City, Wisconsin, called Arkham House (named after a recurring town in many Lovecraft stories) for the sole purpose of reprinting Lovecraft's work within the dignity of hardcovers. Though sales were slow to start, the paperback reprints took off during W.W.II and now H.P. Lovecraft is considered by many to be one of America's foremost writers of horror—equal in stature to Edgar Allan Poe. In time, Arkham House began publishing collections of other Weird Tales authors and is still a viable publishing house to this day. Following Derleth's death in 1971, James Turner became editor in 1974.

5. From 1825 to 1875, there arose a style of uniquely American landscape painting known as the Hudson River Valley School. These works were astonishingly photographic in detail while at the same time rendering nature in such romanticized and noble hues, with such immaculate emphasis on light and atmosphere, that the paintings were like windows into paradise. As the sobriquet would indicate, many of the original paintings depicted the Hudson River Valley in upper New York State. Among the foremost practitioners of this school—such as Thomas Cole, Albert Bierstadt, Asher Durand, John Kensett, and Thomas Moran—was Frederick Church, whose vast canvases portraying Niagara Falls, towering South American mountain ranges, and erupting volcanoes inspired awe in those who viewed them. Toward the end of his career, Church built his home high on a hill overlooking the Hudson River. Designed to resemble a Persian palace, he called it Olana.

6. Derleth and Wandrei felt compelled to leave out chunks of Lovecraft's correspondence for a variety of reasons (irrelevance, length, etc.), replacing the deleted prose with glorified ellipses.

7. Saratoga Springs was where Lovecraft's wife Sonia H. Greene (S.H.G.) convalesced from nerve problems and other symptoms following a stressful employment episode.

8. Lovecraft had a fierce interest in astronomy. Over the years, he provided many articles on the subject to the *Pawtuxet Valley Gleaner*; the Providence, Rhode Island, *Evening News*; and the *Providence Tribune*.

9. Many people, Lovecraft included, believe that "The Colour Out of Space" is his finest work. The story details the horrific events that follow the arrival of a meteorite in the area "west of Arkham."

10. In the course of his biographical sketches of Holmes, clear references are wanting regarding the location of Watson's war wounds, the number of his wives, and the chronological sequence of the narratives, among other proofs that the good doctor had his own share of foibles.

11. At the end of the nineteenth century, the expression "romance writer" had a completely different meaning than what we are used to today. During that era, the term "romance" conveyed the meaning of "imaginative adventure fiction."

12. Notwithstanding note 10, Watson explains in *A Study in Scarlet*, " . . . I served at the fatal battle of Maiwand. There I was struck on the shoulder by a Jezail bullet, which shattered the bone and grazed the subclavian artery."

13. Church's marvelous landscape *Cotopaxi*, which features a distant violent Ecadorian volcano, was exhibited June-August 1865 at McClean's Gallery, London. There is some indication (though this is more difficult to corroborate) that the painting made an encore appearance at McClean's during February-March 1870, which would fit nicely into the chronology of Quatermain's life, being the first time he had visited England since he was three years old [see *Allan and the Holy Flower*].

14. That Church chose to share the privacy of his family's personal sitting room with Quatermain and Watson is telling of his admiration for them. Yet this admiration must have been based solely on their immediately observed characters since neither had attained at that time the prominence that the future held for them. Quatermain's name would have meant nothing to Church, since Quatermain's memoir *King Solomon's Mines* had not yet been published, and wouldn't be for four more years. And Watson's first biographical memoir of Sherlock Holmes would not see print for another six.

15. During his prime, Church traveled far and wide through Mexico, South America, the Arctic, Europe, and the Middle East, so with regard to worldliness, Church would hardly be called an amateur.

16. El Khasne, the ancient treasury house, made cameo appearances in at least two delightful fantasy films—Ray Harryhausen's *Sinbad and the Eye of the Tiger* (1977) and Steven Spielberg's *Indiana Jones and the Last Crusade* (1989).

17. *El Ayn* (*The Fountain*) (also known as *Constantinople*) is currently part of the collection of the Mead Art Museum, Amherst College, Amherst, Massachusetts.

18. Of the Khoisan people indigenous to South Africa.

19. It is important to mention that Quatermain lived in a world of empire, a world and a time whose values were far different than those of our so-called "color-blind," "politically correct," and enlightened culture. It would not have crossed his mind that his choice of expression, the words he used, might be demeaning or hurtful. But, putting this bias of the period aside, Quatermain was as fair-minded as a human being could be.

That said, it is likely that Quatermain did not dwell on the subject of his servant as he related the story in Church's sitting room. Furthermore, it is improbable that Watson knew much of Hans so early in his friendship with Quatermain. Perhaps Watson did not, in ignorance, trouble to consult with Quatermain, who otherwise "indulged him by responding to his every question" during the voyage home, or, perhaps Watson did inquire only to be rebuffed by Quatermain for private reasons. Or perhaps it is as simple as the fact that the document was being prepared as a rather informal record of a private conversation with Frederick Church and intended for him as the principal audience as opposed to a formal book. In either case, as Hans is not introduced with any detail in this narrative, though in pages to come he will have an important role, I have chosen to place here passages from two of Quatermain's 18 previously known memoirs that were recorded during his retirement in England, *She and Allan* (which describes an adventure following the one in hand chronologically by about one year) and *The Ivory Child* (which follows this one by seven years), describing Hans in some detail not only in a physical manner but also in terms of his relationship to Quatermain.

> *She and Allan*: "Hans, I should say, was that same Hottentot who had been the companion of most of my journeyings since my father's day. He was with me when as a young fellow I accompanied Retief to Dingaan's kraal, and like myself, escaped the massacre . . . .
>
> "One good quality he had, however; no man was ever more faithful, and perhaps it would be true to say that neither man nor woman ever loved me, unworthy, quite so well.
>
> "In appearance he rather resembled an antique and dilapidated baboon; his face was wrinkled like a dried nut and his quick little eyes were bloodshot. I never knew what his age was, any more than he did himself, but the years had left him tough as whipcord and absolutely untiring. Lastly he was perhaps the best hand at following a spoor that ever I knew and up to a hundred and fifty yards or so, a very deadly shot with a rifle . . . ."

> *The Ivory Child*: "The truth is that after the death of Hans . . . there was no more spirit in me. For quite a long

while I did not seem to care at all what happened to me or to anybody else. We buried him with honor and when the earth was thrown over his little yellow face I felt as though half my past had departed with him into that hole. Poor drunken old Hans, where in the world shall I find such another man as you were? Where in the world shall I find so much love as filled the cup of that strange heart of yours?

"I dare say it is a form of selfishness, but what everyman desires is something that cares for him *alone*, which is just why we are so fond of dogs. Now Hans was a dog with a human brain and he cared for me alone . . . . Now Hans never cared for any living creature, or for any human hope or object, as he cared for me. There was no man or woman whom he would not have cheated, or even murdered for my sake. There was no earthly advantage, down to that of life itself, that he would not . . . forgo for my sake . . . . That is love *in excelsis*, and the man who has succeeded in inspiring it in any creature, even in a low, bibulous, old Hottentot, may feel proud indeed. At least I am proud and as the years go by the pride increases, as the hope grows that somewhere . . . I may find the light of Hans's love burning like a beacon in the darkness, as he promised I should do, and that it may guide and warm my shivering, new-born soul before I dare the adventure of the Infinite."

20. There is irony here insofar that January 6 is Sherlock Holmes' birthday, according to Holmsian scholar William S. Baring-Gould.

21. By the Portuguese explorer Vasco da Gama in 1498 on his epic voyage to India.

22. In recent decades, there have been serious attempts to show that Sherlock Holmes manifested symptoms of Marfan's Syndrome, a hereditary condition affecting ligaments, muscles, and the skeletal structure to the degree that its sufferers possessed excessively tall, lean body types and long thin fingers.

23. Luna Holmes played a preeminent role in Quatermain's life. Indeed, she is an essential element in four of his memoirs, *Allan and the Holy Flower*, *The Ivory Child*, *The Ancient Allan*, and *Allan and the Ice Gods*. Insofar as it has never been shown that she was not a relative of Sherlock Holmes, I think it can be safely assumed that he and she were cousins not too distantly removed, which would account for his presence at Castle Ragnall.

24. The bones in question, the genus *Australopithecus*, are still housed at the British Museum, and recent potassium-argon dating has shown them to be 3.4 million years old.

25. In the decades following the time period of this memoir, scholars began calling this hypothetical document the "Q" document, Q being short for *quelle*, which means "source" in German.

26. Scholars, as a rule, assume that Gaspar, indeed, all the Magi, or Wise Men, did not exist at all, and was created out of whole cloth by Matthew and later elaborated on.

27. Recall that Quatermain's name first came to public attention with the publication of *King Solomon's Mines*, which was a memoir of a journey that followed a map, the origin of which his second wife, Stella, at least, considered dubious at best.

28. Two or three years after Quatermain's visit to Olana, he recounted the entire adventure of Heu-Heu to Sir Henry Curtis, Captain John Good, R.N., and H. Rider Haggard while they all rested after a long day's sport at his estate. Immediately afterwards, Haggard wrote down the tale from memory. Forty years later, a delay that need not be detailed here, that transcription came to be printed under Haggard's byline as *Heu-Heu or The Monster*. As an aside, it is worth noting that *Heu-Heu* contains some scenes similar enough to scenes in the classic films *King Kong* and its sequel *Son of Kong*, that there has been speculation that the printing of *Heu-*

Heu may have actually inspired the creation of those two now-classic films, at least to some extent.

29. Quatermain's first wife was Marie Marais, the daughter of Henri, and Maraisfontein was where they met as children. Such was the pain associated with her demise and this whole chapter of his life that he seldom ever referred to it. Even the brief mention here was unusually candid, but it nonetheless sheds some light as to why he would hang an unused swing from his porch. See his memoir *Marie* for further details.

30. Sir Richard Burton was one of the great European explorers of the nineteenth century. He was the first to discover most of the great lakes of central Africa. But it is his 1853 adventure into Mecca and Medina disguised as a wandering dervish, or slightly mad holy man, for which he is most known. Within these venerated cities, he visited the most sacrosanct shrines of Islam, adventures which he documented in his *Personal Narrative of a Pilgrimage to Al-Madinah & Meccah*.

31. Burton was fluent in 29 languages and a dozen additional dialects.

32. This list of supplies for a desert trek is very similar to a list compiled for chapter 5 of Quatermain's *King Solomon's Mines*, from which we can deduce that he had a tried-and-true method for desert travel and stuck to it.

33. As described by Quatermain, two-fifths of this adventure took place in what is now the nation of Eritrea, which officially split from Ethiopia in 1993.

34. Now former editor, both because he left Arkham House to begin his own publishing concern, Golden Gryphon Press, and also as he passed away in 1999.

35. Tomasso Masini da Peretola's nickname was "Zoroastro," a name given to him by Cardinal Ridolfi because he was a dabbler in everything arcane.

36. It was this entire episode of the meteorites that seemed to capture H.P. Lovecraft's imagination to the highest degree (see the "Preface: The Prodigious Phone Call."). As editor, I deliberated at length whether to retain his revisions in this volume, but in the end decided that to include HPL's unedited, sometimes florid passages would be a radical change of style that could only be obtrusive within Quatermain's pragmatic narrative. Perhaps in a future edition, I will include an appendix that will focus on these passages and relate them to "The Colour Out of Space."

37. Wolfram von Eschenbach wrote the epic *Parzival* around 1200, wherein he says, "A valiant host lives there, and I will tell you how they are sustained. They live from a stone of purest kind. If you do not know it, it shall here be named for you. It is called *lapsit exillis.* By the power of that stone, the phoenix burns to ashes, but the ashes give him life again."

38. Indeed, there is much discussion among biologists and exobiologists today that the amino acids that helped generate life on Earth may have been delivered by meteorites that were derived from comets and, most especially, from cosmic dust.

39. Today these nomadic people are called the Afar, which is what they call themselves. They are a pastoral people but can be ferocious when angered. Their way of life has changed little since Quatermain's experience with them.

40. Matthew 7:13. Indeed, Luke 13:24 says much the same thing. It is ironic, therefore, that the verse that popped into Quatermain's mind is, in fact, one of those that are conjectured to be Q material.

41. In verifying this, I found references to Jewish marriage customs of two millennium ago. Typical of these is the essay entitled "The

World of Jesus" by Roland de Vaux (Director from 1945-65 of the École Biblique et Archéologique Française) that appears in *Everyday Life in Bible Times* published by the National Geographic Society: "Boys marry at 18; girls when they reach puberty, officially at twelve and a half." In addition, one can find in the extant copies of the *Infancy Gospel of James* (Christian Apocrypha—originally written no earlier than 150 A.D.) references to Mary's age when she was visited by the Holy Spirit that vary from 12 to 17, depending on the manuscript.

Furthermore, in 1858, Bernadette Sobirous consistently described her Marian apparitions at the French town of Lourdes as being a girl about twelve, a description that the press, clergy, and other commentators refused to accept because it was wholly unorthodox and too dissimilar to popular Marian iconography. As a result, the media of the time steadily increased the apparent age of the "Immaculate Conception" (as the apparition called herself) until that age settled at "about twenty," at which point everybody became content.

42. Though nobody can know just what was on Mariam's mind with regard to these words to "Will Scott," her reference to "two score years" does coincide with the events recorded in Leo Vincey's *Sherlock Holmes on the Roof of the World; or, The Adventure of the Wayfaring God* (see Appendix A) wherein Holmes' path happens to cross that of a mysterious Issa, who, it is suggested in that book, may be Jesus Christ.

43. In *The Moonstone*, Cuff tells an acquaintance, " . . . the roses get it. I began my life among them in my father's garden, and I shall end my life among them if I can."

44. Detailed in *The Ivory Child*. Also see note 19.

45. Quatermain's further adventures in the company of Professor Maria Mitchell is documented in the memoir that follows, *Allan Quatermain at the Dawn of Time; or, The Adventure of the Star of Wonder*, of which I am in possession, and which includes still another unknown tract with a similarly spiritual tenor.

46. Word has it that these two became inspired to visit far off Kafiristan in central Asia, at least this was reported by Rudyard Kipling in his East Indian newspaper *The Backwoodsman* in a piece titled "The Man Who Would Be King."

47. It is worth noting here, as an aside, that four years after his delightful evening with Church and Watson, Quatermain encountered another "rose of fire," one of an entirely different sort to be sure. As recorded in his final memoir, *Allan Quatermain,* having tired of retirement, he returned to Africa in search for adventure. His journeying took him into an underground river where he experienced:

> "[A] huge pillar-like jet of almost white flame . . . sprang fifty feet into the air, when it struck the roof and spread out some forty feet in diameter, falling back in curved sheets of fire shaped like the petals of a full-blown rose. Indeed this awful gas jet resembled nothing so much as a great flaming flower . . . . Below was the straight stalk, a foot or more thick, and above the dreadful bloom . . . which gleamed fiercer than any furnace ever lit by man . . . For yards and yards round the great rose of fire the rock-roof was red-hot . . . . My eyes seemed to be bursting from my head, and through my closed lids I could see the fierce light . . . . [I]t roared like all the fires of hell . . . ."

48. It must be noted here for the record that when my copy editor read this remark, his marvelous reaction was: "You mean to say that after reading of the discovery of the Grail and the living Virgin Mary and a lost valley containing the Library of Alexandria and the missing link and a lost gospel, your primary emotion was only that Hans's evil omens didn't come true?"

49. But I will take this logic one step further. Quatermain's description of the probable weapon used to kill Lidenbrock, that of a sharp instrument such as a scalpel, and also the description of the

wound, along with Sherrinford/Moriarty's apparent total lack of concern, all ring familiar. I believe that it is quite likely that another chapter of Sherrinford's life would play out sixteen years later on the streets of Whitechapel—a chapter that would attain its own very special and infamous notoriety.

ALLAN QUATERMAIN AT THE DAWN OF TIME

Or, The Adventure of the Star of Wonder

At the Heart of Which is a Ghost Story Experienced in 1873 By

Hans the Hottentot

Aide-de-Camp to Allan Quatermain and His Father Before Him

As Immediately Related to, Then Later Recounted in 1882 By

Allan Quatermain

Author of "King Solomon's Mines," "She and Allan," ETC.

To His Friend and Companion of Harrowing Adventures, Who Set Down the Tale as It Was Told to Her, Later Bequeathing It to Her Mysterious Cousin "M"

Lady Luna Holmes Ragnall

Heroine of "The Ivory Child" and "The Ancient Allan"

1905 Annotation and Apicultural Commentary By

M* *Ably Assisted By* SS‡

(Please see the footnotes below)

Including a Letter By and Extracts From the Journals Of

Maria Mitchell

America's First Woman Astronomer

Entire Monograph Assembled, Edited, Supplemented, and Annotated By

Thos. Kent Miller

Editor of "Allan Quatermain at the Crucible of Life," ETC.

---

* Some authorities have argued from internal evidence that "M" is the initial of a pseudonymous name used by a certain Great Detective during his retirement in Sussex.

‡. The same authorities sometimes suggest that "SS" are the initials of a neighbor, fellow honey fancier, and occasional assistant of M during this late interlude.

NOTE: The section of Quatermain's *Dawn of Time* memoir that I've titled "Hans' Story" is, I believe, the core of this book and everything before it is introduction, or prologue. Thus, all pages leading up to "Hans' Story" have been numbered with lower case Roman numerals, which is the convention for numbering introductory material in most books. "Hans' Story" is where you will find page number 1—*195 pages into the work.*

The *Thebes*

Contents

List of Illustrations

Astronomers used the James Clerk Maxwell Telescope to detect cosmic ashes from the dawn of time. It comes from stars that died more than 10 billion years ago. It is the first time stellar dust has been detected at such an early stage in the evolution of the Universe, say British scientists.

—BBC News

Oh, Star of wonder, Star of night/
Star with royal beauty bright/
Westward leading, still proceeding/
Guide us to the Perfect Light.

—John H. Hopkins, Jr.

Suddenly, in the air before them, not farther up than a low hill-top, flared a lambent flame; as they looked at it, the apparition contracted into a focus of dazzling lustre. Their hearts beat fast; their souls thrilled; and they shouted with one voice, "The Star! The Star! God is with us!"

—Lew Wallace in *Ben-Hur: A Tale of the Christ*
Book I Chapter V

Dedication

To the Alexander F. Morrison Planetarium of Yesteryear,
California Academy of Sciences, Golden Gate Park,
San Francisco, California, Circa 1960

*From the late 1950s through the early 1960s, during which time my
mean age was 15, I lived on the San Francisco Bay Peninsula in
California and would often ride a Greyhound Bus the twenty miles
or so north to San Francisco and take in an epic road-show "event"
movie, such as* Ben-Hur, Exodus, King of Kings, *or* The Wonderful
World of the Brothers Grimm, *which in those days were presented
in huge movie palaces and were treated with the sort of reverence
that we expected for Broadway theatrical productions. One could
not merely buy a ticket and enter the theater. It was necessary for
me to purchase tickets long in advance at the sole bookstore in my
hometown. These moments were really big events in my young life.*

*Around this same time, a star suddenly burst onto my life. It was
joy and tranquility and peace and awe and amazement and
wonderment all wrapped up in one. It was the Alexander F.
Morrison Planetarium in San Francisco's Golden Gate Park. The
planetarium was part of the vast California Academy of Sciences
complex that included the Steinhart Aquarium, and was just across
from the De Young Museum.*

*At the Morrison in those far-off days, after you paid admission,
you entered a domed theater big enough to hold perhaps one
hundred lounge chairs. The dome was lit in such a way as to
simulate a gold- and orange-tinged dusk, and classical music played
softly through invisible speakers. On a platform in the middle of the
dome was the most fantastic single object I had ever seen up until
then, and its fantastic quality never lessened, no matter how many
times I saw it. This was the planetarium projector, and it looked
rather like a giant insect. It was this elaborate mechanism (built from*

scratch soon after World War II by Academy optical technicians) that projected thousands of stars of varying brightness onto the inside of the dome.

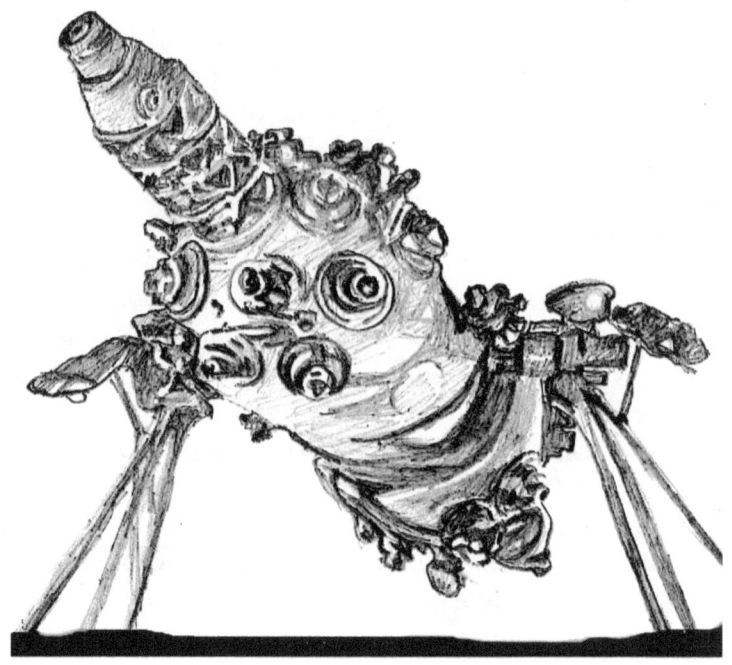

The star projector of the Morrison Planetarium circa 1960.

Once the round theater filled, the doors closed, the light of dusk faded as night arrived, and then, miraculously, before my eyes, the stars slowly came out (and I had to remind myself that we were indoors and that outside it was broad daylight) while the classical music continued softly. When it was completely dark, and the heavens sparkled with myriad crystal points as though seen from the top of the Rocky Mountains, the presenter, who was at a discreetly placed podium near the edge of dome and not noticed by most of the audience, began to speak in quiet tones and presented a family-friendly astronomy lesson that utilized all sorts of multimedia tools—

film, slides, models, animation—all pointed out with a magical red arrow of light wielded by the speaker.

But this calm ambiance simply went away in the early 1970s as commercialism crept into this bastion of science and learning, and, in lieu of the carefully crafted air of relaxation and peace, advertisements were projected onto the dome. Away went the tranquility that I had always prized. Away went the deliciously orchestrated merging of dusk into night accompanied by serene classical music.

More recently, the entire California Academy of Sciences has been renovated, and the 2008 version of the planetarium entered the 21ˢᵗ century by going entirely digital—with the result that the projector I so loved and admired was boxed up and put into storage more than a decade ago, as I've lately learned while trying to establish its location. Attempts by Academy staff to interest outside collectors or other museums have been, sadly, for naught. Can it be that the magnificent star projector that so touched my life will simply be forgotten?

I mourn this loss to this day, more than 40 years later.

It is to the memory of that institution, the Alexander F. Morrison Planetarium, at that moment in time, that I dedicate this book.

Thos. Kent Miller
December 2013

[T]here is in life an element of elfin coincidence which people reckoning on the prosaic may perpetually miss.
—G.K. Chesterton

Preface

By Thomas Kent Miller

i

Thrice in the last five decades, recognition of the name Allan Quatermain has experienced a revival.

A century ago there were bestselling authors much as there are today, but human nature being what it is, before very long something like 95 percent of those popular authors had been utterly forgotten or, at best, relegated to the domain of the cognoscenti. For example, do the names Mrs. Henry Wood, Bertram Mitford, Elizabeth Stuart Phelps, Allen Upward, and Marjorie Bowen sound familiar? I suppose not, yet, in various studies, we are told that Wood (1814-1887) attained sales of 5 million copies; that Mitford (1855-1914) wrote more than 40 novels, many of which sold briskly and were well reviewed; that Phelps (1844-1911) was an extremely popular writer in her day who had achieved phenomenal success; that Upward (1863-1926) was a prolific best-selling author of mysteries and novels; and that Bowen (1885-1952) had more than 180 novels and collections to her credit. In other cases, once-successful authors may not be utterly forgotten—just *almost* utterly forgotten. One such almost utterly forgotten bestseller was Allan Quatermain, who was the author of the African memoir published in 1885, *King Solomon's Mines*, which became an international best-seller overnight—the most popular book of its day (sort of *The Da Vinci Code* of 1885).

Quatermain himself, however, never enjoyed the benefits of this popularity, as he, with some stalwart friends, even before the book was published, had already returned to Africa seeking adventure and had lost all communication with the civilized world. It was while on this journey that Quatermain received a wound that proved fatal . . . but he died slowly enough that he had time to pen his final memoir titled simply *Allan Quatermain*.

Following the publication of *King Solomon's Mines* Quatermain's close friend Henry Rider Haggard came into possession of that final memoir and various other manuscripts and autobiographies, most of which Quatermain had dashed onto paper to wile away his time (and left behind) during his three years of retirement in England. Rider Haggard, who became in effect Quatermain's literary executor, arranged for these memoirs to be published, piecemeal, as they had a habit of popping up unexpectedly, the last in 1927.

Thus, from the mid-1880s to the mid-1920s, that is to say, for a forty year period roughly a century ago, the name Allan Quatermain was common currency. During that bygone era, most literate persons in England recognized the name and attached to it certain striking images of African adventure, as did readers throughout the world once the translators began their work.

However, even before the last of his books had been published, cultures and time had moved forward and changed, and, as is natural, the name Allan Quatermain faded from the consciousness of the public at large, though he was one of those lucky few who wasn't totally forgotten because, on one hand, most public libraries usually kept a copy of *King Solomon's Mines* lying about, and, on the other, there have been at least five movies based on that memoir; however, it is the exceedingly and extraordinarily rare movie-goer who would be able to identify the author of the original book!

And thus it stood for about 50 years until in the mid-1970s, when the Newcastle Publishing Company of North Hollywood, California, reprinted a few of Quatermain's out-of-print books, which stimulated a minor revival that lasted a decade.

Thirty years after that, and more than seventy years after the last of Quatermain's books had appeared, around the turn of the twentieth century into the twenty-first century, writer Alan Moore and illustrator Kevin O'Neill resurrected the name when they made Quatermain the primary character amongst many resurrected Victorian characters in their series of extraordinarily popular and clever graphic novels, *The League of Extraordinary Gentlemen*.

And before long, Sean Connery was playing Quatermain in a popular movie based on the series.

Meanwhile, however, a decade before the League came into existence, in the early 1990s, a long lost Quatermain memoir had come to light, and it was my good fortune, in 1994, to be offered the opportunity to edit and shepherd that memoir into publication. The provenance of that manuscript is most interesting. Beginning as Quatermain's oral account of an 1872 adventure told before a roaring fire in a sitting room in upstate New York, it was put into writing by Dr. John H. Watson *(a full month before he'd even met the great detective!)*; and then bestowed onto Frederick Church, the great landscape painter of the mid-19th century. Following Church's death in 1900, the memoir remained in the possession of his heirs, though stored in a wine cellar for 25 years. By chance, H.P. Lovecraft was presented by the heirs with the opportunity to prepare the manuscript for publication, and he enthusiastically accepted. However, it seems he lost interest in it, and it basically fell off the earth for 65 years. After Lovecraft's death, the box of papers that contained the manuscript was misplaced and the manuscript's very existence remained unknown until it came to light in the early 1990s. At that point, Lovecraft's original (posthumous) book publisher, Arkham House, took on the responsibility of deciding how best to deal with it. However, its then editor had a full plate, and based on his awareness of my prior editing of *Sherlock Holmes on the Roof of the World*, he asked me if I would be interested in taking up the challenge.

Of course I grabbed at the chance and eventually, after its own thoroughly bumpy and exceedingly convoluted publication road (that included, believe it or not, an abortive and embarrassing $75 million movie titled *The Rose of Fire* with Michael Caine, Gene Hackman, and Sigourney Weaver that I had absolutely no responsibility for), the scholarly book that I had originally envisioned and had labored to prepare finally appeared as *Allan Quatermain at the Crucible of Life; or, The Adventure of the Rose of Fire*—an adventure involving both Quatermain and the Great Detective. Thereupon, Quatermain's memoirs of his 1872 travails gained the notice of anthropologists and conservationists around the world—the end result being that Quatermain's words helped to literally change the face of Africa and revolutionize public awareness of human origins, all of which is detailed in the prefaces of that book.

Thus, you can imagine what a staggering shock it was, after all this time, to learn that all the while that I was editing both *Sherlock Holmes on the Roof of the World* and *Allan Quatermain at the Crucible of Life*, with absolutely no awareness of it, by some miracle of chance, I had in my possession still *another* unknown Quatermain memoir.

That new memoir is now the book you are holding, *Allan Quatermain at the Dawn of Time; or, The Adventure of the Star of Wonder.*

ii

I am a pack rat.

Without this defining aspect of my life, I wouldn't be writing these words, I wouldn't be beginning this book.

In the early 1980s, my wife and I bought our first house in the Emerald Lake district of Redwood City, California. Emerald Lake is a forested, rustic pocket of turn-of-the-century log houses in an otherwise normal suburb of San Francisco. As it happened, by pure chance, down the road apiece, around a few bends, lived E. Hoffmann Price--making him my neighbor. Price was a popular and successful contributor to pulp magazines from the 1920s to the 1950s. His first sales were to *Weird Tales* magazine, whereupon he became a friend of many popular writers of the day through correspondence. Before long, he was selling stories to a long string of magazines with titles like *Spicy Detective, Adventure,* and *Magic Carpet.* In time, he developed a wanderlust that he sated by automobile "touring," then a new pastime, and he drove around the country meeting his colleagues and friends, writers and editors, such as Henry Kuttner, Seabury Quinn, Clark Ashton Smith, Otis Adelbert Kline, Robert E. Howard, and H.P. Lovecraft. In the 1950s, however, the pulp magazines faded, and Price gave up writing as no longer lucrative and began work as a microfilm technician with his local government. He'd lived in his house for

about sixty years, for nearly all the time he had been writing for the
pulps.

I had first met Price in his home in 1977 where he regaled
myself and two friends for hours with tales of his myriad adventures
the world over and plied us with various liquors. One of those
friends and I wrote a profile of Price that ran in a local magazine,
and eventually an expanded version was printed in the fanzine *The
Weird Tales Collector # 6* . This was thirty-five years ago.

Later, after we became neighbors, Price and his wife and my
family visited one another often in the course of the next four years.

Then, on April 25, 1986, a life-altering event happened in my
family's life, and we unexpectedly and literally moved overnight
from northern California to southern California, a distance of 450
miles.

Thomas Kent Miller and E. Hoffmann Price approximately 1985.
(Photo: Jayne Miller)

During the few hours (literally) when this was happening and
while I was away from the house, Price came to visit, and my wife,
who was in the midst of chaos, received him, apologizing that I
wasn't around. Price gave Jayne a thick manila envelope and asked

that she give it to me. Within moments of his leaving, she threw the envelope in a box and promptly forgot totally about it, never mentioning this incident to me, as she had far more important things on her mind. During the next year, we sold our house and I moved my family and our belongings nine times (again literally). In the end, my wife and I settled in a small southern California community, where we have been living since. As things quieted down, I finished up the last editorial tasks on *Sherlock Holmes on the Roof of the World* and shepherded that slim book through publication in 1987, the centenary of the Great Detective's first appearance in *Beeton's Christmas Annual.*

Of course, many wonderful books and other treasured possessions vanished from my cognizance during all that 1986 shell game of packing and moving, and moving and packing; much of it was stored and languished in unopened boxes (eventually tattered boxes) in various places. That was more than a quarter century ago as I type, and treasures are still resurfacing to this very day.

It was in 2008, then, 21 years after *Roof of the World* was published and 14 years after Quatermain's Ethiopian memoir *(Crucible of Life)* had come to my attention, that I was rummaging in our rent-a-storage unit in a nearby town looking for some *Weird Tales* magazines that I knew I had somewhere. I opened a box . . . and there on top was a fat, faded-manila envelope that I didn't recall ever having seen before. In a broad, bold hand, my name was written in capital letters in the middle of the envelope in faded blue ball-point pen. When I opened the envelope, I found the following extraordinary note to me from E. Hoffmann Price clipped to a somewhat smaller envelope with a seriously rusty paperclip. Within this second envelope was a succession of five other envelopes, each smaller than the previous, a circumstance exactly analogous to a set of Russian nesting dolls.

The note read thusly:

Dear Tom,

I was puttering under the house recently and came across the enclosed, which has been tucked away in my basement since 1936, surviving floods and mud and other disasters where other possessions, such as cartons of <u>Weird Tales</u> and <u>Adventure</u>, didn't. Bob Howard's dad, Isaac, sent it to me within a few days of Bob's suicide and of the simultaneous passing of Isaac's wife. Those many years ago I perused it, and could not for the life of me determine why Bob had thought to send it to me. During my correspondence with Isaac over the years before his own passing in 1944, he told me how Bob had spent upwards of a week organizing his files and even made funeral arrangements, so it seems logical that at that transitional moment, shipping me the enclosed was something he felt was important. Nevertheless, frankly, I could not decide what to do with it, and as is common in this kind of instance, I eventually did nothing at all and soon forgot about it. You know that Dr. Howard sent me a trunk of Bob's papers that I eventually sent to more capable hands, and it never occurred to me to add this packet to that collection. Now that it has surfaced again, I thought of you. My assessment is pretty much the same as Bob's. It is hard to think of it in any other manner than as a hoax. I am letting you have it as you are interested in our doings during those days and maybe you'll be able to do something practical with it.

April 25, 1986

Inside the second envelope and clipped to the third was this short handwritten note from Robert E. Howard's father to Price:

Cross Plains, Texas
July 3, 1936

Mr. E. Hoffmann Price
Redwood City, Calif.

Dear Mr. Price:

I am so sorry to write you again so soon after my letter of the 27th. However, Robert, I think, wanted you to have this package. At the least he had it all wrapped and sealed and addressed to you. I am enclosing his sealed envelope herewith.

Yours truly,

Dr. I.M. Howard
Box 313
Cross Plains, Tex.

In that third envelope was this note from Robert E. Howard to Price, the first of seven missives clipped to the fourth envelope:

Cross Plains, Texas
June 9, 1936

Dear Ed:

The contents of this package are quite extraordinary, so much so that I can only assume it is an elaborate turn-of-the-century hoax. I received it via an antiquarian bookstore located in Ireland. I doubt the bookseller was the architect of the joke. Anyway, it is too out-of-the-ordinary to merely toss away. Therefore I bequeath it to you.

I've included the pertinent correspondence that resulted in my possession of the envelope and its contents

Very truly yours
Bob

Then there came this series of six linked formal letters. Those written by Howard are all carbon copies:

[carbon copy]

Box 313
Cross Plains, Texas
April 2, 1930

W.H. Smith & Sons Ltd.
24 High Street
Newtown, Powys
Wales

To whom it may concern:

I was recently intrigued by your advertisement that I happened to see in a travel magazine. I am writing to enquire if you have the following book that I would be able to purchase, <u>The Romance of Early British Life; From the Earliest Times to the Coming of the Danes</u>, by G.F. Scott Elliot, and published by Seeley and Co. (1909) which is not readily available in the states, though I have seen a copy in a library. In lieu of that particular title I am also interested in anything touching upon Celtic history and folklore, especially during the era of Roman occupation.

Yours Sincerely,
R.E. Howard

5 May 1930

W.H. Smith & Sons Ltd.
24 High Street
Newtown, Powys
Wales

Dear Mr. R.E. Howard
Box 313
Cross Plains, Texas
USA

Dear Mr. Howard:

Thank you for your correspondence dated 2 April.
However, W.H. Smith & Sons stocks only books of
contemporary interest. I suggest that you try the following
bookstore that may be able to help you: Hodges & Figgis
Books, 56-58 Dawson Street, Dublin.

All best regards,
E. Fitzgerald

[carbon copy]

Box 313
Cross Plains, Texas
July 6, 1930

Hodges & Figgis Books
56-58 Dawson Street
Dublin, Ireland

To whom it may concern:

Mr. Fitzgerald of W.H. Smith suggested I contact your shop
to enquire about the availability of <u>The Romance of Early
British Life; From the Earliest Times to the Coming of the
Danes</u>, by G.F. Scott Elliot, and published by Seeley and
Co. (1909). I am also interested to know about Celtic
histories and folklore in general.

Yours Sincerely,
R.E. Howard

7 August 1930
Hodges & Figgis Books
56-58 Dawson Street
Dublin, Ireland

Mr. Robert E. Howard
Box 313
Cross Plains, Texas
USA

Dear Mr. Howard:

At this present time, we do not have in stock the title you enquired about on 6 July, though I will make a point of communicating with other stores to check its availability. In the meantime, I can recommend the following ($3.00 each after conversion) which we do have in stock:

<u>The Witch Cult in Western Europe</u> by Margaret Murray
<u>The Romance of the Rose</u> by Guillaume de Lorris
<u>Fairy Faith in Celtic Countries</u> by W.Y. Evans-Wentz
<u>The Welsh Fairy Book</u> by W. Jenkyn Thomas
<u>Celtic Folklore: Welsh and Manx</u> by John Rhys

I look forward to hearing from you,

Yours sincerely,
Edward Nicholson
Manager

[carbon copy]

Cross Plains, Texas
Sept. 6, 1930

Hodges & Figgis Books
56-58 Dawson Street
Dublin, Ireland

Dear Mr. Nicholson:

Thank you for your response to my enquiry. I am in fact most
interested in two of the books that you list. I enclose my United
States Postal Office money order for $8.00, which should be
sufficient funds to cover also postage and handling,

The Welsh Fairy Book by W. Jenkyn Thomas
Celtic Folklore: Welsh and Manx by John Rhys

I look forward to receiving these unique titles.

Yours truly,
Robert E. Howard

24 October 1930
Hodges & Figgis Books
56-58 Dawson Street
Dublin, Ireland

Dear Mr. Howard:

Many thanks for your order.

    Also, though I am taking a chance, I nonetheless feel certain that you must be THE Robert E. Howard, the author of "Skull-Face," etc. I frankly feel honoured that you should do business with my store. As a small gesture of appreciation, I am enclosing along with your books an odd item that, in point of fact, was already part of the inventory of the store when the current owners purchased it from Mr. Webster more than 25 years ago. That this item is old goes without saying, but its authenticity is highly suspect. I have shown it to some experts and they all have spent a few minutes examining it and then smiled and told me it is a rather sophisticated hoax and worthless. Because it doesn't appear that I can sell it to anyone with a clear conscience, and because it has been in the store for so long, I am, rather impulsively I admit, including the item in question along with the books I am sending you. As a well-known author of fantasy and the like, perhaps you will have better use for it than I. It is a sort of diary, or purports to be.

    In any event, it is now yours.

All the best,
Edward Nicholson
Manager

The fourth envelope, to which these last seven letters were clipped, bore the Dublin address of the Hodges & Figgis bookstore in the top left corner. I opened this envelope, mindful of its age and brittleness, and I found yet another envelope, this time with no accompanying message. In the center of the envelope was scribbled "To JW" and nothing else. Opening this envelope I found still another with a single defaced formal typewritten letter attached. A hand-written note was scrawled at the bottom of the letter. This is that letter along with the note (in italics and boxed) at the bottom:

Mellis & Mellis
Solicitors
50 Broad Street
London

21 Dec. 1905

[HERE IS A SQUARE HOLE CUT WITH A SHARP BLADE IN THE PAPER
WHERE THE RECIPIENT'S NAME AND ADDRESS WOULD HAVE BEEN.]

Dear Mr. [ANOTHER HOLE]

Our late client, the Lady Luna Holmes Ragnall, requested
that we hand-deliver this envelope to you following her death
in 1884, but not before we could determine, by whatever
means at our disposal, and as soon as possible following
such determination, that you had conclusively retired from
your career as a consulting [ANOTHER HOLE]. It was her final
request. Please do not hesitate to contact us should you have
questions.

Respectfully yours.
Anderson Mellis

am:lbn

*What a hoot cousin Luna sent me this ms.—via her solicitors
21 years after the fact. And thus, after more than 3 decades,
I'm again crossing paths with dear old Quatermain!*

When I opened the next envelope, I found a small diary of indeterminate color because it had long faded into a sort of grey. Placed between the cover and the first page of the book was a fat bulging envelope that we would call legal-sized today. The words "To My Cousin—Please Read BEFORE Negotiating the Contents of This Old Diary" had been written on the envelope in the pleasant script that I would soon come to know so well. However, I set that smaller envelope aside and gave the diary a careful examination page by page.

As I had already worked with two similar documents professionally, I saw quickly that this was neither a joke nor a hoax. Rather, I saw that it was authentic and priceless. It was, quite amazingly, another new Allan Quatermain memoir, this time telling of an experience in west Africa. Examination showed that it comprised an oral account by Quatermain told to Luna Holmes in her bedroom in Ragnall Castle and written down by Luna herself. This document, as you have just seen, was eventually delivered to Luna's presumed cousin via her solicitors, Mellis & Mellis, but that cousin's name had been carefully expurgated—no doubt at the direction of the person we will come to know as "M"—from the various documents that had come into my possession. The cuttings, that is to say the holes, had edges that were either yellowed or browned depending on the paper type, affirming for me that the mutilation had happened long ago. He, that is the cousin (we presume the male gender), is known to us only as, as just mentioned, "M". The only conclusive or apparent information we learn about M is that he was somehow affiliated with beekeeping, and that he rather rudely ordered about an individual identified only as "SS".

The *vast* almost incalculable irony is that I had actually *possessed* this memoir for two years, stuffed in an envelope addressed to me and packed in a box gathering dust in a garage, even as I was finishing up my first book, *Sherlock Holmes on the Roof of the World*, in 1987—and there it remained for another 26 years, unknown to me and packed away in that moldering cardboard box until I finally stumbled upon it in our storage unit 17 years *after* I'd received that momentous call from James Turner that resulted in the publication of my second book *Allan Quatermain at the Crucible of Life* and all the earth-shattering events that fell from that!

After examining the contents of the diary that first time, I picked up the bulging legal-sized envelope that I had found in the diary and which I had set aside. It contained a letter to M from Lady Luna Holmes Ragnall consisting of nineteen sheets of feminine note paper topped with the Ragnall crest, which still retained a faint aroma of roses. Following that were letters from Professor Maria *[Editor's note: Pronounced Ma-RYE-ah]* Mitchell to Luna and another from Quatermain to Maria. In the mid-1800s, Maria Mitchell had risen to fame as America's first woman astronomer and subsequently taught at Vassar College. She also figured prominently in *Allan Quatermain at the Crucible of Life*.

Here follows the contents of those letters followed by Quatermain's memoir as set down by Luna Holmes. The reader will note that in these documents as I am presenting them there are a number of small separate boxes with text printed alongside Luna's entries. These are an attempt to represent the numerous handwritten marginal notes that appear throughout the letters and diary. These notes are all dictated by a person identified only as "M" to another identified as "SS". It appears, thus, that SS must have read aloud Luna's documents to M (SS apparently being conversant in the same singular shorthand that M had taught Luna), while M regularly interrupted to give terse instructions or make some comment or another that SS was obliged to copy into the margins. You will observe that many of these notes appear to focus on the minutia of beekeeping and have nothing to do with either Luna's record or Quatermain's tale, though these notes grow in prolixity, profundity, and relevance as Quatermain's story draws out.

The first of these boxes is a request to SS to send the diary and associated materials to a "W". Of course, while we don't know who either SS or W was (aside from whatever one chooses to deduce from the scribbled "To JW" on the corresponding envelope), we can certainly make educated guesses. However, the fact that the diary languished in a Dublin bookstore for 25 years indicates that something went wrong. Anything is possible; maybe SS did not ship it, or maybe W mislaid it, or maybe some mischief occurred while the package was en route, that is, *between* points SS and W. All we can say for sure is that M requested it be sent to W, and not much afterward, it found its way to Mr. Webster's antiquarian bookshop.

Thus, Luna Holmes' diary traveled as follows: She wrote it in 1884 and soon thereafter put it in an envelope labeled to go to her cousin. She may have hand delivered that envelope to the offices of Mellis & Mellis with instructions that it be delivered to her cousin only when certain conditions had been met. The envelope, therefore, was tucked in the solicitors' safe for more than 20 years, whereupon they delivered it to M in 1905. M did not keep it long and requested that it be sent to W. It apparently did not get to its destination, but instead it further languished in a Dublin bookstore for another 25 years. Then it was sent to Robert E. Howard, who kept it for six years before he made sure it was sent to E. Hoffmann

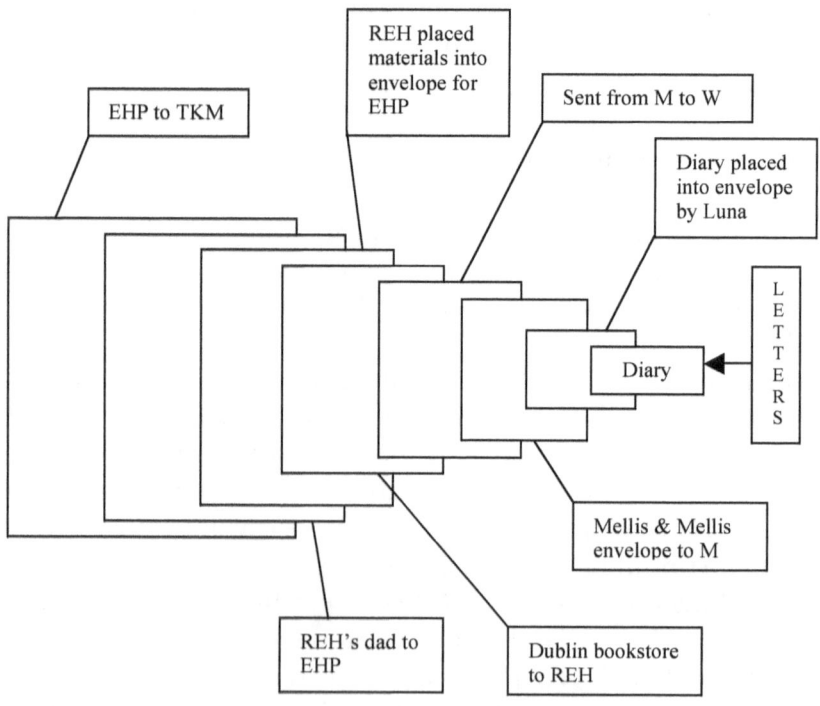

The succession of envelopes shown schematically.

Price, who, for lack of any other reason to treat it any differently, kept it under his house for about 50 more years and then delivered it to me, who unknowingly possessed it for another 22 years or so in a succession of garages and storage units. Therefore, from the time the diary was written to the time it arrived at my front door was slightly more than a century, and two more decades passed until I stumbled upon it! In round numbers, that's a journey of 125 years.

Thus, in the fullness of time, so to speak, I burrowed my way through that astonishing succession of envelopes, shown schematically here, finding at last the old diary that the Lady Luna Holmes Ragnall had grabbed in her haste to find writing materials on which to record her friend's African adventure and which diary she arranged to be delivered to her cousin via her attorneys, along with her scented explanatory letter and some others, all of which follow here as forewords to Quatermain's tale.

First Foreword: A Letter
FROM LADY LUNA HOLMES RAGNALL
TO HER UNNAMED COUSIN

18 August, 1884

My dear cousin:

Boo!!

I'm haunting you now perhaps long after my passing because I wish you to have something of mine. I am requesting my solicitors to deliver it to you only after all principal parties are gone . . . and after they have deemed (through whatever sources) that you are no longer active in the [A HOLE] business, per se, for I have no wish to distract you from your proper affairs.

The gentlemen who have delivered this packet to you—per your request—have no idea of our blood relationship.

At best, from your viewpoint, the enclosed diary will be a curiosity, I suppose.

SS—
Send W all this material from my dear departed cousin. It's astronomically interesting, of course. I'm quite positive that he will want to add it to his files for eventual embellishment.
—M

(See footnotes on the title page.)

I doubt I have mentioned him to you since your and my paths cross so infrequently, but I have a friend by the name of Allan Quatermain. He recently came into a fortune having to do with—I speak the truth!—King Solomon's Mines. He tells me that he has written the whole thing down and that he expects it to be published as a book next year (that is, next year from my point of view—heaven only knows when from yours). With that fortune he bought an estate in Yorkshire.

Allan's and my association has been long and multifarious to say the least! In fact, now I do recall that he and you were both at a garden party held here at the castle in the summer of 1870, though you were but a lad, and Allan is rather shy in social situations, so it is doubtful that you will remember him.

You know of course that I left nothing whatsoever to you as was your request, and, further, I've never mentioned my relationship to you since you made it clear that time years ago how utterly inconvenient my dropping your name could prove to you. Even disastrous!

Though I have bequeathed my monies and possessions to Allan from my heart, I strongly suspect that he will decline—for much the same reason as yourself—namely the inconvenience of riches would impinge on his quiet life. Besides, he is rich already from having cashed in those diamonds that he and his friends brought back from King Solomon's Mines.

However, getting to the point, the thing that I want to give you, and which I believe you will find rather interesting, is the attached ms. written in my hand in the shorthand that you taught me, as Allan relayed the astonishing events of his experience in west Africa.

You will be interested in learning how I happened to hear Allan's adventure!

As you know, as a woman and a noble one by marriage, I can be fickle. And during the evening in question, I had suffered through indignities unimaginable from those horrible Atterby-Smith relatives of Lord Ragnall, who have been harassing me about what they believe is their rightful inheritance—namely all of it! The fact is that I would have embarrassed myself if I hadn't in a fury stomped up those stairs before I could lose my temper, leaving poor Allan to suffer the load and no doubt ponder the peculiar ways of my sex *[Editor's note: See* The Ancient Allan*]*.

Be that as it may, in only a little time I felt lonely in my rooms and asked Alfred [Luna's footman] to fetch Allan. Arriving a little while later, he seemed confused but as docile as a puppy dog. I just needed company, you see, after having to endure those awful people, and I had no intention beyond merely chatting about whatever came to mind—anything but a certain adventure he and I shared some time ago for quite a duration. Now of course, you don't know, or at least I shouldn't think that you would know, that due to various factors having to do with my being kidnapped and being forced to take on the role of priestess of the Kandah tribe in Central Africa, my senses are now ever heightened and it was easy enough to see that poor Allan—who had fought in infinitely more terrible mêlées than I can ever imagine—felt distinctly uncomfortable being alone with me in my chambers behind closed doors. Thus with the intent of distracting him from his immediate plight, I poured him a drink and asked him some leading questions hoping he would tell me in some detail of one or more of his other expeditions that did not involve me, particularly of the curious ones—(by that I mean expeditions over and beyond those ordinary hunting and trading ones by which he plied his trade of hunter and guide, usually with the end being some poor young elephant was left orphaned, though, once when I admonished him on the subject, he admitted that such wanton killing was beginning to give him pause)—for I knew of course that some of his adventures were especially unique.

Picking a subject at random, I asked him to elaborate on some points he had mentioned earlier in the day regarding K.S.M. and the safari leading up to the mines. (Oh, I'm putting the cart before the horse! He had earlier told me that he'd only just finished writing a manuscript that detailed that journey in all its particulars and that he would bring it over for me to read if I was interested.) But, just then he told me how he was tired of that subject and preferred not to discuss it then.

Perhaps, I suggested, over the years he had encountered other lost treasures—wonders to stir the soul. Then I was amazed to see dear Allan become wistful. He was quiet, using his fingertips to make tracks through the condensation on his glass. In time, I saw that the pattern he was making was that of stars, or rather, a star repeated over and over. Finally I had to interrupt his reverie and ask what was he thinking, whereupon he said, "Well Luna, there was a time in west Africa that had more than its fair share of the out of the ordinary about it."

"And the stars?" I asked, for I am nothing if not bold, but you already know that, dear cousin.

"Stars?" he responded confused, and when I pointed to his glass, he frankly blushed. "Oh, I gave myself away! Your questions following so close on one another brought to mind the other time I had a fortune in diamonds in my hands—or, I mean, one fabulous diamond. I didn't have it long enough for it to be christened any particular name, but I thought of it then and still do as my "Star of Wonder." It was mine to do with as I wished . . . but as you can easily conclude, the one thing I didn't do with it was bring it home and cash it in."

"Heavens! Why on earth not?"

"You know what they say, my dear, 'And therein lies a tale!' and to tell it properly would require most of the night."

"Well." I said, "do you see me doing anything else of importance?"

A simple enough argument that won the day, and for several hours I was treated to the joy of beholding a new Allan Quatermain, one that I was not acquainted with—a loquacious Allan Quatermain!

He refilled his glass, stretched his legs toward the blazing fire in my bedroom hearth and quietly began his story. After a few minutes I realized that I was missing the chance of a lifetime and that this was an opportunity to capture all the spirit of the man, so I interrupted him to ask if he wouldn't mind if I took down his words, to which he assented.

When I had grabbed an old unused diary from my corner press and with some pencils in hand, I spent a few minutes hastily summarizing what he had already narrated. All the time I was catching up, he sat silently, apparently in thought. When I was done, rather than continue his story, he communicated the following, as I recall it from memory:

"You know, Luna, here is a queer thing. There are three people who are no longer in this world who touched me to such a degree that mentioning their names or the circumstances that I shared with them in common conversation feels like irreverence. Thus, to remember their loss, or, rather, the loss of them which is my loss, brings down on me a torrent of emotions that I would prefer to avoid."

"Allan," I say, "please tell me."

"Well, there are my two wives, Marie and Stella, and the third is Hans. With regard to Marie and Stella, I want you to know that during my leisure time here in England at the Grange, which is about *all* I have these days, I have jotted down some memories of them and there are two volumes that are devoted to their lives as I knew them—but that is all I wish to say on that subject—Luna, are you crying?" *[Editor's note: See* Marie *and* Allan's Wife.*]*

"No, Allan. Well, yes. Yes, I was, as I can only imagine the strength and devotion of such women must assuredly be beyond my ken!"

Allan smiled reflectively, or at least as I imagined it to be, and said passionately, "No more!" Then after pausing to reflect for a minute or two, he asked, "You remember Hans?"

"Clearly and with much fondness, I have wonderful memories of Hans," I replied, as that old Hottentot was more like Allan's shadow than his servant, and we had shared some little time together before his passing, through the agency of an enraged terrible and giant elephant *[Editor's note: See* The Ivory Child*]*, though admittedly I was not on my best form, having been recently kidnapped, drugged for months on end, and suffered indignities numerous and unmentionable.

But Allan continued, "I was about to say that with

people who never knew Hans, there is no point at all in mentioning him, because one really needed to know him and experience him and have a clear picture of him in mind, or else the exercise of discussing him in conversation is pointless . . . ."

Again, Allan seemed lost in thought for a while.

"But you were saying about Hans."

"Well, here is that queer thing that I meant to say—and, Luna, since you did in fact know him for some time, I can speak comfortably about him to you. Well you remember how exceedingly bright and astute he was, despite never having any formal schooling in the European sense, at least none beyond the lessons my father furnished to all the staff of our Cape Colony station where he performed his duties as a Church of England clergyman. What I'm trying to say is that I can never remember Hans saying, that is speaking out loud, anything to any European either *in* his own language or *about* his language, which is called Khoi. It's that distinct clicking language that the Hottentot people use along with Bushmen and a few other native groups. Of course, as you know first hand, he and I could speak fluently to one another in English, Dutch, Arabic, and Zulu, and he, as I, could communicate in a whole spectrum of languages as one must be able to in order to survive in the distant reaches of Africa where we trekked. I bring this up now because the story I have to tell depends greatly on the nature of his own native language, the language of his birth, which is extremely difficult for Europeans to reproduce . . . . I'm sorry to be wandering, Luna, but there is a point, or rather a story, or perhaps anecdote is a better term to which all the preceding is preface. There was the time in 1873 . . . ."

The tale that he told that night of an adventure with his manservant Hans astonished even I, who have known and seen so terribly much: I who am not easily astonished due to the peculiarities of my own life and certain adventures I endured against my will.

But I have finished my little introduction to what follows. Knowing you, I expect it has some points of interest, and as I dispose my will, there is nothing else I can imagine doing with Allan's record of Hans' encounter with—what?

Your loving and eternal cousin,
Luna

P.S. I must be growing feeble because there is another item that is for all intents and purposes a prequel of sorts to Allan's long story and which I have been meaning to also give you. I am tiring, so I will say this in as few words as I can. Within a few days of Allan sharing his story with me, I impulsively wrote to Professor Maria Mitchell, the noted astronomy professor at Vassar College in New York, who you will learn when you read the diary, was a major participant in the events Allan described. I don't know what I expected, but . . . lo! she responded. I attach her epistle here along with my record of that evening. Her letter, which is actually several, is an admirable introduction to Allan's tale. And, now that I have already said farewell, I hasten to do so again, as I don't wish to appear flighty.

> SS—
> The honey is crystallising again in the farther hives. Check temp.
> —M

Luna

Second Foreword: A Letter
FROM PROFESSOR MARIA MITCHELL
TO LADY LUNA HOLMES RAGNALL

8 January, 1884

Dear Lady Ragnall:

Thank you for your extended message of this last November. Oh, I wish I could say how delighted I was that you wrote and that I have heard much about you from our mutual friend, and that aside from that, I am honored beyond human word's ability to convey the extremity of my pleasure—but, alas!, none of that would be true because (1) my social circles are limited at best, (2) my knowledge of the intricacies of the British hierarchy, of peers and knights and so forth is abominable, and (3) I can't recall that Allan ever mentioned you—and as a result, I have never heard of you, though I don't doubt for one second that you are in fact who you say you are, and that as a natural consequence of that status, you must be richer than Croesus.

Please forgive my clumsy manner of introducing this letter, for I am in fact so happy you wrote and I often wonder about dear Allan, and heaven knows that correspondence was never his forte and I wish to respect his privacy at all costs.

> *SS—*
> *Let's repurpose the wax. Put on calendar to discuss.*
> *REMEMBER!*
> *—M*

It seems that we have in common that we have both experienced intimate and long adventures with Allan and his man Hans. Mine were twofold, first in east Africa on the Horn and close beside the Red Sea and the second was in west Africa, just a stone's throw from the Atlantic Ocean on the border region between Sierra Leone and Liberia. However . . . however interesting my experiences were, I cannot imagine the degree of yours. Being kidnapped as you have described and suffering the lot of being drugged and violated body and soul—I cannot fathom it! And to think that you have been able to retain some semblance of sanity and normalcy, for which I much admire you. It seems that it was the courage and persistence of both Allan and your husband, Lord Ragnall, by which you survived. God protect them both—the one in life and the other in Heaven.

In my own case, Allan's and my first meeting was pure happenstance, unwittingly arranged by the highest powers of both government and church, and as full as it was with incident, it lasted only a few days. In the second instance, Allan and Hans, again unwittingly, stumbled onto a scientific encampment of which I was part. Of course, upon their unexpected appearance at the gates of the place, my scientific colleagues would have turned them away if it had not been for my insistence that they remain. But once having entered, due to the situation, Q and H were obliged to be our guests for some weeks, but of course, he has already explained or confided to you this much or else you would never have gone to the trouble of contacting me! Nevertheless, of course, he, or they, he and Hans, were not privy to anything much more than the surface details of daily life in the encampment, or laboratory, and despite my high regard for Allan, neither could I then, nor now, say too much as I am ever bound by oath.

Yet, as you are so close to him, it is incumbent on me to share something with you. There is so much I want to share with you, but all that must wait because I have something particular to say, and Heaven only knows how, if I get sidetracked and if exhaustion sets in due to the digression, it may be a whole day until I can circuitously get back to my point. What I wish to share needs to be done now and not put off. It is namely this:

Twelve years ago in the summer of 1872, after Allan and the rest of our little group parted at the edge of the Red Sea and once I was home and had begun my life again—though, as it turned out, this would not be for long—I received a most unusual letter from Allan. Indeed, it wasn't really from Allan at all, because he was mainly the agent by whom another wanted to speak to me, but I will not put the cart before the horse. I wish now to include here that letter of a dozen years ago. The reason is that I believe that the message so revealed (despite its flattering reflection on my own person, which modesty would have me exclude, but which act would render the message meaningless) must be shared, that is to say, must become known to another beyond my poor humble self. I think there is something here (despite its strangeness) that ought to be better known and so here is the letter. It is odd because, there is a letter within a letter within a letter but you will see for yourself.

Now, I must wind down this note, as I am very excited that Mr. Matthew Arnold will be presenting in just a few hours his views on Emerson to an expected group of 600 students and townspeople! I've been looking forward to this lecture for some time, and must now get ready.

Yours,
M. M.

Third Foreword: A Letter
FROM ALLAN QUATERMAIN
TO PROFESSOR MARIA MITCHELL

July 1872

My dear Maria:

I am sorry to impose on your normal life in America so soon. I am doing so, however, at the request of a mutual friend. But before that—as I have this unexpected opportunity to communicate with you—something I would not have ordinarily thought to do—not because of avoidance nor rudeness, but because I do not like myself to be imposed on, therefore I tend to assume that any outreach from me to anybody would be construed as an imposition—I wish now to state how pleasant I found your company during our odd little safari three or four months ago. I need not remind you that you were the only woman in our group of a dozen opinionated and some disingenuous men, which might have been an intimidating circumstance for many a woman, but never seemed to faze you in the least. From first to last I must admit you had inspired in me the greatest respect and admiration not only for the heights to which you have risen in academia, as well as your scientific attainments, but for your honest ability to participate in our group without resorting to the feminine tricks that your gender, regardless of race, can do so well, much to the bafflement and embarrassment of us poor men. As I said, I am taking this opportunity now to sing your praises because this correspondence has been pressed on me, on one hand, and because it is only right to speak the truth in a world so absorbed with self-advancement and appearances and so much other nonsense that it is often difficult merely to live and let live and be content within our own skins, and I must say that Hans *[Editor's note: See "Introduction: H. Rider Haggard's Character Hans the Hottentot" in the second book of this trilogy,* Allan Quatermain at the Crucible of Life*, for vital information about Hans.]*, in his own way, feels much the same as I and seldom does a day go by that he doesn't mention you with his own brand of fondness and admiration. ("Baas, remember that crazy lady who risked her life, first, seeking that pile of rocks they called the Heaven's Dead, and, then, by thrusting herself into a man's battle and thereby winning the day, much to the chagrin of many men, including many of those tall, skinny desert folk, especially of the one whose head she lopped off; well, if ever you chance to talk to her in a letter, tell her that I believe she did the right thing, and that my only regret is that I didn't think just then to kick that fool's head around just for fun until my foot ached!") But the true reason I am writing now is that another member of our troop is requesting that I do so (though, please note that his message includes an addendum addressed to me from Zikali, that awful Zulu wizard Shaka once named "The Thing That Should Never Have Been Born").

It is Bayushtiak *[Editor's note: See* Allan Quatermain at the Crucible of Life*]* who asks that I communicate with you. Here following are the impressions he wished me to convey to you, and that I will leave you with. I tried to keep true to his intentions, neither taking away nor adding any thought or statement of consequence of my own or by extrapolating any more than I ought, though I was sorely tempted to soften the edges of his remarks, which I believe sprang forth during moments wherein he forgot himself, and during which his words were colored by some dreadful experience or experiences perhaps having to do with betrayal, I would imagine, or else some other onerous happening, of which I don't presume to comment one way or another.

Still, his positive remarks are kind and reflect some of my own feelings *vis à vis* both you and Mariam *[Editor's note: Again, see* Allan Quatermain at the Crucible of Life*]*

I have nothing more to add here and now, but I do hope our paths cross again.

Your friend,
Allan Quatermain

A Tribute to Professor Maria Mitchell
From Bayustiak the Zulu Warrior

Macumazana—

It has been my experience that women as a rule, by and large, are evil creatures, prevaricators who are not loath to be false time and again with regard to the men in their lives in order to get their own way, but mostly to hurt men for the joy of doing so and merely to raise themselves up. I have loved many times and have deeply regretted each time, for all there is at the end of that black cave is boundless sorrow. With a woman the pain is all the more searing because each time it is always the one you least suspect, because she can wield magic and blind you and cause you to forget and she will laugh all the while. O, Macumazana, the great spirits did ill by creating these creatures, for some shine like the sun and lift the soul and make a man feel he is one with heaven; others are ugly or malformed or overtly evil or vindictive, and no-one would ever think differently about these last, but, O, Macumazana, all of them, every last one is nothing more or less the seed of death and pain and suffering.

Were that the spirits had thought better of their plan!

[Here I broke in and said, "O, Leopard (for you remember he was called, that is to say his honorific title was, "The Steaming Hot Breath of the Crouching Black Leopard"), why are you making a speech to me, of all people, who knows well of what you speak, for, with only— five exceptions (here I confess I counted on my fingers), I would manifestly agree with much of what you say. From women often comes confusion and despair. But why are you, without warning, thundering so in my ear?]

Because, Macumazana, for months now, ever since we returned from that land of more wonders than can be remembered, I have been aware of my mind slowly changing in some measure with regard to these opinions of women which I have just stated and that I have held so true for so long, because not long ago, I—indeed you as well—met two women who broke the mold, who are unlike other women, neither of whom I believe could ever harm a single hair on any man's head. Of course, one is not a true woman but the girl who speaks in tongues and who has so much wisdom, and the other is the sky talker. I have never encountered such two stalwart, apparently honest women who seem not to have some ulterior motive and whose existence almost balances the unbalance caused by all the others. I say "almost" because, on balance, even these two pure souls cannot save the race from the folly that women cause! The beauty of some women is like the sweet sap of fragrant flowers that betrays some poor little insect to feel intoxicated and be off guard so that they let themselves be fooled and in the end must inevitably be not so much destroyed, but eaten alive. O, only suffering and doom is the fruit for any man who is attracted to any woman. It is the wise man who imprisons his women in a *kraal* and does not suffer them to leave. What good is a woman except to make babies and what is the good of that when half the babies grow to become girls, then women. O, evil begets evil! It is an old story!

Still, I want you to tell sky talker that I am quite fond of her and that I am sure that I need not ever fear any evil originating from her, and that she is truly different and I am honored to have known her, and I wish you to convey that to her with those magic markings that you white people often use in the manner that we Zulus employ runners and messengers and, too, as we use the fathers of fathers and the mothers of mothers [that is, elderly repositories of tribal lore]. Tell her I hope to see her again in the Land of Fires where we are all bound.

And now, Macumazana, I also have a message for you from the Opener of Roads [that is, Zikali].

[Here, my Zulu friend was quiet for a time, his head and face lowered, clearly trying to focus. And when I saw his face again, his eyes showed only white, and he spoke, the timbre of his voice having changed, and thus his wizard master, the dwarf Zikali, chose to send me a few chosen words or remarks that I place here on paper, as they have points of interest.]

A Message to Allan Quatermain
From the Zulu Wizard Zikali, "Opener of Roads"
Through the Medium of Bayushtiak the Zulu
Warrior

Ho, Ho, Macumazana:

"The Steaming Breath of the Crouching Black Leopard" ho, ho, tells me he plans to seek you and speak to you. Well, as I am never one to let slip an opportunity, I am giving him a message to repeat to you. I don't know if he will remember it or not, and even if he doesn't, there will be no harm. For their own mysterious purposes, the spirits that continually enshroud me have caused me to see a little into the future, and then they showed me the end of the world, or maybe it was the beginning, I don't know, for they are all the same to me (and O, I fought it, as there are some things I would rather not see nor know about). What I saw was that little yellow monkey of a fellow who is as close to you as your own skin—the one called "Light in Darkness"—earnestly listening to matters that were, or rather will be, far beyond his ken. But, you know I must know all things knowable so I eavesdropped, or rather, again, will do so, over your man's shoulder and heard what he heard, and more, I saw something he couldn't see! O, ow! And what I looked at turned around and looked at me and I knew the uttermost fear that a being could know. It knew I was there and stared at me and I could not have closed my eyes if I had tried. Moreover, we stared at one another for what seemed an eternity and I feared, O, I feared. By now you are wanting to know why I am telling you all this business through the agency of my servant. It is because I have little choice. As I have slaves, so there are things to which I am a slave (yes, I confess this, though you will think I am making up only another wizard's trick). That Spirit, who is the Spirit to which the other great spirits bow, took pains to lay hands on my heart and commanded just this: that I bear witness from afar to that which Light in Darkness will someday tell you after a certain incident, and confirm to you that such matters were not the drunken dream of your servant, but rather accurate reporting. Thus I do not yet know the secret but must needs to wait as you must also do now that I have told this to you. Well, be that as it may, I am bored speaking to you through my servant. Farewell, Macumazana, Watcher by Night!

[At this point Bayushtiak's eyes rolled back into place and he shook his head and drew in a sharp breath and looked bewildered, or as much so as such a man can appear, but only for a moment, and I asked him if he remembered what he had just spoken, and he replied, "O, no, Macumazana, those who are the vessels of the words of the Opener of Roads do not live long if they remember, and, thus, being a man of some sense, I cannot remember anything at all." Which was just as well because I believe that Zikali was playing me the fool yet again and was in the midst of some elaborate joke and I could see him making that horrible sound that was his laughter and rocking back and forth on his haunches, making merry at my expense!]

Editor's Note

Here follows Lady Luna Holmes Ragnall's diary, which she bequeathed to her mysterious cousin, an individual we know only by the initial M. The diary was written in the personal shorthand that M seems to have taught her, and with time and effort, money and expertise, I was able to have it rendered readable. Here are the contents of the actual diary in which Lady Luna Holmes Ragnall recorded Allan Quatermain's adventure as he told it to her.

The epigraphs, chapter titles, illustrations, and captions are my additions, because they offer perspective that would otherwise be missing.

Prologue
By Allan Quatermain

After this Lady Ragnall [retired], having instructed Moxley to show us the smoking room . . . . Over the rest of the night I draw a veil . . . . [W]hile pretending to help myself to whiskey and soda, slipped through the door and fled upstairs. I arrived late to breakfast . . . .

—Allan Quatermain in the *The Ancient Allan*

Here I will stop this tale, for to describe all my adventures and experiences on my way to the West Coast would take another book, which I have neither the time nor the inclination to write.

—Allan Quatermain in *The Treasure of the Lake*

First Prologue Chapter

The Whale

There was the time in 1873, deciding to follow the advice of John Arkle, a man who was central to a story *[Editor's note: See The Treasure of the Lake]* irrelevant to the one I'm about to tell, as to the direction of travel when leaving the country of the Dabanda and the Holy Lake of Mone in Central Africa, I, with Hans,* turned west with the intention of reaching the coast around Sierra Leone and locating an expedient ship or some such with which to return to South Africa and Durban, our home.

That journey took more months than I care to recall and can be divided into two distinct chapters. There was the actual trek between the country of the Holy Lake and the southeastern region of Sierra Leone contiguous with Liberia, a journey full of incident both good and bad, but totally separate from the subject of this tale. And then there were our experiences on the coast.

As we headed out of that amorphous and still largely unexplored region that we call for convenience Central Africa or Darkest Africa, despite my own journeys which *in toto* covered very little ground when considered geographically, we began to hear rumors from the various villages and occasional safari of a tribe of great white witch doctors and of the peculiar magic they wielded that required the building of a railroad for transport. When I asked what it was that was being transported, I received no clear answer but eventually concluded that it consisted of some sort of heavy equipment.

And since it was our encounter with those so-called white witch doctors, which description, by the way, could not be further from the truth, I will skip the fairly routine matters of signing papers, greasing palms, and stating intentions to officials, and get to the root of the episode.

----

* Editor's note: See "Introduction: H. Rider Haggard's Character Hans the Hottentot" in the second book of this trilogy, *Allan Quatermain at the Crucible of Life* for vital information about Hans.—T.K.M.

With our retinue of wagons, oxen, and bearers, Hans and I entered the port community of Freetown, which was then in 1873 a growing hub of trading, with the aim of booking passage on the first vessel heading south. At this point we sold the wagons and oxen and dismissed the bearers and sold the various goods we'd accumulated on our trek from the various peoples we'd encountered.

That left only Hans and myself in this foreign land, as certainly neither of us had ever been this far west, and so the sights were new and different, and, of course, we were always comfortable around each other, having shared so much over the years.

In due course, I had us booked onto the commercial trading vessel *Carlson*, which was expected to arrive in some weeks, and was thence bound to various ports along the west African coast, making stops at Cape Town and Port Elizabeth and then on to our home Durban, of which I saw little enough due to my livelihood. Thus Hans and I had time on our hands, and then I remembered those white witch doctors of which we had heard rumors. I mentioned to Hans that I had half a mind to scout about and see if there was any substance to these rumors.

"Baas! You can go wherever you want! But I intend to stay comfortable at that rooming house you fixed up, for it reminds me of the missionary station of the Predikant, your Reverend father, where I met you years ago when you lost your way in the spirit world and arrived in this land, which is really the very last place a sane spirit would venture, but who am I to judge such things, as I am only the drunken yellow dog that the Zulu cannot be bothered with."

"Or perhaps," I said, "you've noticed that the saloon is only a couple of doors down, and one way or another you will become drunk on square-face [Luna, you remember that by square-face, he meant gin], since my moderating influence would be gone."

Hans looked struck and said, "Baas! You think so little of me, your servant!"

"It's not a matter of what I think, Hans. It is what I *know*."

"Well, Baas, since you put it that way, and since I promised your Reverend father, the Predikant, that I would watch over you and protect you for as long as the spirits allow—and let me tell you a secret, Baas, even after I am swept into the Place of Fires, I will bargain and cajole with whomever it is necessary to do so, so that I will still be with you, which is something you can depend on."

Thus we argued for a day or so, with Hans ever trying to change my mind about my little side expedition, and which he came close to succeeding and winning me over to his side, but then my sense returned. I said, "Be my guest if you wish to get drunk when I'm not here to get you out of your scrapes! Do as you please!"

And in the end, days later, he and I were marching south without bearers through the forested region that there served as a buffer between the town and the black jungle. My internal navigation system is usually pretty good and I seldom get lost, even in places I've never seen or ever known, but this time as forest transitioned from jungle and the sky was a great stage where various brands of air collided and rolled and changed the color of land and hills, I confess that I lost my bearings, though my plan had been simple enough, namely to keep as much as possible within sight of the majestic ocean on our right.

"Baas, smell it! The sea of the west! Smell the salt!" Hans' wrinkled little face was turned upward and his nostrils quivered, and a glow spread across his face.

He was quite correct. After suffering through a maze of steamy jungle on one hand, followed by arid desert on the other, we finally found ourselves exiting a dank forest within view of a hilltop. Hans ran ahead, as he does when he is excited, and in a few moments I heard him cry out, "Baas! Come quickly."

I remember that the sound of his voice was muffled by the sea breeze that refreshed my face. I ran to the top of the hill only to find that it was not a hill at all, but a rise that fronted on and ended in a sheer cliff overlooking a small crescent-shaped bay with mighty waves crashing on the rocks far below. I then fixed my attention in the direction Hans was pointing.

"See, Baas, a great whale coming up to breathe!"

Greatly disappointed, for though I knew not what I expected, it was certainly more than a mere whale, of which I had seen many over the years. Nevertheless, I acknowledged that there certainly was a large vortex of water below.

"Hans, is that all? Have you not seen as many whales as I?"

"Yes, Baas, perhaps even more, but never have I seen such a whale as the big black brother yonder. He is a mountain, this whale, but wait, you have not seen anything but his splash. You have not seen him with your own eyes. He should rise to the surface again any moment."

Impatiently I watched the swirling waters. Then suddenly the waters parted with a mighty frothing and a titanic blue-black-maroon mottled monster fully two hundred feet in length exploded into sight, leaping straight into the air and spouting a prodigious tower of spray and foam nearly half its length across the sky.

"Great God!" I exclaimed, "Such a fish!" Just then the great whale hurled itself back into water and submerged again causing a grand swelling of the waves, and all at once its mighty double-bladed tail heaved into the air, then smoothly slipped under the churning waters.

Hans and I were mesmerized by the sight, so much so that he was speechless, which is rare enough to be sure. Even as we watched, the waves roared and parted once more and the great blunt nose of the blue-black hide poked up from the madly swirling blue-green waters, snorted a blast of spray arcing through the air, then submerged again.

Such a proud spectacle to see! Frolicking there in nature's bosom, skipping about the waters joyfully, was the earth's largest creature, the hugest fish which God ever made. The greatest of the great whales. Fully three times larger than the greatest I had ever seen. Then Hans and I found ourselves being showered with a watery mist and bits of foam as the wind carried the beast's spout up the cliff face. When it settled on the surrounding rocks, it vanished in wisps of steam. Over and again we watched that cavorting monster cross and recross that crescent bay.

But one could only be so mesmerized for so long before more practical matters intruded, and we continued on the path that would lead us to our quarry, at least as suggested by some local natives we had met.

Half a day after this, we heard faintly at the edge of our hearing, or more accurately, Hans' hearing—for his ears were more attuned than mine, and have been as long as I knew him which was long indeed, since my childhood—the distinct chug-chug of a locomotive and then a piercing whistle. Within a day we encountered the wide tracks. Hans ventured up and down the tracks for some distance but saw nothing worth reporting except more track. Insofar as it was late, I decided to throw up some prickly sage and set down our packs and rolls and make a fire, in other words to set up camp, right there near the tracks so that we would be able to learn about the train, and maybe even get a ride. Sure enough, the next morning we heard the whistle again and eventually saw a locomotive appear in the distance with one passenger car and several flat trucks loaded with equipment, all of which was covered with canvas, or oil cloth, as we could not at that distance identify its nature.

I'm sure the engineer saw our camp, but the train's momentum did not waver as it grew closer, so I said, "Hans, stand in the middle of the track and wave your arms to stop this fool train. Don't you agree that it would be at least polite for it to slow down?"

He looked at me and said, "Baas, I don't mean any disrespect for your Reverend Predikant father—who I served for years, or to you for that matter—but you can stand in front of your own damn train!"

In the end we both watched, helplessly, close alongside the track and made futile gestures. However, I don't believe that engineer would have hesitated running us down, if it came to that, for though it slowed a little in a perfect riot of squealing, sparks, steam, and the acrid stink of burnt metal, and so forth, it showed no intention of stopping, and Hans and I had to jump for our lives. As it raced past us, I noticed the name of the railroad company emblazoned on the side of the engine—Kingdom-Elias R.R.—in elaborate ornate and scrolled lettering. The mustached engineer was shaking his fist at us and had thunder in his face. As it roared by, we saw its one passenger coach along with two or three indistinct faces staring at us from within. To their credit, they seemed confused, and I gave them the benefit of the doubt.

Thereafter, assuming that the track must end somewhere, or, at the very least go through somewhere, Hans and I chose to follow the track in the direction that the train had raced off. The country all around was a patchwork of all kinds of terrain both high and low and of foliage both tropical and temperate type, but I couldn't help but be impressed that in every case, if there was a hill or other formidable obstacle in the path of the track, the train builders had drilled right through solid rock with tunnels rather than move the track around the obstacle, even in instances when the terrain included more than enough land to facilitate that approach.

For three or four days—I don't remember now, as these things do tend to blend together after a while—we continued down this deserted metal path, but a path that showed every indication of being recently created and used often enough.

Then all at once the wind shifted and Hans' little body reacted as though it was touched with a hot prod.

"Baas! I smell roasting meat—and beer! May the Predikant, your Reverend father's heaven, that he loved to talk about so long and so often, be praised for I am tired of biltong and warm water."

"Perhaps we are finally approaching the origin or destination of the railroad," I ventured. "Or perhaps that tribe of white witches is around the bend!"

But Hans had already run ahead and he didn't stop until he was out of sight due to the undulating nature of that landscape. "Hans, you monkey, come back!" I cried, but heard no response. Rather irritated at my servant for his impetuous behavior, especially as I valued his gun in this unknown territory and it was certain that two guns were better than one in the event they were needed at all. The end of it was, still following the wide track and stepping around a stand of trees, I finally found Hans, sitting on an outcrop of rock and twirling his filthy hat and grinning.

"Well, Baas, it is nice of you to finally join me, for as you can see, we have company, which can only be to the good as I am hungry and it seems that my nose did not fool me," and he gestured in the direction of the sea which was again visible from this vantage point. But that is not all I saw! Down below and in the distance a mile or so ahead and built at the bottom of a kind of valley that ended at the Atlantic Ocean, was what appeared to be a town of sorts, or village, at any rate a thriving community, or at least that was our first impression of the place as we viewed it from on high from the top of one of the cascading natural walls that formed the north face of the valley. My gaze lingered and then I spotted in the distance half hidden in the ocean mist the oddest sight.

At the far end of the community, I thought I could see through the mist a small Greek temple. But then the vision disappeared, leaving me to rub my eyes and wonder.

Such a proud spectacle to see! Frolicking there in nature's bosom, skipping about the waters joyfully.

Second Prologue Chapter

The City Where There Shouldn't Be One

I said I thought there was a village or town down below us, but in a few moments I realized that the distance and the mist, or what I at first thought was mist, had deceived me. In a moment I began to understand what in fact it was that hovered below in the valley that opened to the sea! What I had interpreted as mist and dark clouds was in fact smoke billowing from heaven knows how many chimneys from numerous large buildings, which at first I took for factories. I rubbed my eyes, and looked at Hans, who was likewise studying the sight, his eyes moving rapidly, calculatingly. It is interesting how one often sees what one expects to see, rather than what actually is. Though any kind of village was unexpected, still when we saw first a cluster of buildings away in the mist, we naturally assumed on some level that the cluster was relatively contained, that is, smaller rather than larger. But when our eyes took in the sight, and expectations vanished, the vast operation below became evident. Our path fell steeply into the valley and ran straight into the middle of a veritable small city throughout which huge construction projects were underway. By far most of the activity was somewhat north-west of the city. It took me a moment to grasp the scale of the scene, but when I finally understood just what I was seeing, I counted nineteen towering steam shovels at work grabbing claw loads of rock and earth and dumping it all into a hundred or more waiting train cars that were attached to a dozen waiting steaming and smoking black locomotives, most waiting their turn. This screeching and clanging equipment was at work excavating an enormous hole in the ground,

> SS—
> *We need a new smoker, as repairing ours won't do at all, as it would be only a temporary solution. We should have a spare in any case. Put it on the list.*
> —M

a vast bowl-shaped pit that somehow reminded me of active volcano craters or titanic meteorite craters, of which I have seen my fair share! The roar and piercing whistles of the locomotives and the cry of the earth being rent and disemboweled were horrible.

Excavating an enormous hole in the ground, a vast bowl-shaped pit.

Then I saw that the clouds were made of just as much dirt and dust from the excavation as black smoke from the chimneys—and it hung over everything and severely blocked the waning late-afternoon sunlight—already turning crimson—slanting in from over the sea, casting long red shadows upon the whole scene, magnifying my impression of vulcanism. And once my brain was able to assemble all the pieces, what I saw was this: The buildings with the chimneys surrounded the pit and were arranged equidistant from one another. Massive pipes with enormous valves extended from each building and were intended, it seemed likely upon first observation, to pour some material or another into the pits, but the pipes were not active at that point.

The tracks for the trains I have mentioned were mainly laid so that they began between the "factories" and ran to the edge of the pits and were situated so that the excavators could dump their claw loads into the railcars. They mostly jutted out at first rather like the spokes of a wheel for a distance and then they all veered gently to the southeast and disappeared into the nearly opaque, poisonous, roiling red air towards wherever they dumped the debris, I suppose.

It was an uncanny sight to find this immense hub of activity where there was supposed to be nothing at all. "A tribe of white witch doctors, indeed!" I muttered to myself, which act stimulated Hans to make his first utterance since this sight had come into view.

But then, as my senses became acquainted with the waves of sensory imagery that assailed me, I blinked and stared and realized that *in the distance was a second giant pit* being excavated with just as much activity as the one below where Hans and I stood.

"Baas!" Hans was saying, "I am not as well-traveled as some, and Durban is as big a town as I have known, but I remember your father, the Predikant, telling stories to his poor staff about white men's kraals many times bigger than Shaka's, many times bigger than Durban, and I have never ventured out of the land of my fathers, but I do have ears and I have heard from many white men of big towns, and I suppose I am seeing such a place being born down below even now!"

"I suppose so, Hans, for such a sight is as new to me as it is to you. But be quiet now, as I need to think."

And, as it was now growing dark, Hans and I retreated and found a sheltered spot in a hollow to sleep, and at dawn we were trekking down the hill following the easiest path, as now that we saw our destination, we no longer needed to confine ourselves to following the train tracks. In so doing we traveled into some ravines and such so that we lost sight of the town for most of the distance. But toward midday, we came to the crest of a hill, and there, right before us, so close you could almost touch it, was the vital and bustling community, doing its best to live and work despite the huge disturbance and the construction going on all around it. Up close, it seemed still larger than it had from a distance. What passed for the passenger train station was off to the right, and the locomotive we had seen—it was the same because I recognized the number on its side—steaming and huffing and puffing, presumably nearly ready to

In the distance was a second giant pit being excavated with just as much activity as the one below.

move out and run down whatever poor innocent pedestrians happened to get in its way!

From our vantage point, we could look straight over the main street, which was pressed earth, with sixty or so spartan buildings with shops. At the end of the street a second street crossed and formed a T. At that crossroads and facing down the main street was the tallest building that was within our view. Perhaps two hundred men and women were on the streets, none strolling, each with a mission and walking with purpose in various directions. None seemed to be taking in the sights. There was no loitering in this place. Despite the crowd, the ebb and flow of its movements were remarkably organized, and I felt that the architects of this mysterious metropolis knew what they were doing and had planned well.

In addition, I was amazed to see that a dwarf-sized railroad system crisscrossed the town. You heard me right, Luna: a miniature railroad system with tiny engines and cars. This turned out to be a transportation system, a handy way to move people and equipment around within the limits of the town. The locomotives were perhaps ten feet in length, yet looking for all the world like their big brothers that hauled rubble from the pits. These were driven by men and women who rode the engines much as they would ride horses, their legs hugging and pressing hard into either side of the black metal engines. All in all, it proved to be a very efficient tram system.

Instead of horse-drawn hansoms and carriages
or omnibuses, the laboratory used small trains
powered by tiny locomotives on which sat the drivers.

In a moment, Hans was pulling at my sleeve, and he said reflectively, "Baas, do you see someplace where they sell square-face, for I am thirsty, and what is the use of a town like this unless it has a saloon?"

I inspected what I could see and had to admit that there didn't appear to be a saloon, at least within our view. But I ventured a guess. "Maybe that tall building has something of the sort."

Well there was nothing for it but to continue ahead, but before we started, I peered into the distance, hoping to see the temple that I'd noticed the day before, but I couldn't see anything of the sort. In a couple of hours, we emerged from the undergrowth through which we had traversed onto a road paved with stone. This led into the town, which was just ahead. But now I noticed a queer fact that was not obvious from the distance. The entire town had a tall fence around it, and as we got closer, I saw that there was a fence within a fence and that it all bristled with barbs, such as you hear about being used on American cattle ranches. And every few yards there were guard towers and armed guards, as though the place was a prison camp. Yet, from what we could see from the distance, the populace, while seemingly industrious, also seemed free to go their own ways.

Frankly I was more than a little confused.

In a few minutes, around a curve and at end of the road, we saw a guard's station and gate with three stout fellows in military uniforms, but of a stripe I was not familiar with.

"Baas, what do you suppose these big men are guarding? And do you see their many brothers with guns on those towers? Perhaps it is gold or diamonds, but then again not even the Bank of Durban has so many guards. What could be more valuable then gold or diamonds?"

"Our skins for one thing," I suggested.

"O, Baas, that's easy for you to say, for you are the great Macumazana, but I am only a shriveled yellow monkey as the Great One never fails to remind both of us, and the skin of a monkey is hardly worth more than a rusty nail!"

"Hans, you are worth more than a rusty nail to me, even if you are shriveled."

"Baas, yes, you are right. I am worth more to you because I have saved your life more times than I can remember."

"Perhaps that is so, Hans, but I have saved your skin just as many times!"

By then we had marched right up to the guard shack.

The tallest of the three guards questioned us, or I should say questioned me, in the manner that all such men question the arrival of unexpected newcomers. I explained that I was Allan Quatermain and that Hans was with me, and that we had come out of the jungle after a very long trek from Central Africa and that we were there only because we had stumbled on the place by accident and insofar as it was the first sign of civilization that we'd encountered, would it be too much to ask to be treated with civility and be offered food and drink at the least?

The spokesman looked doubtful, but at least he was not belligerent, and sent one of his colleagues off with a message. I suppose he would have been within his rights to have sent us packing, so I counted our blessings—at least in the beginning!

> SS—
> *Remind me to do a monograph on the various races of bees—the better to forge a meaningful dialog with the looming authorities who seem to revel in their ignorance of the apiarian universe. Such thoughts could also be condensed for one of the journals.*
> —M

Hans and I waited in the hot sun. Hans sat on the ground in what shade he could find, but I was too proud and stood on principle. Literally. We waited thus for almost an hour. I could see that our presence there had aroused the curiosity of passersby on the other side of the double fence, but nobody did more than slacken their walking pace a bit, stare a moment, then continue about their business. My patience was running thin, when finally I spotted two men approach the gate from the inside. The gates were opened for them, and they came through and advanced up to me.

Third Prologue Chapter

Maxwell

$$L = 4\pi m^2 a\{\log_e 8a/r + 1/12 - 3/4(\theta - \pi/4)\cot 2\theta - \pi/3\cos 2\theta$$
$$-1/6 \cot^2\theta \log \cos \theta - 1/6 \tan^2 \theta \log \sin \theta\}$$
$$+ \pi m^2 r^2/24a\{\log 8a/r(2 \sin^2 \theta + 1) + 3.45 + 27.475 \cos^2\theta$$
$$- 3.2 (\pi/2 - \theta)\sin^3\theta/\cos \theta + 1/5 \cos^4\theta/5 \sin^2\theta \log \cos \theta$$
$$+ 13/3 \sin^4\theta/\cos^2\theta \log \sin \theta\} + \&c$$

—James Clerk Maxwell in *The Dynamical
Theory of the Electromagnetic Field*

The man who seemed to be the leader was about my size, that is to say, rather small, but he had a high forehead with a slightly receding hairline, long swept-back grey hair and long extremely bushy grey mutton-chop whiskers, which were quite the rage back then. His hair and beard were so profuse that they connected with hardly a trace of facial skin showing except a little on either side of his nose and around his eyes. The other man was about the same age but had a rounder face, that is, they both seemed about 40 years of age, though the second man sported a trim beard, rather like mine, in fact. This first man came right up to me and held out his hand, which for the sake of politeness I took and shook in the accepted European manner. I make this specification because when one lives in Africa as long as I have, one learns that the common handshake is not by any means a common method of greeting, and, in fact, how one presents one's hands at the beginning of an acquaintance could well spell the difference between life and death . . . but, Luna, I suppose you of all people know this! Also, I had reservations about simply greeting the man, particularly after his having made us wait in the sun for an hour. He spoke and I was surprised by his strong Scottish accent:

"Allan Quatermain! I have heard of you. Yes, I dare say, that there are few who reside on this continent who have not heard of the great white hunter!"

I often hear this sort of remark, or compliment as I suppose it is intended to be, but learned long ago not to take it seriously, for if I did, my head would swell and I could not fit into any of my hats again! But more than that, such things that are heard about me are usually second or third hand and generally not representative of the real me. Thus I chose to ignore his remarks and said, "Sir, I am afraid that you have me at a disadvantage."

Naturally this always embarrasses the speaker, which put me back on top of the social order, and indeed, this is exactly what happened. Blushing, he said, "Forgive me, Quatermain, but my name is James Maxwell, James Clerk Maxwell." He stopped and showed every sign that his name ought to have been familiar to me and that I ought to have been impressed. But since neither was the case, I merely looked back at him with a blank face. Then he quickly motioned toward his companion and said, "And this is Giovanni Schiaparelli," and seemed again to wait for some sort of reaction.

Of course, this second name meant as little to me as the first. Schiaparelli didn't speak, so I could only guess that he was Italian. I nodded to him and said to Maxwell, "Mr. Maxwell, obviously I can't help but wonder what all this is about. None of this is supposed to be here, or certainly I would know of it."

"Yes, yes. We are involved in some research of a scientific nature, and we established this laboratory only a few months ago. Just a moment, please." Here, he and Schiaparelli moved off and whispered together for several minutes. Then Schiaparelli went back in the direction they had come, hurrying through the gate without saying a word to us, and Maxwell returned. "You know, Quatermain, we don't normally have callers, as you can imagine, and I wish I could be more gracious, but I must cut this interview short. I'm terribly glad we had an opportunity to meet, however briefly. Where are you off to now?"

Taken aback by both his attitude and the question, I think I sputtered some sort of response that I cannot recall. Hans took me by the elbow and said in Dutch, "Baas, I don't understand why these men are being rude and did not invite us inside so that we could rest our feet, have some cool drink, and even offer us a place to lay our poor heads." I couldn't have agreed with him more, and was about to say so, when his bloodshot eyes grew round and his wrinkled old face beamed and he smiled, whereupon he said, "Say, Baas! That merciful Spirit of which your Reverend father, the Predikant, never ceased to remind all us poor servants who manned his station, has looked down from his throne, or up from the Place of Fires, I know not which, and has seen our sad case and has come to our rescue!"

"Hans," I responded, "stop your nonsense and let us make ready to leave this inhospitable place."

But the little Hottentot continued his gaping, and said, "It may be nonsense, Baas, but I think you will think otherwise when I tell you that I see someone who will make this sick looking white man swallow his thick tongue. See over there, through that crowd there, there is a face we know well, very well, indeed, leaving that building."

Shaking my head in befuddlement, I followed Hans' pointed finger, and, indeed, spotted not only a familiar face but a dear one as well.

"Maxwell," I said to the man, "before my servant and I turn around to go, having been turned away by a degree of insensitivity rare, indeed, nearly unprecedented, in a civilized man, please note that I see an old friend inside your fence whose attention I would like to catch, if you don't mind."

He looked off in the direction I had indicated and seemed puzzled. "Excuse me?" Maxwell said.

And seeing that she was about to round the corner of a building, I called out loudly, "Maria! Maria Mitchell! Professor Mitchell!" which succeeded in getting her attention. She looked our way, double-took, stared, smiled, no, grinned broadly, waved, and rushed over to the gate.

"Allan Quatermain! My God! It is so good to see you! How did you know to look for me here? It is so good to see you! And Hans! Neither of you look one iota different since our Abyssinian adventure last year. Well, perhaps it is closer to two years." Then to

Maxwell, "Well, Doctor, what is going on here? Don't you know Allan Quatermain?" There followed an awkward exchange between the two, with Maria finally putting her foot down and demanding, "What are you waiting for? I insist that you escort these men through immediately!"

You see, dear Luna, early in the previous year, I had been hired by several British gentlemen to take them to Ethiopia, which at that time I had never visited. It would be a couple of years later that you and I and Lord Ragnall would travel over that hellish desert to finally come to the little port where we then embarked on separate vessels to return us to our respective homes. It was while on that earlier expedition that our path crossed with Professor Mitchell and her party, and it worked out that the two expeditions were merged before we plunged south into that desert for reasons it's not necessary to go into now. The point being that Maria is an American astronomer, and we were well-acquainted, and it was the purest serendipity that Hans had spotted her just at that particular moment. If he hadn't, if he had been busy yawning or being otherwise distracted, there would be no tale to tell now, and we would be discussing other things!

Well, there was a bit of give and take, with the guards pointing out some particulars of their bylaws and about the minutia of our arrival, and Maxwell holding quite firm.

It was pretty much of a stalemate, when another man approached the gate from the inside and, muttering something to the guards on that side, passed through just as Maria attached herself to him, so that, in a flash they both had come outside and she began exchanging affectionate greetings with me, and also Hans.

SS—

My word . . . the charming Professor Mitchell takes the stage. My recollections of her are most vivid. A different sort of woman, SS, insofar as she was knowledgeable in the makeup of the heavens. What woman in a million . . . nay! . . . 100 million can rise to such heights! What a shame! Maria has been gone these many years and the world is poorer for it!

—M

Fourth Prologue Chapter

Barbicane

"It appears to me by its rocky and barren character to offer all the conditions requisite for our experiment. On that plain will be raised our magazines, workshops, furnaces, and workmen's huts; and here, from this very spot," said he, stamping his foot on the summit of Stony Hill, "hence shall our projectile take its flight into the regions of the [Lunar] World."
—Impey Barbicane in *From the Earth to the Moon*

This new fellow was yet another with a beard, not as full as Maxwell's nor as well-trimmed as Schiaparelli's. However, he seemed utterly out of place as he was attired formally in tall shiny top hat and tails and smoked a cigar.

"Hello, Maria, won't you introduce me to your friend?"

"Where have you been Impey?" replied Maria, not responding to the inquiry. "I have been looking for you for days."

"Didn't anyone tell you, I was tying up some loose ends 'over yonder.'" This was the first reference that I heard to the mysterious "over yonder," which while not mentioned often, would occasionally slip out in hushed tones, succeeding in rousing the curiosity of both Hans and me at the outset of this adventure.

"Well never mind. You're here now. Impey, this is my old friend Allan Quatermain. You cannot imagine the scrapes we've been through together!" Here she winked at me, and in my mind's eye I saw her swinging and jabbing a glass sword—decapitating a Danikil tribesman two years before! But that is another story, Luna!

"And Allan, this is Impey Barbicane! He sent a missile to the moon five or six years ago. You may have read about it. He is the world's greatest engineer—the chief engineer and architect of all this." Her hand gestured in all directions.

"Maria, that's not entirely true. Isambard Kingdom Brunel's work inspired much of what I have done!"

Now there was a name I had heard of and was impressed with, even having been isolated at the bottom of Africa from the stream of technology that Britain seemed consumed with. Brunel had built some of the greatest ships of his day, the *Great Western* and *Great Eastern* among them, and the *Great Western Railroad*, not to mention gigantic tunnels that crossed under rivers, and enormous bridges that crossed over them. Now that I had heard Brunel's name, a little of the mystery I was feeling faded, as Brunel was quite adept at building the impossible. Though Brunel had died some years before, it was clear to me then that this man Barbicane must have been a protégé.

Anyway, the end result of this exchange was that Maria won the day and Hans and I were shepherded in.

Before long we were established in the tall building that we had seen from a distance, which, while not a hotel in the normal sense of the word, nevertheless served a similar function and we called it that out of convenience, and Hans and I had the grand opportunity to bathe and refresh—or rather, I did, for water seldom touched my manservant except when it was necessary to ford some wild stream or another. This building was typical of the rest of the structures in this so-called laboratory, as Maxwell had called it, that is, the building was made of freshly sawn lumber and other rude materials and had clearly been thrown together in great haste. Indeed, the whole laboratory was *being* constructed in front of our eyes!

When we, that is, Maria and I, met again, it was in what passed for a sitting room of the hotel. Hans was there of course, but he preferred to plant himself unobtrusively in the corner as he was wont to do, as you know, your having known him so well. Maria and I did not just then have the opportunity to converse in private as Maxwell soon joined us, and then it was time for tea.

During that ever-so-civilized ceremony, Maria suggested to Maxwell, "James, Allan's discretion is second to none. In fact, there are things that we have experienced together (here she looked meaningfully at me) that even you have never dreamt of, and of which neither he nor I can ever speak, as we have given our oaths."

"That may well be, Professor Mitchell, but we have a responsibility to discharge, and until such time that is accomplished, there is no room for any who were not invited and who have no professional credentials to speak of. And besides, we ourselves have all given our own oaths with regard to *our* project."

"Well, then," she said, "I suppose my services and my specific areas of expertise are not needed." She stood, and said to me, "Come, Allan, please wait for me to pack some essentials and I will join you." Maxwell also stood, a courteous reflex I suppose. Maria walked up to him and stood eyeball to eyeball!

"Professor, that is not acceptable!" Maxwell said. "If for no other reason, I cannot allow a woman to trek through that horrid wilderness outside our gates!"

At that, Maria laughed heartily! "Ha! James, I assure you that that 'wilderness,' as you call it, is nothing at all compared to the places that Allan and I have shared! That jungle beyond our fences and those desert sands are as formidable as this tea-party, I assure you!" As she spoke, she stared into the man's face.

Taken aback, Dr. Maxwell could only gulp air for a few moments as he composed himself. "Maria, notwithstanding the dangers outside, this project needs your experience and abilities for good reason, and it would be a great disadvantage to our group if you were to leave us."

"Wonderful, then I want your promise that, in due course, Allan will be allowed to know what we are doing." Then she looked at me, embarrassed.

"Allan, I'm sorry, but I assume too much! I was so happy to see you that it didn't occur to me that you only happened upon this place by chance and that you have your own plans. I don't mean to impose on you or force information upon you that you would rather not know."

"Professor Mitchell," I said, "no plans I have are so important that I can't delay them to spend time with a charming dear friend." Here she blushed and I regretted my impertinence.

[Lady Luna Holmes Ragnall: Here, Allan is pausing to reflect, I think, and I don't want to lose momentum, thus I am writing these words to keep my pen moving . . . ." Allan," I say, "you romantic devil! I can see that your fondness for Professor Mitchell transcends mere acquaintance." This stirs him out of his reflection, and he says to me, "My dear, don't be foolish. I am impervious to such designs." And I say to him, "Bosh!" and now he is getting back to his narrative.]

"Very good, it is settled!" Maria had said. "James, until which time as Allan can be told the essentials, please let my friends" (here she turned and looked at Hans pointedly for Maxwell's sake) "have the freedom to move as they please through the laboratory."

"Why do you call this place a laboratory?" I asked.

Maxwell responded: "Well, rightfully, that is what it is. It certainly doesn't have any claim to permanence, though. This is all a temporary arrangement built to support our special studies. It is indeed a scientific laboratory."

"I cannot wait until I know something more about your purpose here, Doctor Maxwell. Professor Mitchell called you thus. I should hope I'll avoid getting ill during my stay, as I would not wish to impose on you."

"Oh, no, Allan," Maria exclaimed. "Doctor Maxwell is the world's greatest living physicist."

Now it was Maxwell's turn to blush. "I wouldn't go that far, Professor Mitchell. Certainly I learned from the great Faraday himself."

"Don't be modest, James." She turned to me and said, "James is the world's authority on electricity and magnetism, and has shown that they are interrelated in what he has called the electromagnetic field. James' brand new tome, *A Treatise on Electricity and Magnetism,* was published only this year, and there are those that say that it will transform the world!"

"Maria, please!" groaned Maxwell.

"Furthermore, James is this laboratory's chief scientist and all aspects of the work here not related specifically to building and engineering are his responsibility."

And that was the beginning or our adventure, dear Luna. Do you find it interesting thus far?

[Luna: "Allan," I say, "I am thunderstruck and amazed. What on earth could two renowned astronomers (for I am worldly enough to know that that is Giovanni Schiaperelli's field) and the world's greatest physicist *plus* the world's greatest living engineer, all be doing in an isolated and well-guarded facility on the west coast of Africa?"]

Well, there is so much more to tell. In the coming days, I met many famous and notable scientists. (Or so I would determine them to be in later years as I happened across their names in newspapers, or in other sundry manners. Among them were some astonishingly bright young men who had been drafted right out of school to aid in this endeavor—youngsters named Edison, Hertz, John Thomson, Nikola Tesla, Max Planck, and others.) The core of the team consisted of a number of absolutely dedicated astronomers, physicists, and engineers, all specialists in the narrow fields of electricity, magnetism, and electromagnetic waves. It was quite a select group. It seemed all the world's most brilliant men in these fields had been brought to this one small area. Of course, you are wondering, dear Luna, why this was so. What on

SS—

It's a shame that Q doesn't tell us more about Tesla et al. But, of course, he had no way of knowing during his stay that they would add so vitally to the great repository of essential knowledge. Lest I forget, we must sort out the pros and cons of moving the robber hives away from the productive ones! Let's revisit this when Mrs. H visits next week. She has learned much on the subject during her holidays here. I would hate to make a major decision without the benefit of her guidance and common sense, which I admit I have found most useful as the years creep up on me.
—M

earth could possibly have prompted all these geniuses to have come together in this manner? Well it took some time for me to glean any part of it, with Maria's help; still I am not at all sure that I really had any idea of what went on there during all the time Hans and I were detained—yes, detained, for in the end, once we were let in, we were not allowed to leave, much to Maria's chagrin.

Hans and I had been there only a few days when the first thing of consequence, from our perspective, occurred. Remember that during this time we were never told anything other than what I have already told you, nor could I even imagine what was going on all around me. The excavation of the pits and the construction of the laboratory went on ceaselessly. The constant smoke and dust made breathing difficult. There was a sort of class structure in place. The scientists and their assistants lived and worked in the main laboratory grounds that we knew from first hand knowledge, but the laborers and skilled craftsmen lived in separate areas and were transported by trains.

As I've already said, there were trains everywhere. And these were of three types. There were the ordinary trains with carriages of the type that you see coming into and leaving a busy urban train depot, though these were neither ornate nor plush and largely utilitarian—spartan I think is the word. The one that almost ran us down was of this sort. Then, of course, there were the dozens of work engines that hauled away the debris deposited by the huge excavators busy at the two pits.

And then there were also the miniature trains that I mentioned before. These were utterly unique, and, frankly, captivated both Hans and me. The entire laboratory, or at least the part we would inhabit for the duration, was crisscrossed with a web of tiny tracks on which traveled this miniaturized railroad system, which, as I had seen earlier, you recall, carried people from place to place. Instead of horse-drawn hansoms and carriages and omnibuses, this place had small electric trains pulled by tiny smokeless locomotives on which there was installed a kind of saddle to seat the drivers, both

men and women, who had available an array of levers and knobs
and wheels—and best of all, bells and whistles that they used to warn
pedestrians and which neither Hans nor I ever ceased to enjoy
hearing. Behind the engines, there were attached a dozen or so
small open cars, each holding fifteen or twenty people on benches.
And of course these trains had regular stops, though one could
always wave one down or ask the driver—engineer?—to make
unscheduled stops.

By the way, eventually I learned, and was astonished to find out,
that the population of the laboratory and its work crew and their
families, all of which required this complicated transit system
numbered somewhere in the neighborhood of 40,000! Most of
whom we never saw, as they were busy out of sight.*

During breakfast of our fourth or fifth day there, with Maria,
Maxwell, Barbicane, and myself at a table overlooking the Atlantic
Ocean. I ventured, "Professors, Mr. Barbicane, as we approached
this . . . laboratory . . . from atop the hill, we thought we saw
something odd off in the distance to the south. It seemed to be a
columned structure, a sort of temple, or at least that is how it
registered in my humble mind, through the mist or smoke."

Maria and Barbicane looked at one another and smiled, then
Maria said, "Allan, what you saw is an interesting aspect of this
place. Come, and Impey and I will show you." They looked at
Maxwell, but he said he was needed at the workshop.

---

* Editor's note: The rapid growth of the laboratory as described by
Quatermain is not as uncanny as it might seem at first reading. A
comparably scoped but more recent effort was the Manhattan Project.
On September 17, 1942, U.S. Army General Leslie Groves was
ordered to build an atomic bomb. At that moment in time all that
existed were a few equations and some small experiments done in
universities. *Two years and ten months later,* on July 16, 1945, the
Trinity bomb detonated in New Mexico. In between, there had
sprung into being—literally from *nothing*—the plutonium plant in
Hanford, Washington, with a workforce of 45,000 and the Uranium
235 plant at Oak Ridge, Tennessee, with a workforce of 24,000, and,
of course, the bomb development facility at Los Alamos, New
Mexico, with several thousand more.—T.K.M.

In a few minutes, Barbicane, Hans, Maria, and I were waiting outside for a westbound miniature train. We boarded and rode it through the main part of the laboratory.

When our conveyance reached the outskirts of the place and began its return leg, Barbicane asked the engineer to stop, whereupon we got off and strode through a guarded gate much as the one by which we had entered several days earlier and I was reminded how heavily guarded the facility was! We found a gravel path that we continued on for a half mile or so ducking in and out of stands of trees. Very soon we heard a roaring very like a waterfall, and smelt a tang in the air. The path entered a glade, and there in the middle of the glade stood the totally anomalous sight of a temple, for want of a better word. It was circular and comprised of ten columns. It stood 35 or 40 feet high with an inside column-to-column diameter of about 20 feet. It looked Roman or Greek, I'm sorry but I've never been educated to tell the difference. It stood in the middle of a broad circular pool with half a dozen shooting fountains.

The path we were on led to a footbridge and we crossed over the pool to the temple itself. There squarely in the middle between the pillars was a sort of circular well comprised of a wall about four feet high, and when we looked over the wall into the well, we saw and heard and smelled huge volumes of water spouting from two pipes in the well's sides. The sound was thunderous! I'm sure that millions of gallons a day must have crashed out of those pipes mingling and plunging down the 20-foot-deep, blue-tiled well. I cast my eyes downward, savoring the power of the raging waters. I stood entranced and wrapped in spray, delighting in the wonder of it all.

"Maria," I finally asked, "what is this place? What is the meaning of all this?" By which I meant the whole massive enterprise, of course; but I was not yet to receive a direct answer. Instead Maria looked at Barbicane who said: "Quatermain, you have not seen anything yet, as you have been here only a few days, but you will soon see and learn things on a scale never before conceived by the mind of man. What we are doing here makes my experiment of sending a manned projectile to the moon and back

The sound from the well was thunderous!

again look like a mere backyard romp. Let me say for now that we who are involved in this project are performing an experiment that requires an enormous amount of energy. Vast amounts! As a consequence, we . . . well . . . *invented* a system that creates electricity in quantities inconceivable before now except perhaps by the mind of God. Where, you ask, does such electricity come from? Well it so happens that electricity can most conveniently be produced by the downhill rush of millions of gallons of water. Thus our engineers, to the purpose of diverting and harnessing immense quantities of water, built a titanic dam high up in the Loma mountains 200 miles to the east, damming the Rokel River and turning a convenient valley into a reservoir. They are the Columbiad

Dam and the Columbiad Reservoir, respectively (named after the cannon that was central to my Luna project). To control the flow of the water released from the reservoir a huge gravity-driven network of 11 further dams and reservoirs, tunnels, pump stations, aqueducts and water conveyance pipelines were also built, all of which move 300 million gallons per day and generates over 2 billion kilowatt hours per year of hydropower electricity, which is transmitted here via a 200-mile long network of power stations housing generators, transformers, and dynamos—machines that never previously existed—not to mention the power lines that funnel it all here.

"So, to answer your question," Barbicane continued brightly, "we built this temple—we call it the Atlantis Water Temple—as a monument to that effort. Right here, this very spot, is the terminus of the underground water pipe that begins near Mount Bintumani. This is the final destination of the Rokel River water, water that is spawned by the dense rainforests water skirting the Loma Mountains. When it flows out of this well, you can see that it is expelled into the ocean, for it is not the water that is needed, but the electric power it generates. It was all completed just a few months ago, even though, amazingly, it was only conceived and designed two years ago!"*

"Two years!" I cried. "Surely something so vast would require decades of effort and more money than I can begin to conceive of."

"Yes, Allan, that is so . . . unless there is a well-to-do patron, sufficient motivation, and a clear deadline," Maria said.

---

*Editor's note: The whole gargantuan enterprise described in these pages took less than two years to complete. The construction of the vast energy production system, of necessity, commenced months in advance of the main laboratory. A fascinating analog to this system is the controversial Hetch Hetchy Aqueduct System in northern California, which became operational in October 1934. Requiring 30 years to plan and 20 years to build, this mammoth engineering project still provides fresh water to the City of San Francisco by diverting, storing, and transporting Tuolumne River water from clear across the breadth of the state. The difference here is that the production of enough electricity to run the city's services was its secondary priority, not its true *raison d'être*.—T.K.M.

Well, Luna, what can one say when confronted with such staggering information? Standing there I literally shook from the shock. My companions seemed to understand and gave me a moment to pull myself together. Then I spotted a legend that had been carved into the stone above the columns. It was Latin and read:

IN ASTRIS ES VESTRI POTENTIA ET GLORIA

I asked Maria what that meant and she told me: "In the stars are found your power and glory."

After a pause, I said, "A moment ago, I asked what all this is about? Mr. Barbicane has answered in a manner I could never have imagined in a hundred years, but what I meant to ask was: What is this place? I mean the whole laboratory? Why are you here?"

She looked at Barbicane who could only shrug. Then she said, "Allan, notwithstanding my having taken your side recently, let me say that the details are not for me to share. For now, I can say that we are performing some electrical experiments that include an aspect of astronomy, which of course, explains my presence . . . . Come, let's take a walk so I can hear myself think." She needed to raise her voice over the din of the roaring water. Just then Barbicane made his excuses and went off, leaving me alone with Maria. We then continued on the trail on the farther side of the temple.

Of course, Hans was there, too, but unobtrusively as was his tendency when discussion ascended into realms beyond his comprehension (and frankly beyond mine, as well, if truth be known, but I had the knack of being able to look interested or at least to keep a poker face)—but I was saying that Hans kept to himself.

When we had walked to a spot on the trail that was quieter—and drier, too, as the air around the well was forever filled with a cool mist—Maria began to fill me in: "I was asked to join this project not long after my return to Vassar College from Ethiopia, and when I arrived here, construction of the buildings had only just begun. I've been here at the laboratory now for only about eight months, but when I arrived here, there were only a few shacks and a beach."

Frankly, what she had just said was far more than I could comprehend, but then an image flashed into my head that helped me grasp the vastness of what she was saying.

"I suppose," I said, "it wouldn't be far different from Field-Marshal Lord Napier's Ethiopian campaign—the history of which you recall was an important factor in our last experiences together: 280 ships, 32,000 men, 20,000 mules, and vast amounts of materiel and they set up shop on a beach and—boom!—a small city sprang into being overnight. Locomotives were hauled in, and elephants, and huge piers were built . . . .   Remembering that, it doesn't surprise me at all that so much has happened here so fast!"

"Excellent, Allan. Frankly I had not thought of that, but it is an excellent analogy."

Now that I had a picture in my head that worked for me, I continued, "I have so many questions. What are the pits that are being dug? Is it more construction, or are they looking for something? What is it all for? Something to do with astronomy, but how could anything require as much energy as you tell me is being generated. And the aqueduct you described would take years and millions to plan and build. It is all impossible, yet here it is before my eyes!"

Maria looked very serious and then said, "Well, what I can tell you is that we are building a telescope, a very special telescope, one like the world has never seen."

"A telescope!" I cried. "All this for a telescope!" Of course, Luna, the telescope I saw in my mind's eye was a tube such as one held up to one's eye.

"Actually, Allan, we are involved in a project as big as the world, quite literally. The instrument that is being built here has no comparison. And that instrument, that is, the telescope, is at the heart of this project."

"That is all well and good, but why are *you* here, Maria?"

"Well Allan, after our adventure in Abyssinia, I returned to Vassar, where, as you know, my role has been to teach something of the stars and planets to inquisitive young women. However, because of the meteorite specimens I brought back, I became a bit of a celebrity and received many invitations to present at schools in

Boston, Pennsylvania, New York, and the like. Also I wrote and submitted, and had published, half a dozen papers to scientific journals, and I was quite pleased with the response from the science community. Of course there were a few naysayers who accused me of everything from carelessness to outright fraud. However, I'm happy to report that on balance, my supporters were legion. I had been back about six months, and then one day I received by courier an unexpected proposal. That letter alerted me that I would soon be invited me to join a special project. There was no description of either the project or my proposed responsibilities. Though I ignored the note, a few weeks afterward another courier appeared at my door, and this time the message offered some particulars about comets that grabbed my attention. It seemed that these were of particular interest to the people who wished me to join them. Of course, they could not have chosen a better ploy: I became fascinated, but still hesitant, as my responsibility lay just where I was, especially as I had only recently been away for a prolonged time.

> *SS—*
>
> *On the subject of journals, I must finish that monograph on the bees' dancing language. It ought not be so difficult to finish as that slippery Chaldean paper of mine!*
> *—M*

"Here is where they offered an inducement that could not be ignored. They offered to build a new observatory on the Vassar Campus on the condition that the experiment they were conducting achieved the desired result. Well, what was I to do? I believed that these people made the proposal in good faith, as the college board was already meeting with their representatives by the time I made up my mind to pursue the invitation. In time I had boarded the steamship *de Grandin*. My destination was the Greenwich Observatory. When I arrived, I received the surprise of my life. At the observatory I was received by James Clerk Maxwell himself! He told me that he had selected me especially and that I had been brought over for the sole purpose of his asking me personally if I wanted to join a select group of physicists and astronomers who were gathering in west Africa to conduct a vital experiment. Allan!

James is probably the most esteemed living scientist. Whatever residual concerns I still had about this enterprise, regardless of what it truly was, evaporated on the spot, and I became a dedicated member of the team. Very quickly after my arrival here, machine shops were built with the ability to produce the most sophisticated, delicate instrumentalities imaginable with complex components, even devices for computational work based on the engines of Charles Babbage." She was quiet for a time and merely gestured all around. "I am anxious to see what will become of it all."

By this time, our little walk around the temple had concluded and we passed through the guard gates and returned to the laboratory. Once inside, Hans, who had accompanied us on this whole astonishing tour, but who had not said a word, and thus I had almost forgotten he was with us, spoke quietly in Zulu to me, "Baas, I have seen and heard this day much more than I could ever care to. And, as you know, I understand nothing this fine lady ever says. Whenever we are around her, my head feels stuffed with babble and pains me, and it seems to me that she is about to tell you still more that will undoubtedly be far more than your poor old Hottentot servant would ever want to hear. Thus I will occupy myself looking for what passes for square-face in this poor place!" At which point he scurried around the corner of a building before I could put in a word one way or another.

Maria noticed Hans' exit and looked at me questioningly, but I only shrugged. Then a messenger ran up to her with a note in an envelope. She read it, seemed delighted and said, "Allan, you are being invited to the workshop. Maybe they will now explain rather more to you."

Maria took me to a low building that didn't seem to have a door or windows at ground level, or none that I could see, and we descended some stairs to reach an entrance. Once inside, there were more stairs going down and then we were far below ground. We went down a hallway and through some double doors, and thus entered a room—a room they called the workshop—wherein Maxwell was in the midst of writing some mathematic calculations on a large board and lecturing to the many men in attendance, including Barbicane, but stopped when he noticed we had entered.

Maria didn't waste her time nor her breath. "James, I hope you intend to give Allan some information so he doesn't stew in his curiosity. Allan needs to understand what we are doing here. I just explained how I was lured here against my will." She smiled as she said this.

"I see," he said, looking rather unhappy and looking at Barbicane, who nodded. "Well, Mr. Quatermain, since you are here and a close friend of Maria's, we'll let you in on what we are doing. I can give you an overview now. It is an exercise in astronomy that is quite well-funded by an agency that would prefer to keep its identity secret for now.

Then, Luna, Maxwell paused and reflected and seemed confused. "Well, Quatermain, I hardly know where to begin or how to explain it all."

Fifth Prologue Chapter

The Star of Wonder

Τοῦ δὲ Ἰησοῦ γεννηθέντος ἐν Βηθλέεμ τῆς Ἰουδαίας
ἐν ἡμέραις Ἡρῴδου τοῦ βασιλέως, ἰδοὺ μάγοι ἀπὸ
ἀνατολῶν παρεγένοντο εἰς Ἱεροσόλυμα λέγοντες·
Ποῦ ἐστιν ὁ τεχθεὶς βασιλεὺς τῶν Ἰουδαίων; εἴδομεν
γὰρ αὐτοῦ τὸν ἀστέρα ἐν τῇ ἀνατολῇ καὶ ἤλθομεν
προσκυνῆσαι αὐτῷ.... ἰδοὺ ὁ ἀστὴρ ὃν εἶδον ἐν τῇ
ἀνατολῇ προῆγεν αὐτούς, ἕως ἐλθὼν ἐστάθη
ἐπάνω οὗ ἦν τὸ παιδίον. ἰδόντες δὲ τὸν ἀστέρα
ἐχάρησαν χαρὰν μεγάλην σφόδρα. καὶ ἐλθόντες εἰς
τὴν οἰκίαν εἶδον τὸ παιδίον μετὰ Μαρίας τῆς μητρὸς
αὐτοῦ, καὶ πεσόντες προσεκύνησαν αὐτῷ....

—Matthew 2:1-2, 9-11

"Where to begin . . . ?" Maxwell repeated, mumbling. He looked at Maria. "Have you mentioned anything of the mechanical nature of our work?" "Well," Maria said, "I said that we were building a kind of telescope . . . ."

To which Maxwell said to me, "Well, but of course that probably wouldn't mean much to you, I suppose . . . so I suppose the easiest thing to do is to explain the whole thing chronologically." Here he stepped over to one of the many bookshelves in the room, and took down a Bible. (Incidentally, you know, Luna, that I pride myself in my knowledge of the Old Testament.) Anyway, he opened the book to where there was a ribbon bookmark and opened his mouth as if to begin to read, but instead he looked at me first and said, "Matthew, chapter two."

Then he read, "'Now when Jesus was born in Bethlehem of Judea in the days of Herod the king, behold, wise men from the East came to Jerusalem, saying, "Where is he who has been born king of the Jews? For we have seen his star in the East, and we have come to worship him."'" His finger ran down a few lines and he continued, "'. . . lo, the star which they had seen in the East went before them, till it stood over where the child was. When they saw the star, they rejoiced exceedingly with great joy; and going into the house they saw the child with Mary his mother, and they fell down and worshipped him.'"

He slapped the book shut and looked at me. I shrugged and said, "Yes, the Nativity . . . and . . . ?"

"The point of interest here is the star—the Star of Bethlehem. It is astonishing how many myriads of men have devoted unfathomable amounts of energy into trying to understand the nature of that star." Here Maxwell sighed deeply. "So very much time and energy and effort has been dedicated in attempts to understand those few words that are mentioned almost in passing in the gospel. Of course there are those who claim that the author of Matthew (you know, of course, that the apostle Matthew probably was dead and gone when this gospel was composed late in the first century and, therefore, the gospel can be thought of as a kind of forgery . . . .) simply made it all up and there was never any star or magi or any of the rest." He paused and shrugged before he went on.

"I don't pretend to know one way or another; nevertheless, we have been charged to conduct this experiment under the assumption that it is true. In a nut shell, all this is intended to study the Star of Bethlehem, and we are building a special kind of telescope in order to do just that." Here he paused.

Frankly, I did not know how to respond. I certainly was never one of those men who expended much on that point. I had never given the Star of Bethlehem any thought at all. It simply was part of the festivities that made up Christmas, along with trees and ornaments, ribbons, toys and children. The star was always shiny with rays of light, usually depicted by a circle of pointed beams. I certainly had never considered that it might be something that anybody would want to study. But instead of saying any of that, I said, "And . . . ?" *

---

*Editor's note: At this point in the narrative, Quatermain attempts to recollect details of astronomical hypotheses as presented by Maxwell to him in the laboratory workshop. However, either due to Quatermain's blunted recollection of unfamiliar concepts or

Luna's lack of comprehension—probably both—the next several passages (four pages of Luna's diary) are, for all practical purposes meaningless gibberish. There is no point reproducing those remarks here, but I was confronted with a problem: How to determine the gist of what Maxwell was trying to convey without having to guess what Luna's scribbled notes were, in turn, trying to say. It was at this point that I had, what I thought, was a clever idea. Insofar as I knew that Maria Mitchell habitually made daily entries in her diaries or journals, it only made sense that *somewhere* there must exist her own words that could help give us some sense of the information presented to Quatermain. Without going into details, after months of inquiries (both digital and traditional), I succeeded in obtaining copies of her journal pages from that period and from the exact days in question—but these particular entries cast no light whatsoever onto the astronomical concepts that Maxwell was flinging about. Nevertheless, Maria's entry on August 19 adds significantly to the texture of this tale, particularly because of its insights regarding Hans the Hottentot, and thus I am grateful that I have been given permission to reproduce her entries in the next chapter, the first supplement to the prologue. Nevertheless, regarding my quest to discover what precisely Maxwell had told Quatermain that day, I did in fact strike gold because I was concurrently investigating another interesting vein of inquiry, the results of which will be offered in the subsequent chapter, the second supplement to the prologue.—T.K.M.

First Supplement to Prologue

Heavens Above!
An Extract from the Journals
of Maria Mitchell

August 14, 1873

Oh heavens above! Allan Quatermain appeared out of nowhere today! He and Hans would have been turned away if not for my fortuitous arrival. I am so delighted!

August 19, 1873

After completing a chapter of my comet probability analysis for James—more than 500 pages so far—I joined him and Allan and Impey for breakfast. Later we gave Allan a bit of a tour, as he had asked about the Atlantic Temple.

We showed Allan (with Hans in attendance) the temple and explained the power needs of the laboratory and how we generate it. He seemed impressed with the classic form of the structure itself and also the enchanting waters as they thundered into the well of the temple, but he seemed pretty nonplussed by Impey's description of the dam and the reservoir and all the rest. But what other reaction could there possibly be, since he had no idea about our real work here—no context.

In time, Impey left us to run some errand, and knowing I could not put off poor Allan any longer, I suggested we take a walk. He, Hans, and I followed the trail around the temple and before long we found ourselves heading east, going in the direction of the Lomas Mountains, which is the source of the electricity that James and Impey have so ingeniously tapped. Of course we couldn't see them as they were 200 miles away over the horizon. At some point I suddenly realized that the ground was no longer jungle nor forest, but dry and sandy. It was a very odd experience to be marching over another desert landscape with Allan and Hans. It seems that we three had been doing this just yesterday, though of course, it was almost two years before, which, come to think of it, is not such a long time after all. I explained to Allan how it was that I was here at the laboratory, and he made some cogent observations. Then he grew silent and slowly pulled out his pipe and filled it with tobacco from a little pouch. Since he seemed lost in thought, I quickened my step and joined Hans. Though usually shy and reticent with people he didn't know especially well, he didn't seem uncomfortable with me alongside. He kept his eyes focused on the faint trail we were following. Hans had picked up a stout stick, I supposed to fend off venomous snakes or spiders or whatever indigenous creatures crossed our path. His dried, dark body was covered by a pair of baggy, brown trousers, a plain woolen shirt, and his battered, stained hat. The invisible wind, or rather breeze, bore away the sweat that beaded on our brows. Our regular pace of walking had become hypnotic, so I was all the more surprised when Hans addressed me.

"Lady Baas, you are a school teacher. Tell me about school, as the only school I have ever known was the bench on the porch of the station which was the Predikant's, the Baas' Reverend father's, in the Cradock district. I remember that we all sat there, the Predikant's servants, like myself, and field workers and any others from the nearby districts that could be persuaded to listen, and the Predikant then told us about the word and laws of the Great Baas in the sky, and talked about the Great Book a lot. How is the school where you teach different?"

Glad for the fellow's curiosity, I explained, "Well, Hans, my school is a very great one full of young women eager to learn, and also older ones like myself, who seek answers to all the world's mysteries, and then try to share the answers that they find with others, such as you just described."

He seemed to think about my response for a few moments, after which he spoke again: "Ah, so. As wise as Baas' Reverend father was, and he was very wise, he did not know anything about, say, my own father and grandfather and what they taught. But of course, everything I ever learned from them was wrong, as the Reverend Predikant never let us forget. And when we failed to pay attention he would first be patient, but after a while he wasn't so patient with us. He scolded me much, especially when he caught me drinking square-face, of which there was always a supply at the station, as the Predikant used it as medicine."

I asked, "What sorts of things did your father and grandfather teach you, Hans?"

He glanced up at the sun, and through squinting, jaundiced eyes seemed to weigh everything about the environment around us, or so it seemed to me. Then he continued:

"They, who were old and smart and told us about the thousand white and yellow sparks that fill the sky, and of the spirits, and of times past and how the world came into being. These are the things of my blood. But they are all wrong, and my father and grandfather lied, but what would you expect from a pair of worthless old Hottentots, anyway?"

This last statement took me aback, and I asked, "Why would you say that, Hans?" Then he answered that Allan's father, who, it was obvious he held in the highest esteem, was clearly wiser than his own father or any of his own kind for that matter, but then he added, "But, Lady Baas, what I mean is that all these stories, regardless of who said what, can be only so much mist, and who's to say what the truth really is?" Here he looked at the ground pensively and then indicated that he was inclined to think that "the opener of roads," whoever that might be, knew more than anybody, but that on balance, probably Allan's father was closer to the truth, though of course, he, Hans, couldn't say for sure. What a fascinating person is Hans! No matter what he says, it always sounds like he is arguing with himself to the degree that in the end he says nothing at all or comes to no real conclusions. Still, I was truly touched by his opening up to me after his own fashion.

But then I remembered that Hans always spoke deprecatingly of himself, but that once you got to know him you discovered that all that was just show, and in fact he thought very highly of himself and his abilities and his family. I looked over at him and reflected on this and studied his leathery hide and his face, which was a network of deep furrows. He was certainly loyal and a good shot and had much common sense, to the degree that he often got Allan out of otherwise avoidable scrapes. Just as I was thinking this, the earth shook a little. It was a momentary earthquake, I think, or maybe one of the excavators had dumped an especially large load on the ground. Whichever was the case, Allan, who had caught up with us, and Hans too, seemed to take it in stride and said a few words to one another in one of the African languages they so often use.

When we returned to the laboratory, Hans scampered off.

Then I learned that I had got my way! James and Impey had broken down under my onslaught of common sense, and they invited Allan into their inner sanctum to explain what we are doing here at the laboratory. Of course, the Great Physicist needed to simplify virtually everything for the benefit of the Great White Hunter, and James chose his words most carefully and was in fact quite eloquent. After reading Matthew as a sort of required preamble, he went into some of the simpler theories revolving around, and interpretations of, the Matthaean passages and some other particulars concerning the Star of Bethlehem. When James had concluded his rather pedantic explanation, Allan merely stood riveted, his eyes wide. When he spoke, he stammered, "But the cost . . ." and James responded, "Oh, our sponsor can afford it."

[Editor's note: Please see the next chapter to read a summary of the theories Maxwell doubtlessly laid out to Quatermain—as, astonishingly, rendered by Pope Pius IX himself in 1871 in a secret encyclical letter.]

Second Supplement to Prologue

*Deus Infinita**
Secret Encyclical Letter of Pope Pius IX,
December 25, 1871

Introduction

Deus Infinita—whose ways are eternally wise and whose cup is
infinitely full of truth and mercy—to the extent that everything that
was, is, and will be are but your divine whim and whose being is
infinitely more than the entire existence of man from Adam through
the Four Horsemen on this planet and the planet itself and of the
wide and various and ever-changing space occupied by that planet.

All-knowing God, you bestowed on your earthly children the
ability to learn and grow and then decipher your handiwork. In the
fullness of time, at the same moment that you created the universe,
you created Mary who would bear your son—Mary, who of all
persons was the only one to be conceived immaculately, who in her-

---

* Editor's note: From the hints and clues dropped by Maxwell,
it was easy enough for me to determine that their mysterious
benefactor, or sponsor, was probably Pope Pius IX, which led
me to formally request an examination of the so-called Secret
Archives of the Vatican, which were, in 1881, made available to
scholars. The trip to Italy was a blur, of course, because I am
very focused when researching. I spent several days in the
cavernous Archives and, with the help of some enterprising
assistants, laid my hands on the Secret Encyclical Letter of Pope
Pius IX, issued Christmas Day 1871, that sparked everything
that resulted in the laboratory and all its associated marvels. I
present here the Pope's declaration as a separate chapter. You
will note that it was written in an unremittingly stilted and formal
manner; nevertheless, as it is at the core of Quatermain's tale,
and therefore of this book, I am pleased to provide here the
first English translation of this historical document.—T.K.M.

self would be conceived your most precious son—thereby equating for eternity, Father, Mother, Son and the Holy Spirit: Perichoresis of the Holy Four. Thus, following the great news offered to Mary by your angel, she gave herself with infinite humility so that a boy child was born by the working of divine fate, in the time of Augustus Caesar, in Bethlehem. All the world knows that you made signs in the heavens to accompany the birth of your son, which Matthew in his perfect holiness later documented, for he showed us, all your earthly children, the miracle of the Star in the East, which went before the Magi and stood over where the Child was and which caused them to rejoice exceedingly so that this sign would forever be known and open to all peoples. No other Child was ever born to woman who was heralded with such infinite distinction.

This sign you placed in the heavens to make clear to the lamentably wretched thing that is the human race that your wisdom is all embracing and triumphant over the armies of the Evil One and to guide the Holy Men from the East and then be promulgated by Matthew to the whole world for the rest of time. During recent centuries, at the request and urgings of our predecessors, various learned of our order have scoured the literature both classic and modern to better understand the infinite plan of the ineffable God. Thus were old closed doors opened and old decisions reevaluated.

Being mindful that the College of Cardinals of the Holy Roman Church in 1822 declared that the "publication of works treating the motion of the earth and the stability of the sun, in accordance with the opinion of modern astronomers, is permitted" and that in 1835 the Holy Roman Church went further by allowing to be read the work *Dialogue on the Two Great Systems of the World* by Galileo Galilei and which reevaluated man's position in the universe, we humbly admit the centuries old error of assuming that the heavens revolve around the earth. Galileo was preceded by Nicholas Copernicus, contemporaneous with Johannes Kepler, and followed by Isaac Newton and others whose observations and calculations enriched the world both physically and intellectually, and when these factors have been weighed on balance and compared to both classical knowledge and extrapolations of possible inevitable advances, our committee, which wields vast classical and contemporary knowledge and which is led by His Grace, His Eminence Alberto Cardinal Cigliutti, whose fields include Physics, Astronomy, Electromagnetism, and Communication at a Distance, has concluded that it is possible to make a clear determination of the nature of Matthew's star, which is Mary's star, which is God's star for all space and all time, and which shone upon the place where the immaculately conceived Mary gave birth to the most holy perfect being—part god, part spirit, and part man.

The Root Divine Reasoning

It is widely known that there have been many theories concerning the nature of the Star that guided the Magi. There are arguments in favor of various celestial phenomena, such as a planet or planets, or a conjunction of planets, or a triple conjunction of planets, or a massing of planets, or an occultation of planets, or a comet, or a nova—or even a combination. Each of these ideas and more has received attention over the centuries. Of special note are the observations of Johannes Kepler, whose mathematics and access to pertinent, and even rare, written records were second to none and who was able, by the Grace of God, to calculate the positions of the stars and planets within the various constellations and nebulae going back in time millennia or, in truth, going forward for millennia. Therefore, Kepler showed that it is simple enough to describe the appearance of the skies during the birth of Jesus, which information has aided incalculably to the absolute determination of what the Star truly was, proving its nature as a physical, measurable phenomenon.

Kepler, though blessed with divine skill and faced with astonishing truths, published unwarranted conclusions (likely due to the tenor of that period and hoping to avoid the fate of his acquaintance Galileo), ignoring his own discoveries and choosing to deny the real, physical, and measurable nature of the Star. Rather, he elaborately conjectured in *Opera Omnia* that the Star could only be a divinely produced miracle, a miraculous light placed but a comparatively short distance above the heads of the Magi, for their benefit alone. We reject such naïve conclusions. We say it is a great pity that the times dictated the circumvention the self-evident truth!

Conjunctions and Triple Conjunctions

First, as to the phenomenon of conjunctions. It is now commonly known that insofar as the planets are in different orbits, some closer to the sun than ours, and others more distant, then it is clear that they will appear to move across the sky at different speeds and at changing intervals, each making one full orbit in the course of their own prescribed years. Thus, when it is said that two planets are standing in conjunction, that means that from our perspective as God's divine creatures inhabiting our Earth and peering up into the night skies, it appears during the period of conjunction that one planet is passing another in the infinitely black sky while close together, much as in the manner of two ships at sea, which, we are told, is a common enough experience. However, very infrequently a triple conjunction* occurs. In this case one planet appears to pass another planet three times in a row, with the central passing appearing to be backwards.

This happens thus: Jupiter, for example, appears to be moving westward in the sky from night to night. But when Earth, which is nearer to the Sun, passes in front of Jupiter, there is a period of a few days when Jupiter looks for all the world as though it is moving backward in the sky, or, indeed, eastward. Now, a triple conjunction of, for example, Jupiter and Saturn occurs this way: First, Jupiter appears to pass Saturn in the normal course of events, but then the Earth continues in its orbit so that the line-of-sight shifts, causing Jupiter, which is closer to Earth, to appear to, uncannily, reverse its path and pass Saturn a second time. Naturally, though, the Earth simply continues on its path, and the two outer planets resume their original westward motion, which causes Jupiter to appear to pass Saturn a third time.

By virtue of the mathematics, inspired by the aforementioned Kepler, we can say with assurance that a triple conjunction of Jupiter

---

*Editor's note: The term "triple conjunction" is often erroneously applied (even by those who should know better) to a quite different celestial event—the triangular massing of three planets, discussed next.—T.K.M.

and Saturn occurred in 7 B.C., the dates of each passing being May 29, September 29, and December 4.

Massing of Planets

The massing of planets is when three planets are in such a position that one can see three all at once, close together, forming a bright triangle in the blackness. There is no more awesome sight in the heavens than a massing of planets. It is an event to quicken your pulse and cause you to hold your breath—an unforgettable sight. *And does not this massing, all at once and so close together, prove the infinite wisdom and ability of God to symbolize His three natures—father, son, spirit?* But let us not forget that such a sight is made manifest to us (such humble beings) only by virtue that we are standing on Earth, that is to say, the Mother, who is always with us, yet is seldom recognized or seen.

Kepler famously observed during the autumn of 1604 the triple conjunction of Jupiter and Saturn—and then only 13 days later the massing of Jupiter, Saturn, and Mars.

Furthermore, Kepler himself was able to calculate that in February of 6 B.C. those self-same three planets formed a tight triangle and could be seen plainly in the twilight.

Regarding the Nature of the Magi

It is important to determine the nature of the wise men from the east who saw and followed the Star so that Matthew could record for all time that most holy event. It is common to think that there were three wise men, and that they had names—Gaspar, Balthazar, and Melchior—or many variations on those names. However, in the spirit of truth, the gospel doesn't say anything about their number or their names. These features have come down to us through tradition, variously attributed to histories and embellished scriptures dated from 1,000 to 1,500 years ago.

Also, in the spirit of truth, there is no historical evidence that these Magi ever existed; however, for the purposes of this Encyclical Letter, we suggest that Matthew reported accurately. Therefore, the consensus of informed opinion from a whole spectrum of authorities is that the Wise Men may well have been Zoroastrian astrologers.

These men would have hailed from Persia and have studied the night sky. They would have carefully watched the constellations, stars, and planets at all times, constantly alert for celestial signs that would foretell events to come. Both triple conjunctions and planetary massings, being singular events, would have been most distinctive and full of meaning for them.

These priests, for they would have fulfilled that role within their religion, would have noted these planetary groupings—the triple conjunction and the planetary massing—either of which in and of themselves could have seemed as divine heralds to the Wise Men of Persia. Thus both events, that is, the cumulative events of 7 B.C. and the other of February 6 B.C., occurring in sure succession (the former in the constellation of Pisces, the fishes, that relates to the Hebrew people), would have had still more terrific meaning. Could either of these celestial events or their close proximity or juxtaposition in time be considered the Star of Bethlehem?

Considering Novae

Again being mindful that the great Danish celestial observer Tycho Brahe saw and recorded at length and in detail his famous brilliant nova *[Editor's note: That is, a supernova, a term not coined till 1931]* of 1572, that which the Chinese before him had termed "Guest Stars," and which he described in his volume *de stella nova,* thus coining the word *nova,* there is merit in remembering that his protégé Kepler, when studying the remarkable triangular massing of Mars, Jupiter, and Saturn in Autumn 1604 (having also studied a triple conjunction of Saturn and Jupiter during Christmastime 1603), observed on October 10 the birth of a brand new star—never known, never seen, never recorded, a star, as bright as Jupiter *between* Jupiter and Saturn—his own brilliant nova!

Kepler, being inquisitive and logical, wondered whether this new star could have been created by the triple conjunction and the massing, or by just the massing. Certainly, this new star could easily have passed for the Star of Bethlehem if it had sprung into being

1,600 years earlier. So, Kepler, who was among the first humans who had the skills and tools to make this determination, wondered if any similar celestial events had transpired at the time of Christ's birth. And, lo!, his instincts were correct. He discovered both *the* massing of 6 B.C. and *the* triple conjunction that had preceded it. But instead of yielding to incautious vanity and claiming that he had discovered the nature of the Star of Bethlehem, he published instead that, despite these unique phenomena being clustered in time, he believed that the Star of the Magi was nevertheless a true miracle that originated in the upper atmosphere and had nothing to do with the observed and calculated celestial phenomena.

On a New Miracle

In 1871, John Williams, Assistant Secretary of Britain's Royal Astronomical Society, published his voluminous list of comets—*Observations of Comets, from B.C. 611 to A.D. 1640. Extracted from the Chinese Annals.* The Chinese were more observant than their Western counterparts for centuries, and the list contains data that is in answer to our prayers. There are two points of considerable interest. A comet that Williams lists as number 52 appeared for some seventy days in March and April of 5 B.C. near the constellation of Capricorn. The records show that the comet moved westward across the southern sky. As far as can be told, this was a typical member of the comet family such as we all think of, a ball of blue light with a sparkling tail pointing away from the Sun.

But more important was Williams number 53, which is referenced as a "tailless comet." It appeared in the constellation Aquila in March and April of 4. B.C.—almost exactly a year after 52, but this was no ordinary comet. This was infinitely more spectacular, an exploding star so bright that it hurt the eyes to view it. Could Williams number 53 be the star that appeared to the Magi to shine over the Holy Family that first Christmas season? Could 53 have been Kepler's hypothetical brilliant nova that he then disparaged?

Therefore, following the careful weighing of the afore listed information over the period of time granted us by the Divine Father, we are not in a position for mere speculation and conjecture, but we do declare that the publication of John Williams' holy book at this particular moment in time* stands as divine proof that number 53 is in all reality the One Star. We further declare that the consequent revelation is that the Star of God that illuminated the world was born in the constellation Aquila and gives us cause to rejoice and to accept a charge from God that we must now peer into his mind. Thus we make bold plans.

The Charge

After much deliberation through both lone meditation and conference, we have decided that, just as John preceded Jesus in the hills and streams of Galilee, His Star was the true herald of his birth—a spectacular event not to be ignored, which, like vast legions of angels with trumpets, would be seen and honored as no event before or since has ever been honored. Yet the herald itself would have its own heralds, and thus we can state with assurance and as fact the following:

The new star or brilliant nova in Aquila during March-April of 4. B.C. called Williams 53, was and is the true Star of Bethlehem, the Star of God, the Star of Christ, the Star of Mary.

Furthermore, fittingly, the Star itself had heralds, which we declare were as follows:

---

*Editor's note: This expression *"at this particular moment in time"* needs some explanation and some of Maxwell's words, as recorded by Professor Mitchell elsewhere in her journals help us understand. "In terms of our chronology, we must veer away from the sky to note that our sponsor, who has a natural interest in these matters, became quite ill in 1868 and thereafter, his death seemed imminent; however, he lingered, and his dearest wish was to learn about the nature of the Nativity star. But he couldn't do more than just wish simply because there was no information. But when the Williams catalog was published, he and those close to him felt the finger of God had given them a sign that they could then do far more than merely wish." In fact, Pope Pius IX died on February 7, 1878.—T.K.M.

• The triple conjunction of Jupiter and Saturn in 7 B.C., that gave the Magi cause to believe that something vital would soon happen amongst the people of Israel.

• The great massing of Jupiter, Saturn, and Mars in February of 6 B.C., that formed a tight triangle—an arrowhead pointing to the birth of a new era.

• The comet of March-April of 5 B.C. (Williams number 52) that would have further emphasized the import of that which was due.

And whereas all these heralds of the Herald Star were transitory and meaningful through their clustering in time, and have moved on and have lost their meaning, the Star itself, the celestial Herald of Christ, we now know to be fixed in the sky. We have conferred and are in agreement that that which *was* must *still be* and if we are ever to understand the mind of God we must look in Aquila, for this is our opportunity.

It is therefore decided that every effort must be made to do whatever is necessary to learn of what is now in Aquila. Though the Star that flared brightly over Bethlehem 1,900 years ago cannot be seen with the unaided eye, we can rest assured that it still remains and that a thorough study of its divine presence cannot help by benefit mankind. That which *was* must *still be*.

The Declaration

Therefore it can only be viewed as infinitely wise and useful to paraphrase ourselves and draw upon our own words from the definition decreed seventeen years ago concerning the Immaculate Conception. What we said then we can say again for the Truth is the Truth, and divine language is divine and deserves to be restated as necessary, and there is no value in assigning qualitative differences, for the one is as infinitely perfect and divine as is the other: The Blessed Virgin is the uttermost perfection of being and Her Star is uttermost perfection, and the one is the other and the other is the one, and we here state again that which needs to be said again.

These words have proven their merit and, through the majesty of
the college of Bishops, have been declared the purest words of God,
of the Holy Spirit, of the Christ, and of the Blessed Virgin:*

"Wherefore, in humility and fasting, we unceasingly offered our
private prayers as well as the public prayers of the Church to God
the Father through his Son, that he would deign to direct and
strengthen our mind by the power of the Holy Spirit. In like manner
did we implore the help of the entire heavenly host as we ardently
invoked the Paraclete.

"Accordingly, by the inspiration of the Holy Spirit, for the honor
of the Holy and undivided Trinity, for the glory and adornment of
the Virgin Mother of God, for the exaltation of the Catholic Faith,
and for the furtherance of the Catholic religion, by the authority of
Jesus Christ our Lord, of the Blessed Apostles Peter and Paul, and
by our own:

["We declare, pronounce, and define the gleaned wisdom that
the Herald of God that we call the Star of Bethlehem and the Star of
the East and the Star of the Magi and other names was, in the first
instance of its conception, by a singular grace and privilege granted
by Almighty God, in view of the merits of Jesus Christ, the Savior of
the human race, made the most glorious star in the Universe and
has confidently been revealed by God and therefore to be believed
firmly and constantly considered fact, and that furthermore, God the
Glorious is awaiting our supreme effort to meet Him through His
Star which is located in the constellation of Aquila and is there now
awaiting our attendance.]

"Hence, if anyone shall dare—which God forbid!—to think
otherwise than as has been defined by us, let him know and under-

---

* Editor's note: In essence, Pope Pius IX is saying here that his
wording from this point will in part be a repurposing (or borrowing) of
perfect language he had already promulgated in 1854 in his historic
document *Ineffabilis Deus*, which was his Apostolic Constitution on
the Immaculate Conception, in other words, his declaration that the
Immaculate Conception was a matter of fact and no longer something
that could be argued about. The sections where he deviates from the
earlier text are here bracketed and italicized.—T.K.M.

stand that he is condemned by his own judgment; that he has suffered shipwreck in the faith; that he has separated from the unity of the Church; and that, furthermore, by his own action he incurs the penalties established by law if he should dare to express in words or writing or by any other outward means the errors he thinks in his heart.

"Our soul overflows with joy and our tongue with exultation. We give, and we shall continue to give, the humblest and deepest thanks to Jesus Christ, our Lord, because through His singular grace he has granted to us, unworthy though we be," *[the wisdom and knowledge of how to proceed in this most urgent matter as timing is of uttermost import and God Ineffable has granted us the vision at the auspicious moment in time wherein and so that we can, with effort and expense, forever pull off the veil of mystery that has surrounded the Blessed Star for nearly two millennia and finally see forthrightly and unobscured the Might and Mind of God His Father and finally understand the point of all life and matter and soul and space and spirit, the sun, moon and stars, and all else that claims descent from the Most High.]*

Given to the Select at St. Peter's in Rome, the twenty-fifth day of December, 1871, in the twenty-fifth year of our pontificate.

Pius IX

Sixth Prologue Chapter

Hans Finds the Diamond

Just as Maxwell was concluding his ridiculous business about the Star of Bethlehem, I noticed that Hans had made an appearance. He was standing by the door to the workshop, trying not to be noticed in his typical chameleon manner of blending into his surroundings—yet at the same time gesturing frantically to me. When I felt I could politely withdraw to the side of the room where he was, I excused myself to find out what sort of trouble my servant had got himself into. I found him to be sopping wet!

"Hans, how on earth did you find me, and what happened to you?"

"Never mind that, Baas! You know I have my ways! Baas! Listen. This will not be the ordinary sort of chatter, chatter by reason of which the Great One takes great pleasure calling your servant a little yellow monkey, or dog, depending on his mood. Again, listen! Not finding any square-face in this place which is so like so many army barracks, and I admit I didn't look that hard because I knew that if I was lucky enough to find some, I would doubtlessly do something foolish and then you would find cause to be angry with me, and of course I didn't want that to happen—"

"Not that that ever stopped you before!" I interrupted.

But he seemed not to notice and rambled on: "I decided to visit that place that our teacher lady friend and that tall fellow with the tall hat who spoke funny [referring to Barbicane's American accent I supposed] took us, the place of the crashing waters. I was looking into the waters and then thought I saw something sparkling down at the bottom. I looked and I looked again and again and I felt certain that there was really something shiny down there—not like the visions I sometimes swear to have seen when I've had too much square-face, which as you know all too well is truly seldom."

"Get to the point, man, or I will find reason to get angry with you right here and now," I said grinning all the while, but also being conscious that my absence from the group was causing some looks to be cast our way.

"Well, Baas, my curiosity got the best of me and I decided to take a look, but I knew that if I jumped into that whirlpool that I would be instantly swept out into that hole high in the cliff that dumps into the sea, at least we were told of such a hole and I doubt not its existence or the fact that if I were to be swept out of it, I would be dropped far into the ocean and you would never find me again, or if you did I would most certainly be broken and crushed and have joined your Reverend father, the Predikant, in the Place of Fires. So I hurried back through the guard gate as they knew me and I found a stout rope and returned to the spot, made the rope fast to the thick tree branch you saw me pick up this morning and which I used as a staff such as I've seen pictures of Moses do in the Book that your Reverend father, the Predikant, showed often to all those on the station when they had the time. Then I placed the pole across the top of the well, secured myself as I know that Baas would want me to and climbed down where the current nearly swept me away, but luckily I had wrapped both ankles and wrist securely to the rope and was able to get my balance. Then I held my nose and went deep into the water head first and felt around with my hands in search of whatever the shining object should be. Well, after a time and trying several times, in the end, and seeming like I had half-drowned, I caught hold of it and climbed back to safety. When I saw what I had caught, I forgot the rope and all else and raced back here to find you."

"Well, what is it? What was worth all that trouble?"

"Just this, Baas." Then his hand dropped into his pocket and he pulled out an object palm up. My surprise was total, and what can I say but this was like life—my life, the tree of my whole life—had just been topped by a shining star! A star unimaginable! Hans was holding out to me a huge natural diamond—far, far larger than a hen's egg! Immediately I recognized it as probably the largest diamond ever found. I quickly grabbed it from Hans' grubby hands and slipped it into my own pocket. I was speechless. Perhaps I even cried. I could hear my heart pounding in my chest. Hans looked frightened.

"Baas! What are we to do? I didn't think that anything so shiny could turn my belly so! I think, that now that you have seen it, it would be best to throw it back where I found it."

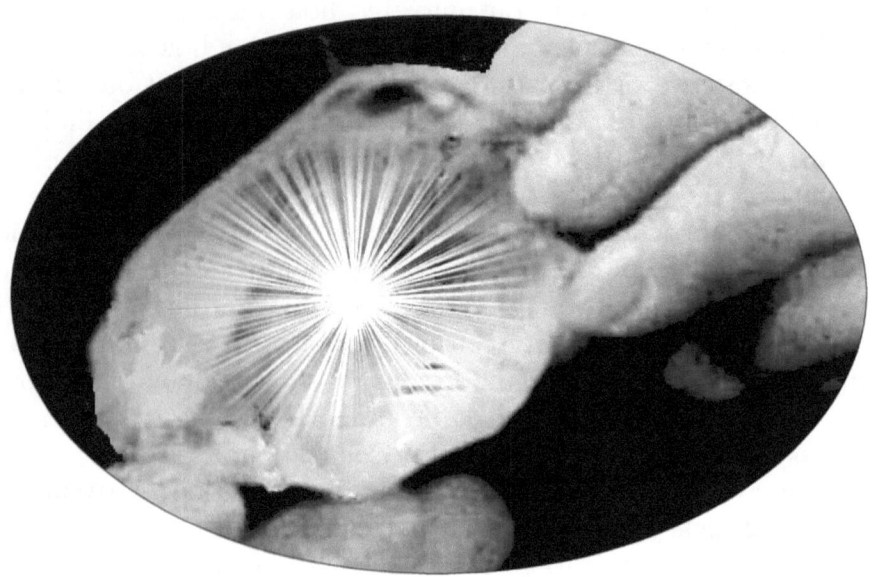

From the sketchy details that Quatermain provides Luna, it is likely that the diamond found by Hans in the temple well was the famous Jonker Diamond, which was found 60 years later in the Elandsfontein region of South Africa *(see "Select Bibliography")*. How the stone got from Quatermain's pocket at the laboratory on the west coast of Africa to Elandsfontein, some 4,500 miles away— well, therein lies this story.

"Are you out of your mind?" I asked harshly through my teeth, trying to be inconspicuous.

"Baas, is there something wrong with your mouth suddenly? It is all twisted?"

"Well, what do you expect? Suddenly we are millionaires and set for life. It's the most outrageous and wonderful thing that could ever have happened."

"Well, perhaps you are a millionaire. But for myself I would rather be the trusted servant of a good shot, and if I had to, then I would prefer to be the servant of a good shot who happens to be a millionaire. I still say we ought to throw it back where we—that is *I*—found it."

"Stop being so foolish!"

Luckily, by this time the sun was getting low, and, since Maxwell's lecture seemed to have reached a conclusion, I could naturally plead exhaustion. It was dark and we went off, with Hans trailing behind, to the hotel where we had long settled in.

The next morning, we were both up early, which is normal for us. Hans insisted on taking me to the temple to show me exactly how he had found the stone. However, just as we were passing through the gate, Maria caught up to us, to my dismay, as I wanted just then to hear Hans' story alone. However, she and I fell into conversation. As we approached the temple, which commands a view of sea, Hans ran ahead to the cliff's edge, as he forever does when there is the possibility of something exciting ahead, just like a child.

> *SS—*
> *I swear, SS, Hans' brain was keen. As much as I admire the adventurer, his sidekick interests me more. Now that I say that, I realise that the two of them together show the qualities of a group mind not so different from hives!*
> *—M*

"Baas! Baas! Lady Baas! Over here, You must see this with your own eyes." Suddenly he was shouting, and the whole scene gave me a weird sense of *déjà vu!*

We rushed around the temple and through the forest where there was a path and joined my servant. "Baas! Look, do your eyes see what mine see?" And he was pointing and gesticulating wildly. When I looked in the direction he was indicating, frankly, I couldn't believe my eyes.

"Baas! The whale we saw the other day, there it is again, or its twin brother. And its game has changed. It has risen and is asleep on the water's surface."

Sure enough, I looked down and saw that the sea waters were calm and devoid of ocean surf, and there it was, that marvelous gargantuan whale we had spied at the outset. It was down below and it did seem to have come to rest.

"Surely it is exhausted," said Hans. "In fact, I too, in its place, would need to rest after such sport as we saw, Baas! Can you imagine its weight? But look: it seems to have died. Yes, already it is stiff. As still as a ship at anchor. Death must have come quickly. Our monstrous friend must have been a fool for a whale or a very old man!"

Dumbfounded, I could only lamely mutter, "Yes, but in either case it clearly over-exerted itself."

I turned to Maria, who was by my side. As her reaction was only to wear an inexplicable smile, I turned back to the scene with the whale.

"Oh, you have spotted one of our little toys! Gentlemen, meet the *Nova*, the king of the seas!"

I looked at her hopelessly, my jaw dropped open. "What? Toy? Toy? What do you mean?" And then I suddenly realized what the truth must be. "You mean that's a ship? A ship that you built?"

"Well I didn't build it personally, of course, but Impey supervised its construction based on some documents that were . . . well, uncovered." Here she seemed to struggle to hide a smile.

"Is *that* what all *this* is about?"

"No, of course not!" Luna, here Maria almost looked at me pityingly. "Do you forget so fast that we are bound to study Christ's star. The *Nova* is merely a tool to help us build our telescope."

Frankly I could not speak, and for once in his life, neither could Hans!

"Come, Allan, your seeing the *Nova* was probably premature, and I think that Maxwell will need to explain this part of the puzzle as well!"

Seventh Prologue Chapter

All the World's a Stage

"Perhaps you are entitled to know about our submersibles, too." The scientist hummed and hawed and seemed tortured, but then he finally spit it out. "The fact is that this complex you see all around us is only half of our project. There is a similar facility 4,500 miles west on the coast of Ecuador on the west coast of South America and, of course, we must stay in as close communication as possible. While we have successfully—through veiled buffer agencies—persuaded various governments that the establishment of a trans-Atlantic telegraph cable linking the two continents is vital, that link hasn't been completed quite yet. In the meantime, our urgent requirement for fast communication and transportation forced us to improvise."

Vividly aware of the huge diamond that was burning a hole in my pocket, I wasn't able to pay attention as I should have. Clearly Maxwell was frustrated that I didn't have more to say, so I forced myself to say something.

"Doctor, geography beyond southern Africa is not my forte, but I do seem to recall that Ecuador is on the other side of South America, that is on the Pacific side. If I stretch my imagination, I can conceive some sort of a cross-Atlantic communication line, but it's impossible to see how any cable or ship, no matter its shape, could easily move back and forth between Ecuador and Sierra Leone without being forced to navigate the Straits of Magellan at the bottom of South America."

"Oh, that is easy. We simply utilize the cross-Nicaragua underground river."

"The what? I don't understand," was all I could venture.

Maxwell said, "I can best explain by means of an illustration. Please step over here." We walked to a far corner of the room where there was a large table, and I only realized when we were right on top of it that the table top was a very large map. More specifically, it was a map of the Atlantic Ocean with South America on one side and Africa on the other side.

"Yes, that is exactly what it is. Now look at it closely. Do you see anything peculiar?"

I looked again and went over it with some exactness, but there was nothing that jumped out at me. When I delayed in responding, Maxwell said, "Look especially at the two coast lines."

I did and then I did see something. "The coasts almost look as though they could fit together, like two puzzle pieces."

"Yes, that is exactly what I hoped you would notice. Quatermain, there is in fact every reason to believe that in the distant past, the two coasts were connected, and that some unthinkably titanic convulsion millions upon millions of years ago split that landmass into two pieces and that the two continents have been drifting apart ever since.

The positioning of the continents as postulated by Abraham Ortelius (1596), Lilienthal (1756), DeBrahm (1771), Snider-Pellegrini (1858), and Alfred Wegener (1912), though it wasn't recognized generally until the 1960s, following the acceptance of sea-floor spreading as a mechanism.

Well, Luna, frankly that was the most wild and preposterous claim I had ever heard, and, being in a sour mood, I said as much, instantly being regretful of my outburst, but Maxwell went on probably because he didn't hear me in his enthusiasm.

"Well then," he continued, preening like a peacock, "let us go on to the next point. As you see, if there had been in the distant past a large deposit of a mineral, say silver, and whatever force split the landmasses happened to bisect that deposit of silver, then it stands to reason that if such a deposit was located today on the west coast of Africa, that one could find a comparable deposit along the northeast coast of South America."

Here he took a stick and pointed to the two areas just mentioned.

"As it happens," he continued, "the experiment we are performing here requires, in fact, two masses of silver that are some thousands of miles apart. We chose this location for our laboratory partly because of the proximity of one such silver mass (undiscovered to date of course and thank goodness or it wouldn't have lasted long). We sent some of our associates to South America to seek the other half of the silver lode in Brazil, but they were unable to isolate any such deposit, a fact we found perplexing. However, applying their geological and geographical knowledge, they did in fact find the deposit we were seeking in Ecuador."

"I still don't understand," said I.

"If we can agree that the two coasts seem to fit together like puzzle pieces, then here is another perspective that is not so obvious."

Here he pulled the continent of South America off the table (as it turns out that they were in fact pieces of a puzzle rather than a drawing as I had first supposed), and turned that continent 90 degrees and set the top of the continent adjacent to west Africa. I was amazed to see that this was an excellent fit as well!

"Thus you see that there are other possibilities," Maxwell continued. "This agreement of geography may well have preceded the more obvious one by some millions of years and it is this configuration which interests us."

Here he pointed his stick very deliberately. "You can see that Ecuador, then, would have abutted right up here to where we stand on the coast of Sierra Leone!"

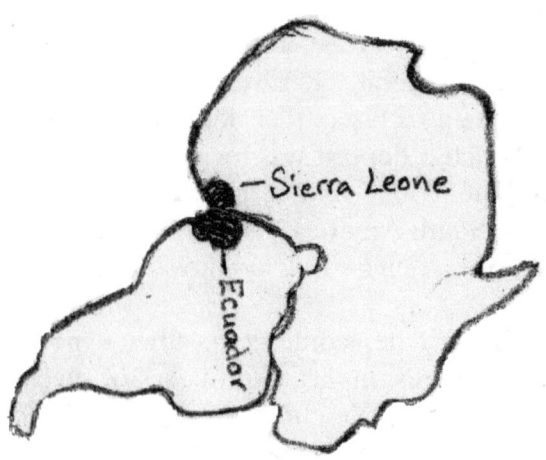

Interestingly, this general configuration was suggested more than a century after Quatermain's adventure by Jerome E. Dobson in "Spatial Logic in Paleogeography and the Explanation of Continental Drift" in *Annals of the Association of American Geographers*, Vol. 82, No. 2 (June 1992).

When Maxwell had finished, I pondered his remarks and privately thought his thinking was flawed and that the whole thing was coincidence and it was preposterous for a noted scientist to take any of it seriously, but this time I kept my feelings to myself and merely nodded sagely. I don't recall now, but I may have also asked a few questions, enough to give him the impression that I understood what he was talking about.

"Thus," he went on, "just when it was becoming clear that we needed to somehow transport to and from, and to communicate with, the other laboratory 'over yonder,' which we would build in Ecuador, we began to cast about looking for a solution, and when we found it, it was two-fold! We found convincing evidence in a recently discovered document that a submersible had been built and was perfectly operational some two millennia ago. We also in the same document learned of the subterranean river under the southern portion of Central America that connects the Atlantic Ocean with the Pacific Ocean.

"But where did you get the plans? How could you even imagine that it was possible?"

"The solution came from an unexpected place," Maxwell said. "The British Museum, it seems, has a cache of codices and scrolls recovered from Ethiopia a few years ago, scrolls that had been saved from the Library of Alexandria 16 hundred years ago."

Luna, I cannot tell you the shock this man's words sent through me. Remember that Maria Mitchell and I had trekked in Ethiopia a year or two before. Well, in fact it was during that expedition that I had heard much about those self-same scrolls that had been rescued by Richard Holmes, the curator of the museum, who had accompanied Field-Marshal Napier during the 1868 Ethiopian campaign. But that is a wholly different adventure and needs to wait for another day. (Actually now that I think about it, I did already tell that story in the presence of two notable gentlemen in New York State of all places, shortly after I settled into the Grange. One of them, my friend Dr. Watson, took ample notes and, in fact wrote up the whole story and posted it to the other gentleman, the landscape painter Frederick Church.) *[Editor's note: See* Allan Quatermain at the Crucible of Life*].*

> *SS—*
> *Ha! Quatermain tells us of his shock! His shock couldn't be more than mine—seeing that I was also on that expedition! Since my brother can accomplish virtually anything at all that he desires that has to do with the British Government, I must see these millennia-old plans for a submarine boat myself! After all, after that B-P affair, am I not within my rights? I'll have him send me photographs!*
> *—M*

[Luna: Frederick Church! Allan, you never cease to surprise me!]

Ah yes. I know John kept a copy—a copious thing, I fear. I'll see if I can borrow it to show you. In any case, it was at this point that Maria turned to me there in the presence of Maxwell and Barbicane and winked, whispering, "Isn't it interesting how these things happen?"

I couldn't just let that go. "Maria, I distinctly remember that you used the word *uncovered* earlier! *Uncovered* indeed!"

She winked again. "I didn't think it was my place to tell you . . . and besides, I wanted to see your face when you were told."

Maxwell, meanwhile, ignoring our little *tête-à-tête*, was continuing: "The scrolls telling of the submarine boat described an astonishing design that incorporated great speed. That was our inspiration, and so we challenged Barbicane, who was well underway with the planning of both laboratories."

I exclaimed, "You mean to tell me that the Ecuadorian laboratory is as immense as this one with the same energy requirements?"

Here Maxwell looked meaningfully at Barbicane, who answered, "Yes. Pretty much insofar as it was necessary to dam the Sumatara and Chambo Rivers, and develop the same sort of reservoir and power complex, though it was somewhat simpler to build the gravity driven aqueduct system due to the rivers' descent down the Andes being significantly steeper compared to the equivalent descent from the Loma Mountains here." Here he vaguely pointed in the general direction of the mountains 200 miles east of where we stood.

Then Barbicane cleared his throat and continued on the subject of submersibles, "When our sponsor, who had learned quickly of the British Museum's new Ethiopian acquisitions, approached us with a possible solution to our long-range transportation and communication problem, in the form of the 2,000-year-old papyrus scrolls, I was intrigued. And the part of my brain that is irrefutably an engineer began to spin plans instantly. But I had a second exceedingly important advantage that I had not consciously connected with our problem. You may remember, of course, that six or seven years ago, the newspapers were full of reports of sea monsters destroying ships—" He looked at me for affirmation, but I had none to give him.

I said, "Doctor, I haven't heard anything about sea monsters, and even if I had, I wouldn't have paid any attention!"

"But surely the furor—"

"I spend months at a time in back country. A hunting expedition to the Chobe River or my trading among the tribes of Nala and Wambe would have coincided with that time frame. It is not uncommon to be on safari for a year. Thus your furor may well have come and gone while I was trying to earn a living."

I admit I was a little put off by Barbicane's remark because I had become bored with the cosmopolitan style of the man who was assuming that everybody must know just what he knows and who can hardly fathom that there are some people whose livelihoods don't conveniently intersect with newspapers and magazines.

He went on, unfazed, "As I was saying, in any case, the United States government became determined to hunt the creatures down or know why not! The upshot is that accompanying the naval task force was a Professor Aronnax, a French naturalist. Their mission had considerable success, though it was not the sort of discovery and resolution that the government could allow to be reported. Nevertheless, through mutual friends I was able to meet with Aronnax, and he described in detail the true nature of those so-called sea monsters. It turns out that there was only one of the creatures and that it wasn't a creature at all, but an armored submarine boat named *Nautilus* that was designed, built and commanded by one Captain Nemo. In the end, I pumped the professor for every scrap of information and data he could recount as it interested me immensely. Remember that our meeting was *before* the singular nature of the papyri scrolls had been discovered and, in fact, *before* our sponsor had any notion of what the future held for him. So, you see, I was the right man for the job. They had hired me in the first instance to build the laboratories. Building the *Nova* and the *Stella* was merely an adjunct to the larger project, but a most useful one. My principal contribution, I think, was the adaptation of the submersible's motive power from steam to stored electricity."

"*Stella!*" I had gulped, I remember, then cried forcibly. "You mean *there are two of them?*" (Mind you, Luna, it was as difficult then as it is now to say that one special name aloud.)

"Certainly," Barbicane said. "Since we had all the infrastructure in place, the dry docks and so forth, it only made sense, and they have both been immensely useful. In fact, I have just returned from 'over yonder.' Everything is coming along fine, I'm happy to say!"

SS—

Drat!! I received the package from my brother! Disappointment!! The world has been robbed! All he could send me were photographs of the few bits of charred remains of the document. The original scrolls and the detailed, annotated English translation, along with a multitude of other treasures, simply burnt—burnt away, vanished, destroyed, along with an entire wing of the museum during the fire of 1902! Destroyed! What he was able to send is lacklustre at best, only some disconnected phrases that mean nothing in and of themselves. I can't even say that these remains are tantalising: "whore and the devil's own bitch," indeed!; "hitting home in the middle of Frigga's quivering abdomen"; "doors overlooking a narrow dock constructed of grates also of iron"; "the propulsion system will take two days to" . . . Bah! A dead end. Too bad, Quatermain! At least I have learned of your adventure these 30 years later. That is something!

—M

Third Supplement to Prologue

*The Twelve Scrolls of Xulê**
(Fragments)
As Translated from the Original Languages
and Edited by Angelina DeMars and Geri Wills
University of Kansas

---

*Editor's note: Reading of M's disappointment, naturally, I was
also disappointed and discouraged. I, too, wanted to see the
translation of those precious scrolls. A submarine boat as early as
1873? Amazing! Now, of course, I knew of the remarkable
Confederate Hunley of the American Civil War, but a full-fledged
operational submarine capable of crossing the Atlantic in mere
days! Impossible. Ludicrous! Then, on a whim, I began to search
the Internet using the phrases that M's brother had provided—
"whore and the devil's own bitch"; "doors overlooking a narrow
dock constructed of grates also of iron"—and within 40 minutes,
PDFs of photographs of papyrus fragments written in Latin and
Greek and called by scholars for convenience *The Twelve Scrolls
of Xulê*, plus an English translation, were sitting on my computer
desktop! The simple facts chronologically are these: As discussed
in my previous Allan Quatermain memoir, *Allan Quatermain at
the Crucible of Life*, the proprietors of the Great Alexandria
Library had the foresight to copy some of its holdings and send
them elsewhere for safe-keeping, some of which wound up in
Ethiopia, thus avoiding, at the end of the fourth century A.D., the
Christian Emperor Theodosius ordering it all burned. In 1868, as
a result of the British sending an expeditionary force into the
highlands of Ethiopia and the subsequent death of the Emperor
Theodore, 900 ancient documents from Theodore's library were
sent to the British Museum. Apparently among them were some
scrolls that included the information that inspired the laboratory's
secret benefactor to suggest to Maxwell and Barbicane that they
plan and build their amazing submersibles *Nova* and *Stella*.—
T.K.M.

However, by the time M had asked his brother, who seemed to have had a high position in the British government, to send copies of the scrolls to M, he was informed that the museum fire of 1902 had destroyed the scrolls except for the few fragments already noted. Then when I followed those same breadcrumb-like clues, I completely unexpectedly discovered *The Twelve Scrolls of Xulê* and the terrible circumstances that led to their discovery. It must be emphasized here that *while the Ethiopian scrolls and the Twelve Scrolls are linked only by conjecture,* still I am convinced that the former must be a copy, or a copy of a copy, of the Xulê documents that had somehow crossed the ocean or oceans from South America and had been deposited in the Alexandrian Library sometime during the 300 years prior to the library being destroyed. Once found, as the reader will see, an international team of experts led by Professor DeMars of the University of Kansas spent two years translating and interpreting the Latin and Greek originals. Given these documents' (seemingly) vital connection to the laboratory, and scientists and engineers who are, or were, pivotal to Quatermain's narrative, I have decided to include the translation here, just as I included similar supplemental material in my previous book, *Allan Quatermain at the Crucible of Life.* The volume *The Twelve Scrolls of Xulê* was a scholarly work intended for scholars and was not much known beyond its core audience. Dr. DeMars and the University of Kansas have graciously permitted me to include here portions of the work, which are in any case fragmentary to begin with, for which I am grateful.

Lastly, I ask the reader to indulge me. Upon reflection, it seems to me that the following almost prescient lines from H.P. Lovecraft are both note-worthy and thought-provoking when considered in the context of the discovery of the scrolls:

> I was confronted by the richly ornate and perfectly preserved façade of a great building, evidently a temple . . . . Neither age nor submersion has corroded the pristine grandeur of this awful fane— for fane indeed it must be—and today after thousands of years it rests untarnished and inviolate in the endless night and silence of an ocean chasm.
>
>   —H. P. Lovecraft in "The Temple
>   (Manuscript found on the coast of Yucatan.)" 1925

Introductory Note
By Angelina DeMars, Ph.D.

The discovery of the twelve ancient and priceless papyrus scrolls of Xulê, maid-servant to Julia, daughter of Caesar Augustus, will, while fragmentary, I'm sure prove to be as notable a discovery as the Rosetta Stone—not only changing our entire interpretation of history, but radically shifting the thrust of science as well.

The importance of this discovery is three-pronged. While the scrolls give us a heretofore unexpected portrait of Julia, they also offer a glimpse into what was likely a pre-Tierradentro empire that rose and fell in the northwest quadrant of South America during roughly the same period as the Roman Republic and Roman Empire combined (less a century or two at either end). Also, we can now surmise, on the strength of the scrolls, that there existed then well-established trade routes that penetrated well into North America, at least as far as Yucatan, spreading culture in both directions.

Mention should be made at this point that the story of Julia as told by Xulê does not adhere particularly to the records of antiquity which historians have, until now, taken as fact. As co-translator and co-editor of the following chronicle, which was composed in the Latin of the period with some Greek annotations in a different hand, I can only testify that the scrolls appear to be authentic in every detail. Doubtlessly, scholars will be arguing for decades in this regard.

Finally, it is known that Julia was exiled in the year 2 B.C., which dates Xulê's narrative to the nascency of the first millennium.

Note that period measurements and nautical terms have been rendered into modern forms to allow for accessible reading.

University of Kansas, February, 1988

Prefatory Note

Though many fine men were lost that terrible May night, it cannot be denied that the destruction of the super-submarine *Leif Erikson* has proven instrumental in turning a fresh page of history of incalculable value.

The following newspaper clippings were compiled to show the reader at a glance the tragic circumstances through which the scrolls of Xulê came to be located.

Since the details of the *Leif Erikson* disaster are well known and on public file, these few clippings are intended to only briefly recount the highlights of the calamitous incident in chronological sequence, thereby putting the finding of the scrolls in proper perspective.

A.D.

The New York Examiner

VOL. 134 NO. 290–NEW YORK, WEDNESDAY, MAY 3, 1985–40 CENTS–FINAL

Giant Trident Sub With 209 Lost In Depths Off Mexico; Navy Denies Triangle Link

LEIF ERIKSON
SEARCH GOES ON

Checkerboard Hunt
250 Miles Off Yucatan
On Tropic of Cancer

U.S. Navy

By Raymond Brown
Special to the
New York Examiner

WASHINGTON, MAY 3 — The U.S. ballistic missile submarine Leif Erikson, with 209 men aboard, submerged last night in the Gulf of Mexico and failed to surface as scheduled, the Navy said today.

The Leif Erikson is a Trident submarine of the Ohio Class, the largest class yet built, and carries 24 armed ballistic missiles, which have the power of destroying 1,300 Hiroshimas.

The vessel, which was making a routine run, is "presumed to be lost," according to Vice Adm. Robert M. Reuben, Chief of Naval Operations.

Two dozen surface craft and as many aircraft are searching the area of the last dive approximately 250 miles northeast of Campeche on the Yucatan peninsula in southern Mexico.

No oil slick or debris has yet been sighted in the search area that includes an undersea valley.

Hope of finding the submarine is centered on the Navy's three deep sea submergence research and ocean engineering vehicles, NR9, Treiste III, and Long John Silver, which are hastening to the 9,400-foot deep waters.

Loss of the $3 billion Leif Erikson, with its 18 officers and 191 enlisted men, would be the Navy's worst peacetime disaster since the loss of the Thresher with 129 men in April of 1963.

Originally launched one year ago as the Alaska on April 11, 1984, the renamed Leif Erikson is 585 feet long and displaces 18,000 tons.

Reuben firmly denied "ill-informed" rumors that the loss of the submarine is connected with the infamous Devil's Triangle associated with Bermuda.

"This tragedy is doubtlessly linked to some mechanical failure," the Navy chief announced to reporters from his Pentagon office at 11 p.m. last night.

Admiral Reuben went on to say that there was "no possibility whatsoever of nuclear explosion or radiation hazard from either the ship's reactors or from its 24 ballistic missiles."

The Leif Erikson submerged last night at 6 P.M. EST near the reef of Triangulo Oeste for a routine deep-diving test accompanied by the submarine rescue vessel Switcher with which contact was maintained through underwater telephone for 27 minutes.

Communications from the Leif Erikson were broken in mid-sentence during a routine depth report that gave the submarine's depth at "approaching its maximum classified capabilities," Adm. Reuben explained.

The Navy has sent destroyers from its Galveston facilities as well as specially equipped aircraft from its Houston air station into the search area with the hope of picking up signals that will aid in obtaining a fix on the missing jumbo submarine.

The Chief of Naval Operations emphasized that the accident would be thoroughly investigated by a court of inquiry headed by Vice Adm. Samuel Ashley, President of the Naval War College.

LEIF ERIKSON HUNTED

Rescue Craft Search Area Of Last Dive In 9,400-Foot Deep Waters

------

By Allan Sunshine
Special to the
New York Examiner

WASHINGTON, May 4 — The Navy said today that its giant atomic submarine Leif Erikson and its crew of 209 "appeared to be irrevocably lost" in the Gulf of Mexico.

Debris consistent with the makeup of the submarine was reported to have been sighted in the area where the vessel took a deep dive test at about 9 p.m. two days ago in water 9,400 feet deep, 250 miles east of Mexico.

"At those depths," said Adm. Robert M. Reuben, Chief of Naval Operations, "rescue would be impossible—even if we were to find the vessel."

The Navy still denies that any sort of nuclear leakage or contamination is to be expected following this tragic incident.

NAVY RULES OUT REACTOR FAILURE

Leif Erikson No Radioactivity Hazard, Navy Says

By Allan Sunshine
Special to the
New York Examiner

WASHINGTON, May 6 — Naval officials ruled out today the possibility that the loss of the atomic submarine Ohio Class Leif Erikson had been caused by any problem in her nuclear power reactor.

Officials also gave assurances that the vessel's power plant was "in absolutely no way a danger to either people, the environment, or sea life."

HOPE ABANDONED FOR 209 ABOARD LOST JUMBO SUB

Board Of Inquiry Launches Investigation Into Mysterious Disappearance

---

NO SIGN IN 72 HRS— OIL SLICK UNRELATED

Bathyscaphes Continue Search Relentlessly

By Allan Sunshine
Special to the
New York Examiner

WASHINGTON, May 7 — There is little possibility that survivors will be located from the lost atomic submarine Leif Erikson, the Navy said today.

"We have officially abandoned hope," Adm. Robert M. Reuben announced to reporters from his Pentagon office at 11 p.m. last night.

Reporter Claims
Sub in Collision

GALVESTON, Tx., May 8 (AP) — A Russian submarine collided with the Leif 2Erikson and caused its destruction, the Galveston Lone Star Tribune reported yesterday.

A reporter for the newspaper claims in a copyrighted article to have heard the recording of the last message from the Leif Erikson before it disappeared.

The reporter, Ashley Neville, indicated that the source of the "bootleg" tape was to be kept confidential. The recording clearly reveals that more than one submarine was involved in the tragedy.

The Navy has gone on record calling the report "ludicrous and an example of someone's imagination running wild."

The New York Examiner

VOL. 134 NO. 297—NEW YORK, WEDNESDAY, MAY 10, 1985—40 CENTS—FINAL

Sub Lost In Collision With Russian Counterpart

NAVY BRASS COMES CLEAN

Russians Silent

INQUIRY BOARD A SHAM

By Lloyd Overholtzer
Special to the
New York Examiner

WASHINGTON, May 9 — The nuclear submarine Leif Erikson was destroyed in a collision with a Russian missile-firing submarine in the Gulf of Mexico, Vice Adm. Samuel Rankin, the Navy's Director of Undersea Warfare, admitted today.

Following the revelation of the collision and the resultant brouhaha, the following small articles and equivalent stories were relegated to the back pages of the world's press.

GEOPHYSICISTS HELP IN SEARCH

Will Map Sea Floor Echo Soundings To Pinpoint The Submarine

A LONG TEDIOUS JOB IS FORESEEN

By Allan Sunshine
Special to the
New York Examiner
ABOARD U.S.S. SAND DOLLAR, May 11 —
A team of geophysicists is on the way to the scene of the Leif Erikson disaster tonight.

The experts will help to mark the approximate spot where the nuclear submarine went down and map the ocean floor with echo sounding equipment.

The Sand Dollar, the fastest destroyer that is based at the Naval facility in Galveston, Tx., was expected to reach the scene by first light. However, rough seas may slow the operation.

BATHYSCAPHE LOCATES LOST ATOM SUB

At Depth Of 9,400 Feet

By Allan Sunshine
Special to the
New York Examiner

WASHINGTON, May 12 — The bathyscaphe Long John Silver photographed an object yesterday that has been positively identified as a section of a conning tower instrument panel of the type installed in the Leif Erikson, the Navy announced today.

Other debris, mainly bulkhead sections, hatch covers, and misshapen tubing, was also located in the same vicinity.

"There seems to be little doubt that the remains of the Leif Erikson have been located," said a Navy spokesperson.

MYSTERY DOME FOUND NEAR SUB WRECKAGE

5,000-Year-Old Structure

Special to the
New York Examiner

CAMBRIDGE, Ma., May 14 — The three Navy bathyscaphes photographing the wreckage of the submarine Leif Erikson yesterday stumbled upon the submerged ruin of an ancient dome-shaped structure, possibly an observatory, predating the Preclassic Mayan period by at least a millennium, the Navy disclosed today in a special news conference.

Found at a depth of 9,400 feet, the structure "precedes the Classic period Maya by millennia," according to Harvard University archeologist, Dr. Bruce Edwards. "We estimate it to be at least 5,000 years old," Edwards said.

"The edifice was originally built on dry land, probably a very narrow peninsula that unaccountably subsided geologically recently," the scientist said. "For convenience's sake we call it a dome, but the fact is that its shape and size are somewhat elusive."

A Navy source, who spoke on the condition of anonymity, said that "there seems to be some sort of sonar anomaly. If I didn't know better, it's like the structure is surrounded by an invisibility shield, like a Romulan Bird-of-Prey," referring to a type of space

PAPYRUS SCROLLS FOUND IN DEPTHS

Special to the
New York Examiner

CAMBRIDGE, Ma., May 20 — Among the artifacts retrieved by Navy bathyscaphes from a sunken pre-Mayan dome-like structure are a series of sealed jade jars containing papyrus scrolls, Dr. Bruce Edwards of the Harvard University archeology department announced yesterday.

The dome, discovered May 13 by the three Navy bathyscaphes making a photo-reconstruction of the debris-littered sea floor following the Leif Erikson disaster, appears to be a 5,000-year-old observatory.

Since the temple sank into the depths of the Gulf of Mexico at least 1,500 years ago, this startling discovery "gives a shot in the arm to the diffusionists' theories that the American empires were influenced by Mediterranean contact," Dr. Edwards explained.

"The scrolls were preserved in watertight jars made of a type of white jade found only in proximity to Colombian and Ecuadorian volcanoes," he said.

After being properly treated with preservatives, the scrolls will be turned over to University of Kansas philologist Dr. Angelina DeMars for translation.

"The text is written mainly in the colloquial Latin of Augustus' time, with some Greek annotations," Dr. DeMars told reporters.

Dr. DeMars hopes to have the translation prepared for publication in two years.

The Twelve Scrolls of Xulê
Prelude

Dying

I am Xulê, and I am dying. I am from the woodlands of Strobe and my skin is black as the coal of Britannica; I am sick, and my dying will be slow. The sword thrust I received in my belly last month at the hand of a skull-faced Taaxipalkul barbarian will be my death. Even as I write, the pain is comparable, I think, to the worst that the cyclonic fires of the Phlegethon, River of Hades, could inflict in several score incarnations. A fortnight I have been delirious, or so Campachix the Surgeon informed me upon my awakening from the swirling greyness. For greyness is all I remember following the moment the barbarian miraculously sidestepped my driving battle-axe and plunged his glass long-sickle through my loins.

For many hours after my emergence from the delirium I lay weak and gasping upon my pallet, seeing nothing but the planked ceiling of an adobe hut, listening to old Campachix prattle on and on about how fortunate I am to be such a giant of a woman; how a lesser woman, sheathed in less substantial muscle than I, would have died instantly from such a wound. Campachix, while a dedicated man of medicine, has the misfortune, however, of being a totally honest man. His string of lies, though uttered with marvelous fervor, became more transparent with each word he spoke.

After I had lain still for some time, feeling a measure of strength finally return to me, Campachix came to my side to change the hot compresses he periodically applied to my throbbing, hairless scalp. Yet once again he was making further assurances that my life was as good as eternal when finally I grew tired of his mutterings and abruptly reached up and grasped his wizened, red throat with one hand and declared that if he insisted on insulting my intelligence for one second longer, I would send his soul as herald to my own arrival at the steps of Hell.

Being not only a man of dedication, but also a wise man, he instantly perceived that my desire for the truth was sincere and that, even in my considerably weakened state, I could easily snap his throat with but a twist of my wrist. Presently, though his eyes had snapped shut at the touch of my fingers, they now bulged open like great yellow moons threaded with red, and a thin, gurgling sound proceeded from his ashen lips which I took for a plea for mercy. I released my hold and pushed him gently aside, at which point he took in a prodigious draft of air, his one hand rushing to his throat while the other pressed against his middle.

"Xu...Xu...Xulê!" he ejaculated. "Mercy, my friend. For well over two years I have served you and your mistress with unswerving affection. I have ministered to your wounds, and on platters of quintessential gold I have given you my counsel. You, who have the strength of ten jaguars, have been as mother, daughter, and sister to me. All this you know well, yet you come within the space of a snake's tooth of murdering your devoted servant. Whatever slight cause you may have had for such an act I honor and respect, yet I deem that, similarly, your respect for me, Campachix, should inspire you to treat me with measured discretion at the very least."

I gazed up at his thin, long-chinned face, stared into the brown irises of his eyes, all the while listening intently to the nervous jingle of the tiny bells on his elaborate, feathered headdress, and regretted my action. I considered the possibility of avoiding apology by feigning a relapse into coma. Instead, following a deep breath, I let a great ponderous growl emerge from deep within the corded muscles of my throat, a sound that has shocked many an adversary into fatal hesitation. Campachix involuntarily took a long step back, then caught himself and stood his ground.

"My physician, ally, and trusted friend," I began unconfidently, "in the course of defending this fair land of Yokatix-Mezel,* the

---

* Editor's note: Probably a pre-Tierradentro civilization between Olmec (1200-300 B.C.) and Early Classic period Mayan (A.D. 300-550), known to be situated in the vicinity of Colombia, mainly, and Ecuador, somewhat south of the area traditionally associated with the Maya and somewhat north of the Peruvian Incas.—A.D.

Nation of White Jade, I have contracted a wound, which, despite your maternal prattling, I sense will be my death. Admittedly, I am not a surgeon, yet I detect a contrived note in your ceaseless optimism. I insist, therefore, that you confide in me your honest appraisal of my injuries. If, having only just wakened from a fortnight of sickness and delirium, I lost patience at your interminable hawking of my goddess-like health and allowed my more bestial nature to predominate, I ask your forgiveness."

I swallowed thickly then, for only twice before had I ever admitted to fault, one of those times at the prodding of a full century of Caesar's legionaries!

Campachix then admitted that the barbarian's serrated blade had opened my innards in such a devious fashion that, though the outer wound appeared healed, there remained a continual, slow bleeding on the inside for which there was no available remedy. Picking each word with finesse, he explained that death was inevitable. It may take many months, but it was certain that I would progressively waste away and die.

Though, as I have said, much of this truth I had already perceived, Campachix's words, despite their silken delivery, stung nearly as badly as the bite of the blade itself. I do not fear death, or, better, I cannot look upon death disdainfully, yet the sure knowledge that my path thenceforth was to be unswervingly guided by the haunting specter of slow death caused all the muscles of my body to go tight as stone. I closed my eyes and, with a wave of dismissal, begged Campachix to leave my side so that I might think— and reflect alone upon my direful fate.

But I get ahead of myself. It was three days ago that I first wrote that I awoke from the grey delirium. It was somewhat later when I lost my patience with Campachix.

My first thought when I awoke was of Julia. "Where is she?" I asked when I saw that she was not by my side.

"Aboard *Thebes*," was Campachix's reply.

"I would have preferred that she had remained by me . . . ."

"Do not fret, Xulê. Your mistress will return before long. For a full fortnight she lived by your side, eating and sleeping on a mat laid on this very spot where I stand. She would only leave after the learned Moab prevailed upon her the urgency of the matter."

"Matter? What matter is more important than her concern for me?"

"I know only that the earth shook badly, and Moab insisted that they leave immediately for the bottom of the bay in *Thebes*."

"And what of Frigga, she whom you call the Jade Princess?"

"The Princess accompanied Moab and Julia, my friend. That was three days past—only hours before you awakened."

"Is there more to tell, then?" I asked.

"Only that as they sped away to the mooring of *Thebes*, The Bride (I should say that Julia often claimed to be Nerio, Bride of Mars, in other words, a goddess, and who am I to say otherwise, I who worship her!) charged me with your care and bade me tell you, when you awoke, that a crisis of unutterable singularity has sent them to the floor of the Great Bay of Mezel."

I lay quiet then and knew in my heart that my friends had good reason for quitting this woman's side in her hour of need. After a time, my thoughts turned to the defeat of King Ponamyak and the barbarian army of Taaxipal . . . for doubtless, brooding on this subject of my mistress' desertion could only beget woe for all.

Now I asked, "How is it we stand champion against Ponamyak? Surely we were blessed by the gods that morn!"

The surgeon, who had fallen into thoughts of his own, looked up and answered, "Indeed! If fewer had died I would call it a miracle. As it is, the gods saw fit to stage an epic with a handful of spectators . . . . But you ask how! The answer we learned from the Taaxipalkul wounded. King Ponamyak's warriors, having partaken of the mescal cactus, fought well and as madmen so long as it was dark. But, when the first arc of the sun appeared, thrust out of the sea, these same madmen saw not the sun, but the cruel mouth of a heinous creature racing upon them to savor their flesh. It seems such visions are common to all who are simultaneously drugged."

Now, when I heard this tale, it struck me so funny that I laughed—or tried to—a gesture which I instantly regretted, for the effort caused me a paroxysm of anguish of unparalleled extent.

When the seizure had passed for the most part, Campachix wiped my face of the tears of pain, and I muttered my hate for Ponamyak and his whole infernal breed. Not so much for my wound or the ceaseless skirmishes did I hate the Taaxipalkuls, but for their cowardly attempts at conquering the peace-minded Nation of White Jade.

And for what?

For the amassment of sacrificial victims for the sloshing altar bowls of the ravening, several-headed snake goddess Bemxote!

"By Greenox!" I was finally able to articulate, calling upon the Janus-faced and capricious forest god of my clan. "If only that fierce creature had been real. Perhaps it would have made feast of Bemxote as well!" But, now I dared not so much as smile, but only lay back and stayed quiet as well as I might.

It was at this point that Campachix began his incessant harangue concerning my recuperative powers.

"Ah, Xulê, when you are better, you will be that creature! You will lead Yokatix-Mezel to victory . . ." ; et cetera, et cetera, et cetera.

✦ ✦ ✦

It is two days since I last picked up quill and scroll—that day Campachix confided in me the nature of my ailment.

And the fifth since Julia, girl-child of Augustus, departed for the depths of Mezel Bay on her enigmatic mission. On a journey of mystery she has embarked, and Xulê has no answers! Xulê has no conception of the reasons!

O, Moab, learned captain, take care of her, daughter of empire, daughter of Rome!

Now, as I await her return, and being confined to my pallet fully against my will by Campachix and his pretty wife, Meyexican, I will further exercise my writing prowess—for scribe I am as well as warrior and gladiator—and record on this papyrus for eternity and for all the future worlds of men the journey of Julia across the Great Sea.

Part One

Exile

Most days, having nothing better to do, Julia would climb the only mound that passed for a hill on our insignificant islet and comb the horizon for hours in search of an unwary merchant or fishing vessel to hail. In two years, though several were apt to approach, none could be persuaded to land, their prurient crews always being reminded of, or giving second thought to, Caesar's decree that whomsever sets one foot on Pandateria without his express Imperial authority loses his eyes, tongue, and all four limbs.

It was on such a day, Julia attentively watchful and ripe with hope, the sun high in a typical Mediterranean clear-blue sky, that our fantastic travels and adventures began.

Within sight of the Italian coast, the barren chunk of rock called Pandateria *[Editor's note: Known today as Ventotene]* pokes out of the sea fifty miles due west of the Bay of Naples. Despite its consisting of little else but grey sand and shattered razor-edged stone, it bears signs—dusty furrows and dead hedges—of being cultivated in decades past. The only things that grow there now, however, are an occasional brittle grapevine, a rarer prickly bush with holly-like berries, and a few sprigs of some sort of yellow grass.

Biting winds whirl unceasingly about the seaward crags and meandering dunes, singing and moaning through the burned-out ruin of the old villa on the northern end of the island, driving deeply into the ancient sea-carved grottos and caves which provide the only other convenient shelter.

Here it was that Gaius Octavius Caesar, the August, First Citizen and Pontifex Maximus of Rome, Emperor of all the known world, chose to exile his daughter and only child, the only person he ever truly loved. This was home for Julia for two endless years.

And for what ghastly crime was she convicted?

Adultery!

At the age of thirty-seven, after three husbands and five children, Julia was shown to be in violation of the *Lex de adulteriis*,* evidence of which was brought before her father by her own horrid step-mother, Livia. It was Livia's plan to cast dishonor upon, and thereby discredit, Julia's two sons—who were also Augustus' adopted sons and Imperial heirs—Gaius and Lucius, by which treachery she hoped to raise her own son, and Julia's husband—Tiberius Claudius Nero—to second person of the empire!

The whole matter was especially irksome to Augustus. That his own child would violate the mandates not only of his own devising but those of Rome herself was more than the old fellow could bear. His heart was broken. He behaved hysterically, exposing her before all of Rome and imposing the mandatory penalty on her!

Now, this affair becomes particularly interesting when one realizes that all the charges brought against Julia were perfectly true— that she was, in fact, involved in, or experimented with, to a very great degree, her own special species of copulation with an assortment of men, an activity she fondly refers to as her "sport."

Though Augustus loved his daughter more than a man can say, he loved Rome more. So, here was a man pitiably torn between the two things of the world for which he cared most, knowing that the mightier of the two must prevail. Doubtlessly, his hysteria turned to madness for a time, and in the end he lashed out at the cause of his torment. Julia must be banished for the good of Rome!

Never again would her name pass his lips!

Thus it was that Julia, my mistress, was thrust from all the civilized world and forced to live out the rest of her life on a bit of rock with nothing but the fishes, seagulls, field mice, and sand crabs for company. That is, except for myself, Xulê, most stupendous woman warrior of all Black Strobe and Nubia combined! How

---

* Editor's note: This refers to one of several laws framed by Augustus himself in the year 18 B.C. aimed at strengthening a demoralized Rome. In particular, the *Lex de adulteriis* was meant to reestablish harmony and virtue in the Roman family by threatening the unfaithful wife and her lover with lifelong exile and the confiscation of a significant part of their property.—A.D.

many men has this one woman slaughtered in the arena? More than I can count—and all I have to show for it is a few scars. I don't count the fine scars on my breast, which were self-inflicted. Here is the reason: there had once been in the arena a Northwoman whose flesh evaded my blade by only the smallest fraction no matter how I pressed my advantage. She laughed in her contempt, for the only thing that prevented my blade from contacting her was the impediment of my own body. Her laughter didn't last long though because the next time I parried, my fury was boundless and my short sword came down and whisked off those minor obstructions in the merest blink of an eye. Can you imagine my joy when my thrusting blade curved back up and smoothly entered her far better than any man, the momentum carrying the point straight up with demonic force through her torso, wiping the laughter off her face by piercing her throat and neatly slicing off her jaw? O, the lucky girl who has known the love of Xulê!

Yet, it came to pass that two years of the sentence was all Julia suffered. Two years of anguish and loneliness unimaginable! Two years with little else to do but hate and loathe her father and everything for which he stood.

Nevertheless, those two years were far from wasted. In that time, having little else to do, she and I both fired by ever-growing thoughts of revenge, each day for hours on end, I would instruct my mistress in the use of the Roman short-sword, the Northern long-sword, spear, axe, bludgeon, and the like. Every day we practiced, whetting her skill, and putting muscle on her slight frame. For in all of Julia's life, with the exception of her "sport," her time was spent weaving, spinning, bearing children, and the other household duties considered traditional and proper for aristocratic Roman women. But now, I, Xulê, taught her the cunning of the gladiator. And being that Julia is intelligent and lithe of muscle by nature, her proficiency developed rapidly. At the end of two years, I can say in all honesty that she was nearly my equal in swiftness of thrust and agility of parry. Often, in practice she has succeeded in striking the blade from my hand with deadly precision. In point of fact, when her blood is hot, she strikes like lightning.

So it was, then, that sweet Julia, daughter of Rome, stood atop the sand-hill fronting our cave on the southern coast of the island one bright morning, gazing out to sea. Enchanting it was to behold the figure of this woman standing tall in the distance, her long, tapering legs taut and spread wide, her elbow-length auburn—but prematurely silver-streaked—hair swelling bewitchingly in the gusty-breeze. Standing naked on that high crest of quartz sand, she clutched her long-sword solidly in her right hand, while shielding her eyes from the glare of the fiery sun with her left. Turning her golden goddess-like form toward one end of the small island then slowly back again, she searched for that unsuspecting Greek or Carthaginian fishing boat or trader to hail. For two long years, Julia had not been able to indulge in her sport, and my mistress, knowing her own needs, never ceased to look for man or men who could service those needs—the ultimate heinous fate of those poor souls seeming not to interest her one whit, her need was so great! Though not the noblest of attitudes, I tended to give her the benefit of the doubt and thought of this as her one foible. Fortunately, no man ever took the bait, as I have no doubt that Augustus' spies would have found him out!

As I crouched inside the mouth of our cave cleaning our breakfast fish and watching her golden body glisten in the sun, I saw her suddenly hesitate in her pivoting search of the sea. Then she raised her sword high into the air and waved it in a wide beckoning arc.

Knowing something different must be in the offing, I leaped up and ran with long strides all the way to the top of the hill. Reaching my mistress' side, I did not hesitate to fix my attention on the sea towards which she pointed with her outstretched blade. By Greenox! I was expecting nothing less than a fleet of Macedonian warships, but all I saw was choppy waves in our little bay.

"What is it, mistress?" I asked. "There is nothing that I can see."

Julia looked up into my eyes, her freshly washed hair scattering like wind-whipped fire in the rising breeze. "By all the gods, there was something out there, something big, but it has disappeared. At first I thought it was an island rising."

In the end, I impatiently marched back to the cave and that day proceeded just as any day. Shortly after nightfall we wrapped ourselves in pelts and huddled by the blazing fire, and I teased her about her "island."

Julia wasn't happy, and she said, "Ah, my big, beautiful comrade-in-arms, have you so little imagination, no romance for the unique and marvelous things that so seldom touch our lives these days? Can you not believe that I saw something out in the bay?"

I replied that I had more than abundant imagination, but she ignored my sarcasm. Sleep then came over us.

We were pounced on in the dark of night and pinned to the ground in our sleep! We had no way to anticipate this outrage. Then we were dragged struggling to the beach. Out there in the bay, we saw a large mass like a floating reef moving rapidly in the bright moonlight—a mass that wasn't supposed to be there! A mass lit with yellowish light *from the inside*. We were so amazed that we both stopped struggling and simply stared. Then we were in for a still bigger surprise. Julia made sense out of the scene before I did.

She cried out, "It has jaws and they are opening! And by the specter of my great-uncle, is that a boat emerging from its mouth?"

Indeed, before our eyes, the thing had come to a rest, agitated seawater splashing against its moon-lit shining blue-black hide. And out of its peculiarly stiff, gaping mouth a spry little boat was being driven by the oars of ten men! As soon as the boat emerged fully, I began to recognize that the great mass resembled a whale—wonder of wonders!—a great fish! The boat pointed its prow toward the beach and cut swiftly through the rolling waves. From atop the hill where Julia and I were held captive and observed these marvelous proceedings, we saw that in the center of the small craft, surrounded by the pumping oarsmen, sat the small, slumped figure of a man dressed in a simple, white Greek robe.

We saw also that the boat would touch the sand of the beach in a short time. Then as one, the men released us shouting with excitement, Julia and I, neither of us wearing so much as a rag around our loins, sprinted into the surf. Side by side we waded out, gleefully waving and calling out all the while. Then, when the boat came between us, we pushed and tugged at the craft till the oars touched bottom and the oarsmen, freedmen I saw now from the manacle scars on their wrists, leaped over the side and leaned their backs to the task, and together we pulled the boat onto the beach. In all the excitement, only the Greek, which we saw clearly now was the case, remained undisturbed and dry.

No man of them, however, uttered a word to either Julia or me during this first encounter, the old Greek only staring fixedly ahead with a faint smile on his lips. But no sooner did the boat come to a rest than he stood up and waited till one of the freedmen, a lieutenant I supposed from the heavy knot in which his hair was arranged, offered an arm, which the Greek took. Clutching up the folds of his robe with the other hand, he stepped from the boat, then casually glanced from my naked form to Julia's.

He lifted his hand to his mouth, coughed slightly, then spoke. "Julia, my dear, daughter of Octavias Caesar, you must pardon our intrusion."

From where I stood, I could see Julia's eyes open wide at the sound of her name. The master of the boat evidently saw this as well, for he said quickly, "Yes, Julia, I know who you are. Indeed, I was sent here by your father on a mission of mercy."

"I do not understand, old man," Julia exclaimed. "My father has publicly stated that he would never again speak my name. Indeed, I was to be exiled with no other human contact but Xulê here, my protector, for the rest of my life."

"Indeed, Julia, that is so. Yet, what Augustus saw fit to tell Rome and that which he held close to his heart were two entirely different matters."

"Then I will be allowed to return home?"

"No, I'm afraid not, but he has gone to great pains to see that your life of exile be less strenuous then he originally indicated to the Senate."

"Less strenuous!" Julia nearly screamed. "Less strenuous than two years of solitude, of loneliness unimaginable! It seems a little late for missions of mercy. How would you like to live with nothing but sand crabs and seagulls for company for two years? If it had not been for Xulê, I would have died for want of companionship. Don't talk to me of less strenuous! Speak no vile hypocrisies to me, old man!"

"Nevertheless, my dear," the old man continued, seemingly unaffected by the outburst, "all these two years past, your father has secretly been the architect of a rather intriguing deception, designed principally to allow you to regain at least a portion of your freedom— a plan which you will doubtlessly accept gratefully once you hear the details. But first, let my men and me be welcomed into your home. A moment of leisure for ourselves after a long sea voyage . . . and a surprise for you."

"But who are you?" Julia finally found the wits to ask. "And what in the name of Jupiter is that monster yonder? Fish or ship or the handiwork of demons? Great gods, man, if you are master of that monster, as I take it you are, are you man at all . . . or monster yourself?"

The Greek laughed, more I gathered from the sudden change in my mistress' expression than from the content of her accusations.

"You need not concern yourself over such matters, my dear. I am quite as human as you, if not so young—and *Thebes* is merely a ship of my own design. Shall we go?"

"It's all beyond words," Julia said as we walked, her lovely limbs swinging gracefully in time with the sea sounds. "It's so good to see new faces again after all this time."

"Yes, so good! I too crave new faces and talk," I said, "especially if that talk deals with freedom—for you, at least, if not for me."

"My name is Moab," our guest explained once he had seated himself in the shelter of our cave. "I am a Greek, who but recently was residing in my homeland in a small coastal town called Poros. It was there that I built *Thebes* ever so discreetly so as not to attract attention, directing the efforts of my dedicated men.

"I am a naturalist primarily, but can make do with mechanical devices. In recent years, I have become particularly interested in solar eclipses, which, of course, can be easily predicted through calculation, but, by far, the majority of them occur over open ocean. When I found that there was no ordinary means by which I could quickly cross the seas, I endeavored to develop a fast craft, and while I was at it, I thought I could build it suitable for exploring the vast mysteries of the sea below the surface. As you have seen, I succeeded admirably."

"And you fashioned your craft in the guise of a whale for reasons of camouflage, no doubt," Julia offered.

"Yes, but also to decrease water resistance so as to improve speed. It is the only one of its kind in the world, so far as I know—unless old Job's Leviathan is to be believed!—and quite comfortable I might add. With it I can do my eclipse studies wherever they may happen and travel at depths quite unattainable prior to its construction. Yes, yes, depths absolutely unheard of. It is also, needless to say, your means of escape."

Julia's face still showed confusion. She said, "You say that you calculate the location of eclipses. How can that be?"

"Excellent question, my dear! I can see that your intellect has not been exaggerated to me. Yes, while I do pride myself on my mathematical prowess, I was fortunate to happen upon some plans, in the Great Library at Pergamum, for a mechanism that aids in determining celestial positions. The modified version I built has proven most useful in confirming my own calculations.*

Julia remained quiet far a time, no doubt awed as much as I by both the apparent skill of the Greek and the proposition he offered. Miracles and freedom all at once! It was more than we could assimilate at one time!

"But," began Julia finally, after a long silence, "at irregular intervals an Imperial galley circumnavigates the island, skirting the shore, making certain that I am still here. Sometimes, knowing they have arrived, I keep hidden to see what they do next. But it's no good, for they always send ashore an armed party of mute women

---

* Editor's note: Moab's device may have been based on the so-called Antikythera mechanism, thought to be part computer, part astrolabe, discovered in an Roman-era shipwreck off a Greek Island in 1900.—A.D.

who comb the rocks till they find me. It is the closest I've come to having fresh company. But it is no good at all because no sooner do they find me, they turn around and head back to the galley, which in turn sails off and disappears before long. How can I leave without the whole Imperial Navy raising the alarm?"

"That, my dear, is no problem at all. That is, it is no problem now. Your father has gone to great lengths, great lengths indeed. But, let me explain his entire scheme. In order to save face, it was necessary to prepare for all contingencies. That is why it has taken so long.

"Without making known his motives he sent dozens of specially chosen couriers throughout the empire with instructions to look for innovative inventions, especially sea-going vessels, and new weapons.

"After eighteen months, one of these Imperial representatives learned of *Thebes* from fishermen and, after observing her performance from a distance, immediately impounded her, much to my chagrin, naturally. Within a month, I was told to take *Thebes* to a hidden cove several hundred miles north of here. There, much to my surprise, Caesar himself met me, examined *Thebes*, and explained his needs, which he made quite clear: simply stated, I was to remove you from Pandateria and give you your freedom so long as you never again set foot within the empire . . . and that I was subject to your direct orders and desires—and, of course, even your merest whims so long as we both shall live—which state automatically guarantees my own exile!

"I must say, while sympathetic, to tell the truth I didn't much care for the idea of having to leave all the known world behind, as obviously would be necessary if I agreed to his plan. He made it exceedingly plain, however, that I really had no choice whatsoever in the matter. And whereas I've lived a long and fulfilled life, with great expectations of continuing to do so, I readily saw his point, whereupon I began preparations for an extended sea voyage.

"Caesar then further explained the second part of his plan, namely that he had dispatched a number of mutes across the empire who were to search for a double—a veritable twin—of yourself; then finding such a double, they were to bring her back with them under the strictest guard, by force if necessary, with the intention of training her to mimic your voice and every movement and then substitute her for you—that is, to pose as you—on this island and thereby fend off the suspicions of the watchful galley."

"But that's horrible!" Julia cried. "I could never allow such a thing!"

"Nevertheless," Moab continued, "It was among the barbarians who dwell in the broken country north of the Danube that a woman was finally found who met the desired specifications. She was seized, as a matter of fact, some time before knowledge of *Thebes* had reached Augustus, and was taken to a secret training center on Sicily where she was instructed in her new role—namely, to be you.

"Mind you, from what I understand, she was not a particularly willing student, but in time she picked up enough of your obvious mannerisms—drilled into her by certain of your own tutors and servants—to fool most casual observers.

"Frigga—that is your double's name—is to take your place here and live out the rest of her life on this island as you would have done—"

The old Greek would have said more but Julia's face grew livid, and she nearly thrashed the fellow right there. The way that tiny, slumped-over old man recoiled from Julia's wrath was quite the sight. I would have laughed but for the fact I wanted to hear what my mistress had to say.

"By all the gods," she began, her small fists trembling with restrained fury, "I cannot allow this to be! It is ghastly! I would not wish such a fate on an innocent. For shouldn't I know what life on this god-forsaken cinder is like? It is bad enough that my own father would cause me to live in torment and despair for two years; I cannot allow this guiltless woman to live out the rest of her life in my place, despising every moment of that life, living only for hate as I have done, with not even a friend such as Xulê to console her in her worst moments. I will not live to see such a fate forced upon another! I will sooner stay than see that! Do you understand, foul worm of a man?"

At that moment, the man with a knot in his hair, whom I had taken for Moab's lieutenant, leaped up from the group of sailors who were stretching and lounging outside the entrance of our cave and raced up to Julia. As he rushed past me, I saw his face draw tight into a mask of hate, a sight which made my muscles convulse, and I found myself confronting the man, my hands on his shoulders.

"Julian bitch!" he cried. "No hell-bound offspring of that demon Augustus nor niece of Caesar the traitor can talk to my master like that! By Jove, I'll wring your poisonous neck till your sharp tongue bloats purple before I'll hear such talk again!"

When I heard this, I think I must have blacked out for a time, for the next thing I remember is feeling pain in my arms as six men pinned me to the ground. I ceased to struggle, at which point the men backed off and I sat up to see that the fellow with the vile mouth had decided to go to sleep slumped against the wall of the cave, which I thought was good for him, for otherwise I would have killed him.

Julia, meanwhile, though calmed down somewhat, still glared at Moab, gasping air. It seemed as though she was fighting violently the anger rising out of her heart. Yet, I could tell her mind was entirely on the subject of her double. She seemed, for all appearances, unaffected by the incident that just occurred with regard to the man who had fallen asleep.

"O, man! Where is this woman now?" she demanded.

"She remains guarded in the submersible."

"Then bring her to me immediately. I would see this twin of mine."

Moab gestured to another of his men. "Erasmus, return to *Thebes* and bring Frigga hither. And take Livinius."

Immediately, the man called Erasmus turned and began kicking and berating his fellows in a comradely fashion, relaying and enlarging upon his master's orders.

In a moment, they were all on their way back to the long boat, two of them supporting Livinius the Blowhard, who was slow to keep up.

"Please, you must pardon Livinius' behavior," Moab began to explain. "He is really quite loyal to me, and easily takes offense far too personally, I fear, when criticism is aimed my way. Furthermore, he was once the personal slave of Horatius Claudius Nero, your step-mother's uncle, and, therefore, remains faithful to the Claudian side of your family—despising anything Julian."*

"In that case, I'll pay him no mind," Julia said. "Perhaps, he will become less of a fool someday. In that event, he may learn to call me 'friend.' Well, old man, you tell me my father, the *great* Caesar has engineered my escape and contrived to retain his honor in the bargain. Yet the freedom I wish is not the freedom that is now offered to me. What is a girl to do, ah, Xulê? We should have thought he would pull some trick as this. My father has many faces. I suppose that's why he is emperor of the world. But I will never understand how even one with a multitude of faces could exile his own daughter to a living death. Then again, I suppose that one such as that is capable of anything—anything at all!"

"True, mistress, yet it was he who brought us together. So, though I hate him for the one, I love him for the other, and now that I know that he did not truly forsake his love for his daughter, I find myself almost respecting the man again."

Here, I strolled to the cave entrance, looked around and assured myself that all of Moab's men had returned to their vessel. Then I faced Moab and set my expression in a serious mold.

"Moab, old Greek, listen, I say, to my words. Bear witness to these words which must be spoken! For two years this woman"—here I gestured towards Julia—"Daughter of Rome and, therefore, of the World—and I have lived alone together on this hellish rock. The frustrations of our heinous imprisonment you can never fathom, never having experienced it, yet through our suffering, a suffering of the spirit which I can tell you from hard-earned and bitter experience is a thousand times a thousand times worse than any physical torment, we, myself and this woman, fallen heir to the world, have come together, and grown so that we share a kinship, a sense of nobility, and a knowledge of well-being while in one

---

* Editor's note: Despite the fact that Augustus (great-nephew and adopted son of Julius Caesar, and, therefore, a Julian) and Livia (a blue blooded Claudian) were man and wife, Emperor and First Lady of the empire, the Julians and the Claudians were vehement political enemies.—A.D.

another's company that never can two other people—man and wife be damned!—ever hope to obtain, nay, to imagine, I say! You gaze upon us and see two; we look upon one another and see but half of ourselves. Enough! You are witness now to my words. You, who fate has chosen to be our rescuer, have heard the truth of my bare soul. No, say nothing. Merely contemplate a fact as firm as this cursed rock on which we sit. Julia and I are as one and shall remain so till the gods reclaim their own. And I tell you now, that if I have a say in the matter, Julia shall regain this, her rightful world—she shall be empress of all the lands as is rightfully her due—and I, Xulê, with sword and teeth if need be, will deliver it into her hands!"

"Nay! My friend," Julia broke in. "I shall accept no such gift from you. We will take it together, for it is as much yours as mine, for in fact we are joined in soul as you say, and togetherness is our blessed boon. What say thee, now, old Greek, Moab, our redeemer? You are bidden to speak."

Moab, who had been sitting quietly, staring into space, slowly lifted his gaze. Lingeringly, he looked first at Julia, then deliberately shifted his owl-like, bottomless eyes and took in my own near-Olympian figure.

"Solitude!" he began. "How it can distort the mind! How it can make one hunger for one's own kind! I can well imagine the need you both have to talk to a new person . . . . For instance, I have only been on your island for a few minutes . . . not even an hour . . . and already you both are pouring out your souls to me. Can you be sure I am a sympathetic listener? I think I understand your sadness, for I begin to feel it in this vast welling of words, this tide of emotions. It must have been excruciating, your time on this island, yet I gather from your words that, quite unexpected to both of you, you have found something which has almost made the experience worthwhile (that is no doubt the wrong word)—you have found that which is genuinely and finally the truth that comprises your essential selves. You each have discovered within the other a part of yourselves, a part that has always been missing whether you knew it or not. I can state that with the utmost assurance. No one is ever born whole; that missing piece of the individual is always locked away deep inside another person. It is the task of each person, then, to search for that missing piece. Some succeed; some fail. Yet the road is never the same for any two successful unions.

"I am happy to say that it appears you two have succeeded . . . . Only to discover this, to understand this, it was necessary that you suffer the foulest agony of the spirit so that you would each seek succor within the other. The greater the pain, the deeper you must have plumbed the other till at last you found that which you had no idea you sought: your lost selves, that elusive fragment of your mind and personality which the Creator saw fit to sequester in a safe place till you stumbled upon it in the dark (which is the way it seems always to happen). Though you had never conceived that you were lacking some vital part, when you found it, you soaked and bathed in total joy.

"And I tell you now that having bathed, you have confronted your Destinies. From that moment when you found your lost parts within the other, you became whole—complete as too few men and women ever can be—and being whole, there now awaits you a future to be reckoned with. That I can promise you, but I cannot say more . . . for who truly can outguess Destiny, ummm, my friends?"

Now, I ask you, whoever may someday read this, what would you have done if such a speech had been addressed to you? Julia and I could only sit quietly for a while, the only sounds being the distant roar of the surf and the muffled beat of our own hearts. At times I would, with an effort, look up at Moab, who seemed lost in his own thoughts, or at Julia who would meet my eyes. During the next few minutes, it was as though we could read one another's minds: as our emotions and feelings ebbed and flowed, our eyes were like windows in which we read the softness, the hardness, the confusion, and, finally, the understanding that the other experienced.

After a time which proved to be a far longer time than I had imagined, I realized that I could take no exception to the old Greek's words and was about to say as much.

But then, there came a howl from the beach.

Part Two

Frigga

The long-boat had returned. All at once, Julia and I were on our feet and racing for the crest of a wide sand dune which blocked our direct view. Reaching the top simultaneously, we saw clearly in the moonlight Moab's men splashing and gesticulating wildly at the sea's edge. I sprinted ahead, arriving first at the site of the commotion where I thrust aside three or four of the guffawing oarsmen and beheld in their midst—to my utter amazement!—a blond, lily-white and snarling Julia clothed in snowy linen and brandishing a curving, saw-toothed bronze dirk; and, too, doubled up kneeling in the wet sand was a skinny, saffron-hued freedman who clutched the side of his bloodied head and moaned pitifully.

The next moment, Julia herself came rushing up, stopping dead at the sight of this strange tableau.

"Great Mars! Jupiter and Juno! Xulê, is this real? I cannot believe what I see. It's myself—but a pale version to be sure!"

Hardly had Julia gasped these words than, with the lightning speed that only the hopelessly trapped animal can summon, the woman in white leaped at Julia, and in a flash they were knotted together, rolling in the surf, the crescent dagger lashing furiously through the flying salt foam and churning sea wash. Not once, however, did that driving blade touch my mistress' golden flesh. With one flashing wrist, Julia parried the down-swinging blade over and again, while her other hand grappled ferociously for a fast hold around her foe's alabaster, rock-corded throat.

For a time, I watched the sport with some relish—mindful, of course, of mishap and of possible harm to Julia—but, when I saw that the fracas was not about to end quickly, I took it upon myself to resolve the quarrel by unceremoniously taking up the false Julia by her little waist and ample thigh and holding her high above my head, all the while threatening to crush her spine into pulp if she didn't stop struggling. Needless to say, she had no intention of ceasing her struggles—my threats serving only to add fire to her senseless thrashing. Rather than ingloriously twisting her life out, I chose, instead, to toss her floundering body across the beach (first taking the precaution of disarming her) where she landed in a linen heap amongst a tangle of oozing, red seaweed.

No sooner had Frigga landed, than my mistress, with the speed of a mountain wind, was by her side offering to help her to her feet, there being no animosity on Julia's part. But her milk-like twin scuffled in the sand, then bounded up like an airy sprite in the moonlight with both hands extended and fingers carven into claws, pouncing at Julia's throat. This time, however, Julia was ready, instantly sidestepping so that her twin, of necessity, had to lunge futilely to the side while still in mid-air, a move which put her completely off balance and caused her to crumple headlong into a sand pile. But, in less time than it takes to think of it, she was up again, ripping off her clinging wet garments. In a second she stood naked and white, her feet braced in the sand, facing the equally naked, brazen Julia!

Imagine the sight. Two immeasurably perfect women—Aphrodites both—cast from identical molds standing but a few paces apart ready to pounce on one another, teeth and eyes flashing!

The white Julia's flesh was as smooth and hard as ivory; my mistress' like the finest bronze. They circled, the one snarling, the other watchful. They crouched . . . the globes of their breasts hanging in ideal symmetry, swaying, ripe, and wholesome, as their bodies stepped quickly and agilely over the rocky sand. For a moment, it seemed as though they were dancing, as their hands, legs, and arms moved, weighing the potential of each passing moment, searching for openings in one another's guard.

Before then, I had never seen a more gracefully composed idyll of flesh and limbs and gleaming, glaring eyes than those two women, replicas but for the baking of the sun and the tint of the hair, leaping at once into the air and intertwining their bodies in tight, if inimical, embrace before hitting solidly into the ground. It was uncanny—the pantherish molding of the one mirrored the other, even to the way their forms blended and folded so that their smooth, tight bellies and groins joined as one.

No sooner had Julia's shoulder dug into the sand than she twisted and was on top of her adversary all the while shouting between sobs and gasps that she intended her twin no harm, but she may as well have spit at the moon for all the good it did!

I had never seen a more gracefully composed idyll of flesh and limbs and gleaming, glaring eyes than those two women, replicas but for the baking of the sun and the tint of the hair.

Only now did old Moab arrive at the scene, tut-tutting, coughing and seeming out of sorts generally.

"My, my, Frigga is putting on quite a show today," he said as he moved wearily to my side.

"You mean this sort of thing is a frequent affair?" I asked. "Not 'frequent'," he answered. "'Common' would be better."

"What's the use of splitting hairs, Greek?" I snorted impatiently.

"From the looks of things, I'd say I'm not the one who's splitting hairs," Moab said. "Don't you think it would be wise to break up this . . . uh . . . altercation? Especially since it seems to be for no purpose, your mistress having effectively given Frigga her freedom—at least, that is my understanding. Further hostility seems rather pointless, actually."

"Once already I have tried to break up this game," I replied, alert to any change in the course of the fight, "but to no avail. Now I am content to let things take their course."

And then, Julia launched her knee up with catapulting force, hitting home in the middle of Frigga's quivering abdomen. Things happened quickly then. Frigga, who had been flying through the air at the time, diving for Julia's thighs, crumpled into a ball and crashed into the sand. But even as Frigga's knees touched the ground, Julia's calloused foot smashed into her hard, round jaw, throwing her whole body backwards and twisting. Surely, Frigga's knee would have come disjointed had her body not moved instinctively, flowing with the fall, even as she sprawled unconscious in the liquid sand.

For three breaths, Julia remained poised, muscles ready to attack, before she realized fully that her twin would be no more trouble. Then she, herself, fell headlong into the surf beside her quieted foe.

Instantly, I went to Julia, lifting her up in my arms, as two of the freedmen, responding to a signal from Moab, hauled up the other and carted her across the beach. Within a few minutes, we had both women clothed in dry linen and situated comfortably in the shelter of the cave. Julia had awakened, but lay quietly at my insistence. It was necessary, however, to take the precaution of tethering Frigga's wrists and ankles in case she was still in an ugly mood when she awoke and wanted to display more of her fighting skill.

[Summary: Over the course of the long night, Julia, Frigga, and Xulê learn to trust one another so that by morning they resolve to put themselves in Moab's care. Considering that the absence of Frigga in Julia's stead on the island will surely betray their flouting of the Emperor's will and condemn them, they are cavalier and anxious to quit heinous Pandateria forever.]

Part Three

The Thebes

Moab spoke, "Little more do I have to say except that as we are all exiled, under sentence of death by crucifixion should we return home, let us remain together and be friends. It is to our advantage, I think."

Frigga's hard, glaring eyes rolled up white as she threw back her head and laughed a full, deep, meaty laugh.

"Old beetle, do not fear my wrath, for if death should claim you by using my hand as its instrument, you would never know it. But, I do not foresee the necessity for that course of action, for there is value left yet in your withered old carcass, I suspect. Let us then respect one another—you for my splendor, and I for your genius and enchanting craftsmanship. We shall travel together in peace, my father."

"Fine," Moab said, a shining in his eyes. "Then let us prepare to leave—quickly—for the tide will soon be ebbing."

In less than an hour, Julia's belongings, which consisted of a few chests of clothing, body ornaments, perfumes and other accoutrements—most of which she had not bothered with at all in two years—also, along with all our weapons and what few items I possessed, were heaped in the bobbing long-boat, and we pushed off toward the unimaginable . . . ! Behind us, Pandateria lay heavy in the sea, its baked sands cooling in the late-afternoon sun, devoid finally of human life, far removed already from the human suffering it had harbored for so long. As we pulled away from the beach, neither Julia nor I looked back at any length, for we saw that the whale's monstrous great mouth was opening wide to receive us.

"Meet *Thebes*, King of Fish!" Moab crowed, extending an arm broadly toward the torch-lit maw which loomed strangely ahead of us.

Our boat glided over the submerged lower jaw into a cavern of hanging bristles and combs that from a distance passed for whale baleen but which I could see now was some kind of sturdy tree bark tinted white and pink. At the rear of this mighty orifice, 25 or 30 feet from the tip of the snout, where one would expect to see the cavernous gullet, were two wide, bolt-studded iron doors overlooking a narrow dock constructed of grates also of iron—iron being the principal constituent of the vessel. On the starboard and port sides of this dock were two small slips just wide enough to snugly accommodate our long-boat and another which in all respects was identical. The oarsmen guided our boat into the empty starboard slip, and, no sooner had this been accomplished, the great doors swung outwards and two men emerged, one tall as myself but pale and blond, the other stooped and brown with straight Ethiopian hair. Hurrying to our side, these two caught the line which Erasmus tossed out and pulled the boat firmly into its notch.

When this was accomplished, all the oarsmen jumped out of the boat and disappeared along with the two new fellows through the portal, leaving only Julia, Frigga, Moab and myself standing on the deck watching the red dying light sparkle on the open sea beyond the cavern-like mouth. Uncanny and eerily lovely was the entire scene—as nearly like the holy, many-hued Greenoxite Caves where Pepumsay-Lemox conversed with the gods, as anything I have seen before or since. So engrossed were we in absorbing the colors and the shimmering light in that extravagant environment that Julia and I, at least, failed to notice the fast growing darkness.

Then, however, I noticed that the ceiling, that is, the roof of the mouth, was dropping fast—that the whole mouth was growing smaller! Involuntarily, I jerked around searching for a means of escape. But Moab, seeing my distress, quickly put his hand on my forearm and said, "Xulê, fear not, for we are preparing to leave the bay, and *Thebes* must secure her snout for this to happen with expedience."

I was still wary nonetheless. Despite the wonder of it all, and the many reassurances, I did not like the idea of being shut up inside an iron fish. Yet, to please Julia, I made a pretense of relaxing my guard and watched the final shutting of the tremendous mouth philosophically.

"Follow me," Moab said, "and become better acquainted with *Thebes*. As its creator, I'm sure you will sympathize that I am justifiably proud of my rather elaborate creation. It is unfortunate that Caesar learned of its existence, thus impeding my unfettered dual studies of eclipses and marine habitats. But, perhaps it is better this way. If I had shown my invention to the world, or if knowledge of its existence had circulated during one of Rome's frequent naval campaigns, then I'm sure *Thebes* would have been conscripted for military service. Its usefulness as a tool for peaceful naturalistic research would have been finished in that event—my submersible would have become a war machine. As it is now, at least, *Thebes* can honestly be called an instrument of freedom, and the warring nations are mostly ignorant of its existence."

Julia snorted, "Ha! Thank the gods for small blessings!"

Moab ignored her, continuing reflectively, "Yet, still a creator enjoys some recognition for his craft . . . ." Then, with a grand sweep of his arm and a profuse bow, he ushered us through the great, bolt-studded doors.

The first thing that caught my notice was a refreshing draught of cool air rushing from somewhere within the bowels of the monster machine. Though curious, I mastered my desire to question the master of the boat right away, realizing even then at the beginning that one question would lead to another, which in turn would lead to interminable others as our tour progressed. In point of fact, I desired to be the least nuisance I could, especially as I was sure to learn all I wanted in good time.

Julia, however, suffered from no such inhibition.

"That cool flowing air feels grand. Where does it originate?" she inquired.

"At the moment, a hatch is open at the opposite end of the ship and all communicating compartments are open for ventilation. It is just an ordinary evening sea breeze."

The room in which we now found ourselves was small, no bigger than the docking facility outside to which it was adjacent, and studded, like the doors, with iron bolts in orderly vertical and horizontal rows, a common sight we would soon learn throughout the craft. The light in this room came from a series of tiny flame-jets that glowed dimly inside red glass globes. The effect was to fill the room with a rubyish gloom. No sooner had we entered, than

Erasmus, who was occupied with some strange, notched levers in one corner, ordered the doors sealed. Immediately, two husky fellows, the same two who had helped pull in the long-boat, and who were now busy at some task involving still more levers, moved quickly to obey the order, and the doors were secured with a thunderous clanging. Then, a solid iron beam nearly forty feet long and as thick as my fist and which was fixed to the bulkhead in a sort of hinge arrangement was dropped into place across the doors, holding them firmly in place.

"The seams in the doors are water-tight now," Moab explained. "We have not yet in our journeyings or explorations reached a depth at which the exterior water pressure would prove a formidable risk. Of course, these doors are afforded double protection due to the large space beyond, which forms the whale's mouth and the fact that the giant lips, when sealed, are also air and water tight.

"This compartment, by the way, serves not only as an antechamber but houses the mouth opening and closing controls as well. The mechanism itself, that is the machinery involved, is accessible through floor and ceiling hatches there"—he indicated the locations of the two hatches—"and there. If you are interested, you are welcome to study the controls at your leisure. Only be sure either Erasmus or Livinius or one of the other officers is close at hand, for the instruments are very delicate. You must remember, due to the strangeness of most everything you'll see, to please observe common sense safety precautions at all times. A good rule of thumb is if you don't know what it is, don't touch it. Are we perfectly clear on that point? Good. Then, I have much I want to show you . . . and you have much to see! Come along, come along."

We stepped into a corridor somberly lit with that same disagreeable ruby-red radiance. Frigga then announced, "I'll go to my quarters now, Master Moab. I am acquainted well enough already with your iron whale."

"Yes, yes, go ahead, my dear. Go freshen yourself and rest. We will see you at dinner, then."

But Frigga was already striding off ahead of us, disappearing around a bend in the corridor.

"Till then!" she called out.

Moab now pointed out that the corridor here branched off into six small metal rooms, three on either side, five of which were officers' quarters, and the last on the starboard side being the ventilation and blowhole control room. Glancing inside the latter, we were impressed by a most singular array of iron pipes and valves obscured by a hanging cloud of steam. The two burly, sweaty men who were at work inside turned at the scrape of the opening door, smiled cheerily and tossed up their arms in sloppy salutes, then returned immediately to their labors.

"Our principal motive power is no more complicated than ordinary steam," Moab explained. "Boiling water. But the excess heat, steam and smoke from the furnaces must be expelled. At intervals we allow it to escape through what in a real leviathan would be its blowhole, a trick which helps to maintain the illusion that *Thebes* is a living creature, though a bit of an anomaly, I would wager. . . . The ruse is extremely effective when we wish to avoid unwanted guests, and, I think, the disguise is rather aesthetically appropriate, don't you agree?"

Now we came to the elbow in an L-shaped bend in the passageway and turned right for a short way, then left, where we came to a set of closed double doors. Entering, we found ourselves standing in a dining hall, fitted with six large tables, each table having six chairs—room for thirty-six men at a meal. Each of the tables and chairs, I noticed, too, was securely bolted to the deck.

"Our dining room is equipped to handle half the crew at meal times—the other half maintaining their posts—and is large enough to accommodate the entire crew during briefings and special occasions," Moab explained.

"Wait!" I couldn't believe my ears. "You mean to tell me that your crew consists of over seventy men?"

"Seventy-five, to be precise."

Then we followed the old man into the after-starboard corner of the dining room where he showed us the tiny, but fully equipped galley. He introduced us to Jabez the cook, who we learned was an Egyptian, and who, also, was obviously quite fond of consuming his own plain but palatable preparations. We talked a little, learning that a fresh food storage compartment of considerable size opened off the galley, then we continued on our tour, exiting by the same doors through which we had entered, though we saw that we had the option of using another door should we have chosen.

Then, just as we stepped into the corridor again, there was a sudden sensation of forward movement as though the floor had moved ahead of my feet. Caught unawares, I had to grab at the door jamb to keep my balance. Julia faired better, I suppose since she is smaller than I.

Moab, however, appeared as though nothing at all had occurred, though he smiled at my small predicament. "Livinius," he explained, "is moving *Thebes* out to sea now. We will remain on the surface for a spell to allow the nighttime air to circulate through the vessel. Unfortunately, the one problem I haven't been able to solve as of yet is the build-up of poisonous air and heat while submerged. In fact, this limits our time under water to two hours—no more than four in the event of an emergency."

We followed the corridor directly into the port fin control room. This compartment was fitted with a series of mechanisms that controlled the angle of the one fin, thereby helping to steer and dive the ship. On the starboard side of the craft, we learned, there was an identical room to control the starboard fin, but with the cranks and gears reversed. Also, in each of the two rooms was a great set of spiraling stairs which ascended above the hull—or hide of the whale. Moab now motioned us upward, so Julia and I mounted the stairs, she first. "Jove preserve me! Moab, you have a tidy set-up here. From the beginning, I wondered how you saw to steer this thing. Now I know! You are a wizard!"

Now I, too, saw what Julia perceived. The stairs wound above the ceiling of the fin control room ending in a sort of platform wide enough for two people to stand. And at this point the metal hull of the upper part of the craft was broken by what at first I thought was a circular hole through which I saw the moon and a few bright stars. But on closer inspection, upon reaching Julia's side, I realized that it was no hole at all, but some sort of solid transparent covering in the form of a hemisphere or dome. It was there because I could feel it with my fingers and knock on it with my knuckles, yet I could indeed see the sky beyond.

"By Greenox the Merciful! What kind of witchcraft is this, Greek?"

"'Tis nothing but glass, but of exceedingly high quality, melted from the purest quartz sand, made to my specifications by the most skilled glass-makers in Alexandria."

Though I had no reason to doubt the man, the material I touched for the first time that day resembled not in the least the alabaster-like substance I had learned to call glass. In any case, the configuration of this strange window was such that, while standing on the platform, one's head protruded above the hull allowing perfect visibility in all directions but down. Looking forward, I *saw Thebes'* blue-black snout driving through the dark water, bits of foam glittering white in the frosty moonlight. Turning around, I looked down the length of the titanic beast-machine and saw that we were at a point less than a fifth of the way from the prow. Greenox, such size! Yet, of even greater interest, I was able to see in the distance the tremendous tail flukes of the machine rising above and slapping the surface of the sea with eruptive, powerful strokes—with a slow, regular rhythm—propelling *Thebes* towards uncharted worlds!

Julia coughed, and I realized that my bulk was blocking most of her view. I climbed down and faced Moab squarely.

"Master, how by all the gods do you move this enormous contrivance?"

But he only smiled and said, "You will understand when you see, my friend, in due course, for the propulsion room is the final compartment in the vessel. Patience, Xulê."

We left the port fin control room, following the corridor to the right. We stopped for a moment to inspect the crew's quarters which was a spacious area furnished with crude but adequate wooden bunks. I had seen many such bunks aboard the quadriremes and quinqueremes of the Roman Navy. The difference here being that these bunks had no chains or manacles attached.

Across the hall from the crew's quarters was a storeroom filled to the ceiling with an assortment of salted and dried meats, nuts, and fruits, and barrels of fresh water, which we learned was a by-product of the power generation. A little farther along, the passageway divided, one branch jogging off at right angles to the left. Moab explained that in that direction lay the starboard fin control room. Adjacent to this compartment, just at the point where the hall veered to the right again, was a door quite unlike the bolt-studded, iron-grey doors and hatches we had already grown accustomed to. This door was solid bronze, shining brightly even in the dim red light of the colored globes. Moab made no move to stop here, mentioning only, "This is the Master's Stateroom. You will find that I am frequently there." I thought that the second part of that remark was rather odd, its meaning, by rights, being self-evident. Yet, Moab, as I learned as the days progressed, had his own notions about his personal conduct. As we passed by the door, I noticed a small copper plate was attached a little below my eye level. Emblazoned on the plate was the single word: MOAB.

Next, our host pointed out the guest rooms, two on either side of the passage.

"These will be your rooms, my friends. I'm sure you will find them suitable at least, if not comfortable."

I opened the metal door of the room that he had designated as mine—Greenox preserve me! The place was hung to the hilt with combed lion skins and carpeted with antelope pelts of every brown imaginable. Above the bed, two bronze-headed spears crossed through the heavy, black mane of an especially large lion, while two razor-sharp and bone-handled axes crossed on an adjacent wall. And the bed! The bed was obviously soft! And covered with leopard furs!

By the goddess' fountaining . . . ! A tub! This was a room more properly assigned to a senator or visiting dignitary than to a weathered and much-scarred gladiator veteran like myself.

"Greenox's gushing . . . !" I exclaimed. "Old Greek, what am I to do in a room like this? I'm more used to wooden pallets and flat rocks."

"Xulê, a woman of your obvious worth and loyalty deserves far more than rock to sleep on. I ask you to try it . . . then, if after honestly trying to develop a taste for the simpler comforts of life, you still find the room unacceptable, then we'll make other arrangements."

"That sounds fair, old man. I agree to your terms. I'll try to grow accustomed to the plush comfort of it all. But, mistress, let's see your room. If mine is fit for a king, what must yours be like?"

Julia stepped over to the door of her room, which we learned was the room next to Frigga's, pulled the latch down and slowly pushed the door open . . . .   Gods! This was no room! This was a palace! Rubies and sapphires and a myriad other gems—and braided gold hung in clusters and ribbons from each of the four dark wood posts that supported the embroidered silken canopy. The bed itself was strewn with rich velvets and exquisitely colored fabrics from the four corners of the empire. The carpets were of brightly dyed wools—wine red, amber, cobalt blue, jade green, orchid violet, and more—and woven thick as hawsers. Silken draperies covered the walls, and yard-high mirrors of polished copper set in frames carved in the likenesses of a phoenix, a griffin, and a sphinx adorned the three walls opposite the door. A bureau and stool of solid cast silver sat nicely in one corner, and an ivory-inlayed acacia-wood tub filled another. Even the clothes hooks were of gold!

Quoth Julia, "Moab, my friend, you certainly know how to do right by a girl! You spoil me nearly as much as I was used to!"

To which Moab humbly replied, "The daughter of the Caesar deserves no less, my dear. Your personal belongings will be brought to you shortly. Then you may arrange things just as you like. But shall we continue? There is only a little more."

Our next stop was the library, which was comfortably arranged with hammocks and several stuffed settees. Cushions, too, and vividly hued pillows were cast about to the number of a dozen or more. Built against the walls were numerous scroll-racks and shelves heaped with ancient and modern writings—everything from the Sumerian epic Gilgamesh to Livy's latest works. Of course, the walls were hung with bright material of varied and expensive sorts, and the floor was of rich, dark rosewood. The finishing touch was several white marble busts—of Homer, Hippocrates, Philolaus, the Egyptian Amenhotep, Socrates, and others of the same sort—securely fastened to raven-black pillars at various strategic spots around the room. Altogether, it was certainly a formidable chamber, to be utilized by the best-honed of the world's great minds. I imagined, in fact, that I would pass many a pleasant hour there.

Once Moab was certain we were duly impressed, he led us through one of the library's two communicating doors—the other being to his own cabin—to the main control and navigation room, the nerve center of the entire ship. Here, there were seven or eight men busy at some of the most peculiar instruments I have ever seen: arrays of hanging balances, swinging hour glasses, delicate glass yellow-and-scarlet-liquid-filled tubes, and other paraphernalia which defy my powers of description, and which, to this day, even after living with them for as long as I have, I do not fully understand except to say that they dealt with matters such as the level of the ship, its depth, speed calculations, and increments of time. Some of the devices were even able to determine the position of *Thebes* at all times relative to the sun and stars. From this room the course of *Thebes* was directed. Orders were sent from here to the fin control rooms and to the aft propulsion room via flexible copper tubes which—wherever else they might lead or branch to—all began at the captain's station, a raised lectern which overlooked the entire room. Radiating in all directions, the tubes disappeared into the bulkheads where they led to every compartment and corridor, thereby giving Moab complete control over his vessel. He explained that all he needed to do to communicate with any other compartment was to talk into one or other of these hollow tubes and his orders were conveyed by echoes the length and breadth of the ship, either to individual compartments or to the entire ship, as he so pleased. Naturally, these tubes allowed communications in both directions.

And, of course, the control room was fitted with a spiral stair leading to a glass observation chamber above.

Then we came to the featureless catapult room, a bare, iron space in the center of which were two giant wooden catapults that, we learned, were constantly manned and ready for any emergency, especially wise given our soon-to-be renegade status. Nearby was a store of boulders and barrels of oil placed within easy reach of the artillerymen. This is where they also stored their other weapons—bows, arrows, swords, and suchlike.

"But, Moab," Julia queried, "how do you launch your missiles and flaming oil? The ceiling and hull seem completely solid."

Moab smiled and made a motion to the two freedmen who were standing at attention nearby, and they strode over to a length of rope which hung from a large pulley suspended near the ceiling and began to pull down in swift jerky movements. Then, with a great squeak and rumble, the ceiling moved back slowly and slid up onto the whale-ship's back, revealing the great starry expanse above.

Julia turned and gazed at the old master with an expression of reverence, a feeling I easily shared. Moab coughed, blushed, and hurried out of the catapult room, signaling to his men to return things as they were.

Finally, we came to the end of the passageway, stopping before a door which Moab explained led to the main propulsion room. He pushed the door open and let us through.

Instantly, we were enveloped in an oppressive heat and stench, and blinded by an intense flickering light. Yet, despite the discomfort, the area was filled with song . . . not the knell-like droning of galley slaves, but the lilting chanty of a happy, well-fed crew. Sitting on two benches were twenty men wrapped in towels and rolling dice, laughing and swearing loudly at one another. Another twenty sweating filthy fellows—the ones who were singing— were occupied pushing a massive horizontal wheel. This wheel was about 20-feet in diameter and designed like a chariot wheel with the exception that the twenty thick-beamed spokes protruded out past the rim, providing plenty of leverage for the laboring men.

As they heaved the wheel around, a series of gears, pulleys, and rods were activated that alternately stopped and unstopped two steam vents, which were the heart of the entire propulsion system. The power itself was created by, as Moab had said, nothing more complex than boiling water. In an uncanny way, Moab had devised a means of funneling steam from comparatively small boilers into narrower and narrower pipes and tubes, which steam then emerged at tremendous speed and pressure from the two vents in scalding streams aimed at a circular paddle device that spun and whistled first in one direction then the opposite direction as the two vents were alternately closed and opened. The whirling paddle-wheel, in conjunction with other gears and rods, then lifted the monstrous flaxen and bronze tail-flukes high and then lowered them an equal distance, thus propelling the wondrous craft through the seas. The speed of travel was determined by the speed with which the men turned the great horizontal wheel, thus increasing or decreasing the rate of flow from the vents.

All the excess steam and smoke from the boilers was continuously sucked out of the atmosphere with gigantic bellows and then piped to the front of the ship where the smoke was eliminated through the all-too-realistic blowhole and the steam was recycled into potable water. Then, just as soon as *Thebes* surfaced, other bellows forced in fresh air, replenishing the stagnant air. When the craft submerged, however, it was necessary to dampen the fires, slow the ship down to minimum speed, and send snorkel tubes to the surface whenever possible. The depth to which *Thebes* was able to submerge was limited only by the length of these tubes, though towards the end of our adventure, we were able to circumvent that limitation and descend to depths even unimaginable to venerable, old Moab. But more of that in its place.

This entire propulsion system proceeded smoothly when the vessel was in motion, but a major problem had to be dealt with at all times in order to maintain the safety and integrity of *Thebes*. The hazard was a mechanical one which resulted from the constant motion of the various moving parts—the gears, pulleys, and such. If not continuously lubricated, all these moving parts would quickly wear out. To combat this, four men were specially detailed with heavy brushes and thick grease to circulate among the moving parts, slapping them thick with the stuff. And since nearly all of these parts were suspended in the air between the bulkheads with beams, three of these men worked on catwalks and scaffolding installed over and around the thrusting beams, creaking hinges, and whirling wheels.

The noise level was far too intense to allow normal speaking, so after watching for a time the amazingly coordinated activity, we finally exited through a second door which opened opposite the captain's library. No sooner than the heavy iron door shut behind us, Julia put her arm around Moab's shoulders and exclaimed,

"Pluto's den, I have been there now, by the gods! Your men must be paid well to slave in there voluntarily, Greek."

"You are quite correct, my dear," Moab responded, "though 'slave' is hardly the right word. It has been long since any of these men were slaves or worked for a slave's pittance. In fact, it has not been many years since most of these men were marked for the games—some as gladiators, some as fodder to sate the bellies of starving beasts—but I was sufficiently well-to-do to purchase the most able men I could find, men who could help me build and guide the vessel of my dreams. And having bought them as slaves, I immediately gave them their freedom, offering them a good wage to remain and work with me.

"And such was their faith in me and the project that would culminate in *Thebes*, they stayed to a man. Furthermore, each and every one has pledged himself to our forthcoming adventure. And despite their affection for me, and their willingness to stay with me, I have promised them that should we find a new and hospitable land in which to settle they all have the right to chose to stay or leave as they desire."

"Master Moab," Julia piped, "right now, I want only to wash the sand and sun from my body . . . to lie in a soft bed . . . to swim in cool silk . . . and to decide which of your men I'll first bed down with. I must admit, you seem to have chosen a fine crew . . . a fine crew indeed! Whatever else our voyage might hold, it certainly promises not to be entirely boring . . . no . . . more than likely not boring at all!"

And with this last remark, she turned and strode spritely down the passage to her room, which she quickly entered, pulling the door shut after herself.

Beaming—that is to say, beaming as well as a face shriveled like a raisin can—Moab turned to me and said in a clear, quiet voice: "Julia, darling that she is, will claim a world someday, Xulê. But somehow I feel it will not be this one. One thing I can tell you is that more worlds abound than meet the eye." And with that enigmatic comment he excused himself and stepped into the library.

Left alone, I followed Julia's example and went to my own room, filled with thoughts of immersing myself in a tubful of scented water. But once inside, the sight of a platter of steaming roast lamb and a flagon of crimson plum wine shoved all thoughts of a bath from my mind. Lustily, I sat myself down on the bed and attacked the meal to good purpose. I ate as I had not eaten for two years! As you can well imagine, fish and clams and coarse brown bread are no fit diet for one such as I. Aren't I the most cunning and vicious and able fighter of all Nubia, Black Strobe, and Rome combined! No! Fish and bread and the occasional stringy sea-fowl were not my fare. Give me a shank of roasted meat and a villain to brain, and I'll be content!

Finishing this sumptuous feast, I finally bathed—an elegant experience which I could write about for many feet of papyrus, but will refrain from—and eventually lay my naked, sore body on the down mattress, drinking in its feathery caresses.

I was just drowsing off, thankful for our good fortune and blissfully considering sleeping the night away, when the ear-shattering toll of a gong resounded mercilessly through my skull, quite effectively voiding any such self-indulgent fancies. Then a full, rich resonant voice—not loud, but terribly earnest—filled my compartment:

"Submerge *Thebes!* Down! Submerge! Emergency!"

Hardly had I become aware of the urgent cry, having thrown on a garment, I found myself in the corridor beside Julia and Frigga. Inside of a breath, Frigga took the initiative.

"To the control room," she cried, and we raced down the corridor, men running before us and behind us as they hurried to their stations. My only thought as we ran was—How does one fight a decent fight when surrounded and protected by thick iron walls?

In a moment we burst into the control room. Moab and Livinius were there already, directing five men who were busy pulling controls and cranking wheels.

"More water!" Moab bellowed with a force I hadn't suspected he could muster. "More water! We must submerge faster! Now!"

Submerge? Only now did I realize that the whale-ship was off the level, slanting gradually downward. Great Greenox! We were under water and sinking deeper with each passing second! Of course, I understood intellectually that *Thebes* was designed for just this purpose, but to accept it emotionally was quite another matter. As I stood there in the control room beside the two women, not for one minute did I really believe that we were completely underwater.

"But how?" asked Julia, as soon as she too realized the full implications of Moab's order. "We never did learn . . . how do you control the vertical movement of *Thebes* in the water? What makes it sink, then rise to the surface again?"

She was not questioning anyone in particular, seeing that Moab and the control room crew were working frantically, but merely thinking out loud. Frigga, however, replied confidently, "You see, Julia, *Thebes* has not one hull, but two—a slightly smaller one inside a larger one. The space between the two hulls is completely empty when *Thebes* is on the surface, but when she must submerge, cranks are turned which open vents in the outer hull and water floods in with enormous force causing the craft to sink. The more water that fills the space between the hulls, the deeper and faster *Thebes* will sink. When it is time to come to the surface again, some of the steam from the boiler is diverted from the propulsion system into the space between the hulls and forces the water back out of the vents. When we have risen to an acceptable height the vents are closed and we're back at the surface."

"Ingenious, even if I do say so myself," we heard Moab say. "Thank you, Frigga. Your explanation was quite concise."

We turned, but Moab was already busy consulting one of his men, passing out instructions and inquiring into the moment-by-moment state of the ship.

Livinius, I saw, was engaged in supervising the four men who worked rapidly with the mechanisms set into the forward-starboard corner of the room. At one time, he happened to look my way, and the concerned expression on his face bent into a grim frown. Then he glanced at Julia, but his attention did not linger, turning quickly back to the problem at hand. I didn't need a tutor to know that I had an enemy in Livinius. But, by the looming sight of Greenox, what was life without enemies to slaughter or be slaughtered by?

Just then, a man we had not at first seen rushed down the stairs from the observation chamber above and busied himself with more instruments that I did not understand. Seeing that the transparent dome was not at that moment being used, I glanced at Moab, who looked my way only long enough to nod authorization. I clambered up the steps and saw, when I reached the top, that *Thebes* was indeed under water, that there was nothing but water over and around me, and that I could actually see fish being tossed about, illuminated dimly by the eerie, distorted moonlight that penetrated into the madly swirling sea. Yet, the surprise this vista inspired in me was as nothing compared to the jolt I would experience the next moment.

As I watched, thrilled by the insane beauty of it all, the wooden prow and keel of a 75-foot long galley cut the surface overhead, propelled by the stark rhythm of forty long-oars. Without doubt those on board her who saw *Thebes* slip right under her nose were startled by the momentary sight of such a great whale—but not for an instant could they have realized it wasn't a whale they suddenly saw in the darkness. Even now, the officers and men on deck were probably gawking in wonder at the last bits of white froth that had marked our presence a moment before.

The next instant, the man whose place I had taken in the glass dome returned, pushing himself past me, peering in all directions, then yelling down: "All clear! Ship clear off the port beam." Then, he was back down the stairs again, only to be replaced in a flash by Julia.

"O, Neptune!" she cried. "So it's true then! The sea is now my home . . . below as well as above!"

"Apparently," I responded, "that is indeed the case. If this machine truly works . . . and without killing us . . . it would seem that we, like the fish, will call the great seas our home."

"How I wish Quinctius Crispinus could share this with me," she went on, "or Cornelius Scipio. He too would have thrilled to this sight as too few men can. But, alas! They are dead or are somewhere in exile, aren't they, dear Xulê. And Appius Claudius

Pulcher and Sulla Validus and the rest. All they had offered me was their love, and they all died or were banished for it! Mars above!"

The next instant, there came an ear-splitting crash and the terrible rending of wood and iron being torn like parchment, and the whale-ship lurched wildly to starboard, throwing Julia clear to the deck below. Not having sea legs, I too was left hanging by my fingers to the handrail. Dropping to the deck, I pulled Julia to her feet, and together we lifted up Moab who lay stunned against a bulkhead. He shook his head, putting his hands to his temples, then remembering, he cried, "Full about! Overtake that galley! She's been broadsided! All hands to rescue stations!"

Suddenly, I felt the ship swing about. Once again, both Julia and I were caught off balance. Enviously I watched Frigga strutting around the control room, not seeming to notice the frequent sudden movements of the ship at all. And thankfully, she seemed totally unconcerned with Julia's and my unfortunate awkwardness, as she went around watching and, as I found out later, studying the activities of each of the men working the control mechanisms and aiding them as she was able.

When I regained my footing, I, with Julia right behind me, raced to get another view through the dome. Straight off the bow I could just make out not one, but two ships' hulls. As we moved closer, it became obvious that the two galleys were aligned perpendicularly to one another, and that one was stoved in.

Moab bawled out from below, evidently getting his information from the forward observation domes via the communication tubes, "It looks to be a Persian warship. Probably pirates. And the Imperial galley is sinking fast! Bring us alongside! Full speed!"

So absorbed was I in this drama that I didn't at first notice that we were surfacing. No sooner did I realize this, than the dome broke water and the sky was full of stars twisted by the seas running off the glass. Both vessels were aflame, and many men with sword, spear and crossbow were intertwined, jabbing and slashing. The Roman defenders fought bravely and fervently but their crumpled ship was sinking fast in a vortex of rising flame, and their screaming foes were a horde of demons reaping a plentiful harvest. Yet there would be little pillage, it was sure. There would be little enough time for the victors to regain their own ship and put out the fires before she, too, was lost. The Persians this time would have to content themselves with glory only, for the baubles they sought would soon be food for the fish.

Then, as I watched, *Thebes* came around and picked up speed, moving some distance out. Then she turned and sped back the way she had come, faster and faster, ramming speed surely being her goal. She crashed through the dividing seas on a perfect collision course broadside to the raider. Moab was going to ram the pirates! I couldn't believe this!

Why would he want to help Romans?

Julia gasped as the flaming, groaning vessels loomed ever closer; then, with a horrible shudder and a crack which made the original sound of the two galleys colliding seem like a whisper, *Thebes* smashed into the raider, the whale-ship's broad snout acting as a perfect battering ram!

Quickly, we submerged, only to surface right under the broken hulk of the offending vessel, which was lifted into the air and capsized back into the cadaver- and debris-ridden wash.

We dived once more, than came up again close to the Roman vessel which was all but gone. I could see several men and children clambering about the awkwardly sloping deck, trying to get into a small boat which was bobbing furiously in the water. Suddenly, the galley rolled over and slipped beneath the waves, carrying many flaying forms with it. Though the smaller boat was tossed around a great deal, it weathered this last great upheaval and remained afloat. Amidst the pools of flaming oil and debris, the eyes of all the occupants of the small boat follow their galley as it pursued its unexpectedly defeated enemy deep into Neptune's domain.

As *Thebes* came abreast of the overloaded little boat, Livinius pushed himself between Julia and me and peered out at the survivors of this catastrophe—what looked to be about two dozen souls, mostly children.

"Out of my way, cupids!" he said roughly as he shoved. I was minded to make some comment or other appropriate rejoinder but then thought better of it considering the circumstances and only smiled at him, my teeth gritting like two stones being rubbed together.

Then, as we passed them by quite closely, some of the children saw our faces peering out at them from the innards of the crazed whale and pointed at us with looks of paralyzing fear. Never have I ever seen such faces distorted and twisted so by such terrible apprehension. Even as we observed and began to recognize their intensely overwrought state, at least two children appeared to collapse.

Moab brought *Thebes* about one more time, circled the boat, then, again surprising me, headed far out to sea as though leaving the frightened children to their fate. Then, just as unexpectedly, *Thebes* came about and directed its snout directly at the small craft for all the world as though to ram it!

As we drew nearer, the looks on the children's faces—as on the older survivors—were no longer human but mirrored those most abysmal pits of Hades that even demons fear. Here, I glanced at Julia. Her entire frame had become a single knot of fury, every muscle taut, ready to leap down into the control room and somehow avert the impending disaster, to divert the steaming monster even if she had to kill to accomplish—*

---

* Editor's note: The *Twelve Scrolls of Xulê* end at this point. We may never know whether the Ethiopian scrolls recovered from Emperor Theodore's library and referenced by the secret laboratories in Sierra Leone and Ecuador were in fact facsimiles of the Twelve Scrolls. Furthermore, as I mentioned earlier, their being related as I have made them here is only the purest conjecture; nevertheless the points of similarity are strong, and I hold to my opinion, or theory, that they are one and the same. However, the Ethiopian scrolls may have been complete or at least more complete than the truncated narrative found in the proto-Mayan temple or dome deep in the Gulf of Mexico. We cannot know. But we can say with deep assurance that the fundamental power of the scrolls was in their power to inspire. The *Nova* and the *Stella* were proof of that! —T.K.M.

Important Addendum

It was while I was examining page proofs of this book that I made a critical decision, and Rosemill House Publishers have graciously allowed me to add these few words at this late stage. Not being satisfied with the abrupt ending of Xulê's story, I dedicated 18 months to examining an assortment of ancient texts housed at universities and museums on three continents. Slowly, with the aid of Mr. Gail Morgan Hickman, my agent and, by happy chance, philologist extraordinaire, I am now piecing together what I believe will be the continuation of Xulê's narrative. Since that task is in process and there is neither time nor space here to detail my findings, I offer to notify by e-mail in due course those readers who contact me about the availability of the conclusion of Xulê's story. See the e-mail addresses included in the "About Thomas Kent Miller" section at the end of this book.

Eighth Prologue Chapter

Synchronization and Calibration

Thus it stood, Luna, for several weeks, our being housed pleasantly enough in the laboratory—though effectively against our will—though I, for Maria's sake, chose not to make an issue of the matter. After all, it was not as though Hans and I needed to be anywhere in particular and it was not as though our hosts were belligerent or indisposed overly much to our presence once they got used to our loitering around. They, however, quite ably diverted any suggestion or effort of mine to quit the place. (Well, I say that, but, of course, they would have given much to be rid of us; they simply didn't seem to have much of a choice; they were damned if they did and damned it they didn't.) And truth be told, I found that my curiosity had been piqued after I learned that the hoped for culmination of all this enormous work was expected in an unspecified "short time."

In fact, as you can imagine, Luna, I was torn. On one hand I truly enjoyed spending time with Maria. Though our backgrounds couldn't have been more different, I found I enjoyed the honest and straightforward interest she showed in Hans and me. I'd spent some time with her the year before, as I've said, and she certainly showed her intellectual side then, especially when propounding about the stars and comets, and I was affected then, as I was again in this instance, by her down to earth and straightforward and reliable manner—unlike so many of your sex, who are experts in deceit and prevarication and falseness generally—and I think I can say with some certainty that her affection for me was also sincere.

But on the other hand, I had a fortune burning a hole in my pocket. That diamond was enormous and I have no doubt, looking back on it, that its value would have been far greater than the value of all the diamonds Sir Henry and John Good and I brought back from King Solomon's Mines, which have made us all wealthy, and my life so comfortable here in Britain in my new home, the Grange.

[Luna: Here I had to interject and ask what became of the diamond, as it was clear that the story he was telling occurred a dozen years or so before he in fact became wealthy.]

Ah, Luna, you are the one who asked to hear my story, and if I were to tell you that now, I would have no finish to my story. But since you insisted and I am now well along, I am having fun recalling it all, as I haven't had any need to reflect on these incidents and circumstances to any degree before now. Now, where was I?

As I was saying, beyond my affection for Maria, I'd become interested and now I wanted to see how it all played out in the end. What could all this effort and material and money be for? Can you imagine the fortune all this must have cost—tens of thousands of workers, two 200-mile-long aqueducts, vast dam complexes arresting the flows of mighty rivers high in the mountains, power plants, and not one but two inconceivably large laboratories on opposite sides of the earth, the submersible boats . . . ? Aside from the vague awareness that it all somehow had to do with learning something about the Star of Bethlehem, Hans and I knew nothing and we had no choice but to cool our heels.

The huge pits we had seen being dug on either side of the lab as we approached it had reached a sufficient degree of completion that the scaffolding had by now been dismantled and removed. The excavating equipment was removed, too, and it was then that I realized just exactly what the many plants with chimneys were producing—they were smelting silver, and the insides of the pits, or bowls, were being covered with silver leaf. Thousands of square yards of pure silver. So you see, while Hans and I loitered, we saw a vast fortune in silver coat those two fantastically huge bowls—and there were two others presumably just like them all the way over in Ecuador. The more I learned, the more preposterous it all became. A telescope indeed! I was not so stupid to be fooled so easily any further . . . or so I thought just then, dear Luna.

Eventually in the middle of the bowls grew arrangements of tubing and wires and scaffolding of a different sort and from which all manner of unfamiliar equipment was suspended, all shaped into a pattern I cannot begin to describe other than to say that it was complicated to the extreme.*

At any rate, it was now about eight weeks after we had arrived at the laboratory gates. Maria and Maxwell told me over breakfast that they were ready to calibrate the machine to, in effect, connect both laboratories and the vast machines that they had built—to create one inconceivable machine! I suspected that whatever happened next, it would not be dull.

Maxwell said, "We're going to begin adjusting our apparatus today. It may interest you, though I fear there will not be anything interesting to actually see. We will pull some levers and twist some knobs, and then the four units, two on either side of the world, will be connected for the first time via the submarine cable that the governments have only just finished laying on the floor of the Atlantic Ocean, and then we will have to calibrate for a few days."

So Maxwell and Maria led me back to the workshop. Typically, by the way, as it will be pertinent later on, by then Hans had got into the habit of removing himself each morning and I'd not see him again till the late afternoon. He didn't volunteer what he'd been up to, and if I asked, he declined to answer.

There was much more equipment in the room than the last time I'd been there. New shiny instruments had been neatly stacked on new racks that had been mounted onto the walls and new sturdy

---

* Editor's note: Quatermain's description of the mysterious bowls sounds similar to the Arecibo Observatory in Puerto Rico (as seen in the films *GoldenEye* and *Contact*) at least in terms of shape if not in composition. Thus one need imagine four such radio telescopes forming an immense astronomical interferometer array pointed toward the constellation Aquila, two on the west coast of Africa and two on the west coast of South America.—T.K.M.

islands and tables had appeared mounded with still more equipment. I was led to the back of the room and we entered a dark alcove I'd not noted before, which was the case, I realized, because it had been screened off. Here there were two tables that seemed to be covered with toy buildings. But when lanterns had been ignited, what I saw reminded me of the table with the movable puzzle pieces by which Maxwell had explained the positioning of the continents. These tables were on either side of the room. The one on the right side of the room, closest to me, held not toys, but a model. It was obviously a representation of the very laboratory where we'd been honored guests all those weeks. It was a tiny reproduction of the main points of the facility, or town—the temple, the buildings, the trains and tracks, the aqueduct and power stations, and the two huge bowls that we'd only just seen completed. After I had oriented myself to the model, Maxwell led me across the room to another table with a similar model.

"This is the laboratory in Ecuador. As you see, its general makeup is similar to ours. We simply call it 'over yonder' usually."

And it was so. A small town with its own array of tracks—with two perfectly equivalent bowls!

"Now step back, Quatermain, and view the set up from that raised platform."

I did so and took in the sight before me. It certainly was impressive. I knew that the space between them represented both the Atlantic ocean and the whole breadth of the South American continent.

I said, "And with this you will listen to the mind of God?"

And then I heard an unfamiliar voice. It said in English with an Italian accent, "Yes, that is our hope."

I looked down toward the voice that had surprised me, and there stood a Roman Catholic priest, which was obvious from his collar. I climbed down from the platform and greeted the man.

Barbicane, who happened to enter just then made the introductions. "Quatermain, this is His Eminence, Alberto Cardinal Cigliutti, Prefect of the Holy Office and Vatican Secretary of State. Under the circumstances, his boss, as you can imagine, has a vested interest in our little experiment, and he is here as an observer."

I shook the cardinal's hand and muttered something about an expensive toy, and he responded naturally enough, when I think back on it, "My dear Quatermain, I suppose you are speaking ironically or sarcastically. I can't tell which because my English is not up to such subtleties. Regardless, this attempt to glean something fundamental of the Almighty is one of the greatest works projects since the building of the Suez Canal, which pales by comparison. And it is infinitely more important, as the canal merely makes passage easier between west and east, whereas our goal is to receive the will of the creator of all the universe!"

I said something polite and turned to Barbicane and asked when the show would be on the road. What followed was exactly as Maxwell had predicted. Knobs were turned and levers pulled and orders recorded. To be polite, I hung around for a couple of hours and then retired to the hotel and took a nap.

Ninth Prologue Chapter

They Turn on the Machine

Thus it stood for a few days. Maria, Maxwell, Barbicane, and I would breakfast, then Maria and Maxwell would go straight to the workshop. Though Barbicane inevitably wound up there before long, he would always go elsewhere on inspection tours upon leaving the table.

Then one day I noticed that the hair all over my body had begun to tingle and stand up. Plus there was an unaccountable faint rushing sound in the air like running water that seemed to emanate from everywhere. It was both frightening and distinctly uncomfortable. Soon after I noticed this, I received a message that I was needed in the workshop. Hans, as usual, was nowhere to be found, and I went alone.

Maria met me at the door, clearly very excited. "Allan! All is ready! You're just in time. We need you now to please be a witness. Sh-h-h, James is going to speak." I saw that he and Barbicane and Cigliutti were standing at a chalk board at the front of the room.

"Everybody!" Maxwell called out. Here, Luna, I should say that the room had somehow managed to squeeze in perhaps one hundred scientists and technicians, most of whom were talking and comparing notes.

"Everybody!" They all finally quieted down and Maxwell continued, "The moment has arrived! We've all been working against the clock on an impossible deadline, and we have succeeded beyond our wildest dreams. On both sides of this planet earth we are pointing our telescope toward the constellation Aquila. The power that we harnessed is coursing through all the materials that surround us. Whatever happens next, we will be a better people for it!"

That was all. He stepped over to some equipment and turned a knob. Immediately, everyone in the room began their tasks, including Maria, who had a device over her ears and was listening intently, pad and pencil in hand. The next thing I knew, an array of tubes was flashing and sparks were flying everywhere. There were spinning wheels large and small. Switches were pulled and pushed, and meters and dials were moving like fury. The tingling and buzz that I'd been aware of all day intensified, frighteningly so.

Frankly, I felt more in the way than anything else, but Maria had told me that I was needed, so I remained.

Maxwell was on the raised platform. Cigliutti was next to him. Maxwell began screaming commands. It was controlled pandemonium for perhaps ten minutes.

And then it all stopped, and all was quiet.

Without being told, I knew that something had gone wrong. The room had grown hot and there was an air of disappointment. Maxwell didn't look happy. "All right gentlemen, we will recalibrate and try again in an hour!"

And what I have just described was repeated half a dozen times through the day and the disappointment turned to despondency. But they soldiered on and recalibrated again and again. In time, at nightfall, exhausted, Maxwell announced that they would stop and rest—rather than work—for 30 minutes before continuing.

It was towards the end of this respite that Hans finally appeared at my side. "Hans, where have you been. History is being made . . . I think."

"Well, Baas, if history has to do with spooks, then I have much to tell you. O, Baas! This day I've been haunted by more spooks than—"

But he was cut off, as Maxwell called out. Again, electricity flowed through the whole room, and sparks again flew and containers containing colored liquid began to gurgle and bubble furiously. Hans, despite his endless worldly posing, was clearly in awe of that show of exotic energy.

You could feel the tension increase, and this time the mood in the room swung over to joy.

Slowly, a peculiar steady hissing hum could be heard and soon overwhelmed all the mechanical sounds combined. It was a steady hiss that increased in volume. All the while Hans' eyes opened wider and wider (as mine must have also, truth to tell) and then, suddenly, I felt Hans' body jerk to attention. He seemed absolutely riveted. If it had been a momentary thing, I wouldn't have worried, as such shocks happen all the time—usually a tingling in the spine or a chill—but my concern increased as his eyes grew wider and as he stood thus longer and longer, and then his mouth began to open and close and his lips moved as though he was forming words, mainly without sound—but intermittently he vocalized some clicks that are part of his Hottentot language. I said something to him, but he was able to distinctly communicate "no," by words or change in posture I don't know, but I understood that I ought not interrupt.

Maxwell and the others were clearly riveted as well by the constant hiss that filled the room. I haven't mentioned it yet, but the room was filled with stenographers, listening to every word spoken by every soul in there and recording every one of those words— Hans and me, too, for all I knew. Indeed, there were machines with pens that recorded all the other sounds, and they were responding wildly to the hum or hiss or whatever it was.* I was worried about poor Hans, whose body had snapped to attention and stayed thus for nearly a half hour. But suddenly his body relaxed and folded, and he would have collapsed onto the floor if I hadn't caught him and quietly carried him out of the room.

---

* Editor's note: Though Maxwell and his colleagues could not have imagined its existence, there is little doubt that their magnificent observatory, or earth-spanning telescope, stumbled upon the key (without recognizing it, of course) that has since proven the existence of the Big Bang and the expansion of the universe. They had accidentally isolated the Cosmic Background Radiation (CBR), which formed mere millennia after the Big Bang and which had been extrapolated from Einstein's general theory of relativity and predicted by George Gamow, Ralph Alpher, and Robert Herman in the 1940s. However, the CBR was not officially "discovered," albeit again accidentally, until the 1960s, this time by Robert Wilson and Arno Penzias of Bell Labs in New Jersey, winning them the Nobel Prize in Physics.—T.K.M.

Note

As mentioned at the beginning, on page iii, the following section, titled "Hans' Story," is the heart of this book and everything leading up to this point I consider introduction or prologue. As such, all pages up to this point, as you have seen, have been numbered with lower case Roman numerals, which is the convention for numbering introductory material in most books. Hans' story will begin now with page 1.

HANS' STORY
CHAPTER ONE

Hans Steals the Diamond

Once we were outside and Hans was steady on his feet, I said, "What on earth happened to you in there? It looked like you were hit by lightening!" A simple enough observation and question, I suppose, and here is the gist of his response.

"Baas! Baas! You will not believe! I've seen and heard your Predikant father, and while I did in fact see him, the conversation was all on his side and thus I mainly heard him."

Now, Luna, Hans was always making the most ridiculous pronouncements, especially having to do with things he could know nothing about—statements rife with superstition.

"What is it, Hans? What do you mean? I'll admit that you seem more pale under that yellow skin of yours!"

"O, Baas, you don't know the half of it."

"What do you mean that you saw my father, the Predikant, and that he spoke to you?"

"Baas, I am easily bored by all the chatter that I don't understand and it hurts my head and that is why I always go off somewhere in the mornings. Well, Baas, as you know, they have here a sort of general store and the folk who tend the store are much like you, Baas, and are very neat and take the garbage out to bins during the day. Well, this morning I chanced to be in the area when I noticed that the door had not been fully closed the last time the garbage went out. Out of curiosity, I peered through the slight space between the door and its jamb, and lo! what do I see but a case full of square-face. Your Predikant father will scold me, I'm sure when I reach the Place of Fires, but I could not help myself nor could I control my hand as it squeezed between the door and its jamb of its own accord and grabbed two bottles. I told my hand and arm that they had sinned but that didn't stop them from uncorking the bottles."

"Hans, you silly fool, stop the speech. You are trying to tell me that you stole a couple of bottles of gin and got drunk."

"Yes, that is it exactly, Baas."

My thought was to shrug off this admission, as it was hardly the first time Hans had transgressed the rules of life as laid down by my father.

"Yes, Baas, but this time it was far more than that. First of all, as I was getting drunk, I felt very guilty—far more guilty than I have ever felt before while stealing square-face and getting drunk and sinning before the spirit of your Predikant father who I served so faithfully since you were a boy, Baas!

"One other thing, Baas, as I slept this morning, I dreamed of that pretty but evil diamond that I found in the temple pool. Do you remember that diamond, Baas? Do you remember who found that diamond and nearly drowned for the sake of that pretty stone? Thus, while you still slept, O, Macumazana!, I took the stone that you always keep wrapped with paper and string from your pocket where you always keep it so that it won't get lost, and I substituted an ordinary stone also in paper and string."

"O, no, Hans, don't tell me you lost it!"

"O, no, yourself, Baas. No, I didn't lose it. But, of course, my guilt was doubled now because I had two thefts on my conscience and was drunk besides and knew full well that your Predikant father was looking up at me from the Place of Fires and that he frowned very sadly as he did so. As all this is going through my mind, I wandered over to the temple because the falling water and rising spray and thunderous roar always seem to relax my mind, and because of my great guilt, I very much needed to calm my head down."

Now I knew precisely what Hans was saying because I have myself felt a special tranquility when I have been at the temple, and, as such, I was sometimes drawn to it myself unaccountably.

He continued: "As soon as I got there, Baas, everything changed. The sun that had been hot and bright went behind a cloud and all became dark and cold. I shivered and my knees felt weak and I sat down on the marble floor with my back to the well and pulled my knees up to my chest and huddled up to myself."

Luna, Hans then paused in his story and looked inquisitively up to the skies, probably toward the Heaven that my father taught him about, and also toward the ground, where many Africans—including Hans' Hottentot forebears, of course, believe their afterlife will be played out—in the "Place of Fires" . . . .   But, I'm sorry, Luna, you already know this. Also, I fear I'm repeating myself."

[Luna: That's quite all right, Allan. I wish I could forget most of what I had never asked to learn.]

As I was saying, Hans paused and then he said, "Now here it becomes confusing, Baas. I probably fell to sleep, but I cannot say for sure. Well I remember the sudden cold and my shivering, and I looked over toward the forest edge and I saw something sparkle. At first I thought it looked like a cloud of embers. Then I realized that it *was* a cloud of embers, and I thought I saw someone step out of the burning cloud. Then I was afraid because I realized that people don't step out of embers and then I knew that it was a spook. I was still cold and didn't want to see the spook, and so I closed my eyes. I think they were closed for a long time, but, of course, after a time I had to open them. I saw that the cloud of embers was still there and that the figure that had been emerging from it had not moved from where I first saw it, but now that I'd opened my eyes, it began to walk toward me, neither slow nor fast and I knew right away who it was, Baas. It was your Reverend Predikant father."

"You were drunk, Hans."

"Perhaps you are right, Baas. So in that case I saw your father while I was drunk. But he was a spook, I'm sure, just the same, Baas. Now, you know how much I hate spooks, even if they disguise themselves as your Predikant father. So I shut my eyes once more and covered my face with my hands, and put my head between my knees, and rolled over on my side and faced toward the well wall.

"Well," Hans continued, "eventually I opened my eyes and looked to see your father still walking toward me, but by then I'd learned that pretending it didn't exist did no good, so I decided to watch and wait. That it was your father, or perhaps a spook who did a good job of seeming to be your father, I had no doubt. In time, he stopped right in front of me and patiently waited for me to pay attention. Finally, I was able to say something."

"What did you say to him?"

"I said to your Predikant father, 'Whoa, Baas! Why are you here? What do you want of me?' And he said, 'Hans, my old friend, do not be scared. I need you to do one or two things for me.'

"'Ask me anything, O, father of Macumazana,' I said, "'and you know I will try,' and he said right back, 'The first thing I need you to do is *remember*. It is important to remember everything that you will see and hear and feel this day and convey it to my son.'"

"What did he mean, 'the first thing'?"

"I will get to that soon, Baas. There is much more to tell you."

"Hans, why on earth would my father choose to make himself manifest to an old drunken Hottentot like you, rather than to his own son, if anything you say is true?"

"I don't know Baas, except you know I loved him and he loved me and charged me to take care of you for as long as I lived, a charge I have happily and faithfully fulfilled to this day, and I hope many more, because I care for you as I cared for him, and as you care for me—though you would never say so to me—though mayhap some day when I am no longer here, you will tell anyone who will listen."

"Is there more, Hans?"

"Yes, Baas. Even as I looked, the embers washed over him and in a minute he was covered with them and, in another minute, both he and the embers began to fade, and then they were all gone, and it was as though none of it had ever happened, and I was left wondering if I had dreamed the whole thing . . . . Except that I was still cold and shivered, and I had not moved from my huddled position, and so I knew that it had happened, and right now I am this very moment doing just as your Predikant father required of me: I am remembering and telling you about all that happened at the temple well."

He was nearly panting due to the struggle of telling me all this. I asked, "And all the while, you were clutching the diamond?"

"O, yes, Baas. Never for a second did my fingers loosen from around that pretty stone."

"That pretty stone, as you call it, Hans, will make us both more wealthy than it is possible to imagine."

"Yes, Baas, of course it will. But you should know some other things." Here he gulped and looked all around as though startled. Recall that after Hans' legs had given out from under him, I had led him outside and behind the laboratory building.

"I closed my eyes again, Baas, for a long time, and then opened them half expecting your Predikant father to be standing there again, but, of course, he, or rather, his spook, was gone. Then there was silence for a time. It seemed a long time, and then another voice, a new voice laughed loudly, or rather, an old voice as we both know it well. It said, 'Hans, you yellow dog, attend me!' It said again, 'Hans, attend me!' And then I understood that this new voice was the Great One." That is to say, Luna, the wizard Zikali, also known as "the Opener of Roads."

"'What is it that you want, you old devil?' I cried, knowing perfectly well that he was even then squatting in his hut, as he hates to travel in the flesh because he finds it so much more convenient to let his spirit fly. The voice said, 'I am here with you, as real as if you were standing next to my hut.'

"'So what? You say this, but why should I believe you, as the Baas always tells me that you are nothing but an old cheat? I'm probably hearing things due to my having been thinking a lot about square-face and also drinking it.'

"'Stop yammering, little yellow man, and attend me!'

"This seemed a simple enough thing to do and the wisest course of action, so I did not argue. As you know, when dealing with the Great One, one's first response is to run the other direction because he is so ugly, also so powerful, also for fear he might 'sniff' you out."

"What do you fear being sniffed out about, Hans?"

"Baas, you know that I have my follies as does every man, though some men (and women too) have more follies and therefore are more fools than others and therefore may be prone to seizures of guilt, and I cannot deny that I have done many things in my dirty and slothful life that I'm not proud of. In any case, I determined to merely do as Zikali asked, or rather ordered!

"'Listen to me, you fool!' he droned on. 'When next you see Macumazana, be sure that you pay attention and listen to everything that you hear all around both of you. Listen to the very air itself! Listen and be surprised! Listen and become wise. Be most careful and listen with your ears and listen with you heart! And then when all is done, tell Macumazana all that you heard and all that you saw.' He seemed more than usually mean and angry, Baas."

"Then, Baas, it must have been that I sleepwalked. I soon realized that I was no longer at the temple anymore, but that I had somehow got into one of those long tunnels that connect the big bowls with the laboratory buildings. And then I heard the voice of your Predikant father again, Baas. I could not see him, but it was his voice all the same."

"What did my father say this time to you, Hans?"

"He said, 'Something more, Hans: Hide the stone! Now, Hans, hide the stone in the tunnel. It's important! Trust me, Hans!' Of course, I did not trust my senses, but no sooner than I heard him say this I heard someone enter the tunnel from the opposite end, and so I quickly found a box on the wall and shoved the diamond into it to hide."

"God in heaven! Do you mean our diamond is stashed in a box in plain sight of the technicians who fill that service corridor night and day and who are even now trying to repair the machine?"

"That's about the size of it!"

Luna, I was so angry at Hans I could have wrung his skinny neck right there. I wanted to go to the tunnel right then and there, but Hans took my arm and held me back.

"But wait, Baas, I, that is we, are not nearly done. There is more! So much more. And I have promised the spooks that I would tell you all!"

He stopped and seemed to gather his thoughts for a minute, and I waited.

"So then I escaped unseen," he continued, "and waited for the corridor to clear out so I could retrieve the stone, which I had hid

for no better reason than the command of a spook who sounded
like your Reverend Predikant father. I hid for a while but the tunnel
was always full of men, thus I came looking for you."

"And when you found me, you promptly passed out!"

"Not at first, Baas. Much happened before I became so weak
and would have hit the floor if you had not caught me. Remember,
Baas, that just as I walked into the room, all the Baases with the
beards and their servants and, too, the star lady of whom we are
both so fond, were growing happy even as I came in, or they seemed
relieved like a great boulder had flown right off their shoulders.
Remember that I had just joined you and that we were standing
there in that big room with the lightning that jumped off the walls
like fleas. And as we watched it all, there came a sound—a sort of
hissing sound from out of the lightning—that began quietly and soon
filled the room, and it seemed that it was this sound that made all
the Baases so happy. You saw! After standing shocked for a minute,
with their eyes bugging out, they all got busy again, even more so
than they usually are, and as they did things the sound changed,
quieter, then louder, then almost shrieking, then a whisper."

Luna, frankly I was amazed that Hans had noticed so much—far
more than I, who was mainly irritated by the whole proceedings.
Nevertheless, it was just as he described, now that he called it to my
attention.

"Yes, Hans, all those things happened. What is so important
that you must tell me now, even before we go fetch the diamond?"

"Baas, just this! As that hissing sound began I began to hear a
faint voice, a small voice, like a small cat caught behind a cupboard
door on the other side of the house. It seemed far distant and so
low, but it was accompanied by a quiet drawn-out drumming sound.
I could hear the voice, the drumming, and the hissing all at once."

"I tell you, you were drunk, Hans."

"No, or rather yes! But not like this have I ever been drunk,
Baas. The distant voice said, or rather whispered because it was so
low and almost drowned out by the other sounds, the most strange
thing. It said it was *the holy trumpet* announcing, heralding, *the
most divine voice yet to come* and I was drunk because it, *the
trumpet*, had made me get drunk, and that it wanted me to be
drunk, the better to hear with. And no sooner did I understand this,

than the voice just disappeared altogether like when you think you might be hearing something in the distance, but then the wind changes direction and it is gone and you are left not knowing if you heard anything at all."

"What did the voice you *might* have heard want you to hear, Hans?" I couldn't believe that I was asking such an inane question! But when no reply was forthcoming, I asked, "And everything you've said about this strange voice was something you *heard*— through your ears—and nothing that you *saw*?"

I don't know what made me ask a question with such a self-evident answer, but Hans responded, "Good question, Baas. I don't know. It almost felt as though I was hearing it through my *skin*. And then, as I said, it was gone."

"Where is all this leading, Hans?" I asked, my temper growing short.

"Only this, Baas! Ha! All those silly fools with all their machines and whale-boats and brains were trying to hear some sort of message from the Great Baas in the sky. They told us so! Well, they succeeded, *but they did not recognize it and will never do so!* Yet I, Hans, poor yellow dog drunken Hans, heard the Great Baas' voice and it spoke to him."

"What on earth are you talking about, Hans?"

"Only this, after the small voice that said I was *supposed* to be drunk came and went, I could hear the hissing more clearly, and I paid attention. At first it was low, but then it became louder and terrible like a room full of snakes, and then the hissing changed and became the flapping of giant wings—just like great wings—and then I thought I could hear words coming from somewhere, but I couldn't make out where they were coming from, but finally I understood that the voice was the hissing sound! I was amazed and at first forgot that I was supposed to remember everything that happened. You will not believe me, Baas, but I swear on your Reverend father's grave that it is true. The hissing sound that filled the room, mixed with popping and crackling sounds, was speaking to me in my own Hottentot click language! O, how I wished then that I could claim to be more drunk than I was. I became scared—very, very frightened, as scared as I have ever been—and then the fear died and I began to feel like I do sometimes when we have reached the top of a tall hill and there is a great green valley below us, or a raging ocean blown around by a storm. What I felt, Baas, was this: It was like a great claw was scraping and tearing at my soul, the very soul your Reverend Predikant father was always telling us about, but I was not so much afraid of it or even hurt by it as I was full of curiosity about what it was and I ached in other ways, not with pain and hurt as you would expect great talons to do, but I ached with yearning to know more. But of course it wasn't really a claw, I just said it felt like one."

"Hans, this story is indeed much different from your normal run of excuses for getting drunk, but I am losing interest. If you have a reason for this story, you had better tell me now."

"Just this, Baas. As I said, the hissing spoke to me in my own click language. The voice came through clearly and spoke at length and gave me a message, and it repeated the message several times so I would remember it forever, and once I had memorized it, the language of my fathers faded and changed and again became mere scratching and gibberish."

"Well, Hans, are you going to take all day? Give me the message if you really have a message to give me."

SS—
After I met Hans 30 years ago, I was fascinated by his clicking language and did a monograph on it—never printed of course and I lost track of it years ago. It was a paper much like the one I always planned to write about the Chaldean roots of the Cornish language. In any case, my conclusion was that Khoi (the name of Hans' language) was a strong candidate for the first human language! *Imagine that!* [Editor's note: M's notion is borne out by several linguists and anthropologists, including John Reader: "[I]t is generally agreed that the roots of the mother tongue [first heard on the savanna 100,000 years ago], must have been set in Africa perhaps among the ancestors of the Khoisan" (in *Africa: A Biography of the Continent*, p. 110. New York, Alfred A. Knopf 1998).]—*M*

HANS' STORY
CHAPTER TWO

The Message Vouchsafed to Hans

And this is what Hans told me those many years ago:

"'O, Hans the good!'

"Yes, Baas, that is what the voice said to this old yellow monkey, as the Great One usually enjoys calling me.

"'Hans the mischievous. Hans the child. Hans the wise. I wish you to be the vessel of my message to all the people.'

"Here, Baas, despite being haunted by spooks for half the day, I was more surprised to be spoken to by the lightning, or rather by the clicks buried in the lightning, and I responded, 'Great Baas, as you must be or you wouldn't be speaking to me thus. Why are you playing with my head? Leave me alone.'"

"Hans," I said, "I was watching you and I did see your lips move, but it was some time later that you spoke out loud."

"I don't know what to tell you, Baas. I'm only saying what I know, and what I was told I was supposed to repeat back to you."

Chastened, I said, "What else did this voice say to you?"

"Only this, Baas: 'Hans, your fathers and their fathers and their fathers, and also all the mothers, all the way back to the dawn of time, have watched the stars and the sun and the moon move across the sky. Also, your people and all peoples have noted that sometimes the moon will precisely cover the sun, and the light and warmth will vanish! Can anything be more frightening? I ask.

"'Listen, Hans the faithful! Perhaps fear of hunger or of cold or of enemies or of pain or of death can be as frightening. But these are all things that are part of life and are expected, thus assumed, and though they may be feared, they are not strange. For does not every man [i.e., person] fully expect his lot to be touched by these fearsome things at some point during his journey?

"'However, the greatest joy in a [person's] life, indeed, in a whole people's life, is warmth and light from the sun. Thus the fear that comes from the sun vanishing and the world growing dark is the most fearsome thing of all for there is no way of knowing when such a terrible thing will happen. It is not like the sun setting and rising.

"'Or at least this was so up until the various peoples discovered by their industry *my secret pattern*. Man [i.e., humans or humankind] has become fully [human] because he sought to know when in the future the circle of the moon would cover the circle of the sun and plunge the earth into darkness. Behold! In time, each people built tools and discovered the pattern in the randomness. They learned when the fearsome thing would occur, and they became less afraid. They found the secret that I had buried deep within the complexities *I'd created just to goad [humans] to seek it.*

"'I tell you that [humankind's] seeking to predict when the moon will cover the sun is what has made [humans human]. *This is the key that honed problem solving far beyond that needed for mere survival. From this has sprung all that makes [humans human].*

"'Thus peoples built grand temples and pyramids and statues and standing stones to observe the sun and moon and sky, and, sometimes, they enslaved whole peoples to build their observatories. Hans, this took many thousands of years, during which time people have done much for both good and ill. *But remember that it all began due to fear of losing the sun during the day—a fear I instilled by making certain that the moon exactly covers the sun. I created a problem that [humankind] needed to solve and thereby progress!*

"'Surely nowadays many people have studied that age-old problem and have for centuries grown to understand thoroughly the remote—I say again—*remote* probability of any such equality in size of the sun and moon, so small a probability that the fact of this equivalence is on the surface preposterous. Yet, too often people just shrug and call it coincidence. *Too few reach the next logical conclusion. If such a thing is preposterous, and yet exists nonetheless as a fact of life, what could it mean? Perhaps it means that someone wished it all to happen in just that manner. But who could wish up suns and moons and propel [human] advancement?*

"'Who indeed? [Humans] now have clear reason to *know* me. I am right there in the maths and calculations that they treasure so much, but they can also be stubborn, can take things terribly for granted and rationalize. Still, Hans, people will someday understand that *something is happening, has always been happening, that defies reason . . . yet has a cause and that cause is me—for I am that I am!*

"'But first there must come a drawn-out time when the blind will lead and these words I am saying will verily be *the light in the darkness.* Old Hans, share my words. Remember all that I've said and share it with your Baas, Allan, O Hans the child, Hans the wise!

"'For you are my messenger.'" *

SS—

Did you notice that it's Christmas? Happy Christmas! In any case, having just read the interesting new paper by a certain A. Einstein and now Quatermain's memoir with Hans' mentioning eclipses brings to mind certain matters that had once piqued my interest concurrent with my interest in the Cornish and Chaldean languages, both preoccupations of which came to a head during the excursion W and I took onto the Cornish moors, but ultimately came to naught as the distractions at that time were piling one onto another. The region where we were staying was one of those Celtic lands that are dotted

---

* Editor's note: While some readers might take exception to the idea that a message in the Khoi embryonic language could be embedded 13.7 billion years ago in the Cosmic Background Radiation with the intention of it being heard by one small Hottentot who just happened to be in the right place at the right time, be advised that, while definitely awesome, this scenario is not unique. Futurist and science-fiction writer *(and creator of the geosynchronous communications satellite that is at the heart of current world culture)* Arthur C. Clarke died on March 19, 2008. Virtually at the same time Clarke died, there appeared in Earth's skies for 30 seconds the light from an exploding stellar source labeled GRB 080319B that just happened to be the most powerful blast ever observed in the universe and which exploded 7.5 billion years ago (3 billion years *before* earth formed). This seeming coincidence becomes something quite different when you factor in Clarke's 1954 award-winning short story "The Star," the main plot point of which was that the light from a distant supernova (that vaporized an entire noble civilization) traveled 3,000 years and finally reached earth just in time to shine brightly over Bethlehem.—T.K.M.

with stone monuments and rings that had in centuries or millennia past sprung up all over that charming land. I was then just beginning to see a glimmer of purpose in the erections that dealt with eclipses, a purpose that stimulated me to venture down avenues of which I'd heretofore paid little attention. In connection with the longitude and latitude of these constructions, I couldn't help but notice that on or near December 21 and June 21 certain of the stones lined up in thought-provoking ways. This led me later to peruse all manner of almanacs and volumes in the British Library, and certain facts took shape that directly pertained to the stones. For one thing, eclipses of the sun occur roughly every 18 months in some part of our world. Naturally these experiences affect humans of all walks of life, often by exciting some of the more primitive emotions such as fear and awe. This reaction is partly a consequence of a remarkable coincidence. The diameter of the moon happens to be 1/400 of the diameter of the sun. But the moon's proximity to the earth is 1/400 of the earth's distance to the sun. The result of this, during a solar eclipse, is that the disc of the moon perfectly covers the disc of the sun—causing any number of atmospheric effects: strange glowings in the resultant darkness, cold, wind, and so on. What must stone-age man have thought of this extraordinary intrusion? Furthermore, I concluded then (an opinion that hasn't changed) that Stonehenge and its brethren were built and conceived as instruments with the primary purpose of predicting the occurrence of eclipses. The builders of these ancient observatories most certainly made all their calculations under the assumption that both the sun and moon revolved around the earth as even I would have assumed had not W set me straight on the matter! This is only a natural conclusion because, for all major purposes, the sun and moon do appear to behave in just that fashion. Now it happens that one of those obvious facts of life that most people entirely take for granted, never thinking of, is the equivalent sizes of the sun and moon! Nevertheless, this illusion of apparent equivalence of size owes nothing to physical or universal laws; there is no simple *definable, materialistic explanation for the relative placements of the sun and moon—no discernable cause. It is merely a coincidence!* Yet, it is just this coincidence that causes such an awesome fearsome eerie spectacle that stone-age man was inspired to engineer and build their vast calculators. Considering the incalculable import that the equivalent solar-lunar magnitudes have had on our Western culture and civilization, it would be ludicrous to deny that this exceptional coincidence has meaning! One need only to look at the ratio of measurements to become aware of the remarkable relationship that, presumably blind chance has provided:*

$$\frac{\text{Sun's Diameter}}{\text{Sun's Distance From Earth}} \qquad \frac{\text{Moon's Diameter}}{\text{Moon's Distance From Earth}}$$

$$\frac{865,400 \text{ Miles}}{92,956,500 \text{ Miles}} \qquad \frac{2,160 \text{ Miles}}{239,000 \text{ Miles}}$$

$$.0090 \qquad\qquad\qquad .0090$$

In other words, a pretty damn peculiar one to one ratio! Hans' mysterious voice seemed to know what it was talking about? I wonder!

—M

---

* Epigraphic Reprise: "[T]here is in life an element of elfin coincidence which people reckoning on the prosaic may perpetually miss."
—G.K. Chesterton

Note on the Back Matter

So far as I know, there is not a page numbering convention to distinguish back matter from the principal part of the book or from the front matter. That is a limitation of book design, as I believe the following chapters need to be considered separately from the preceding material. Thus, I really have no choice but to create my own back-matter numbering system, which will comprise capital Roman numerals.

First Afterword Chapter

Wrapping Up

While at the time, Luna, I honestly feared for Hans, years later when I happened to think upon the odd words of his soliloquy, a memory came with a shock, an electric shock, an eerie shock that shook me to my soul—because just such an eclipse as Hans described in principle saved me and Sir Henry and John Good from serious trouble during our adventure to King Solomon's Mines. We had got in trouble with the Kukuanas in that region and would have certainly been slaughtered had not Good remembered a notation he'd glimpsed in the almanac that he always carried with him. That almanac identified that the following day at one o'clock there would commence a total eclipse of the sun. Well, we there and then claimed to be great wizards with mighty powers and declared that we would extinguish the sun to prove it. We succeeded in creating doubt, sufficient to postpone our executions, and sure enough, the solar eclipse happened right on schedule, with all the resultant reactions in the native mind that Hans had listed out. *[Editor's note: At the "37ᵗʰ thousand printing" of* King Solomon's Mines, *someone—an editor? a publisher?—changed all references and descriptions in the book of this solar eclipse to that of a lunar eclipse! To what avail is anyone's guess.]* But I won't go into any further detail now as that adventure was the first that I wrote up—even before I retired to come here—and my agent thinks it will likely be publishable before long. Thus, Luna, you may soon be able to read all about that adventure in all its boring detail.

Well, getting back to what I was saying, no sooner had Hans divested himself of all this nonsense, than he scampered off as he was wont to do. Naturally, I hurried to the service corridor he spoke of and loitered for ages waiting for the place to clear out so I could fetch the diamond that Hans said my father had told him to hide there. I could just see into the tunnel from where I stood and I spotted the box mounted on the wall perhaps 50 feet from the entrance. Before long, the corridor didn't clear out so much as there was a chance moment when perhaps a dozen stressed, sweating,

coughing individuals had gone their separate ways, and for a brief
time the spot I needed was accessible! I ran in and made a beeline
to the box, opened it, and, to my delight, found the paper-wrapped
stone, pulled it out and thrust it into my pocket, and only then did I
feel in a position to breath again, ever since Hans began to tell me
his ghost story, as I suppose you would call it.*

Well, there you are, Luna. There isn't much more to tell. Hans
and I had stumbled onto a most strange enterprise, become
reacquainted with an old friend, had been detained against our wills,
spent time with some notable scientists and engineers, and observed
with our own eyes the expenditure of uncounted millions to build
enormous pieces of equipment the like of which I can never
adequately describe let alone understand in terms of purpose.

All I can say for sure is that Hans believed to the day that he
died that he had touched something divine, or rather that something
had touched him, and he felt satisfied that he had conveyed to me

---

* Editor's note: Here Quatermain makes an aside that is intrusive to
his story, but is interesting nonetheless, so I'm culling it out and here
making it a footnote: "Speaking of ghost stories, Luna, now that I've
settled into the Grange and I'm noticing the so-called civilized genteel
society around me, I find that the ghost story is all the rage. All the
popular magazines make a point of publishing ghost stories, especially
in their Christmas numbers. I'm saying this because I simply cannot
get over the huge gap that exists between your average Londoner and
my African acquaintances for whom ghosts, spirits, witches and
witchcraft are assumed to exist and taken for granted. Here, ghosts are
treated abstractly (spiritualist societies excepted, of course), but
virtually my whole life has been lived amongst peoples whose daily
existence revolves around the supernatural. For them, the spirit world
is utterly real and alive and is as much a part of their lives as servants
and hansom cabs in Piccadilly are for us. Thus you see that the point
of a ghost story would be completely lost on most of my African
friends and acquaintances! But, of course, you know this already!"—
T.K.M.

that which he had been ordered to memorize and convey back to me, but what of it? What would I do with such irredeemable nonsense? Except forget it—as I have in fact done until now, and in fact, it makes my heart sore to remember Hans at such a low ebb. It was likely some sort of trick perpetrated by Zikali just to prove a point—of what I can't imagine—though in later days, he denied any direct involvement. Of course, he knew all about everything that Hans claimed to have experienced, as he is prone to do with anything that is remotely mysterious. Thus I sit before you today wondering what Hans' experiences or hallucinations all meant, if anything?

I'm close to the end. Poor Maxwell and Barbicane and Cardinal Cigliutti tried over and again to receive some sort of signal from the star in the constellation Aquila, and never heard or measured anything of consequence more than that continuous hiss that I've described. Hans and I remained there for a week further to keep Maria company, but in the end, it was clear that their expensive toy was a failure and that nothing could come of fine-tuning their instruments any further. Heartbroken that all their immense effort, manpower, and expense to hear some whisper from God about the divinity of His son was for naught, they rallied and began to make plans to destroy it all.

Barbicane suggested to me that Hans and I should leave quickly and be well on our way at the end of 24 hours because they had no choice but to erase the laboratory from existence. He did not elaborate, but I could tell he was deadly serious. One wonders what the fate of it all would have been if the experiment had been a success. Certainly I'll never know.

I sought out Maria, and we said farewell, which was of course sad, but I was glad to be on my way finally, and she was clearly happy to be returning to her former life as a professor of astronomy in America. She told me that she and Maxwell and the rest would be boarding a British naval vessel and be leaving before dawn. She told me that they were left with immense amounts of data of an unknown sort, and that she would remain in touch with Maxwell, and perhaps they would be able to extract something of scientific value from the whole experience.

Second Afterword Chapter

Allan Throws the Diamond Away

The next morning, from the top of the same hill from which we first saw the town, as we thought of it then, but which we came to know as an unprecedentedly prodigious laboratory, we spied a ghost town. In the distance out over the ocean was a great naval ship in full sail and moving rapidly toward the horizon.

Then in an instant, the whole facility exploded. With heaven knows how much dynamite—I suppose it must have been dynamite, which was new and controversial then—they destroyed everything they had labored so hard to build. Even the temple that had captured our hearts from the start vanished, as well the incredible aqueduct that fed into it, and presumably all the dams and reservoirs, too, high up in the mountains. It all jumped into the air in fire and smoke that rose it seemed without let-up. Hans and I watched for a time, having very mixed emotions. When the smoke cleared, we saw that some structures had escaped the brunt of the blast, and we could still make out clearly the two bowls on either side of the make-shift town. Of course, I suppose all that silver leaf with which they had covered the bowls must have been stripped away and carted off. In the years since then I've heard rumors of huge pits and ruined buildings being swallowed by the jungle in that region, thus I conclude they never did finish the clean-up and erasure of their occupation. With regard to the two submersible boats, of which Hans and I saw only one, the *Nova*, we never set eyes on it again, and I simply have no idea what became of them. I would think that they'd be too valuable to scuttle outright, but, as I said, I just don't know. Likewise, I never learned or heard anything more about an equivalent base of operations in Ecuador, not that I was ever in a position to banter with those who would know about anything of the sort in South America!

As we turned to leave and descend the hill, Hans said, "Baas, somewhere in this very strange tale there must be a lesson similar to the sort of thing that your Predikant father used to drum into the heads of all the poor workers and students, of which sometimes I was counted."

"If so, Hans, I'm at a loss to see it. The whole affair seems to have been a detour with little enough value."

"Well, then, if you, Baas, the wise Macumazana, can find no meaning in any of this, then I say curse it all!"

And thereupon, he vented his anger and frustration by cursing just about everything.

"Curse this hill and that great fish. Curse the natives that told you of the white witch doctors. Curse the white witch doctors and all their machines. Curse the temple and the river that ran to it and the mountains from which it was born and curse the rain that fell on the mountains and made the river. Curse that hen's egg of a stone that the river brought down for me to find. Curse me for finding it. Curse its pretty shininess that tempted me so. Curse Zikali for knowing full well what would befall us as he always knows such things. And curse you, Baas, for getting us into this mess to begin with."

By now Hans was breathless and his eyes were red and bulging and I decided it was time for me to step in and calm my servant down. But he wasn't quite done, after all.

"And curse the noise from the sky in which I heard voices, and curse the voices, and curse me for hearing the voices!"

Then our life regained some of its normalcy. I decided that I had seen more of west Africa than I cared to and decided not to go back north to catch a ship back to Durban. We hired some porters, reequipped ourselves with oxen and wagons and trekked southeast to see what trading situations I could set up and also to hire myself out as the hunter that was my chief occupation then.

Some months later, Hans and I found ourselves on the outskirts of Zululand, and over a fire we chatted about the sundry challenges we had overcome that day because, as you know Luna, any day in the rough country of Africa is tantamount to a test of endurance. While we sat thus, in time I became absorbed by the flickering wood fire and simply stared into it, when Hans voiced the very subject that was really on my mind.

"How will you spend the money you will fetch from the great stone that I found, Baas?"

Well, I began by mentioning a certain mansion that had come onto the market in Pretoria after its then owner—an officer in the Army had perished in battle—I know not how. Having no wife or other heirs to speak of, his executors had put the property up for sale a year before, and so far as I knew there had been no takers, as apparently the asking price was exorbitant by any standards. So I fantasized in my response to Hans that I intended to march into the responsible agent's office and state that I wished to purchase the house at its current price, and oh, by the way, here is cash on the barrelhead, and a gratuity besides!

"And then, you Hans," I said, "can be head servant and the whole world will be at our beck and call!"

Of course, Hans saw through my weakness and my dreams of avarice.

"Baas, forgive me if your humble servant disagrees with you, but I don't understand why you are happy by such a future. I think you are better off giving the pretty stone back to the earth gods, for they will doubtlessly be very unhappy when they discover that their plaything is missing, and they will track us down and cause us much grief. May your Predikant father forgive me for speaking of such forbidden gods, but still I think we will not hear the end of their anger and our lives will be less than worthless in time—even in the big house that you dream of! Friends you never knew you had will hound you. Offspring that I never knew I had will likewise cause me no end of trouble. And what is the use of being head servant when all the servants will be forever plotting against me and sneaking their filthy hands into my pockets, as you, too, will find out—but the hands you will fight off will be the bigger hands of bigger men, even men with six and eight hands, like insects, and moving so fast that you will never know that they emptied your pockets until it is too late—and then we will regret that we ever carried that cursed stone away from the place where we found it!"

Hans was clearly in one of his lecturing moods, which he slipped into whenever he thought he was wiser than either my father or me, so I just let him have his tirade, after which I figured I would give him a drop of gin or not depending on my mood. I forget what I did then.

A few days later we were crossing the Mambuzo River. The sun was straight overhead. I remember that it was a crisp beautiful day and that I didn't mind one bit that I was soaked up to my chest due to the necessity of crossing the river. And, then, on impulse, I reached into my jacket pocket where I had kept the diamond all along and pulled it out. I unwrapped the soaked paper that was covering it and discreetly held it up to the sun and squinted as the sun's rays penetrated its magical substance. But I knew then that the sun's rays were harsh and were never intended for men to stare into for long. Then I clenched the diamond in the fist of my hand, swung my arm around a few times to limber up and hurled the stone into the deepest part of the river as far from me as I could.

Hans, who notices everything, looked at me with eyes as big as saucepans and his jaw dropped.

"Baas . . . Baas . . . ."

"Quiet fool," I countered, "can't you see that I decided that your wisdom won the day."*

Picture this, Luna. We were both standing in the middle of the river. The water was up to his chin, as he was so much shorter than me (imagine me talking of comparative heights!). Behind us were

---

* Editor's note: Again, from the sketchy details that Quatermain provides Luna, I suspect that he had had in his possession the Jonker Diamond that would be found *again* 60 years later in the Elandsfontein region of South Africa, near the area where he threw away the stone into the river. If so, then Hans' predictions about the destiny of the finder of the stone held true, because Johannes Jacobus Jonker, the 62-year-old who found the diamond on his claim, did not enjoy his wealth and soon lost it.—T.K.M.

two wagons and on the shore in front of us, our other two wagons had already been secured. A dozen porters were all around us, half drowned as we all were, but they were ignorant of the little drama that was being played out between Hans and myself.

"But, Baas, you threw away your big house and the servants that I would boss around!"

"Yes, I did, Hans." I glared at him and we thenceforth did not talk about it again. And, Luna, until tonight I have never spoken a word of this whole matter, and that is pretty much the end of the story."

[Luna: Allan, what a remarkable tale. I don't know what to think! The vastness of the project! The cavalier manner in which it was destroyed. My mind cannot contain it all; not to mention the cavalier way you tossed away your diamond—your Star of Wonder!]

And don't suppose, Luna, that my mind has ever been able to grasp any part of it either, despite Hans and I being in the middle of it all. Still, here I sit a wealthy man as the result of finding untold riches in diamonds. It seems I was fated to experience all these trappings . . . and much of the downside, as well, just as poor dear old Hans predicted, for good or ill I don't know yet!

[Luna: Here I reminded Allan that ironically the very reason we were sitting in my room at that moment was because of the necessity of my getting away from those dreadful, grasping Atterby-Smith cousins of Lord Ragnall (exactly as Hans described!) who are plotting and scheming downstairs even as I write, and who truly believe they and not his wife ought to have inherited his wealth! Yet, this journal must end somewhere, so here are the last words I will record from this evening.]

Luna, I sorely miss Hans! O, dear, I hope, as I so often pray mantra-like to myself, I hope I do find the light of his love burning like a beacon in the darkness as he promised I should do, and that it may guide and warm my shivering new-born soul before I dare the adventure of the Infinite. O, Luna, I've been so lost without him!

Epilogue

Since this narrative says virtually nothing about the "over yonder" facility other than it was along the coast of Ecuador, I spent four months combing newspaper archives on both sides of the Atlantic. I believe I was successful in that I found the following 1915 item, which speaks volumes without my having to say another word!

In the Footsteps of Alexander Von Humboldt
Continuing Coverage of the Third Challenger
Expedition to South America

TITANIC METEORITE CRATERS SPOTTED

Challenger Says "They're Recent"

By E.D. Malone
Special to the
London Daily Gazette

ECUADOR, October 24 —— This morning as we ventured north along the west coast of South America, the dense jungle which had been our constant companion for some days unexpectedly cleared and we, who had just topped a low peak, viewed below us two enormous craters, the remnants of an interplanetary collision, according to Professor Challenger, who declared that no force on earth could have been respon-

CONGRATULATIONS!

You have just reached the end
of what may well be
your first haunted book,
and I dearly hope that
the impressions you've received
and
the experiences that resulted
have all been for the best.

If you enjoyed this book, I highly recommend two classic short stories by M. R. James, "Canon Alberic's Scrap-book" and "The Tractate Middoth," Thomas Bontly's more modern yet intensely thought-provoking *Celestial Chess,* and Tom English's exhaustive and massive anthology *Bound for Evil.* To explore the extraordinarily rich world of Victorian ghost stories, I cannot rate more highly the three anthologies *The Mammoth Book of Victorian and Edwardian Ghost Stories* and *The Virago Book of Victorian Ghost Stories* both edited by Richard Dalby and *The Oxford Book of Victorian Ghost Stories* edited by Michael Cox and R. A. Gilbert.

Select Bibliography and Suggested Further Reading

This book is a love letter to subjects I adore and have been interested in my whole life. But it didn't come easily. It took 11 years of trying desperately to pull words and sentences out of my head.* I liken it to pulling taffy through a keyhole on a cold day! I can see myself at the dining room table for hours on end for years struggling to put words into Quatermain's mouth. I assembled countless thick folders and piles and binders and boxes of outlines and notes and tentative text, most hung together with lots of Scotch tape and staples. Yet, it is hard to believe, it is finally done! Is it any good? Frankly, I don't know. My goal was to offer to a few readers a good time and food for thought. Only you can say if I succeeded. Still, I'm very clear that countless genre writers of similar material can write prolific rings around me faster and better. I can only claim to have done my utmost best.

While a lifetime of reading and viewing for both pleasure and research is behind every page of this novel, specifically for *Dawn of Time*, I've read or viewed at the very least, hundreds of books, magazine and newspaper articles, videos, websites, and other media on the pertinent topics—certainly most available studies—and it would be impossible to list the mountains of material that influenced me before and while this story was being crafted. However, some works either have special meaning for me or could be particularly useful further reading for interested readers. Thus, I studied my shelves to cull out some representative works to share and quickly learned that there is just too much! Therefore, frustratingly, I list here a mere sampling *with the understanding that nobody responsible for any part of these listed works has anything whatsoever to do with the unlikely extrapolations and fantasies that I present in this novel:*

The Manhattan Project

Groves, General Leslie M. *Now It Can Be Told: The Story of the Manhattan Project.* New York: Harper 1962 (Boston: A Decapo Reprint).

Jaffe, Roland. *Fat Man and Little Boy.* Paramount Pictures 1989 (film).

Kunetks. James W. *City of Fire: Los Alamos and the Atomic Age, 1943-1945.* Albuquerque: University of New Mexico 1979.

Los Alamos: Beginning of an Era 1943-1945. Los Alamos, New Mexico: Los Alamos Scientific Laboratory. (reissued by Los Alamos Historical Society; 2nd edition, February 1, 2008).

Rhodes, Richard. *The Making of the A-Bomb.* New York: Simon & Schuster 1986.

Rhodes, Richard. *Dark Sun: The Making of the Hydrogen Bomb.* New York: Simon & Schuster 1995.

Taurog, Norman. *The Beginning or the End.* MGM 1947 (film).

---

* *Crucible of Life* took 15 years. Preceding it, the slim *Roof of the World* took four years.

The Hetch Hetchy Project

"Here's to You. Down the Hetch: Through Granite by Gravity" in *Phoenix*. San Francisco: San Francisco State University, December 3, 1981.

The Hetch Hetchy Water and Power System: Origin, Development and Future. San Francisco Public Utilities Commission 2005.

Leonard, James H. *San Francisco Water and Power.* San Francisco: Hetch Hetchy Water and Power System c. 1980.

Righter, Robert W. *The Battle Over the Hetch Hetchy: America's Most Controversial Dam and the Birth of Modern Environmentalism.* New York: Oxford University Press 2005.

Wurm, Ted. *Yosemite's Hetch Hetchy Railroad: San Francisco's Water and Power Project.* Fishcamp, California: Stauffer 2000.

Maria Mitchell

Albers, Henry (ed.). *Maria Mitchell: A Life in Journals and Letters.* Clinton Corners, New York: College Avenue Press 2001.

Gormley, Beatrice. *Maria Mitchell: The Soul of an Astronomer.* Grand Rapids: William B. Eerdsmans 1995.

Mitchell, Maria and Kendall, Phebe. *Mitchell. Maria Mitchell: Life, Letters and Journals.* Boston: Lee and Shepard 1896 (A Kessinger Reprint)

Stonehenge and Megaliths

Alexander, Caroline. "If the Stones Could Speak: Searching for the Meaning of Stonehenge" in *The National Geographic Magazine* Vol. 213. Washington, D.C.: The National Geographic Society, June 2008.

Hawkins, Gerald S. *Stonehenge Decoded.* New York: Dell Publishing 1965.

Hoyle, Fred. *From Stonehenge to Modern Cosmology.* San Francisco: W.H. Freeman 1972.

Wernick, Robert (Bernard Wailes, consultant) and the Editors of Time-Life Books. *The Emergence of Man: The Monument Builders.* New York: Time-Life Books 1973.

Victorian Africa

Burton, Richard. *Wanderings in West Africa* (two volumes bound as one). New York: Dover 1991 (first published 1863).

Moorehead, Alan. *The Blue Nile.* New York: HarperCollins 1980.

Patterson, John Henry. *The Man-Eaters of Tsavo.* Stilwell, Kansas: Digireads.com 2005 (first published 1907).

The Khoisan People and Language

Reader, John. *Africa: A Biography of the Continent.* New York: Alfred A. Knopf 1998.

Wade, Nicholas. *Before the Dawn: Recovering the Lost History of Our Ancestors.* New York: The Penguin Press 2006.

Isambard Kingdom Brunel

Brindle, Steven. *Brunel: The Man Who Changed the World*. London: Phoenix 2005.

Rolt, L.T.C. *Isambard Kingdom Brunel*. London: Penguin 1989.

The Star of Bethlehem

Alexander F. Morrison Planetarium. *The Christmas Star* (Booklet No. 6). San Francisco: California Academy of Sciences 1959.

Brown, Raymond. *The Birth of the Messiah: A Commentary on the Infancy Narratives in Matthew and Luke*. Garden City, New York: Doubleday 1977.

Clarke, Arthur C. "The Star of the Magi" in *The Challenge of the Spaceship*. New York: Ballantine 1961.

Hughes, David. *The Star of Bethlehem: An Astronomer's Confirmation*. New York: Pocket Books 1979.

Kidger, Mark. *The Star of Bethlehem: An Astronomer's View*. Princeton: Princeton University Press 1999.

Maier, Paul L. *First Christmas: The True and Unfamiliar Story*. New York: Harper & Row 1971.

Williams, John. *Observations on Comets, From B.C. 611 to A.D. 1640*. A Nabu Public Domain Reprint 2010.

Robert E. Howard and E. Hoffmann Price

De Camp, L. Sprague; De Camp, Catherine Crook; and Griffin, Jane Wittington. *Dark Valley Destiny: The Life of Robert E. Howard, the Creator of Conan*. New York: Blue Jay Books 1983.

Howard, Doctor Isaac M. *The Collected Letters of Doctor Isaac M. Howard*. Plano, Texas: The Robert E Howard Foundation Press 2011.

Price, E. Hoffmann. *Book of the Dead: Friends of Yesteryear: Fictioneers & Others*. Saul City: Arkham House 2001.

James Clerk Maxwell

Balchin, John. *Science: 100 Scientists Who Changed the World*. New York: Enchanted Lion Books 2003.

Hart, Michael H. *The 100: A Ranking of the Most Influential Persons in History*. New York: Citadel: 2001.

Mahon, Basil. *The Man Who Changed Everything: The Life of James Clerk Maxwell*. Chichester, UK: John Wiley & Sons 2004.

Maxwell, James Clerk. *A Treatise on Electricity & Magnetism* (two volumes). New York: Dover 1954 (first published 1873).

Pope Pius IX

Ambrosini, Maria Luisa with Willis, Mary. *The Secret Archives of the Vatican*. New York: Little Brown 1969.

Pius IX. "Ineffabilis Deus" in *Mother of Christ, Mother of Church: Documents on the Blessed Virgin Mary*. Boston: Pauline Books and Media 2001.

Julia, Daughter of Augustus, and Ancient Rome

Casson, Lionel. *The Ancient Mariners: Seafarers and Sea Fighters of the Mediterranean in Ancient Times*. Minerva Press 1959.

Coolidge, Olivia. *Roman People*. Boston: Houghton Mifflin 1959.

Fast, Howard. *Spartacus*. New York: Howard Fast 1951 (a 1960 Bantam Book).

Kubrick, Stanley. *Spartacus*. Universal-International 1960 (film).

Stobart, J.C. *The Grandeur That Was Rome* (5th ed.). New York: Praeger 1971.

Big Bang, CBR, Interferometry, and Planetariums

Gamow, George. *The Creation of the Universe*. Mineola, New York: Dover 2004 (First Published 1952).

Hey, J.S. *The Radio Universe*. New York: Pergamon Press 1971.

Norton. O. Richard. *The Planetarium and Atmospherium: An Indoor Universe*. Healdsburg, California: Naturegraph Publishers 1968.

Singh, Simon. *Big Bang: The Most Important Scientific Discovery of All Time and Why You Need to Know About It*. London: Fourth Estate 2004.

Tyson, Neil Degrass and Goldsmith, Donald. *Origins: Fourteen Billion Years of Cosmic Evolution*. New York: W.W. Norton 2004.

Solar Eclipses

Menzel, Donald H. and Pasachoff, Jay M. "Solar Eclipse, Nature's Super Spectacular" in *National Geographic Magazine* Vol. 138. Washington, D.C.: The National Geographic Society August 1970.

Monsman, Gerald. Annotation to *King Solomon's Mines* by H. Rider Haggard. Buffalo, New York: Broadview Press 2002.

Steel, Duncan. *Eclipse: The Celestial Phenomenon That Changed the Course of History*. Washington D.C.: The Joseph Henry Press 2001.

Beekeeping

Bodmer, Rudolph J. (ed.). "The Story in a Honey Bee" in *The Book of Wonders*. New York: Presbrey Syndicate 1915.

Grout, Roy A. (ed.). *The Hive and the Honey Bee*. Hamilton: Dadant 1949.

Hambleton, James I. "Man's Winged Ally, The Busy Honey Bee" in *The National Geographic Magazine* Vol. LXVII, Number Four. Washington, D.C.: The National Geographic Society April 1935.

Maeterlinck, Maurice. *The Life of the Bee*. New York: Mentor 1954 (originally published 1901).

Murayama, Hashime. "In Field and Hive" in *The National Geographic Magazine* Vol LXVII, Number Four. Washington, D.C.: The National Geographic Society April 1935.

Continental Drift

Dobson, Jerome E. "Through the Macroscope: Geography's View of the World" in *ArcNews*. Redlands, California: Esri Winter 2011/2012.

Sullivan, Walter. *Continents in Motion*. McGraw-Hill. 1974.

The Maya

Highwater, Jamake. *Journey to the Sky: A Novel About the True Adventures of Two Men in Search of the Lost Maya Kingdom*. New York: Crowell 1978.

Mysteries of the Maya: The Rise, Glory and Collapse of an Ancient Civilization. National Geographic Magazine. Washington, D.C.: The National Geographic Society April 2005 *(among NGS's countless fine Maya pieces over the years)*.

Stephens, John L. *Incidents of Travel in Yucatan* (two volumes). New York: Dover 1963 (first published 1843).

Von Hagan, Victor Wolfgang. *Maya Explorer: John Lloyd Stephens and the Lost Cities of Central America and Yucatan*. San Francisco: Chronicle Books 1990.

Immense Engineering Enterprises

Ambrose, Stephen E. *Nothing Like It in the World: The Men Who Built the Transcontinental Railroad 1863-1869*. New York: Simon & Schuster 2000.

Broggie, Michael. *Walt Disney's Railroad Story: The Small-Scale Fascination That Led to a Full-Scale Kingdom*. Pasadena: Pentrex 1997.

Burleson, Clyde W. *The Jennifer Project*. New York: Prentice-Hall 1977.

Clarke, Arthur C. *Voice Across the Sea*. London: William Luscombe 1958.

McCullough, David. *The Path Between the Seas: The Creation of the Panama Canal 1870-1914*. New York: Simon & Schuster 1977.

Nineteenth-Century Explorations of Ecuador and Colombia

Sachs, Aaron. *The Humboldt Current: Nineteenth-Century Exploration and the Roots of American Environmentalism*. New York: Penguin 2007

Sanz de Santamaria, Pablo Navas. *The Journey of Frederick Edwin Church Through Colombia and Ecuador April-October 1853*. Bogata, Columbia: Villegas Asociados, Universidad de los Andes, Thomas Greg & Sons 2008.

Von Humboldt, Alexander and Bonpland, Aime. *Personal Narrative of Travels to the Equinoctial Regions of America During the Years 1799-1804* (three volumes) London: George Bell 1908.

The Jonker Diamond

TheLazareDiamond. *The Cutting of the Jonker Diamond*. (YouTube video based on 1936 Movietone News footage) 2010.

Tourneur, Jacques. *A Miniature: The Story of "The Jonker Diamond"*. MGM 1936 (short film).

Useful Reference Fiction Found in Many Editions:

Clarke, Arthur C. "The Star"

Doyle, Arthur Conan. *The Lost World* and "The Devil's Foot"

Heard, H.F. *A Taste for Honey*

Verne, Jules. *From the Earth to the Moon* and *20,000 Leagues Under the Sea*

Note About the Typeface—This book is mainly set in Baskerville Old Face, based on the serif face designed by 18th century typographer John Baskerville.

Appendix

The Gospels of Issa, Gaspar, Mariam, and Hans (Combined)

There are few persons, even amongst the calmest thinkers, who have not occasionally been startled into a vague yet thrilling half-credence in the supernatural, by *coincidences* of so seemingly marvellous a character that, as *mere* coincidences, the intellect has been unable to receive them. . . . [S]uch sentiments are seldom thoroughly stifled unless by reference to the doctrine of chance, or, as it is technically termed, the Calculus of Probabilities.

—Edgar Allan Poe in
"The Mystery of Marie Rogêt"

Insofar as four heretofore unknown gospels have happened by pure chance to arrive years apart at my front door, it would be immensely hypocritical of me not to state forthrightly that such a coincidence has given me great pause. Of course, being no Biblical or Christian scholar, I am certainly in no position to determine the veracity of these texts; furthermore, one must bear in mind that all any of us has to go on are the rough-and-ready translation (from Aramaic) of Horace Holly (filtered through the sensibilities of Leo Vincey), the two sets of passages presented to Allan Quatermain by Richard Holmes a decade apart (in regards to the latter, my repeated inquiries to the British Museum have elicited no response), and the two sets of pronouncements made in the presence of Quatermain, which he decades later recalled and verbalized extemporaneously as aspects of long anecdotes shared with friends. Nevertheless, I am now taking the liberty of merging the tracts as they seem to me to have points in common; it does not hurt that they, as well, express my own long-held core convictions.

✦ ✦ ✦

The Gospel of Issa

1. Is it God or is it I who guides this brush? God fills me as milk warm from the goat fills a cup to overflowing.

2. Long ago I ceased to be merely the man who is the son of my parents. I was young when God showed Himself to me:

3. That was the time I ceased to be the son of my parents. I became then an instrument of the Lord. I, Issa, son of Joseph, the carpenter of Nazareth, ceased to be.

4. My whole will from that time forward focused on the fact of God's gracing me with the indisputable awareness of His presence.

5. Why me? What did I ever do to deserve the acquaintance of God? My time and my life have been for these last eighteen years fully a matter of trying to understand what was and is happening to me.

6. I am filled with God. But tell me, if you empty a fig of its meat and fill its skin with mandarin orange pulp, are you left with an orange?

7. Then I am no more God than the fig is an orange. But as that fig, transformed, knows more of oranges than a natural fig, so I know more of God than a natural man.

8. They will say, I think, that I am the son of God. Others will say I am a fraud!

9. I know that the Lord has chosen me for some other than ordinary purpose. I can see glimpses of it, but the details elude me.

10. These things are fact, not to be ignored by me or anyone.

11. I know clearly how the prophets must have felt; what they must have known. As God spoke to Abraham and Moses and Isaiah, so He speaks to me.

12. I truly know that I am to do my Lord's bidding; I am to be the instrument of His will.

13. My Lord wants me to wander through the East and absorb everything I see and hear.

14. So be it. Such is what we have done for nearly eighteen years. Here I am with my brother Didymus Judas Thomas in the land of the Bon, the mightiest mountain country that my Father has created.

15. We have traveled far, about as far from home as is imaginable.

16. I have learned much: the tenets of Hinduism, Buddhism, Confucianism, yoga. These are all fonts from which I have drunk mightily.

17. What is it now that I am supposed to do? Is it time to return? Home has beckoned for months now.

18. Is there anything else to learn in this high land of false magic and superstition? Will I know what to do when the time comes?

19. Now, however, I write this account as You have asked, or, rather, ordered, for my Father does not ask.

20. I am here, Lord; but I don't know why. I have learned much, but I don't know why. We have traveled far, and I don't know why.

21. Everything is so different than that which I was taught as a child in Nazareth.

22. Is it that I am loath to admit to myself what your purpose is for me?

23. In our wanderings, I have noted a common theme. A tenet that explains so much—that answers so many of your children's unanswered questions.

24. Whether in China or India or here in the loftiest mountains, so long as I am in the East, I hear of death and rebirth, and of the soul using the body much as I would ride in a vehicle:

25. How after death, the soul must be born again. Though in a new vehicle, or vessel, according to the merit that the soul exhibited in its previous existences.

26. It is a meritorious approach to existence certainly. Much as a school boy moves from one level of learning to another higher level, so, too, a death marks the potential for a move, for the coming to a crossroads;

27. But as some children need to repeat an entire season of lessons due to slothfulness or poor behavior or inattentiveness, so, too, a soul must sometimes repeat a wasted life in order to attain the merit to move on.

28. Attainment of merit is simple, surely. To do onto others as you would have them do onto you.

29. If a man or a woman follows this tenet for a lifetime, he or she will achieve merit and be closer to God for having done so: In this life and in the next.

30. To be One with the Father, that is the purpose of existence: base man must rise above his baseness to sit at the right hand of the Father.

31. Yet it is slow. God's time is not man's time, nor woman's. A human lifetime is but the single beat of a fly's wing in God's measure.

32. The miracle is that God notices, and more than this, that God cares.

33. But God does care. If God was not Love Incarnate, perhaps all of human existence could have begun and ended without the Father even knowing.

34. But God does know and God does love.

35. Patience is the foundation.

36. An hour, a day, a month, a year, seven years, a single lifetime is not enough.

37. I have had arguments, or, rather, discussions with my brother Thomas.

38. It is self-apparent, I will say to him, that the punishment for the curser is that the soul will forget its previous life and will be cast down into a body that will spend its time continually troubled in its heart;

39. That the punishment for the arrogant and over-bearing man is that the soul will forget from whence it came and will be cast down into a lame and deformed body so that all despise it persistently.

40. Then Thomas will ask, "And the man who hath committed no sin, but done good persistently, but hath not found the mysteries, what will happen to him?"

41. And I reply, "He will seek the light and will find it."

42. Surely, then, my destiny is to teach of these matters and others, such as the righteousness of humility and of seeking and others of which I have learned during our long sojourn.

43. But to whom? Surely, the people of our fathers, the people of Abraham will make naught of such matters.

44. Oh, my brother and I have seen so much in these last years.

45. By caravan, we followed the silk road to Bactra and from thence to Kabul and Palitara. I have seen the holy cities of Juggernaut, Rajagrina, Benares, and Kopilavastu.

46. We have journeyed through many nations and supped with many peoples.

47. I am filled to overflowing with the wisdom of the ages.

48. You told me that I am Your tool. Well, use me! I have much knowledge and have acquired marvelous techniques. What is it all for? I am tired.

49. (Could it be that it was I who recently wrote here of patience?)

50. I know now that I am to teach. Well, then, let me teach! How much more must I learn? I have seen your many faces!

51. Eloi, Eloi! I am lonely. Despite the companionship of my brother, Thomas, I am tired of being a stranger in a strange land.

52. I have learned without doubt that You are Love, but I do not love. I have teachers but no friends.

53. I am feeling sorry for myself, for I am lonely and too wise.

54. I know God as well as I know Joseph, the husband of my mother, Mariam.

55. In the beginning, when I was very young, He would speak to me, and I would respond.

56. He spoke to me and it was clear enough. Not in words would He speak, but in signs and symbols and, sometimes, in dreams, too, He made His wants known. Learning the language of the signs was the challenge.

57. What is school if not a challenge for the student?

58. As a child who does good is rewarded, and is punished for having done bad, so, too, God shows pleasure when a sign is read correctly and displeasure when a sign is misread.

59. Usually some coincidence that inspired wonder would be my reward for right interpretation; a sense of foreboding being the clue that there was misreading.

60. I needed always to plumb my feelings and try to understand what God was trying to say. In time, I built a whole vocabulary.

61. But now I am lost in the mountain country of the Bon people.

✦ ✦ ✦

62. My brother, Issa, is dead. I, Didymus Judas Thomas, who has been my brother's companion for nearly eighteen years as we traveled through the strange lands of the East, am now alone. I am afraid. God has deserted us.

63. Issa was attacked in a dark alley by robbers and was clubbed to death. The morticians here, who feed their dead to the birds, have him in their care now.

64. I cannot bear to stay in this foreign land one day longer. I am leaving for home, Judea.

65. I have much to carry; I leave behind much; my burdens are heavy.

The Gospel of Gaspar

66. Thus Gaspar says:

67. These are the words of Gaspar the Ethiopian.

68. I am dismayed. A significant portion of my life has been given to the study of one man, and more and more frequently I hear reports concerning him that are blatantly false or twisted far beyond the simple truths.

69. Why is this? Can there be so many whose self-interest outweighs the simple truth?

70. In all things, Jesus the Nazarene said, 'Treat others as you would have them treat you. Do good and give as you can without expecting a thing in return. Your reward will be great, and God will call you his children. Show mercy even as your Father shows mercy. Do not judge, for how can you judge? What right do you have to judge when you have no understanding why a person is the way that person is? Remember, the standard you use will be the standard used toward you.'

71. The one God is real, a spirit that is at the core of everything and everyone. God is always observing how you treat and judge others and how your actions and words, or inaction for that matter, affect others. This spirit doles out according to your actions. Hurt and you will be hurt, love and you will be loved, cause someone to

cry in suffering and you will be made to cry with your own suffering. This circle of doing followed by God's response may be experienced immediately or may be held off for a future lifetime, according to the will of God for his own reasons.

72. Jesus explained the way of the world in a simple manner, with parables that even children can understand. He was proud of his ability in this respect. He told his followers and all those who would listen, "Blessed are the eyes that see the things that you see, for I tell you that many prophets and kings have desired to see those things that you see and have not seen them, and to hear those things that you hear and have not heard them."

73. And yet I, Gaspar, mourn, as none of this do I hear from the caravans. Instead I hear about magical wine and multiplying loaves and fishes. Where is the word of Jesus the Naserene, who told us not to worry about our lives, what we will eat, about our bodies, or what we will wear, for isn't life more than food, and the body more than flesh? Did he not remind us of the way lilies grow, that they do not work or spin, but that even Solomon, in all his splendor, was not as glorious?

74. And Gaspar said:

75. Where is the word that tells us how to listen to God, that tells us that God speaks in a special language. When you see clouds in the west, you know that rain will come. You know that wind blowing from the south is always followed by blistering heat. You know the ways of your home and its land and you can read the sky. So why can't you understand the signs that God brings you?

76. God's language doesn't use simple words like fig or tree or wall or camel. Instead, he uses symbols. For instance, if he shows you a circle, you know from common sense that a circle has no beginning or middle or end. It is whole unto itself; therefore, if God shows you a circle, you know that he is gracing you with wholeness and completion.

77. In the same way, a home or house is where you live your life, where you are aware, and where it is that you know all that you

know. So if God shows you a house, you know he is showing you your very awareness, or if he shows you an underground vault or perhaps the depths of the sea, you know these places are lightless and the realm of dark and he has graced you with a warning that you need to beware of that which you cannot see, of that which is below your awareness.

78. God communicates to you in two ways. One is obvious and the other is less so. Both are common but only one is spoken of, though even then rarely understood. Through all time, people have spoken about God talking to people in dreams. But what is not said is that, even in dreams, God does not talk in an ordinary way using the dreamer's ordinary language. Dreams are full of symbols that mean something personal from God to the dreamer; it is the dreamer's duty to discover what is being said.

79. The other less obvious way that God communicates, the way that people seldom speak of, is his placing symbols in our paths during our waking hours. Most such symbols are ordinary and self-evident. So you ask, how is a person to recognize that this or that ordinary thing is a message from God?

80. It is not difficult at all. God causes us to notice such symbols by having them occur in the same space or time as other symbols so that two or more ordinary things coming together is not ordinary at all. When this happens, we feel a jolt of wonder or awe or even love. We all have these experiences, but I tell you, as sure as I am talking to you, that God is thus trying to get your attention, to speak to you. If in your heart you feel such a crossing of paths is wonderful, then I promise God is talking to you.

81. Therefore, fortunate are you to see what you see, for these are the visions of the prophets, and many are the kings who wish to see what you see, or hear what you hear. But they never do, for they seek too hard and are not pure of heart.

82. In this way, there can be nothing that is covered up or nothing that is secret between you and God. The secrets of your mind are held up to God, and God whispers back, or sometimes shouts, as the occasion deserves.

83. But again, it is your duty to understand God's words to you, of what he is saying especially to you! Whether it's easy or hard, God rewards the trying.

84. Now think! There are many people in your towns, in your nations, in the whole world. Think of all the people of all the many ages who lived in all those nations. Now ask yourself this: why would God trouble to speak so to you, who is but one person among so many? Why would he send you a sign, or speak to you in your dreams? Why would he trouble himself with you?

85. He does so because you are holy as all his children are holy. But few listen. But few heed. Few trust. Few love God as he loves them. Instead they choose to be blind. They choose to be deaf. They choose to be mute. God speaks all the time, but he is ignored by so many. His signs and dreams are ignored. His messages are ignored.

86. Where is the voice of Jesus that explains how the world works and how it should be observed? Where does it say that God approaches and needs to be approached with a serious heart fully open, that this is how God and man come together and that life ceases to be a mystery?

87. Happy are those who show mercy, for, in this life or the next, God will be merciful.

88. Happy are those who have open hearts, for, in this life or the next, they will see the face of God.

89. Great are the keepers of the peace, for, in this life or the next, they will be called the children of God.

90. But where is the voice of Jesus, the voice who held all these wondrous truths? Where are these truths? I do not hear of them from the caravans.

The Gospel of Mariam

91. I am Mariam.... I have brought you here to Sinai from your far off homes to share with you, and through you to the rest of the world, knowledge of *the holiest place on earth!* I say again, *the holiest place on earth!*

92. Long have men sought treasures such as the cup from which they believed Christ drank, which is what I caused you to believe was the object of your quest; or the Ark of the Covenant; or for the

true mountain called Sinai; or fragments from my son's tree; and so much more.

93. Well, I, of all people, know well what is holy and what is not and what is more holy or less holy, for I am the mother of God, and you have come to this remote spot at my bidding though you knew it not. You, each of you, came now rather than before or later because the time is soon coming when the people of this world must learn the truth of their own existence.

94. They say that God created man in His own image. There is truth to that, not in the material sense, for the material aspect of God can be better thought of as the entire world on which we stand, and, by extension, perhaps the Universe without as well. No, man is created in God's image in the sense of "mind" and spirit. Of all the creatures on earth, man is the only one that can seek God consciously, or who can arrive at God's door through attainment of merit, for God created man to join with and become God—and the destiny of each man, woman, and child is to attain God, whether he knows it or not, wants it or not, needs it or not. And though some men may not consciously strive for this, in time they will arrive there in any case.

95. Of all of God's creatures on earth, man is the holiest by virtue that only man becomes God, as a child becomes an adult at childhood's end.

96. Have you never gone back to the spot of your birth and wondered at the fact that it was there in that precise midwife's home or there in that very room or there in that exact glade that you came into existence, where you were born into this world? Now I bid you think. At such moments, are you not full of wonder for your very existence, for the miracle of your life?

97. I have brought you here to make it clear that mankind likewise has a place where it came into existence, where it was born, and it is time that all of mankind learn of that place so that all may feel that self-same wonder.

98. The Holy Scriptures tell of the creation of the world and a place that is called Eden....

99. The Holy Scriptures tell of the creation of the world...and they tell of God creating man in the land of Eden and that the act of creation took mere moments. These statements are of course true,

but who is to determine what is a moment in the eyes of God, who measures time in billions of years? Indeed, God created man in a moment, a mere few million years, and he did this feat in a place that you can call Eden for want of a better name. I have brought you here to identify that real place to you and thus to all men.

100. Before I discuss the realm that is the real Eden of the real world, you need to know more of myself.... I will explain somewhat. As all the world knows well, Jesus asked his beloved disciple to care for his mother. That person is myself.

101. There came a time when the Angel of the Lord came to me. It was Gabriel, the same who had revealed himself to me at so many other crossroads in my life. He made me see in my mind a place on the far side of the Red Sea....

102. He said, "Verily, the spot that I am showing you is holy, more so than Ur was where the Lord spoke to Abraham or the Mountain of Sinai where the Lord spoke to Moses. Though these are surely holy places, the spot I show you is holier still, for it is the holiest spot on earth. And verily, you who are the Mother of God, you are bid to attend this veritable womb of mankind, for are you not the holiest person of the world? Thus is it not right that you should live by and in and protect the holiest place? Are you not also the mother of man? Then it is fitting that you reside by and in and protect the womb of man. Verily, I say to you, the spot I show you is the most holy in the eyes and mind of God."

103. The place the angel showed me was a vast valley that ran the whole length of Africa from north to south, a tremendous valley with many lakes. The angel bade John and I to come to this very spot that is under our feet now—indeed, verily even where you stand before me—which is the northernmost gateway both into and out of the great valley.

104. Let me say a wonderful truth. Remember, thee, how the Lord through the burning bush told Moses that he stood on holy ground? Well I say to you that the ground on which you stand is holier still....

105. That spot, which is under your feet, continues south, making up the great valley of eastern Africa, the bowl out of which sprang man, the crucible where the embryonic spirit, or God-in-the-

making called mankind, was forged.... Humans came into being, not all at once, but in stages over time, for that is the way that God performs his miracles, building from the blocks that are available, the stuff of life.

106. My purpose is to share the truth of man's origin with those most able to divine it and appreciate its meaning. After all, we are all the children of God, and God wants his children to grow beyond the quaint stories they tell amongst themselves and to hearken to things as they really are.

107. Listen to me now!

108. If God is as real as, for instance, me, and is by definition divine, and if through the use of the tool called Time, he crafted people in his own image, then it would follow that people are also divine and that the spot where He did his crafting must be holy ground—the holiest of ground.

109. I have drawn you here from afar to tell you my wishes.... First, that all mankind turn away from sin, chiefly your disregard for God and, too, the lust for war. Second, that a chapel be built on the spot of my appearance in my honor. Well, now I ask something similar of you. I ask that all the terrain from where you stand to the southern-most reach of the great valley—the vast bowl that is birthplace of the human race—be designated holy ground and be set aside so all people can come and contemplate their existence, to perceive with their own eyes the spot where God's greatest miracle occurred, and this will make them more mindful of one another and of God, as well.

110. Rest assured that in the fullness of time all these things are possible and will be fulfilled! For you are my tool and, therefore, blessed by God!

The Gospel of Hans

111. O, Hans the good! Hans the mischievous. Hans the child. Hans the wise. I wish you to be the vessel of my message to all the people.

112. Hans, your fathers and their fathers and their fathers, and also all the mothers, all the way back to the dawn of time, have watched the stars and the sun and the moon move across the sky.

Also, your people and all peoples have noted that sometimes the moon will precisely cover the sun, and the light and warmth will vanish! Can anything be more frightening? I ask.

113. Listen, Hans the faithful! Perhaps fear of hunger or of cold or of enemies or of pain or of death can be as frightening. But these are all things that are part of life and are expected, thus assumed, and though they may be feared, they are not strange. For does not every man [i.e., person] fully expect his lot to be touched by these fearsome things at some point during his journey?

114. However, the greatest joy in a [person's] life, indeed, in a whole people's life, is warmth and light from the sun. Thus the fear that comes from the sun vanishing and the world growing dark is the most fearsome thing of all for there is no way of knowing when such a terrible thing will happen. It is not like the sun setting and rising.

115. Or at least this was so up until the various peoples discovered by their industry *my secret pattern.* Man [i.e., humans or humankind] has become fully [human] because he sought to know when in the future the circle of the moon would cover the circle of the sun and plunge the earth into darkness. Behold! In time, each people built tools and discovered the pattern in the randomness. They learned when the fearsome thing would occur, and they became less afraid. They found the secret that I had buried deep within the complexities *I'd created just to goad [humans] to seek it.*

116. "'I tell you that [humankind's] seeking to predict when the moon will cover the sun is what has made [humans human]. *This is the key that honed problem solving far beyond that needed for mere survival. From this has sprung all that makes [humans human].*

117. Thus peoples built grand temples and pyramids and statues and standing stones to observe the sun and moon and sky, and, sometimes, they enslaved whole peoples to build their observatories. Hans, this took many thousands of years, during which time people have done much for both good and ill. *But remember that it all began due to fear of losing the sun during the day—a fear I instilled by making certain that the moon exactly covers the sun. I created a problem that [humankind] needed to solve and thereby progress!*

118. Surely nowadays many people have studied that age-old problem and have for centuries grown to understand thoroughly the

remote—I say again—*remote* probability of any such equality in size of the sun and moon, so small a probability that the fact of this equivalence is on the surface preposterous. Yet, too often people just shrug and call it coincidence. *Too few reach the next logical conclusion. If such a thing is preposterous, and yet exists nonetheless as a fact of life, what could it mean? Perhaps it means that* someone *wished it all to happen in just that manner. But who could wish up suns and moons and propel [human] advancement?*

119. Who indeed? [Humans] now have clear reason to *know* me. I am right there in the maths and calculations that they treasure so much, but they can also be stubborn, can take things terribly for granted and rationalize. Still, Hans, people will someday understand that *something is happening, has always been happening, that defies reason . . . yet has a cause and that cause is me—for I am that I am!*

120. But first there must come a drawn-out time when the blind will lead and these words I am saying will verily be *the light in the darkness.* Old Hans, share my words. Remember all that I've said and share it with your Baas, Allan, O Hans the child, Hans the wise!

121. For you are my messenger.

Afterword to Trilogy

This trilogy of novels is by definition a work of fiction. Furthermore, it is a pastiche of several H. Rider Haggard stories and of, to *lesser extent*, various and sundry tales of the Great Detective. Moreover:

(1) The book you are holding is not a commonplace Great Detective mystery. Rather, it provides our hero with four distinct problems at three different periods—youth, middleage, and two while in retirement. Yet, the narrative never does more than quietly allude to the detective, offering scenes that *imply* his destiny crossing paths with Horace Holly, Leo Vincey, and Allan Quatermain.

(2) This trilogy is structured like a child's nesting toy—rather like a set of Russian nesting dolls—insofar as the reader is invited to explore multiple layers within layers, of framing devices within framing devices, books within books, and narratives within narratives.

(4) Further, this book can be viewed as a kind of light-hearted homage of the once common practice of casting works of fiction in the form of fact for the sake of verisimilitude. Countless authors have indulged in that conceit over the centuries—from Horace Walpole and Johannes Wilhelm Meinhold through Wilkie Collins, Arthur Conan Doyle, Arthur Machen, H. Rider Haggard, Edgar Rice Burroughs, and A. Merritt to, more recently, Ian Cameron, Michael Crichton, Nicholas Meyer, Lin Carter, and Umberto Eco.

(5) This work should also be seen as this author's paean to the progeny of the above literary art form, the pastiche, which often comes equipped with literary conventions such as framing devices, pseudo-prefaces, footnotes, and so forth. My goal has been to take this pastiche convention to a whole new level. None of the apparent ancillary material passage in this book should be skipped over or derided; it is not optional.

(6) At the same time, this trilogy is built on a framework of allusions. For example, the various title pages are parodies of, and allusions to, turn-of-the-century publishing conventions, while the dedications are allusions to H. Rider Haggard's preferred style of trumpeting his allegiance or loyalty or friendship while in his more serious moods, and there are endless allusions to all manner of genre tropes. Of course, this is nothing new, being at heart the same sort of structural foundation employed by, for example, George Lucas in *Star Wars* and Sergio Leone and Quentin Tarantino in their various films.

(7) Now, of course, comes the disclaimer: As all the opinions expressed in this book are not necessarily those of the author, this tale has no further intention beyond providing *food for thought* and a good time! Further, in the tradition of pastiche, any references to historical events; to real people, living or dead; or to real locales are intended only to give the fiction a sense of historical reality; additionally, while some names, characters, and incidents are the products of H. Rider Haggard's and Arthur Conan Doyle's and other deceased authors' imaginations, they are used here solely in the spirit of homage. Other names, characters, and incidents are the products of this author's imagination and their resemblance, if any, to real-life counterparts is entirely coincidental.

Acknowledgments: Please see the first editions of the three volumes that make up this trilogy (see copyright page) for my original musings on this subject. Short of that, the names listed in the dedication (also on the copyright page) were of utmost help. Then chronologically, the following folk provided important input and/or feedback: Norman Siringer and Michael J. Thornton (1962-1963), Steve Greaves (1980), Michael Karman (1995), Henry Nkosi and Patrick McKivergan (2000), Peter Manley (2001) Tabot Debretion Araia (2001), and Sean Wallace (2003). My literary inspirations were legion; some standouts are Betty Ballantine, William S. Baring-Gould, Carl Barks, Lin Carter, Wilkie Collins, Michael Crichton, Clive Cussler, Nelson DeMille, Umberto Eco, Richard Halliburton, Graham Hancock, Donald Johanson, C.J. Jung, Rudyard Kipling, Roger Sherman Loomis, Burton L. Mack, Arthur Machen, Nicholas Meyer, Alan Moorehead, Walter Sullivan, James Turner, Jules Verne, Wolfram von Eschenbach, Irving Wallace, Lew Wallace, and Franz Werfel.

About Thomas Kent Miller

Thomas Kent Miller (often known as Thos. Kent Miller) is author of *Mars in the Movies: A History* from McFarland publishers, as well as the foregoing three H. Rider Haggard/Great Detective pastiches. I am a member of The Friends of Arthur Machen and The Rider Haggard Society. I have written for *The Weird Tales Collector, The Ghosts & Scholars M. R. James Newsletter, Faunus: The Journal of the Friends of Arthur Machen, The Haggard Journal, Wormwood*, Borgo Press, Wildside Press, and Hippocampus Press. I can be contacted at thomaskentmiller@gmail.com.

Since I'm on the last page of the third book of my long-perculating trilogy, which was begun September 10, 1983, I wish to mention here outright for the first time the over-arching concept that has informed the writing from the start (aside from bringing together characters conceived by H. Rider Haggard and Arthur Conan Doyle). But, of course, you've probably deduced that concept already by virtue of having read this volume. The first book, *Sherlock Holmes on the Roof of the World* (1987), intended two things: (1) to bring together the Great Detective and Jesus Christ, and (2) to suggest what might have happened if Jesus had had some dealings with yogis. The second book, *Allan Quatermain at the Crucible of Life* (2005), was intended to (1) broach the idea that the birthplace of the human race, the Great Rift Valley of East Africa, needs to be better recognized and honored and (2) bring together the iconic detective and the mother of Jesus. *Allan Quatermain at the Dawn of Time* was conceived to (1) cause the detective to circuitously cross paths with God (insofar as I'd already had him encounter Jesus and meet Mary) while (2) offering some illuminating notions regarding solar eclipses and, while I was at it, the Universe, and (3) illustrating the curious, illusive, exceedingly patient, peculiar, and roundabout manner in which Fate can sometimes work.

My interests include science-fiction cinema, Victorian and Edwardian ghost stories, 19th-century Hudson River School landscape paintings, and home theater. I live in Southern California.